PRAISE FOR *A* S T R A

"Haunting and powerful are two words that come to mind at the close of reading Roseanna M. White's debut novel, *A Stray Drop of Blood*. Not since Francine Rivers' Mark of the Lion trilogy has a book and its characters captured me so completely. From its rich, historical prose that depicts the era of Christ with startling reality, to a compelling love story that will both jolt and seize your heart, this is one of those rare novels that haunts you centuries beyond the last page. Amid the seething unrest of Roman tyranny and Hebrew uprising, a spellbinding saga unfolds, unleashing startling twists of both fate and heart that will leave you utterly breathless."

Julie Lessman
author of the Daughters of Boston Series

~

"White draws the reader in with irresistible characters and keeps him reading with complex action and a heart-clutching story. Not to be missed by anyone who loves Biblical fiction!"

Marta Perry
author of *Leah's Choice* and *Rachel's Garden*

~

"In *A Stray Drop of Blood*, Roseanna M. White delivers a spellbinding tale that will whisk readers back in time, to the last days of Jesus. Like an artfully-woven tapestry, the story is rich in colorful details of the city and its people... and the fearsome political climate that changed Jerusalem, forevermore. When you've finished this book, you'll want more from this talented author!"

Loree Lough
award-winning author of 74 novels that are "touching hearts and changing lives"

~

"*A Stray Drop of Blood* is a complex and captivating story full of characters I both adored and despised, sometimes at the same time. I loved the rich historical setting and how it wove effortlessly through the plot. The story is unpredictable, addictive, and full of hope even in the saddest of scenes. An excellent debut from Ms. White."

Stephanie Morrill
author of The Reinvention of Skylar Hoyt Series

~

"Prepare to be transported to Rome in the time of Jesus by this powerful debut novel. With a cast of compelling characters and a roller-coaster plot, this is a memorable tale that will stay with you long after the last chapter is read. Abigail's journey of faith and love is nothing short of miraculous. Biblical fiction fans will find it extremely rich and satisfying."

Terri Kraus
author of The Project Restoration Series:
The Renovation, The Renewal, The Transformation

~

"*A Stray Drop of Blood* is a fast-paced story that keeps you guessing until the very end. The unexpected plot twists and action make for an entertaining read . . . If you're a lover of Biblical era novels, then this is the book for you."

Michelle Griep
author of *Gallimore*

~

" I love biblical fiction. I love reading about how the ordinary people really lived during that time and related to each other without haloes drawn around their heads and a chorus of angels singing in the background. And Roseanna White does a splendid job in *A Stray Drop of Blood* of bringing the days and months surrounding the crucifixion to brutal reality through the eyes of a young Hebrew girl. If you enjoy biblical fiction like I do, pick this one up. You won't be disappointed."

Golden Keyes Parsons
author of Darkness to Light Series

To Pastor Chuck,

Blessings to you and through you!

Roseanna M. White

A STRAY DROP of BLOOD

A Novel BY ROSEANNA M. WHITE

WhiteFire Publishing

This is a work of fiction. All characters and events appearing in this novel are ficticious or used ficticiously.

A STRAY DROP OF BLOOD

WhiteFire Publishing
13607 Bedford Rd NE
Cumberland, MD 21502

www.whitefire-publishing.com

ISBN: 987-0-9765444-6-3

Cover design by Tekeme Studios
www.Tekeme.com

Dear Reader,

I've written a lot of books, ranging from humorous contemporary romances to intense historical fiction—with one delve in sci-fi (shudder). But through all those stories crowding my head, this remains the one dearest to my heart. I took great pleasure in reworking this story for its second release and hope that it touches you as the writing of it did me.

The story began for me on Good Friday when I was fifteen. Having just begun a relationship with the man now husband—and getting in a huge fight over it with my best friend—I had a few bittersweet feelings flooding me as I sat down to reflect on the day. As I read the story of Jesus' betrayal, of his crucifixion and resurrection, my heart swelled with the amazing reality of what this Man did for me. And I wondered . . . what would it have been like to be a woman in the crowd? A woman who went there seeking vengeance and instead beheld forgiveness the likes of which she had never imagined? And so *A Stray Drop of Blood* was born. I wrote a short story, which over the next six years became a novel.

Because this story touches on so many subjects you might find interesting, I've put together a companion guide with articles written by me and some of my dear, fabulous author friends, available on my webiste. Go to the "Books" tab, and there will be a link for it. Please visit if you're interested in finding out some interesting FYI about the details behind the story. I also welcome any and all reader comments!

This story is not perfect, but it tries, just as my characters do. I pray we all have the strength to do the same; after all, that stray drop of blood was shed for the cleansing of each of us.

Cheers,

Roseanna

Roseanna M. White
www.RoseannaMWhite.com
www.RoseannaWhite.com/index.php/books/companion_guide
www.RoseannaMWhite.blogspot.com

To my husband, David.
You're my heart, my love, and my inspiration.

ONE

Abigail's tears were unneeded. Mourners enough had been hired by her mother's husband, and their loud keening drowned out her grief. She risked a glance at Silas, who stood with an appropriately sorrowful expression in the corner. Her mother's husband, but not her father. Her father was dead. Mother too. And this family would never be her own.

"Abigail."

She turned to the doorway, where Rebekka, Silas's first wife, beckoned. Abigail darted one last look at the body laid out on the table, but her mother could offer her no protection now. She left the room, following Rebekka's voice down the hall. "She is eight years old. Very strong–she gets that from her father. But beautiful, as her mother was."

Even at eight years old, Abigail recognized the jealousy in Rebekka's tone at the mention of Mother's beauty. She stepped into the room, felt her head go light when she saw the man within.

A Roman soldier.

Rebekka motioned her forward, and though she wanted to remain rooted in place, she dared not. One step, another, and she was under the Roman's full perusal. Deafening silence pounded her until the man nodded and reached to the money purse on his belt. Her fingers clenched, her breath caught, her eyes ceased blinking. If possible, she would have stopped her heart from beating.

Had it come to this? First her father's death, then her mother's, and now she was to be slave to a Roman dog?

The man drew out several coins, but as he handed them to Rebekka, he offered Abigail a smile. And she knew. She knew that she would have more of a home with this Roman than with these people she could never call family.

Something inside shifted, making her shoulders edge back. That place from where tears sprang went cool, ran dry. An image of a cracked, parched streamed flitted before her eyes. That was what she would be. Hard and empty. If her own people would sell her to their oppressors, then so be it. She would be a humble slave. No more whimsy, no more dreams.

It was obviously what *God* intended.

"Does she speak Greek?" The man's gaze stayed on Abigail, though his words were aimed at Rebekka.

"Of course. She is a bright girl, able to obey any command."

He nodded, offered that smile to Abigail again. Strange . . . it was younger than his dignified years suggested, not unlike those of the boys who ran the streets. And kinder than any Roman's smile had a right to be. "What is your name, little one?"

"Abigail." Her voice sounded flat to her own ears. Barely more than a breath.

He crouched down, much like her father had once done when he wanted to speak to her. "Well, Abigail, you are to be my wife's helper. She is a Hebrewess and wishes for a young girl to teach and keep her company. You will enjoy spending your days by her side."

Enjoyment? Perhaps Roman masters could speak of such a thing, but Abigail had long ago given up on it. Ever since Father's death, there had been no joy to be had.

Her eyes sought the ground and stayed there as she followed him out into the early-morning bustle of Jerusalem. With every step that took her farther away from all that she knew, her heart grew heavier. Only God knew what her future held now, and he had never shown her any favor.

But he would not forsake her, no matter how much she may wish it. Mother had died a loyal child of Jehovah, and Abigail knew no better end awaited her. The Lord would not relinquish her. Even if the Roman had not come, she still would have been a slave to him.

Cleopas Visibullis glanced at the waif that trailed behind him and fought back the urge to scoop her up and carry her the remaining distance to his home. Ester would take one look at her and admit her into her heart as a daughter. The thought made him smile. He had known when she begged him to go see about the girl for sale that if he brought her home, it would be as a slave only in the loosest sense.

But with Jason bound for Rome this afternoon, his wife would need the distraction. A companion. The impending departure not only erased his smile, it brought a pounding in his head. In some ways, he knew Rome would do his impetuous son good. But in others . . . would he even recognize him if or when he returned?

They skirted the Praetorium, where Cleopas had served as prefect for two years now. Even before the promotion, he had been a soldier of import. Hence why his home abutted the compound. As they walked, citizens of Jerusalem moved to the other side of the street to avoid him, all Hebrew gazes flicked away.

He cast a glance over his shoulder. The girl still stared at the ground as she kept pace, but she surely knew that the moment she entered his house, her culture would by necessity change. Not as drastically as she may think in this moment, but no one would ever look at her the same, if they looked at her at all.

Simon opened the door for him as they neared, and Cleopas greeted the loyal servant with a nod. "Ester is in her chamber?"

"Yes, Lord, as is your son."

He nodded again and motioned the girl to follow him. Angry voices sounded as they neared the bed chamber's door. His wife's first. "You will not speak that way, Jason. He will be back in a matter of minutes—"

"He should not have left today in the first place. Buying a slave on the day his only son leaves? It is Simon's duty."

"I asked him—"

Cleopas halted the argument with a cleared throat. Ester sat with a brush in hand, eyes glistening with unshed tears, and looked to him with hope. Jason let out a growl and charged past him in the doorway, nearly knocking the girl from her feet.

He would deal with his son in a moment. For now, he ushered the girl forward with a hand on her shoulder. "Beloved, this is Abigail."

His wife's eyes lit, and she held out her hands. Though she looked awe-struck and terrified, the mite stepped forward. Ester smiled. "Abigail. A fine, strong name. First the wife of Nabal, but too wise for such a wicked man. After his death, she married David. It is good to meet you, Abigail. I am Ester."

Abigail dipped her chin, but her spine straightened. "An excellent namesake as well, Mistress. A wise, better queen has never been recorded in all the history of our people."

His wife laughed and tapped a finger to the little one's nose. "You know your history. Excellent. I shall teach you more, and we shall discover much together. You will be well taken care of, Abigail."

The girl nodded, but a tremble moved through her lips. Ester leaned forward and cupped her face with what looked to be the gentlest of touches. "I am sorry you are no longer free, that you have lost your parents. But I am glad you are here." She looked intently into Abigail's face, undoubtedly seeing into the depths of her pain. She gathered her close in the next moment. "My sweet child."

The slight shoulders shook, and sobs tore from her throat. He caught Ester's gaze, gave her a tender smile, and motioned to the door. She had the girl well in hand. It was time to try to do the same with his son.

He found him in his chamber, looking out the window at the busy street. Cleopas paused in the doorway without making himself known. His boy had grown up, stood at a man's height, had a man's strength. But the wisdom had yet to come.

"I am sorry I was not back sooner, Jason."

Jason spun around, a wry smile on his lips. "I should not have grown angry. It is but the first hour. Did I upset Mother?"

"If so, she is soothing her wounds by lavishing adoration on our new little handmaiden." He sighed and joined his son at the window. A few soldiers hurried by, as well they should be. They were late for the morning drills. "I train soldiers every day, Jason. I could have trained you here."

His son shook his head. "We agreed that Rome would be a better option, Father. I can attend the academies there, check on our family's property. Learn of our culture and escape this oppressive Judaism while learning to be a soldier."

"Please do not speak ill of your mother's faith. You are part Hebrew, and you will do well to remember it."

"I have been submersed in it all my life." Jason waved a hand, as if to dismiss it all. "The Jews will never accept me because of my Roman blood. Perhaps the Romans will overlook the Hebrew part and I will finally find a place for myself."

"In Rome?"

"I could regain the status of your grandfather. Our reputation. Expand our estates."

The very thought wearied him. "I would that you just safely return to your mother's arms."

Jason's lips twitched up. "Rest assured I will see you both again, Father. Perhaps someday I will even serve with you."

He would do all he could to make sure of it.

Abigail found that Simon was surprisingly friendly; then again, he had no reason to feel threatened by an eight-year-old girl whose main purpose in the house was to be Mistress's entertainment. So it made sense that he welcomed her into the kitchen with warmth.

"You, of course, will have little need to know the particular goings-on in here," he said with a smile. "At least for a while."

Abigail sent her gaze around the room. There was a woman rushing about in preparation for the soon-coming meal, the fire roaring in its place, and a table laden with a bounty that she told her mouth she would not taste.

"My wife, Dinah." Simon motioned to the cook. "I will introduce you when it is less hectic. For now, I will take you to meet Andrew. He serves the master, so it is imperative that the two of you learn to work well together."

Abigail nodded. She even voiced her question. "Are there only the four of us?"

"There is also Mark, but he will leave this eve with his lord, Jason." Simon led them through the kitchen, to a brief hallway accessible through it. "Your room is through here. It exits also into the corridor directly outside Mistress's chamber. For now it is your own, but if ever another female is brought, you will of course have to share."

Abigail nodded again; they did not stop at the door he pointed at in indication, but rather went to the next one down. He tapped upon the door and waited the two seconds it took to be opened.

A young man stepped out, girded to serve. He looked surprised to see his fellow servant. "Simon."

Simon smiled. "Andrew, this is Abigail. She is replacing Hadassah in our lady's service. I thought she should meet you before the meal."

Andrew nodded and offered her a friendly smile. "This is a good house to belong to. I came here when but a child myself, and I have chosen to serve my lord for life." He offered a view of his pierced ear as proof, the ring in it matching the one Simon had in his own.

Her new Roman master obeyed Jewish tradition with his servants? Though surprised, she said nothing. Instead, she simply offered a small smile and went into her own room when Simon opened the door.

"Go ahead and change." He indicated the tunic folded neatly on the pallet in the closet. "Once dressed appropriately, come back to the kitchen. You will serve our lady today."

He closed the door again behind her, leaving Abigail alone for a moment with her thoughts. She looked around the quarters with a strange contentment. Here she was with a room of her own, people that welcomed her, and, if nothing else, a degree of security. It was more than she had ever had before.

It took her only a minute to shed her clothes of mourning and slip into the rough material that she knew she would have to get used to. Moving back to the kitchen, however, she found that it was actually a comfortable garment to move around in. *That* at least was helpful. As to the task she was about to undertake . . .

"Just do not drop anything," Dinah whispered in a voice that reminded Abigail strongly of her mother. She immediately pushed the resemblance aside and focused instead on the words. "Mirror Andrew, and you will be fine. We send out a platter for each of them. Mark will take the one for Jason, Andrew the one for the master, and you the one for the mistress. Offer it as he does and be sure to keep her glass full. Otherwise, just stand there and be available."

Abigail nodded and accepted the platter that was placed in her hand. Dinah put a hand on her shoulder to keep her back while the menservants went through the portal into the family's dining area, then gave her a gentle push to follow after them.

The tray was heavy; it was strength of pride rather than body that kept her from dropping it. But she managed even to keep it steady as Ester took the portions she desired, smiling.

She followed Andrew and Mark back out of the room moments later. They exchanged their trays for towels and pitchers.

"I will pour for our lady," Andrew said to Abigail. "The wine is still a bit heavy for you, I think."

Abigail wanted to say that she would manage, but she did not. She had been here for perhaps an hour, he for nearly a decade. And he looked as though he only wanted to be kind. So she muttered her gratitude and followed him once again into the outer room.

"You know that Caesar has never cared too much for our family," Cleopas was saying dryly to his son. "It was Augustus who decided we were not equal to our reputation, but I do not look for Tiberius to be any different."

"But I thought you got along well with Tiberius." Jason took a lazy sip from the freshly filled glass.

"That was many years ago, before he and his mother got it into their heads that he should succeed Augustus."

"Well, if _I_ were even the adopted son of the divine Augustus–"

"Jason!" Ester's displeasure crackled through the air like a living spark. "I will not tolerate such heresy in this household. Caesar is no more divine than–"

"Father, please." Jason turned frustrated eyes to his father. "Tell Mother that as a Roman–"

"No." Both voices of argument died at his word. "We will not argue today. Tomorrow, Jason, you will have only your conscience to guide your beliefs. But today, you will respect your mother. Ester, have you attended to what we discussed?"

Ester nodded and turned to empty-handed Abigail. "Abigail, go to my chamber. Under the couch you will find a wrapped parcel. Bring it to me, please."

Abigail wasted no time. She easily found the chamber again, and the package was right where she was told it would be. But her thoughts were elsewhere. Where exactly, she could not say. Somewhere in the past, perhaps back so far as to when her father yet lived. Perhaps she was remembering what it felt like to be in a house where Caesar was spoken of only as the monster he surely was. Perhaps she was remembering simply her own father, and how he reprimanded her with that loving reproach.

Perhaps it was useless to even think about the past. She went back to the outer room with the object in her hands, handed it over, and then retreated to the wall.

Jason's attention was surely piqued, but to his credit, he waited patiently for whatever gift lay under the wrappings to be given with introduction.

Cleopas cleared his throat. "Your mother and I know that this is the time when we need to let you go, son, to make your own way in the world. You are a man now. And while I will hope, pray, and pull whatever strings necessary to see you back here," he paused to exchange a grin with his son, "there is still the possibility that you will fall in love with Rome."

"Or some lady there," Ester added with a twinkle in her eye.

Jason rolled his own but did not interrupt.

"Since we have no daughter, what remains of your mother's dowry will go to you when you wed. We do not want to burden you with too much, so we selected these few things to send with you now."

Ester handed their son a smallish wooden box, ornate in engravings that pictured the ark of the covenant. Jason barely glanced at the lid. He flipped it open and drew out a heavy chain of gold with a pendant of surprising wealth hanging from the end. It was a large ruby, which complemented the words Ester recited as she watched him withdraw it.

"'Who can find a virtuous woman? for her price is far above rubies. . . Favour is deceitful and beauty is vain, but a woman that feareth the Lord, she shall be praised.'"

Jason ignored the proverb and pulled out the other object.

"It was my father's," Ester offered by way of explanation when he slipped the ring onto his finger.

Jason met his mother's eyes. "I did not realize that your family had such wealth."

Ester held his gaze steadily for a moment before answering. "My father was once high priest of the synagogue. When I married your father, he would have no more to do with me."

"But this jewelry–"

"Was his method of paying me to stay away." She averted her gaze. "He was a hard man, but a good one. I am sorry that he died before you could meet him; I have a feeling he would have taken you under his wing as though you were his son, rather than that of the daughter he claimed not to have."

Jason ran his tongue over his lips, looking at a loss for words. Cleopas smiled softly and apparently decided to take pity on him. "Have you sent your belongings to Steven yet? He asked that they arrive before you so the caravan would be ready to leave upon your arrival."

Jason stood, tucking the closed box under his arm. "I will see to it now, sir."

Cleopas held Ester's gaze for a moment longer, then got up to join their son.

"Two days' journey to Joppa," Ester whispered in a voice low enough for only Abigail to hear. "And then the sail to Rome." Her gaze was on the seat that Jason had just vacated. "So long before I will even know if he arrived safely. So long before I see my son again."

Abigail was shocked to see her small hand on Mistress's shoulder and to hear her voice whispering just as softly, "'Rest in the Lord, and wait patiently for Him.' 'For in thee, O Lord, do I hope: thou wilt hear, O Lord my God.'"

Ester's gaze was still focused on the absent, but her hand came up to engulf Abigail's. "'Why art thou cast down, O my soul? and why art thou disquieted within me? hope thou in God: for I shall yet praise him for the help of his countenance.'" Their gazes met, and a smile even crept onto her face. "We will learn a lot in these coming years, you and I. And when Jason returns, he will find two women worth more than any jewels that bedeck the finger of Caesar."

Abigail did not smile, but her face relaxed. It was more than she could imagine right now, growing up beside this woman. So many changes . . . only two days ago her mother had been alive, eager to tell Silas the news of their new child; now Abigail was an orphaned slave who had not even seen her mother into the tomb. How could she possibly see far enough into the future to visualize herself as a woman? How could she survive the night, alone in that unfamiliar chamber that moments ago she had thought wonderful? How could she even now keep the tears at bay?

"I understand that your loss is far greater than mine, Abigail." Ester tilted her head up with a gentle finger. "I may be parting with my son, but he will return. You do not have that hope. And while nothing can replace a mother, I will do all I can to comfort you. We shall help each other through these times." She smiled. "Take the rest of the day to rest. Our house will be busy with Jason's departure, but there is no reason for you to get involved. Tomorrow I will have Simon knock to be sure you are awake with the others, and he will instruct you in the daily preparations."

Abigail nodded and took a step back as Ester rose from her seat. "I will see you in the morning," the elder said in farewell, leaving the room with grace that Abigail knew she could never muster.

She made her way back to her room but did not immediately close the door, as there were no windows to provide light. A lamp sat on the floor, but she had no desire for illumination. So she took a moment to look again at the space, her eyes finding first the other portal directly across from her. She fully intended to open it soon, just so she would know exactly where it let her out. But not yet. First she would take a nap; sleep had been impossible the night before. She took another second to notice the crudely fashioned chest, small but sturdy, in the corner, the only other object in the room. Then she closed the door and let herself drop down on the pallet, settling down with her eyes closed tightly against reality.

"Father Jehovah," she prayed almost silently, "I know you are with me still. And since you will never forsake me, I ask only that you have mercy on your servant. I realize I will never be a man nor even free, but what I am is your doing." Sensing that if she said any more it would be more accusation than worship, she ended quickly and determined to fall asleep.

TWO

Andrew took his master's sword as Cleopas reached for a water skin. The men emptied from the training field, headed for their midday meal. Andrew relaxed his stance for the first time that day and cast his gaze toward the Visibullis house. From this distance, he could barely make out the figures on the rooftop. Ester would be the one pacing, Abigail the small dot sitting down.

Cleopas looked that way too, and his lips curved up. "Ester says their lessons are going well."

Andrew barely contained a laugh. "Abigail says it is useless to teach a slave girl as if she were son of the high priest."

His master's brows arched, amusement in the quirk. "*Our* Abigail said that? To you?"

"To Dinah." He shook his head and looked toward the females again. In the year she had been with them, Abigail had yet to share so big a piece of her mind with anyone but Dinah. Strange as it seemed, he would have sworn it was pride that kept her so humble with the rest of them.

"Well, she shall have to get used to it, my wife will settle for nothing less than a daughter to instruct." Mischief combined with merriment in Cleopas's eyes. "Perhaps I shall take a role in her schooling as well. If she is learning Greek and Hebrew so well, she ought to learn Latin, ought she not?"

Andrew shifted uncomfortably. It was no great secret that his command of his master's language was minimal, in spite of the lessons Cleopas had given him. "Certainly she would benefit from your tutelage, Lord."

"You will sit in on them too, Andrew. More structured, regular lessons will help you as well."

Andrew swallowed back the desire to groan and focused on his gratefulness for a master who took such interest in them. "I am honored by your attention, Lord."

Cleopas chuckled, proving he was not fooled. A commotion behind them stopped any response he may have made, however.

A glance that direction had Andrew stepping back into his place behind his master, reaching for his waterskin as subtly as possible. The unmistakable plume of the general towered over the milling soldiers, headed their way. Andrew focused on invisibility while Cleopas straightened to his full height and snapped to attention. "Good day, General."

"Cleopas." The general stopped beside them with a slight smile. "Your men are in good form. At this rate, we shall inspire Caesar to expansion once again."

Cleopas chuckled and relaxed his shoulders a bit. "Not unless Augustus's will has changed overnight. Tiberius would never disobey it."

The general grunted and shifted from one foot to another. "I trust you have heard that my wife has joined me here."

"Of course. Is she settling in well?"

"She complains of being lonely. When she learned that my prefect was married, she immediately requested that you and your wife join us for dinner on the morrow. I promised to do all in my power to convince you."

Andrew sucked in an unobtrusive breath as Cleopas's shoulders edged back. In all his time in the Visibullis house, Andrew could not recall an occasion when any of his master's Roman friends had made an overture to include the mistress in their social gatherings. And given that all of her Hebrew family had disowned her upon marrying Cleopas, she had become an expert on loneliness.

"We would be happy to join you." Cleopas's voice sounded even, undoubtedly confident to the general. But Andrew heard the thickness beneath the words.

Perhaps a new season was upon them.

❧

Abigail stared at her master without blinking.

Cleopas looked to be battling back a grin. "I know you are capable, Abigail. What are your objections?"

She focused her gaze the ground, as she made it a point to do when she spoke. "I simply do not wish to disappoint you, Master. But your servant is of small mind."

Cleopas laughed, which brought her gaze back to his for half a moment. "If ever there was a child of greater mind, Abigail, I have yet to find her. Ester has kept me updated on your progress this past year, and she is very pleased. You, my child, have a strong mind, and you learn quickly. For example: how long has it been since you began your studies of written Greek?"

"One month, Master."

"One month. And already you can read the letters I have provided and translate them into written Hebrew."

"My mother taught me both languages, Master."

"The spoken versions, though, correct?"

"Yes, Master."

Cleopas turned to Andrew, who stood with a muted grin in the corner of the room. "Andrew, did you grow up speaking both Greek and Hebrew?"

"Yes, Master."

"And have you learned the written forms?"

"Not well. I know enough to carry out your business."

"And how long since I began tutoring you?"

"Five years, Lord."

"Well then." Cleopas turned back to Abigail. "Either I am a miserable teacher in comparison with my beloved wife, or you, Abigail, have a mind for learning. Which do you think, Andrew?"

Andrew smiled at the verbal trap. "I believe that Mistress is a splendid tutor and Abigail a quick learner both; moreover, I hold that Abigail will learn just as quickly under your direction."

There was no point in arguing further, if argument was even a proper name for the small objection she had raised upon interrogation. She dutifully took her place at the table in the kitchen and waited for the two men to get settled. Truth be told, she knew she *could* learn the language. But she should not. Ester had started their relationship as one more appropriate for a mother and daughter, but Abigail knew she was not in that position. It did not matter that the woman had given her softer, more becoming clothing; it did not matter that she instructed her in the arts of womanhood, as well as lessons that should be left to free men. She was a slave girl. It was the portion the Lord had given her. Why try to pretend otherwise?

"Shall we begin with verb conjugations?" Cleopas asked.

"Yes, Master," she replied. "Are they similar to the Greek?"

"Somewhat." His eyes went to his other student, who squirmed as if in pain. Cleopas smiled. "Let us begin."

"Mistress, I will never finish your hair if you do not sit still." Abigail bit back a smile and put a calming hand on Ester's shoulder. The lady's excitement mounted with every moment, but the complicated Roman style she had desired for her hair would never be finished at this rate. It was difficult enough to begin with.

"Sorry." Ester chuckled but held herself still. "I am nervous. All these years, I have been alone, and now I do not know how to identify myself. What if they see the Roman style and think me pretentious? Or if they eye my Hebrew dress and decide I am out of mode? Will they think my jewels–"

"Mistress." Abigail put the pin she had held back onto the table and wrapped her arms around Ester. "What they will see is a woman of great beauty. And they will be pleased to see you trying to show how pleasing you are to be seen with."

As Abigail had hoped, Ester laughed, gave her a quick hug, and drew in a steadying breath. "Well said, little one. Your mind amazes me daily."

"I am but your humble servant."

Ester snorted and turned for her hair to be finished. "So you say. Now, let us finish so that you can change. I have a belt for you, so that we match."

"I will complement you as best I can." She picked up one of the last free lengths of hair, coiled it. Wrapped it into the space she'd left on Ester's head, and pinned it until it was secure. Then she picked up the headpiece of gold that her mistress had chosen and slipped it over her head from ear to ear. "Mistress . . . what will I be doing tonight?"

It was not a question she would usually dare to ask, but she had no desire to make a fool of herself or the woman she had come to adore.

Ester hummed. "I do not know. In all likelihood, they will have servants to perform your usual tasks. Unless they provide other instruction, let us say you should remain close to me to serve in the ways only you know how to do."

With a dip of her head, Abigail fastened Ester's ornate necklace and then stood back to survey her work. "I will make you proud, Mistress. If they care to look, they will see that your handmaiden serves you out of love."

Ester placed a soft hand on Abigail's cheek. "And if they look further, they will see the mistress loves her servant. Now run along, little one, and put on your linen tunic.

Then I will brush your hair."

She had long ago given up arguing about that, since Ester derived such pleasure from it. After a nod, she slipped out, into her closet, and quickly changed.

Within the hour, the family set off into Jerusalem. Abigail took her place beside Andrew, behind the Visibullis couple. Ester traveled a half step behind Cleopas, but still he defied custom by constantly turning his face around to converse with her. Perhaps in Rome they were not so strict about such things.

For a moment, Abigail simply admired the sway of her mistress's hips, the graceful stride with which she moved. But Andrew snagged her attention with a clearing of his throat, and her gaze moved up to him.

He offered a tight smile. "Be careful tonight, little one. I do not believe the master mentioned it to the mistress, but the general's wife specifically asked for them to bring us so that she might see what kind of maidservants are to be had from among our people."

Abigail frowned up at her fellow servant. "Should I behave any differently than usual?"

"No, but I wanted you to be aware. Our house . . . they treat us better than most. The recognize us as people, as individuals. In all likelihood you will be studied tonight as a piece of merchandise, and you are not accustomed to that. I did not want you to be surprised."

She nodded, but her mind flitted back to the cold, hard gazes of Silas and Rebekka. True, she had only been in their household for a year, but even when Mother lived, Abigail had received worse treatment from them than at the hand of these, her legal masters.

Andrew drifted a step closer. "Do you miss your mother much?"

Was she so transparent? Gaze on the ground again, Abigail saw no reason to lie. He could undoubtedly see the sheen of tears in her eyes anyway. "I do. And my father, who died a year before she did."

"And then your mother remarried?"

Small clouds of dirt puffed up with every step of their feet. "My father's friend. We were in debt to him and he . . . Mother said if she did not marry him, he would have taken all we had. I had no brother, no uncles to care for us. We would have been left as beggars if we had not gone to Silas's house. So the day her mourning was complete, they wedded."

Andrew sucked in a breath that sounded as outraged as she felt. "So soon?"

A short nod confirmed it. "His first wife was displeased, jealous. Mother was very beautiful."

"I suppose that is why she sold you."

"Yes." Her gaze went to the backs of Ester and Cleopas, and warmth surged up inside her. "I am blessed that it was the master who came."

"You are indeed." Andrew's tone was low, serious enough to tell Abigail he spoke of something she did not quite understand.

The walk to the general's house was short, though on the other side of the Praetorium. Many soldiers of the Tenth Legion were out and about on the streets, all showing deference to the man in charge of their training as they passed him. Cleopas acknowledged each as if he knew them by name, by face.

Abigail suspected he did. A man to take such an interest in his slave's education surely gave even greater respect to the free men under his command.

When they arrived at the massive abode that housed the general, Abigail followed Andrew's lead and headed to the kitchen at the rear of the house.

A dour-faced man received them. "The bulk of the serving will be done by our staff," he said as he made a motion to a girl behind him. "Since you know your masters best, stay by their sides and we will deliver food and drink into your hands."

His eyes narrowed upon Abigail. She fought the urge to squirm and instead squared her shoulders. He sniffed. "Although perhaps we ought to provide a maidservant for the lady?"

Andrew's hand landed with comforting weight upon her shoulder. "Abigail is strong. She handles everything herself."

She could not have said why his confidence in her warmed a frozen place inside.

Ester followed her hostess outside into the well-appointed courtyard, happy to escape the talk of politics that the men had turned to. She knew her husband was enjoying the chance to socialize with others more recently from Rome–after twenty years in Israel, and ten in Gaul before that, Cleopas undoubtedly missed the customs of his home. But he had chosen to let her run their house in the Hebrew tradition, which meant that his were still largely unfamiliar to her.

Several moments throughout the night, she had felt the difference of her world and his. In things as small as the stola Julia wore over her tunic to the vast difference in their outlooks.

Ester settled onto a stone bench, softened with colorful cushions that a servant undoubtedly took inside every night, and motioned for Abigail to take up her position behind her. She would have liked to urge the girl onto the pillow at her side–would have, had they been home–but refrained. Julia would not approve, and Abigail would feel it.

Julia's maidservant had also followed them out, but the hostess waved her away with an abrupt flick of her wrist. The girl, probably twice Abigail's age, slunk back inside. Julia sighed. "That girl is such a nuisance. I brought her with me from Rome, but she has done nothing but mope since we arrived. I begin to think she had a lover there she did not tell me about."

Ester hummed but made no other reply. Perhaps she ought to comment on the lovely jeweled collar Julia wore. Anything to turn the conversation from the servant's personal life.

Julia's eyes turned to Abigail. "How long have you had your girl?"

"Abigail has been with me for a year." Hopefully her soft smile would prove she was more than just a girl to her.

"Only that long? She is very well trained. From whom did you purchase her?"

Ester shifted, turned slightly so that Abigail would not feel like a shadow behind her. "The poor dear was orphaned, and her guardians could not keep her. Thankfully, Cleopas heard of it and brought her home to me. I have been very blessed to have her."

"She is a pretty child. I have always thought that important–who wants to look at a homely creature every day? So long as they do not think themselves above their stations because of their looks." She narrowed her gaze on Abigail. "Do you dress her so well to entertain yourself, or is she already showing signs of arrogance?"

Ester felt her spine go rigid. "It is Hebrew tradition to treat fellow Israelites with compassion. Especially orphaned children, even if they are slaves. Moses says they are in their position only because of an unfortunate turn, not because they are worth any less than the rest of us."

Julia's face reflected apology and youth. Ester was reminded of the decade she had on her hostess, of the relatively new marriage to the general. "I am sorry," her hostess said, voice soft. "The custom in Rome is quite different, and I am not very familiar with the ways of the Jews. I pray you will be patient with me and help me learn the customs of your people. I will need the education, if I am to survive here for any length of time."

Ester relaxed again. "I will be glad to help. And perhaps you can teach me more of the ways of Rome. Cleopas and I have not had the opportunity to return to his home."

She was rewarded by Julia's bright, young smile. "I would be honored. Thank you."

Ester let a relieved breath ease slowly from her lungs. Finally, after twenty years of marriage, she had made a Roman friend.

THREE

Cleopas noticed the shift in his men before he heard the tickle of a familiar female voice. Their language changed from curses to pleasant observations, their shoulders edged back, their chins went up. He had no need to look over his shoulder to realize that Abigail had stopped by. The greeting of Vetimus, one of his centurions, merely confirmed it.

"Abigail, good morning. Market day, is it?"

Her laughter rang out, incongruous with the clang of swords and armor if familiar to it. "As you well know. Though Michael once again tried to charge me too much for the oranges."

"Because you steal the man's livelihood every time you haggle him down. But more importantly, have you any of Dinah's famous honey cakes in the basket?"

Again, her laughter filled the halls. "Not today, but I have been instructed to invite you and your family to dinner at your earliest convenience."

"Name the day, and we shall be there."

"Tomorrow."

"We shall see you then. And if it is Andrew you search for, you shall find him at the entryway to the field."

"Thank you."

Cleopas turned to Andrew. "I imagine my wife has sent her with the correspondence I forgot this morning. Go ahead and fetch it. I shall be over in a moment with the letter."

Andrew nodded and moved away from the open field, back into the building. Cleopas watched the soldiers for a moment longer, shouting out a command when one flank broke formation. Then his thoughts drifted to the parchment he had received that morning, and his pulse kicked up.

Usually he would bring any news from Jason home with him in the evenings and read it to Ester himself. She had never learned to read Latin, but Jason would write in nothing else. This, however, could not wait. He would entrust it to Abigail, who would not only read it without fault but would be a steadying check on his wife's nerves.

Eyeing the angle of the sun, Cleopas dismissed his men for their meals and spun around to find his servants. Andrew had accepted a few twined letters from Abigail and had maneuvered her into a corner, shielding her from view of the other men. Had she realized his reasoning, she would probably not have stood so happily, chatting.

"Dinah will need my help," Abigail was saying to Andrew, "so we shall have to cancel your Latin tutorial tonight."

Andrew sounded as though he was grinning. "A terrible shame. I shall mourn its loss."

Cleopas rolled his eyes as he moved over to them. Abigail had long ago caught up to him in knowledge, but Andrew still needed the lessons as much as he hated them.

Upon reaching the two, he greeted her with a nod. "Abigail, thank you. I am glad you came. Could you please take this home?" He pulled out the parchment, handed it to her. "Read it to your mistress straight away."

Her eyes sparked curiosity that made it nowhere near her lips. "Certainly, Lord. I shall take it over this moment."

"Have a good afternoon." Andrew stepped back to let her pass and sighed as she left another wave of staring soldiers in her wake. "Your men are beginning to notice that Abigail is no longer a child, Lord."

"Mm." And distracted soldiers were never a good thing. "I think it is time that Simon resume the responsibility of trips to the Praetorium. Though our young friend will not enjoy the curb to her independence."

Andrew grinned and took his place behind Cleopas. "I say we let the mistress be the one to tell her, then."

"You are a wise man indeed, Andrew. That is a sound plan if ever I heard one. We shall let my wife be deafened by her silence and save ourselves the guilt." Grinning in return, he nodded. "Her obedience can be so demeaning, can it not? Were she a man, she would make an excellent soldier."

"Were she a man," his servant said behind him, "I suspect she would soon command us all."

◈

Abigail smoothed out the parchment, wondering what news it held. Surely something important, for Cleopas to send it home midday. But nothing bad, or he would not have delegated the task.

She glanced at her mistress, whose foot swung back and forth as she waited. Abigail smiled. "Shall I read it in Hebrew?"

Ester nodded. "Please."

She cleared her throat and directed her gaze to the words. It was addressed only to Cleopas, so Abigail skipped the salutation altogether. It may hurt her mistress, if only slightly, to know that her son had not cared to include her in whatever was of such import.

"'I have not much time to write,'" she began, "'as I must go soon to the house of a friend to dine. They are an influential family, and it may serve me well to be accepted by them. Titus's father, Caius Asinius, was up until recently a consul, and a very successful one. Of course, some say it is because of Tiberius's excellent mood due to the death of Germanicus that he was met with such ease in his duties, but I will retain judgement on the matter, as I have never had cause to meet the Emperor himself. At any rate, the house of Asinius is one destined to greatness, and I am pleased to be seen as one of their friends. Actually, though, I find Titus a bit intolerable sometimes, as he seems to have the opinion that he is too good to serve as a soldier. He seems to think that his career in war will not be long-lasted, as his father apparently has other plans for him in a year or two. At any rate, it is still Menelaus Casicus I most enjoy spending my time with, but as he is of a family far below our own, originally Greek, I believe, it is not so advantageous to spend my evenings with him.

"'On to the real news, though. I just received my assignments today, and while I am sure you will get the official word soon if you have not already, I knew you would rather hear from me: I am to serve directly under you, Father, replacing Marcus Persibia, the news of whose death has just reached Rome. So I will be on a ship to Joppa within the month, bound home. Tell Mother I am looking forward to seeing her again. Menelaus and Titus have both been assigned in Jerusalem as well; Menelaus to the palace of Pontius Pilate, an enviable post, as he has shown excellent skill in defensive combat. I am not certain where Titus will be; he only said the Tenth Legion and no more.

"'At any rate, that concludes the time I have allotted to this letter, and I must be going to the Asiniuses' now. Give Mother a kiss for me, and know that I miss you both. Much respect, your son, Jason.'"

Abigail looked up from the parchment to see her mistress's face. Ester sat, at the moment, surprisingly still. Her gaze was looking upon something Abigail could not see, something much farther away than Rome. Back six years, perhaps, to the man-child who had left her home with high expectations. Abigail tried to conjure up that image of her first day in this house, but the memory was shrouded in years of growth and change. All she could recall was an impression of a boy with disrespect for the woman she had come to love so much and an eagerness to escape the Law that made Israel a nation blessed by God. The Law she was so grateful to have been taught, that had shown her time and again how fortunate she was to have landed in a house that observed it.

"So long I have prayed for his return, and now I fear it." Ester shook her head, tears in her eyes. "What if he is no longer the son I remember? What if he has given himself to all I warned him against?"

"Do not borrow troubles, Mistress. He seems happy to be coming home. Perhaps it required change for that to be, but it cannot be so bad, can it?"

Ester smiled and gripped Abigail's hand. "You are right. Even so, I need to think, to pray. Leave me for a while, dear one."

Abigail obeyed, slipped quietly from the chamber. And determined to return soon to ensure that her mistress's thoughts did not lead to undue burden.

She headed for the kitchen, where Dinah was hard at work, as always. For a moment, Abigail paused to watch her. In so many ways, Dinah reminded her of Mother. The voice, the way she moved. And since Dinah had never had children of her own, she knew she had a special place in the woman's heart. These moments in the kitchen beside her gave Abigail a feeling of home. Here she was an orphaned slave, but with two women who thought of her as a daughter. One she could work beside, one who could teach her.

Dinah pulled down a stack of clay bowls and started singing a psalm. Abigail moved into the room, joining her voice in the hymn. She had helped in here enough over the years to slip into the rhythm seamlessly. They finished the song together as they worked, then Dinah drew in a satisfied breath.

"Did you hear any news in the marketplace today?"

"Very little." Abigail checked the bread dough. It had risen sufficiently, so she shaped it into loaves. "You know they stop talking when we come. Not that they do not like us, but they know we serve Romans, and I believe it is they that cause most of the grumbling these days."

"Yes." Dinah rinsed some vegetables. "There is much unrest. Andrew mentioned that another rebellion was discovered and quieted just last week."

"I am glad that the master seldom has cause to be involved with such things. I understand our people's cry for freedom, but at the same time, it is a good house we serve. Master is not a tyrant, even if Caesar is."

Dinah laughed. "Speak like that in the markets, and you will be turned over to the high priest for treason."

Abigail shared her smile. "Did Andrew mention who was leading this last uprising?"

"No, I do not believe he knew. I suppose no one mentioned it today?"

"No. The only thing of any interest was the gossip about that teacher."

"You do not suppose he could be a rebel, do you? Simon heard that some are calling him the messiah." Dinah picked up a knife and began cutting the greens.

"The news I heard about him has been more the complaining of the Sanhedran than anything else. Apparently the man healed a cripple on the Sabbath or some such thing. Nothing to indicate that he is planning to free Israel from Rome."

"Yes, well, Simon also said he is preaching spiritual rebirth and salvation, of all things. As if the Law is not enough for us."

Abigail retrieved a bowl from the shelf. "I have heard very little about him, to tell the truth. I suppose I will reserve judgement on the man."

"Mm. Oh, is Vetimus coming tomorrow?"

"Yes," Abigail replied. "I cannot wait to see little Claron again. The child gets more adorable every time I see him."

Dinah smiled in response. "The poor thing. I hate seeing someone so small with such an illness. To think he will never run with the other boys–"

"Do not bemoan his future yet." Abigail borrowed Dinah's tone for the reminder. "Perhaps he will grow out of it."

"Or perhaps that teacher will heal him." Her tone was sarcastic, a reprimand for Abigail's reprimand.

Abigail smiled. There were no words for a moment, just the methodic sounds of a busy kitchen. Dinah was the first to speak again. "I imagine Mistress and Master will be arranging your marriage soon."

"What?" Her hands stilled, and her voice sounded flat and incredulous to her own ears.

Dinah did not interrupt her chopping. "You will be in your fourteenth year in but a month. It is time for you to be a wife."

"But I am a sl–"

"Surely you have caught on in the past years. Mistress did not want to procure a girl to serve here forever. She wanted a companion, a daughter that she could raise." She finally stilled her hands and looked at Abigail. "She wants the best for you."

Abigail had no response. Certainly she knew that most young women her age were betrothed or married. But the very thought of leaving yet another home, one where she loved and was loved in return . . . it did not bear thinking about. "I need to check on the mistress."

It was the one excuse that Dinah would not argue with.

Abigail found her mistress exactly where she left her. She put a small hand on Ester's shoulder. The woman sighed at the touch but did not alter her unseeing gaze.

"It will be all right, will it not, Abigail? When my son returns, I will see that life has shaped him into a good man?"

"Of course," Abigail replied dutifully. "Come now, Mistress, let us get you changed. You are meeting Mistress Julia for the midday meal, remember?"

Ester sprang up. "I had forgotten! What would I do without you, Abigail?" She headed for her closet. "You go change yourself first. I will get everything ready in here."

Abigail knew Ester wanted a few moments to gather her wits again, so she obliged. She went to her little room and lit the lamp, more than happy to slip out of the course tunic she wore to the markets—it was her own rule, not Ester's, that she be seen as a slave by the populace—and into the fine, pale linen she wore at home. She knew that Ester would have a belt for her, as always.

Thinking of such things was far preferable to the topic that Dinah had planted in her mind.

Abigail followed Julia's handmaiden up onto the roof of the general's house. The two ladies were in the courtyard sipping their wine and had dismissed the girls to their own meals. Over the past years Abigail had become good friends with Elizabeth, a Hebrew girl a bit her junior whom Julia had purchased soon after her own arrival.

"Did you see Julia's necklace?" Elizabeth settled down with her bowl. "It is absolutely divine. I do not even recognize some of the jewels."

Abigail nodded and took a bite of food, not bothering to reflect on the lack of respect her friend showed her mistress when out of her company. She would never refer to Ester by her given name to another. She deserved every morsel of respect Abigail could give her. As for Elizabeth—she could govern or not her own thoughts as she chose.

When Abigail made no other response, Elizabeth sighed and grew abnormally silent. Her food remained untouched. Then she said, "The general gave me as wife to Cleon a few days ago."

Abigail was glad she did not have any food in her mouth. "Cleon? The kitchen—"

"The only Cleon in the house." Elizabeth pushed her bowl away. "The old and loyal servant who deserved a nice young wife since his died on the passage from Rome."

Abigail was not sure what to say. "He is . . . a kind man."

Elizabeth nodded reluctantly. "He is very kind, very gentle, and very dull. But I had hoped that when it came time for me to go to a man, it would be to someone more exciting."

Questions filtered into Abigail's mind, but modesty censored most of them. "Such as whom?"

"The general."

Again, Abigail was glad she had nothing to choke on. "What? Elizabeth, he is your mistress's husband!"

"I keep forgetting how innocent you are. Surely you, the one who has been taught the Law, know that all female servants are legally the wives of their masters if he so chooses. Why are you so surprised that I would hope for that?"

She fumbled for an argument. "Well, for one thing, the general is even older than

Cleon–"

"But a general, not a kitchen slave."

"He would never give you his whole heart."

Elizabeth met her gaze, brown eyes meeting brown eyes as always, but with some new spark that Abigail did not like. When the younger spoke, it was more softly than usual. "Do not be naive, Abigail. Someone like us cannot hope for the heart of any man whose heart is his to give. A free man will never give it, and a slave's belongs to his master. We are lucky if we can find favor in our master's eyes. I have already been sold twice. I do not wish to repeat that again."

"I am sorry–"

"Do not be sorry!" Elizabeth stood, slashing a hand through the air. "I am sick of your pity. We both know that my mother was a harlot and yours an upstanding widow. Do not feel sorrow that my first master sold me because his son turned rebel and fled to the hills before I came of age. It will only make you feel better about yourself to pity me, and you do not need that. You have it good enough as it is!"

"Elizabeth–"

"Just wait, Abigail. Someday soon you will understand what I mean."

Abigail felt her brows pull down, the anger bubble up. "Are you a prophetess now? Shall we call you Anna?"

Her friend ignored her. "Maybe the prefect will give you to Simon, since his wife is barren. Or maybe old Cleopas himself will–"

"Stop!" Abigail's voice grew loud for the first time in the conversation, and she stood to emphasize her point. "Speak how you will of your own masters, but mine you will treat with the honor they are due."

"Always the good little slave." Elizabeth turned to face the Praetorium.

Without another word, Abigail left the roof. Surely this day would forever be fixed in her memory as one stained by unwelcomed truth.

FOUR

Abigail glanced once more at the table, set and ready for their guests. She heard the commotion at the door, Simon answering. She slipped behind Ester as she and Cleopas moved to greet Vetimus, his expecting wife, and their small son. The small family had a new luminosity about them, especially little Claron.

When he hopped about without a limp, Abigail forgot herself. "Claron! Your leg!"

The little boy grinned. "It is better! The Lord healed me!"

Ester and Cleopas looked first to each other, then to the parents of the suddenly whole boy. Vetimus put a possessive hand on his son's small shoulder. "Phoebe and Claron were in Capernaum visiting her sister. The Nazarene was there."

"Who?" Ester never heard as much gossip as the rest of them, since she rarely went into town. And Abigail rarely bothered her with the stories of the latest rebel.

"His name is Jesus." Phoebe smiled and put a hand on her son's shoulder. "I have heard the most remarkable stories of the man. I had no idea he was in the city, of course, but as Camilla and I were shopping, Claron got away from me and ran up to this stranger."

"He was nice," Claron interjected in his little-boy voice. "He bent down and picked me up and smiled at me. Then, when Mother came to get me, he put me down again and I could walk!"

"It was a miracle." Phoebe fairly beamed.

Ester, disbelief in her eyes, held out an arm. "Why do we not go in to dinner, and you can finish the story?"

The visitors followed Ester and Cleopas into the other room, but the conversation did not stop. Abigail trailed behind, careful to listen as Phoebe continued the tale. "Some are calling him Messiah, but I do not know exactly what that means. He is a Jew, though, so I was hoping you may know a bit more about it, Ester."

Her mistress looked uncomfortable. "There have been many prophecies, of course, but most are disputed. The general populace holds that they portend a Christ, a man who will come as a king to deliver Israel. Others, my father included, held that the Scriptures speak of no such individual, but rather to many different men who have already come and gone. I do not know."

Phoebe's face fell. "This was no king, certainly. But nevertheless, he healed my child, without even being asked. It was as though his very touch contained magic."

Vetimus laughed. "Have you been in Persia, my love? There is no magic."

"Power, then."

Claron piped up. "I knew he could make me better."

He grinned into the looks of shock everyone sent him. "He is God. And God can heal anybody."

Did Abigail ever have such faith as this child? Not in her recollection. Then again, no messiah had ever healed her.

"Which god, though?" Phoebe shook her head. "Apollo? Jupiter?"

"*God*," the boy insisted. "He made me better."

Cleopas smiled at the child. "Indeed." He turned to his wife. "I, too, have heard of this Jesus of Nazareth. For a while, when people first started wondering as to the possibility that he is a messiah of some sort, there was question that perhaps he was a rebel. We kept an ear on the stories coming in about him but were not worried. It seems he is more concerned with preaching repentance and telling stories and healing people than with Rome. A rabbi."

"I hear he fed five thousand people with just a few loaves and fishes." Vetimus's lips twitched into a grin.

The other adults laughed over that one, and Phoebe's eyes twinkled. "Stories certainly have a way of growing with the telling, do they not?"

The conversation turned to other far-fetched stories they had heard over the years, many of them about senators and Augustus himself. Abigail took the opportunity to sweep the child out the room, as she always did, and into the kitchen.

Dinah had a plate ready for him. Simon and Andrew were doing all the serving tonight so the women would be free to watch the boy.

"I am better!" Claron proclaimed again upon seeing a new face.

Dinah looked from the boy to Abigail.

"You were right." She did not intend her voice to be hushed, but it was so nonetheless. "The teacher healed him."

Dinah just nodded and smiled. "I made your favorites." She bent down to be on a level with him. "Would you like some now?"

Abigail met her gaze again, well understanding the unspoken message within it: they ought to be grateful he was well, and question nothing else. Questions of this sort never had answers one could believe.

◈

The wine was excellent, the food superb. It was no surprise to Jason; he had yet to receive anything but the best treatment when a guest in the Asinius house. His main pleasure came from the others, and the fact that they were all there. Menelaus, for instance, had never even been invited here before, nor had the other two soldiers present, Lentulus and Apidius. To be sure, if they were not all going to Israel together, this gathering would probably never have occurred. But since they were much livelier than Titus, Jason was glad to have them in on this particular celebration.

Caius and his wife, Aquilia, were out for the evening; Jason was certain they wished to have no part of their son's party, but they had made sure he had ample provisions for it.

"Jason, is the food this good in Jerusalem?" Lentulus asked, taking a large bite.

Jason laughed. "In my mother's kitchen, perhaps, but not where you will be. Besides," he added, motioning to the dish in his friend's hand, "you will not find that particular delicacy anywhere in Israel."

"Oh. Pork. Right."

Jason nodded and tasted it himself. He did not consider himself bound by the laws of his mother's people, and had, therefore, no qualms about eating what he wished. "I know I will miss it."

"What are the women like?" Menelaus asked, not for the first time. His gaze followed one of Titus's slaves as she refilled his wine and gave him a sultry smile.

Titus shook his head. "Menelaus, your mind is on but one thing. Have no fear; I am sure there are harlots in Israel, just as in Rome."

Menelaus threw a chunk of bread at his friend. "Spoken as a man who has no reason to pay for what he can find in his own house."

Titus shrugged but smiled, not hesitating to put his hand on the thigh of the slave as she moved to refill his glass. The woman kissed his proffered lips before moving off to tend to Jason's drink.

"I will miss Rome," Apidius said. "And I do not mind saying so. Nowhere else can you find the culture and opportunity. Art. Freedom."

"Drusilla," the rest added in unison, which quickly turned into laughter.

Apidius flushed but joined in the laughter. "You are all just jealous that I have a woman who is worth being a wife."

"And a lot of good it does you." Menelaus stifled his mumble with a gulp of wine. "You are getting shipped to Israel with the rest of us."

"Feel free to stop mentioning it at any time."

"A lot of good that would do, as well."

"Menelaus, you depress me."

The insulted man held up his glass in salute before tossing its contents down his throat, then kept the empty vessel in the air to be filled yet again by the smiling maid.

The woman looked at her master silently. When he nodded, she proceeded to descend into Menelaus' lap, setting her pitcher on the side table in the same motion, and capture his receptive mouth with hers.

"Well, at least one of us is happy." Lentulus sighed, his eyes skirting to the couple and then back again to the wall.

"Why do you two not go elsewhere to spare the other poor gentlemen?" Only disinterest colored Titus's tone.

Jason watched his friend and the tempting slave get up and move out of the room. He took a deep breath, telling himself to be glad Titus was finally accepting Menelaus. But, as that man would say, a lot of good it would do now, two days before they left Rome. Even with these thoughts, though, part of his mind was remembering his own pleasant experience with the sensuous wench now entertaining his friend.

Another slave entered at that moment, one Jason had seen less frequently. She was beautiful, graceful, tasteful. Her clothing was not the sheer and barely-covering material of the other women serving them, but it still showed the curves that put all the others to shame. She went directly to Titus, whispered a word in his ear, waited for his equally short murmur in reply, then departed again without even glancing at the other men.

Jason had seen her before. He did not know her name, since Titus never referred to her or spoke loudly when she entered, but he knew who she was. She was the one maid in this house that Titus would never share; she was his, and his alone. He knew that much, from previous visits where they had exchanged a kiss in addition to the whispers.

He was suddenly glad to be going home to the land he had grown up in, where *his* family was the one with the influence, where these friends of his would have nothing that he himself either did not have or could not get with greater ease than they. It was not that he wanted them to be without, or even that he wanted to be better; he was just ready not to be in the deficit.

It was at least two hours later when Jason decided he had taken his fill of the refreshments and company and sought fresh air in their stead. His retreat led him to the gardens in the rear of the house, probably his favorite place on the estate. The more frequently he was entertained by the Asiniuses, the more appreciation he had for their remarkable grounds.

There was a cool breeze blowing, but the temperature was still warm enough that he was not chilled, simply freshened. He chose not to go to one of the benches, opting instead to walk the maze of paths. The stars were lustrous tonight, dazzling, in fact, in their clarity. There was Venus, now the Evening Star, and there was Saturn, retrograding, as he had learned in his studies.

And there was a noise disturbing his solitude.

"Jason!" It was Caius, so the younger man opted not to be perturbed by the interruption.

"Lord! You are returned earlier than we expected."

The ex-consul moved in closer. "I wanted to catch you before you left. I have an offer for you."

Both curiosity and eyebrows raised, Jason leaned on the stone wall beside him. "Of what nature?"

Caius, too, leaned on the wall. "We both know that the solder's life is not an easy one, Jason. Even if not involved in an active campaign, one still faces dangers."

"I am aware of its risks, sir." What he did not know was his host's point.

"Titus is my only son, and he is my heir. I did not act fast enough to keep him here, but I have every intention of getting him ordered home as quickly as possible; but it could take a while."

He was beginning to catch on. "Lord, your son is an able soldier. He is in little danger."

"In battle, perhaps," the man conceded. "But Titus has a strange disposition that I have never understood. His temper can be unriled when he is greatly insulted but then flares up with no provocation." Caius paused to take a breath. "To be honest, I do not trust him to stay out of trouble in a foreign land. Which brings me to my proposition. You are a man of sound and dependable manner, Jason. And, since solders' pay is nothing to brag about, I would like to satisfy both of our needs. I am prepared to offer you a comfortable monthly stipend in exchange for your keeping an eye on my son."

Jason was tempted to laugh but settled for a smile. "Lord, as Titus is my friend and your family has welcomed me so warmly, I will do all I can to safeguard him. But there is no need for payment. Especially since there is no guarantee we will be near each other in our assignments or that he will even find himself in a position to need my aid."

Caius waved off his objections. "If I wish to waste my money on a deserving friend, then I will. And so long as you simply speak with him on occasion and keep abreast of his social life, which is my main concern, I will be content." With that, Caius put a fatherly hand on Jason's shoulder. "One of my men is a merchant in Jerusalem. I have already sent him instruction. He visits your father's camp monthly. At that time, just relay any information that you think I need to know. But even if there is none, which I honestly hope will be the case, he will dispense your stipend."

"Really, Lord, I have no need of–"

"Then save it for your future or spend it on your friends. I will hear no more arguments." He smiled, apparently quite happy with himself. "I will probably not see you again before you leave, so have a splendid eve and a pleasant trip. It has been a delight to call you a friend. Be sure and return to Rome, son, and when you do, I will give you all the aid you need in whatever endeavors you plan for yourself."

"Thank you, Lord." Sincere gratitude rocked him. "Truly, it means much to be numbered among your friends."

They clasped hands, then Caius moved away, back into his house, leaving Jason with another moment of silence.

It did not last long. The voice that spoke this time was soft, unfamiliar. He had to turn, in fact, to find its owner in the shadows.

"Master Jason?"

Unless the darkness deceived him, it was that slave of Titus's, the one whose name he had never discovered. If possible, she was even more beautiful under the soft luminescence of the stars, her dark hair and olive features blending harmoniously with the night. He made no verbal reply, but when his eyes met hers, she stepped nearer.

"You have agreed to my master's request?"

She had obviously been listening, so should know the answer. But he replied anyway. "I have."

From the closer vantage point he could see that her eyes contained a dangerous light in them, something he would not have expected. This woman was one with a determined will.

"I would add my own request to his."

So even the slaves looked to him to grant their desires. This should be interesting. He pasted on a lazy smile. "Would you ask that I keep him from falling in love with another?"

That spark flickered in her eyes. "I would not. In fact, the opposite." When he straightened, surprised, she smiled. "Things will change when Titus leaves. I would be a fool to expect otherwise. The moment he steps out of Rome he loses his claim to me, and not by my will. But if he does not realize this truth, his return will be fierce."

He could easily comprehend. Caius was known for his love of beautiful women; he may respect his son's property while he was present, but he would not recognize it in his absence.

"The master was right about his son's temper, but I have the understanding he lacks. My lord can be terrible in his jealousy; it inflames him. Please, Lord. There is enough tension between father and son as it is. I would not want it to erupt because of me."

He somehow doubted the direction of her concern. From what he knew of his friend, it would not just be his father that he would grow angry with. And he knew also that *he* would not relish being in Titus's path when he was raging.

"I promise, fair one, to do all in my power to make him forget you." He smiled again.

"I will throw him in the path of every lovely face I see."

She smiled, too, and drew even nearer. When her body was pressed against his, awakening his senses acutely, she gave him a fiery kiss. "When you return to Rome," she whispered, "I will give you the proper thanks." She kissed him again, then moved away, back into the shadows, no doubt to prepare herself for Titus's retiring.

Still burning with her touch, Jason decided to take a few minutes more to calm down before returning to the party. He briefly touched his moistened lips and smiled again. She, if nothing else, would be worth returning to Rome for. Which made him wonder how he could possibly grant her request. Especially since Titus was not one easily persuaded of anything. At least Caius's request would be easy enough; the son did not show his best face to the father, but all his friends knew him as the responsible one.

Well, he *had* tried to persuade the man not to pay him. But when confronted with a determined man like Caius Asinius, one did not stand a chance.

⚜

Ester did not know whether to cross her arms in anger, sigh, or laugh. So she was silent for a moment, then simply said, "Cleopas, it is not that I object."

"But yet you refuse." He was sitting on the bed, his elbow propping his body up with the help of a mountain of pillows.

She sat beside him, her stance one of pleading. "Not for my own sake. You know that. It is simply that—"

"You have been dreaming and planning for so long."

She lowered her eyes in humility. "And you have encouraged my dreams and plans."

"So I have." Cleopas pushed himself up and took her in his arms. "And I do still. But this is an option that had not occurred to me, and I am not certain why. It would be ideal."

"For whom, Cleopas?" She rested her hands on his chest. "For us? For me? Or for them?"

He sighed and rested his forehead on hers. "Think about it. I will give you one month to decide, since it *is* your decision. Unless in that time you come up with something better, we will consent. How is that?"

Ester smiled. "You are a good and fair man, my husband."

⚜

Ester left the sanctuary of her abode with Abigail close to her side. It was rare indeed for her to enter Jerusalem; the years of her marriage had taught her many things, one of which was that her own people, regardless of her continuous love for them, saw her as a traitorous recreant. And since she offered them no argument, their opinion had not changed over the ages. Instead, they viewed her with distaste, and she generally avoided the crowds, contenting herself with the world within her home.

But today she had announced that she intended to take a walk through the city, and that was that. She had not even allowed the girl to change into her rougher garments, so they looked like mother and daughter walking through the streets. Ester tried to rid herself of the unrest that had forced her outside to begin with, but she suspected the cause was lost.

The last time Ester had been in Jerusalem proper had been almost a year ago, and the trip had not been far, only to the palace of the governor, Pontius Pilate, to attend one of his feasts. She had not, on that occasion, really had time to think; she was with her husband, on the way to dinner, her thoughts busy with that. Now, however, she had plenty of opportunity to let her mind take in the goings-on around her: the bustle of the streets, the dust rising from the multitude of hurried steps, the song of myriad clangings and laughings and words and bumpings all joined together into one muted din as they entered the markets.

"*Pe'kanims!*" one merchant was calling out. "*Shkedins, egozims, tzimukims!*"

"*Zay'tims!*" another sang. "The finest in Israel!"

"*Shezifims!*"

"*Charoov!*"

"Abigail!"

Abigail turned with a smile for a vendor. "Michael." She spoke in Hebrew, as did he and the others in the market.

"Are you in need of more *te'enims* so soon?" The man, dressed in a brightly woven mantle, motioned to the ripe figs before him.

She smiled and shook her head. "Mistress Ester just wished to walk."

Though Michael acted as though he had not noticed her, certainly he had. "My apologies, Lady Visibullis. Have you been faring well?" His words had changed to Greek.

Ester forced a pleasant smile, and she answered in Hebrew. "Wonderfully, thank you."

Abigail was giving the merchant a glare that would have withered a lesser man. "Good day, Michael," she bade in a stony tone, in Greek. "And you can keep your figs and pomegranates and grapes. There are others just as sweet elsewhere."

Panic entered Michael's countenance. "A moment, my friends!" This time he spoke in Hebrew. "Again, my apologies. Do not hold my slip of tongue against my produce."

Ester put a restraining hand on Abigail's shoulder when she saw that the girl was practically ready to bite. "It is all right." Her words were not only soft, but in Latin. She knew that most here would not know the words, as she herself was not even fluent.

"It is not. He has insulted you, and that is not to be tolerated. He is but a merchant."

The word for "tolerated" was not familiar, but Ester understood the general meaning. "There are none who would act differently. Do not punish him for the feelings that come most naturally."

Abigail's speech drift back into Greek, her eyes on Michael. "Just because a feeling is natural does not mean it should be indulged."

The merchant was, by this time, looking adequately abashed. "You are my best customer, Abigail, and my friend. Please, I meant no insult. It is simply a habit to speak in Greek–"

"Do not lie to me, Michael."

Exasperation overtook the man's expression now. "And why not, when you did just moments ago? You *know* there are no fruits as sweet as mine!"

Quite suddenly, Abigail laughed. "You are right. And so am I. Shall we forgive wrongs?"

The man nodded, satisfied. "Here. A *tapooz* for my gratitude."

Abigail took the orange with a soft smile. "Thank you, Michael. I will see you as usual in a few days."

The women walked away then. This had been a bad idea. They ought to turn around and go home now, before another merchant could insult her and anger Abigail.

"You do not have to defend me," Ester eventually said as they moved out of the market quarter.

Abigail remained silent for but a moment. "They only respect what they see is worthy, Mistress. If you simply accept their insults, they will think you a coward. If you insult them in return, they will think you a tyrant. I simply wish to help you find that path that is most favorable."

"And I appreciate your efforts. But I *am* a coward, Abigail. I always have been."

Abigail looked over into her eyes. "I find it difficult to believe you, Mistress. Cowards do not–"

"Ester?"

The voice was not loud, and sounded as if from leagues away. But she stopped, shocked, and turned in the direction of the man who spoke. "Jairus."

He was well dressed, still handsome. She knew he had risen to a leadership level in the synagogue, but it had been so long since she had seen him . . . and to see him now, and actually speak to him on the street–her nerves buzzed at the unexpectedness.

He looked incredulous himself. "It has been a long time. You look well."

"Thank you. You do, also." Ester searched her mind for something with which to fill the silence. "How is your daughter?"

"You have not heard?"

Their gazes locked again. "I suppose not. What is it?"

"She died." He said it calmly, though perhaps with a bit of surprise that she knew nothing of it.

"Oh Jairus, I am so sorry! If I had known, I would have come–"

"No, no, it is all right. You see, she is well again." His brown eyes were soft as he shared this news.

"Pardon?"

He smiled. "It was a while ago, now. We were all in a terrible panic, of course, and no one knew quite what to do. The fever had hit her very suddenly, and no one expected recovery. The mourners were already gathered, but I just could not accept it. So I went into the city looking for the teacher I had heard was here, the one they call Jesus. You have heard of him?"

"Briefly." Ester stilled. How strange to have heard nothing of this man, then for him to come up twice in such a short time.

"I am not certain what it was that possessed me to go to him, especially with all of the concern he has been causing the Pharisees. But I found him, and the moment I looked at him, I knew he could heal my daughter. So I begged him to come, and he agreed. But when we arrived, the mourners were wailing, and my wife met us at the door with the news of her death. But the master said she was only sleeping and put everyone out of the house and then simply went in and commanded her arise."

"And she did?" Her disbelief surely showed on her face.

"She did. And now she is in better health than she has ever been. The teacher told us not to tell everyone what happened, but even so rumors have spread. Most have at least heard something about it."

Ester dropped her gaze again. "I am not privy to much gossip. But I am glad to hear she was restored."

Silence reigned for a moment more. Jairus cleared his throat, his gaze flitting to Abigail. "I did not know that you had a daughter."

Ester smiled. "I have not. Abigail is my dearest companion."

Jairus nodded. "Your son, then. He is well?"

She nodded in return. "He has been in Rome these past years, but is even now on his way home to serve under his father."

Jairus moistened his lips and sighed lightly at the mention of Cleopas. "You are happy with your husband?"

Though most would deem the question forward, especially on a street where anyone could overhear, Ester knew no surprise. She smiled. "He is a wonderful man. I love him with all of my heart."

Jairus's face relaxed. "I am glad. All of these years I have wondered, but I never had the courage to ask you. But with all that happened to my little Keren, I have acquired an altered view of life. One should never live with regrets in one's heart. So I knew when I saw you that I could not let another day go by without asking for your forgiveness for my past ill treatment of you."

Ester did not smile again, but she trusted he could see her sincerity. "You have been forgiven for many years, Jairus. It is I that has yet to be excused in the eyes of my people."

He shook his head. "Yet it was you who did no wrong."

She shrugged, hoping to look disinterested in the old pain after all this time. "But I would choose the exact path again if the years were given back to me."

"Well." His hand swayed gently into his leg, obviously at a loss for conversation. "Give my regards to Cleopas, Ester. And best wishes for your son upon his return. And to you, of course, and your lovely companion." He turned to Abigail and smiled. "You remind me of my Keren. I can only hope she will grow to share the same beauty I see blossoming in you."

Abigail blushed and uttered the appropriate words of gratitude.

Ester smiled anew. "It was a glorious surprise to speak with you again, Jairus."

"And you." He nodded in farewell and continued on his way, leaving the two women alone again.

"I think I am ready to go home," Ester whispered.

Abigail was quick to take Ester's arm, for which she was glad. The tears already crowded her eyes.

FIVE

"I will brew you some camomile."

Ester nodded and took a deep breath, trying to regain herself. She was more than happy to simply sit now, her body engaged in no movement but the methodic stroke of her fingers along her garment's edge. Sunlight streamed in through the opening to the courtyard, along with the distant noise of clanging weapons as her husband continued to keep his men trained and ready, although there was no one left to conquer. Nothing but the very spirits of her people, and they would put up many a fight before succumbing completely. It was the rebellions they trained for now, day in and day out, so that when the inevitable assaults came they could be crushed as quickly and easily as possible.

Sometimes it still scared her to think that it was *her husband* training the Romans to kill her people. To crush them.

But she could not think that way. He was doing his job, serving his country.

Just as the Rebel Jews held that they were doing theirs.

Who was right? Who could tell? Who was she to judge?

"Here, mistress, drink this."

Ester's attention was momentarily grabbed by her beloved maid. She took the cup and offered Abigail a smile, then patted the cushion next to her. "I imagine you are wondering about the incident that you just beheld."

"I would never pry into your past." Abigail sat in her normal place and folded her small hands into her lap.

"I know. But I would like to tell you, if you would like to listen. Perhaps you can learn something from my past naivete."

"I wish to share in any story you desire to tell."

Ester smiled, but it soon faded as her mind retraced the past decades, to the time when she was little more than a girl herself. Finally becoming a woman but with little knowledge of how to handle it.

"As you know, my father was high priest for a time, the years of my maturing," she began. "My mother died when I was in my tenth year, so it was only my father who saw to my upbringing those later years. He taught me what he knew: the Law. But never did I sit down with an older woman and hear of how to best grasp the transition into womanhood, marriage. So it was not with grace that I handled myself."

She sighed, searching the room as if for the best path to take in this journey to her past. "I was fourteen when I wandered to this section of the city, where the soldiers stayed. My father had, of course, charged me to stay as far away from the Romans as I could at all times. To go to the other side of the street when one was about in the city, to stay away from the booths when they purchased their goods, and to *never* go near the compound, especially alone. But–" she gave a breath of a laugh– "I had a stroke of rebellion then, I suppose, because at first opportunity, here I was.

"I was trying to act nonchalant, but my courage was not long lasting, and I ended up in the marketplace, which I deemed safe enough. Oddly, though, it was *there* that I met my first Roman centurion."

"The master?"

Ester smiled. "No. A friend of his, who has long since returned to Rome. He was a brash and forward man, more of a boy, really. He approached me and started complimenting me, quoting some poem I had never heard. Needless to say, I was terrified."

They shared a smile, and Ester chuckled. "All I could think was that my father would kill me, and that Jairus would never marry me if I was caught. But I have gotten ahead of myself, I have not even mentioned Jairus. I will go to him now instead.

"I had known him for most of my life. Our families were very close, and it had been long understood that we would marry, although no formal betrothal had yet taken place. Jairus was years older than me, and I found him so intriguing. It had always seemed a bit unreal that I would someday be the wife of he who would someday surely be so powerful. Whenever I saw him I would try to hide my face and practice every virtue I knew to prove that I was worthy of him, but he would never allow it to last long. Inside of five minutes he would have me laughing about something, or engaged in a discussion of the Law. My father scolded me often, telling me that Jairus would never want a wife that spoke as a man. But if he did not, then I could not understand why he drew me into those conversations."

Ester shook her head in the old confusion and took a sip of her camomile. "So, when I was faced with that soldier and frightened that I would anger the two men most important to me, I did what they both taught me to do: I tried to talk my way away. When the boy finished his little line, something, I believe, from Homer, I told him that his barbarian poet was a heathen and completely ignorant of all truth, as were all the philosophers his people so loved to dote upon."

Abigail bit her lip against obvious laughter.

Ester sighed. "I thought he was going to strike me, he was so angry. And he may have, if it were not that Cleopas chose that moment to intervene. He had been listening the whole time at the next booth, but I did not notice him until he put a hand on his friend's shoulder and said to him—I will never forget this—'Did you hear her, Mannas? Finally, one who knows Truth, after all of those horrible dialogues we were forced to read. What luck to happen upon her here, and what fortune that knowledge has taken such a beautiful form!'

"I, of course, took that opportunity to try to slip away, but Cleopas would have none of it. He caught up with me at the edge of the marketplace and insisted on walking me home. I ignored him, but he would not be put off.

"As I had feared, my father was walking up the street when I returned, having just been at the temple, and he saw me with a Roman. I would not even look at Cleopas, I just hurried into the house. But he was brazen back then, Abigail, you would not recognize him. He did nothing then, of course, when he saw my father following me in. But I now know he left only to figure out who I was, who my father was.

"My father was surprisingly silent all that evening. I had expected quite a berating but was relieved. I thought he must have known what had happened, that it was not in accordance with my will that a centurion was with me. Now I think he was probably just mulling it over all the next week, getting angrier as the days went by. His imagination had surely come up with something horrid, that is the only explanation that would partly justify his later explosion."

She paused a moment for a breath and took a bit of the bread that Abigail had brought in on a tray and set nearby. "It was a week later when Cleopas came again. I was at home, my father away at the temple with Jairus, when I heard the knock. I assumed it was a neighbor woman, so I went to answer it myself. When I opened the door, Cleopas stepped in before I had a chance to respond and closed the door behind him." She smiled at the memory now, although it had not seemed so humorous then. "I demanded that he leave at once, but he just grinned—you know his grin. So boyish and charming, though I was not charmed at the time. I was outraged. I gave him no time to speak, just opened the door again and tried to push him out.

"My father was right there, Jairus behind him. I remember thinking how poor my luck was. Then I thought, 'Surely he saw that he just came in a second ago.' And he should have. I do not know how he could not have, but he was so angry that I was worried for a moment he might hurt himself.

"He just pushed his way in and spoke in Hebrew, which he assumed Cleopas would not understand. He said, 'Ester, I could have you stoned for this.' When I asked him why, he looked at Cleopas and said, 'That you would let a Roman defile you—' I did not let him finish. We both knew, or should have known, how absurd his accusation was. I told him I had done nothing wrong, that I did not deserve his ire. He insisted that I had shamed myself and him and Jairus, and that now I would have to pay the penalty.

"And then Cleopas spoke. In Hebrew, although not splendidly. He had apparently decided to pick it up when he arrived and had done remarkably well. He simply said, 'Let not your daughter be hurt. I will marry her.'

"That was the worst thing yet in my mind. I turned to Jairus then with my beseeching, begging him to take me as his wife as we had all planned, and if he was not satisfied with the evidence of my virginity then he could divorce me. I actually said it would be better to be divorced by an Israelite than married by a Roman. I do not know why Cleopas did not grow upset at that, but he did not. He just held his ground and remained silent while I wept and begged and made a fool of myself.

"But my father thrust me away and turned to Cleopas. He said, 'I am High Priest. No daughter of mine weds a Roman. But if you desire that wench, then she is yours.' I thought I would die from the humiliation. I said that he could not disown me, I tried to say something about the heritage of our family, but he cut me off and offered Cleopas the family's jewels if he would just keep me and my shame far from his home. The insult to me was awesome."

Ester paused to take a long breath. "I was crying so hard by the time the conversation ended that I could not hear everything that happened, but it ended with Cleopas leading me from my father's house with a box of jewels under his arm.

"I am to this day not certain how Cleopas managed all that he did in that afternoon, but he somehow convinced the general to let him buy this house and take a wife. He paid for it with a few of the pieces from my dowry, that I know. We were married and came here for the first time.

"The house was in disrepair, and we could not afford any servants so soon, but I was blind to it that night anyway. I was too busy being terrified to care about the state of the place. I did not know what to expect, or what to do. I did not know this man, and yet he was suddenly my husband. And strangest of all, I did not know *why* he had wanted to marry me. He did not know me, and though I was pretty, there were many more so. You, Abigail, are far more beautiful than I was."

"I find that hard to believe." Abigail turned her face modestly away. Ester smiled, since the action made her all the more beautiful, thereby proving her point.

"At any rate, I do not believe that I had ever been so afraid as I was then. When he took me to the bedroom I thought that surely Jehovah would allow me to die then before subjecting me to a Roman's bed." She rolled her eyes at her past self. "Thankfully, he did not. But even though Cleopas was patient and gentle, I indulged in tears the moment I thought he was asleep. Only I was mistaken. He heard my quiet weeping but did not say anything that night."

She sighed yet again, with contentment this time. "The next morning when I awoke, Cleopas was watching me. I know I must have looked a fright, what with red eyes and disarrayed hair, but he just smiled and said, in Hebrew, 'Ester Visibullis, you are going to teach me the Law.' I was shocked and could manage only a meager 'Why?' And he said, 'Because I am a smart man. And I know that if ever I want to please my new and alluring wife, I must first please her God. Because any being great enough to invoke the worship of a woman like you is surely more worthy of praise than a statue in Rome. So you shall teach me of this God you say is the only one, and when I am convinced' he actually said when and not if 'then we will together teach him to our children.'" She smiled, even laughed a little. "Within a week I began to realize that God had, indeed, intended me to be the wife of this man. And within two I was madly in love with him."

She looked to Abigail at the close of her narrative and found the girl with stars in her eyes.

"That is very romantic," Abigail said. "Now, anyway. I am certain it did not appear so beautiful when it first happened. Do you suppose I will ever fall in love so completely?"

Ester laughed. "I have no doubts, beautiful one. You will have your pick of husbands."

Abigail sobered. "I do not see how."

Ester said nothing, just took another sip of her camomile. And buried a grin behind it.

◆

Jason was pleased that both weather and wind were with the large craft as it made the journey across the Mediterranean, the breeze strong and steady, filling the sails and promising a prompt arrival. There were a total of fifty soldiers on their way to assignments, replacing other men that had died or been called home to Rome. All were to become members of the Tenth Legion, although their tasks within that great force would certainly be as varied as the men themselves were.

He lounged with his four friends on the upper deck, basking in the sun for what they knew to be one of a very few days of rest. They were among the youngest of the passengers, having achieved the positions of centurions because of connections rather than years in the field, and it showed in their talk and comradery. Conversation had reached a lull as the sun achieved its zenith, giving Jason's thoughts leave to wander to home.

His smile must have betrayed his musings.

"Look at his smirk," Lentulus said, only one eye partially opened in the bright light. "He is probably thinking of how he can use the advantage of his familiarity with the land to best us."

Jason laughed. "Lentulus, my friend, you reflect your own ignoble goals upon us all. Why would I wish to humiliate you?"

The soldier shrugged. "So you can keep all the women to yourself."

Jason laughed yet again. "I need not cast you down to do that; my natural charm should do the job."

It was Apidius who rolled his eyes. "I expect that if Menelaus has anything to say, he too will have his share of company."

Menelaus grinned. "While our good friend here pines over the love he left behind."

"Am I the only one pining? What of you, Titus? Surely you will miss your woman?"

Titus lifted an eyebrow. "And who would you be speaking of, my friend?"

"You know the one I refer to." Apidius wiggled his brows. "That beauty that we saw so briefly at your father's house."

Titus gave a breath of a laugh. "Women are to be enjoyed while you are with them. But she is only a woman. And even less: a slave. That is nothing to pine over."

"Is there a woman waiting for you in Jerusalem, Jason?" Lentulus asked.

"Only my mother." He stretched, grinned. "But then, I imagine she waits with more faithfulness than any other would have."

The grunts of agreement settled again into silence. Jason closed his eyes just as the others were doing, but his mind did not fall into sleep. The closer he got to the land of his birth, the more vivid were his memories. At first, the clearest remembrance was of his intense desire to leave, to be free of the oppression of the Law that pervaded the land so thoroughly. But as his mind traveled further back, he also began to remember the more appealing things of home. Like the sweet taste of Dinah's unsurpassed honey cakes, the wafting scent of burnt incense and offerings outside the temple, the sun glistening off the alabaster stone and fair sands of the city. And while it was difficult to separate reality from his own images in his memory, he had grown enough over the past years to know that life in his parents' house with his mother's faith had not been as bad as he had supposed. But then, his stay in Rome had affected him in many ways, and he knew too that he was now a Roman and would never be accepted by or even want to be a Hebrew. In childhood he had been seen as the son of a dissenter. Now they would view him as the enemy itself.

He opened his eyes wide enough to glance at his friends. They expected their positions to win them respect, fear, awe. Jason knew, though, much better than they, that more oft than otherwise it gained them only the loathing of those people they would not hesitate to crush if the opportunity arose.

He could not stop the sigh that escaped his lips. This homecoming would mix blessing with curse, he knew. But there was nothing to be done about it.

♦

Andrew looked up from the parchment before him to find reproval waiting on his instructor's lips.

"You are not paying attention," she scolded.

"I am sorry, Abigail." He offered her a small smile. "My mind continues to wander even when my will forbids it."

The slant of her brow said she was unconvinced. "Perhaps if you willed to learn a little more you would not be subjected to such an internal battle every eve."

Andrew grinned and pushed his parchment aside. "I do try, my friend; I am simply easily distracted from studies."

She folded her hands before her. "You are lucky you focus better on the training field, or you may have been killed by now."

He laughed. "We each have our virtues. Mine, apparently, do not incline toward the Latin tongue. I have been studying for years now, and still I can claim little knowledge of it."

"I suspect you know more than you employ."

"Let us hope so; otherwise, it could be said that you are a horrible teacher, and I could not bear to hear such a disparagement."

That, at last, drew a smile from Abigail. "I daresay all would know to blame the pupil."

Simon entered at that moment. "Mistress's wishes for her son's room have been carried out, Abigail. Tomorrow will be the day to clean it."

Abigail nodded. "Have we heard any news of his arrival?"

Simon shook his head. "It depends largely on what weather his ship encounters. But to be safe, I will go with you to the market this week to see to the necessary provisions. They will be too much for you alone."

She nodded, then smiled. "Is our lady pacing yet?"

Simon laughed. "The master has convinced her to sit down for the time being."

Dinah entered then from the store room. "Oh, Simon, I was just coming for you. I have reviewed our supplies. Are you ready to take down my list?"

Her husband nodded and smiled, then picked up the utensils and followed her back into the closet.

Andrew saw the contemplation on Abigail's face, and when they were alone again, he asked, "What has you worried?"

She did not hesitate to meet his gaze. "Do you realize that Dinah is the only one of us that cannot read and write?" He was obviously aware, so simply waited for her to go on. "It is unusual. Most masters do not educate their slaves."

"We have been blessed," Andrew agreed, still waiting for her point.

"Their son has been in Rome these six years, Andrew. What if he does not approve?"

"He is not the master. Why would it matter?"

She shrugged, bit back a smile. "Perhaps I am afraid of change. Perhaps I fear the influence he may exercise."

Andrew smiled outright and put an encouraging hand on hers. "Perhaps you should not borrow anxieties that are not ours."

Abigail nodded, smiled in return. "Sometimes it is difficult in this house to remember that I am a slave. Although at other times it is difficult to remember I was once something else."

"But in your heart, Abigail, you are not."

Her eyes searched his as if for the truth. "How can you be so certain of that, Andrew?"

"Because." He winked and leaned back in his chair. "I am an excellent judge of character."

She rolled her warm brown eyes. "Your insight, as always, astounds me."

Seriousness crept into Andrew, urging him upright again. "When I look into your eyes, little one, I do not see an Israelite bonded in Egypt. I see a woman fit to be the wife of a king."

She laughed. "You are a true and flattering friend, Andrew. Of course, Israel has no true king."

"That is your one fault, my friend, you always get caught by such minor problems."

They both stood, habit telling them it was time to go assist their masters in the day's final preparations. Abigail gathered all of her supplies together. "Sometimes," she said, "I think you are unable to differ between reality and your own imaginings."

It was a common statement, and he responded in the usual way; he tugged her long braid and said, "Someday I will convince you that my view is best."

"You have not thus far."

"Give me time."

"You have had six years."

"Perhaps it will take seven."

"And when it had been seven, you will say eight, then nine, then ten."

"But always will I maintain hope."

They had been walking throughout this familiar discourse and were now at their destination, the closets. They exchanged a smile before slipping silently in to attend to their duties, without disturbing the couple in the adjoining room.

SIX

The entourage was making good time; nothing record-breaking like the time Caesar marched the same Tenth Legion two hundred miles in one day, but a steady pace nonetheless. They would reach Jerusalem by late afternoon, and Jason would sup with his parents this eve. The thought brought a smile to his lips, grateful the runner would arrive hours ahead so that Dinah would have enough notice to make the appropriate dinner. He hoped she still remembered what his favorites were. And, for that matter, that he still liked his old favorites.

"What are you grinning about?" Menelaus took a sip of his ration of water.

"The idea of eating this eve at my parents' table while you lucky boys are tasting of daily fare. Sleeping in a real bed, taking a real bath."

Menelaus gave him an unthreatening glare. "It is absolutely unfair that you get to live in your father's house."

"And you in the governor's palace. Life is full of little cruelties." Titus sat down beside them, Lentulus and Apidius close behind him.

"Do you suppose we will be given the eve off after we report?" Lentulus asked.

"I should think so." Menelaus took another lazy sip. "It is not as though they need us to relieve them in a crisis."

"Good. I am anxious to see the city. What do you recommend, Jason?"

He took a bite of bread and breathed in the once-familiar scent of Israel. "You will find some interesting wares in the marketplace close to the compound. Or if you are looking for entertainment, there is a street directly across from the east gate that can provide." He grinned. "Not that I know anything about that, as I was scarcely more than a boy when I left."

They all laughed with him, content to eat their food and plan an evening of restrained carousing. Titus arched a brow Jason's way. "Are you certain you would not rather join us?"

It was his turn to laugh. "And face the wrath of my mother so soon? No. Thank you."

"Your loss."

"We will see about that. The quiet may be a welcome change."

"He will grow tired of that soon enough." Menelaus knew him too well. "We will not miss his company often, I am sure."

Jason grinned. That was why he had stipulated the "so soon" onto the comment of his mother's anger. He, too, knew it would happen soon enough.

⚜

"Five."

"Seven."

Abigail arched a brow at the merchant, careful to hide the expression from Simon. He had come with her to the markets because they needed too much for her to manage alone, and he was in high spirits. The man enjoyed haggling . . . but was unfortunately not very good at it. If left to his own devices, they would pay a premium for everything.

The merchants, however, knew better than to try it when she was there. This one cleared his throat and scratched his head when he saw her glare. "I mean, five. Of course, five."

Simon let out a victorious snort and handed over the money. Abigail could have gotten the myrtle for less but saw no reason to ruin everyone's satisfaction. "Thank you, Joshua."

"Have a good day, Abigail. Simon."

"Well, that is that." Simon tucked the dye into his basket and flashed a grin at Abigail. "We had better get home. There is nothing like a morning in the markets, is there?"

Abigail chuckled. "Nothing in the world."

It took only a few minutes to near the house again. When Abigail heard her name being called, she turned to see Andrew approaching from the direction of the Praetorium. He jogged over to them, took the heavier basket from Abigail's arm.

Simon opened the door. "Did the master forget something, Andrew?"

"No. The runner just arrived–Master Jason will be here before nightfall."

Abigail drew in a sharp breath and thrust the smaller basket at her friend too. "I must go inform the mistress."

She rushed to the courtyard, trusting the men to handle the food. Ester was not there, so she climbed up the ladder to the roof and found her at the loom, purple wool at her side. "Mistress. We just got the word–your son will be home this eve."

Ester's hands stilled for a moment, light flashed in her eyes. "Dinah will need you in the kitchen."

Kneeling at her mistress's side, Abigail put a hand on Ester's arm. "Are you certain? I could read to you, or sing." Anything to help the woman keep her nerves in check.

"No, dear one. You must help make everything perfect for my son's homecoming. When there is a lull in the kitchen, then help me ready myself, but otherwise assist Dinah. And could you send a note to Julia, postponing our plans for this afternoon? She will understand."

"Of course, Mistress. Please let me know if you need anything else."

Ester smiled and went back to her weaving. "I will be fine, Abigail. I will be at the loom a while longer, and then I shall rest. You have nothing to worry about."

Abigail stood, even though she knew that rest was well beyond her mistress.

◆

The bread was in the oven, the cakes cooling. Dinah had the rest under control, and Abigail took the opportunity to slip away to help Ester. She found her mistress as she had expected to, pacing the courtyard impatiently.

"Come, Mistress." Abigail stayed inside and bade Ester join her. "Let us get you ready."

Ester came in and sat in her normal place for her hair to be brushed, although she fidgeted every which direction.

Abigail laughed softly and put calming hands on her mistress's shoulders. "If you do not calm down, your hair will be a wadded mess. Is that the impression you wish to make on your son?"

Ester tried to scowl into the metal mirror but gave up and laughed instead. "I cannot help it, Abigail, you know that." Then her brows drew together. "His correspondences have been so vague. A soldier's life can be a treacherous one. I see many men scarred in many ways during their service. They often become so cold, even cruel."

"But then, look at your husband." Abigail gathered her mistress's long locks, smoothed them with her hands. "There is none whose heart could rival his."

Ester sighed. "That, precisely, is my fear."

Abigail met her mistress's eye. "What of Vetimus, then? The general? Alexander? Marcus?"

Ester finally smiled. "All right, I admit it, there are many soldiers that are of noble spirit, men of honor. But you must also admit that for every one of those, there are a hundred that are not."

Abigail smiled. "I would not know. My only acquaintances among them are the ones I just mentioned." Satisfied with the level of stillness Ester had managed, she picked up the brush and began her methodic and soothing work. "Will you wear the new stola your husband gave you, with the gold collar?"

"Would that be too much?"

"Is anything too much for your son's return?"

Ester smiled. "Nothing. And you wear your new white tunic. I have finished a multi-colored belt for you."

"Certainly, although I will have to wait until the last minute to change; I do not want to stain the linen with kitchen work."

"You can change right before we dine, then. I will just give you the belt, in case I am busy by the time you are finished with Dinah."

"That is fine. There, your hair is shining as the sun. How would you like it dressed?"

"Just bind it in the Hebrew fashion, it is simpler."

Abigail selected a length of cloth that would complement the stola and wrapped it around her hair. She then fetched the clothing.

As the folds settled across her curves, Ester smiled. "Jason will be impressed with his mother's youthful beauty, will he not?" she asked, winking.

Abigail laughed. "He will be sure to tell all his friends so as to drive them to jealousy over his fine family. A queen of a mother, and a father that they must all obey."

Ester, too, breathed a laugh. "You have made me feel much better, Abigail. But now I fear you must return to Dinah. The hour grows late, and there is still much to be done, I am sure."

"Are you certain you are all right?"

"Go. Let me fret in peace if I will."

With a last smile, Abigail left her mistress's chamber and made her way back to the kitchen, where the pace had picked up again.

"Jason Visibullis, centurion, reporting as ordered from Rome, Lord."

Cleopas looked up from the sword he had been sharpening, a smile ready. Even through six years of change, he recognized that voice. "Jason!" Putting formality aside, he embraced his son with a hearty, happy laugh. "My son! It is good to see you again."

Jason grinned. "You look well, Father."

"As do you." He took a step back to study the younger man. "It is so good to have you back." Cleopas clasped his son's shoulder with a strong hand. "Shall I show you around the Praetorium, or does your memory recall the layout?"

"I have gone over it in my mind many times, I think I will be fine." His smile stretched across his face, his gaze traveled from Cleopas's face to the compound. "Frankly, Father, what I could use is a good hot meal."

Laughter once again bubbled from Cleopas's lips. "Andrew assures me that the women have been in the kitchen ever since they received word of your arrival. Let us go home. Your baggage is there behind you?" At his son's nod, Cleopas motioned Andrew to pick up the burden.

Andrew moved to obey, but question creased his brow.

It triggered his own. "Jason? Where is Mark?"

Jason's eyes went blank for a moment before he regained himself. "In Rome, I suppose."

"You suppose? You do not know where your slave is?" Cleopas tried to control the hard edge of his voice, but the flicker of annoyance across Jason's face proved he had not.

"Well, I have not seen him for two years, Father."

"And why is that?"

"I sold him to the state."

Cleopas stopped in his tracks. "You *what*? Why would you do that?"

Jason sighed, his eyes roaming the sapphire skies above him. "For torture. I had reason to believe he was involved with another slave that was stealing from her master."

"Oh?" Perhaps it was not a direct question, but he trusted his son would hear the meaning the word.

"They had a child together. The wench was accused of stealing her mistress's jewels and trying to run away. Mark would have known if it were true."

Cleopas ground his teeth together. "Do not tell your mother of this. Simply tell her you left him with the woman he loved."

"Gladly." He waited, though he looked ready to move again.

Cleopas sighed and strode homeward. "You gave up the slave I bought you, son. I will not provide another. If you wish one, you will have to find and purchase him yourself."

Jason nodded. "Fine, but there is no need. I can take care of myself."

"In a camp, yes. But who will wait on you at our table? Your quick judgement will cause more work for *my* servants."

"If I recall, Simon seldom had much to do during meals anyway. He can help."

"Simon has his tasks. As do the others." He sighed again. "I will let them figure it out among themselves." They were nearing their home now, and the sound of singing could be heard.

Jason's lips twitched up. He had undoubtedly not heard the sound of women lifting their voices in a psalm, for no reason other than to praise their God while they went about their lives, since he left Israel. "Beautiful."

"That would be Dinah and Abigail. I think they do not even realize they are singing until they see someone else approach. Enjoy it for the moment, for they will stop as soon as we are within sight."

◆

"Mistress, they come."

When Ester sprang up, Abigail fell in behind her, wiping her hands on her coarse tunic as she went. Already commotion sounded at the front of the house, where Simon had gone to open the door. Abigail held back when Ester rushed forward and launched herself into the arms of the stranger.

Abigail wanted to think he looked familiar, but she suspected it was more because of his resemblance to his parents than because she remembered his face from six years ago. He stood tall, like Cleopas, shared the dark hair of both him and Ester. His features were the fine ones of his mother, though stronger. His form showed evidence of the hours of exercise and training he must have put in while in Rome.

She watched as a grin split his face and he caught his mother up, twirling her around.

"Mother! You have grown younger since I left."

Her mistress laughed and pressed a kiss to his cheek. "My handsome charmer. All grown up. Where is the boy I sent off?"

His laugh was full and rich, but Abigail's focus moved to Andrew, who slipped past the family and exchanged a few quiet words with Simon. Both their brows pulled down, even as they started back the hall.

They would be set on unpacking the young master's belongings, and they would certainly make a mess of it. Simon did not spend enough time in the masters' closets to know how best to organize it, and Andrew was filthy from the day's activities. She slipped away to follow them.

Andrew nodded at whatever Simon had said to him. "The master has forbidden the mistress to know, as well."

Curiosity piqued, Abigail stepped into Master Jason's bedchamber right behind them. "What is she forbidden to know?"

"Abigail." Andrew spun around, obviously startled. When she arched her brows, he sighed. "I suppose you may know, since you barely even met the man. It is his slave, Mark. He has been sold to the state for torture."

Her throat closed up. True, she did not know Mark, nor the ways of Rome. But she knew that the man who had sold his trusted servant was now here, in their house. How could she be anything but uneasy about it?

To soothe herself, she moved to the bags Andrew had set down and got to work while Andrew and Simon exchanged what information on the subject each knew. She focused on the belongings to find places for. They were few—not surprising, she supposed, given his soldier's status. He had been wearing his uniform, the armor and red cape. That left only a few tunics to unpack, a toga. One mantle more in the Hebrew tradition, brightly covered. A small chest engraved with the ark of the covenant.

"You need not do that, Abigail," Andrew said after a moment. "I can manage."

"I am done, and you are filthy." She smiled and indicated his dusty feet. "You had better wash up while I change. Dinah will have the meal ready in minutes."

They all left the chamber to tend what last-minute preparations they could.

Jason chose a couch in the room his father had deemed the triclinium and reclined to await the meal. He had made a detour to the kitchen to greet Dinah, had noticed the slaves leaving his chamber. He knew well his belongings would be put away, though he would probably have to reorganize later.

He settled in across from his parents and picked the conversation back up. He had already planned out the stories to regale them with, and they gave him their undivided attention as he spoke of Rome and the journey over. Thankfully, they were not long left without refreshment. Simon appeared with wine and cheese within moments.

Not long after, he smelled the arrival of real food. Andrew entered first and headed for Jason's father, then Simon followed with a tray for him. He nearly missed the arrival of his mother's maid, but the sway of hip caught his attention.

Many lessons had he learned in Rome, and one of them was how to observe a beautiful woman without being noticed–a lesson he had not expected to need in his own home. But employ it he did as he selected food from the platter Simon held.

Abigail, he recalled. His father had mentioned her frequently in his letters. She was young, but not a girl–certainly not the waif he barely remembered from the day he left for Rome. Her hair was dark and shining, bound with a strip of cloth that looked to barely contain the thick mass of it. She wore a tunic of fine white linen, a belt to match Mother's emphasizing full curves and narrow waist. And her face–her face would inspire any artist in Rome. She would make an alluring Venus. Perhaps a nymph.

Jason lounged on his chaise and tasted his first bite of the food of his childhood, smiled. "I had forgotten how excellent Dinah's cooking is. My friends will all be very jealous that I get to feast like a king every day."

His mother smiled. "She will be pleased at the compliment. And speaking of feasting, the general and his wife wish us to bring you for dinner at your earliest convenience."

"Well, my first night watch is not for another four days, so any evening before then will do." He drained his cup, partially so that the maid, who now held the pitcher, would have to come refill it. "Perhaps the day after tomorrow? That will give me time to settle in."

"I will send word."

He nodded his approval and did not glance over at Abigail when she paused by his side. Her voice came quiet and melodious, careful not to interrupt. "More wine, Lord?"

"Yes." She smelled of spices from the kitchen and a lingering perfume he identified as his mother's. When she moved away after topping his cup, he smiled again at his parents. "You have been moving in high circles, Mother. The general's wife is from an upstanding family in Rome. I dined with them a few times at the Asinius house."

"Julia is a dear friend. We hope to meet all of yours soon too."

"Of course." They would be impressed, he knew. A powerful father, a beautiful mother . . . even a tempting maid that he could contemplate at his leisure. Finally, he had come home. They were in his world now, and he would enjoy that luxury.

Gaze sweeping across Abigail as he looked to his father, he very nearly grinned. He would enjoy it very much indeed.

⬧

"What do you think?"

Abigail looked up at Andrew, who was apparently paying no attention to her lesson. The masters still talked and lounged, but when they had been dismissed, Abigail and Andrew had returned to their normal routine.

Or she had, anyway. Andrew's attention was not so easily put on the lesson. "That you are truly a horrible student, but I will forgive you today since we have been so busy and disrupted." Abigail took a sip of her water and did not bother to sort through her own documents. "He really gave Mark over to be tortured?"

Andrew nodded. "He said so himself."

She shook her head. "Then I think my fears may be justified. The young master obviously has a very diverse view from his parents. He could make things uncomfortable."

"He is not the one who has control."

"Tell me, though, Andrew. Was there tension in the air when he shared the news with our master?"

"Yes."

"And would you want to feel that all the time in this house?"

He sighed. "Of course not. But he did say the incident with Mark happened years ago. Perhaps his views have changed, or will. Other than that then, what did you think?"

Abigail's eyebrows raised in question. "What answer are you looking for, my friend? I think he looks much like his mother, he seemed a bit tired, he was very attentive to both of his parents, and I did not see much of the insolent boy I remember from my first day here." She smiled. "Or did you wish something else?"

Andrew met her smile. "Nothing in particular. I suppose it is just that I knew him many years before these six, and I wonder how much he has really grown out of his vices and how much he has simply better hewn them."

Her smile turned to a grin, playful. "Now who is borrowing troubles that are not ours?"

He laughed lightly. "I am merely testing you, trying to lure you into speaking idealistically."

After sharing his laughter, she stifled a sudden yawn. "The day has been long. And does not promise to end soon."

"At least tomorrow is not market day."

She nodded her agreement. "But soon it will be Passover. And the city will be so crowded and prices in the markets will soar and–"

"And you will not have to go out very often, and it is not your money that you will be spending, so just try to enjoy the holiday and the feast."

Abigail narrowed her eyes teasingly. "Easily said by one who does not spend his days in the kitchen preparing this feast."

His gaze turned serious. "You are right. I spend my days learning the way to wage war against my people."

"We both spend our days obeying our master," she said softly. "And you know our lord would never ask you to enter a battle against your own."

Andrew sighed and rested his head on his palm. "He would never ask, no. But how could I chose, Abigail, between the man I have sworn to serve for all of my life and the nation that birthed me? Our master is fair, good, and just. Moreover, he not only recognizes but worships Jehovah. It should not be a choice, my friend. Would that we were all members of the same people."

She opened her mouth to reply, then closed it again. Finally, she said, "Perhaps someday there will come one who erases the boundary between Jew and Greek. Perhaps one day there will be a greater understanding of the Law that allows for the love of God to be extended completely to all."

"You speak of Messiah?"

She nodded. "Mistress does not even know if it is proper to interpret the texts to prophesy one, but it seems, especially to us, to be the only hope of a better world."

"You do not think, then, that Messiah will rid us of Rome?" He seemed almost relieved.

Abigail smiled. "I am only a woman, Andrew, and a slave. I do not pretend to have the answers. But nowhere in the Holy Scriptures themselves have I heard or read of a king come to triumph over nations. I have heard only of a savior come to be defeated."

Andrew leaned back in his chair and blew out his breath quickly. "What a bleak hope it is that we have."

The bubble of laughter lightened her spirit as it rose and spilled from her lips. "It would not be an absolute defeat, friend, just an apparent one."

"Well then, break out the best wine. Our champion has lost today! Let us all rejoice!" He, too, grinned now. "It is good, though, to be here in this house. It is good to hear you laughing with our mistress. And," he added with a magnanimous sweep of his hand, "it is also good that the young master has returned. At the very least, it should break the monotony."

He stood, and she followed suit. "But I like monotony."

"You will be fine."

"But we have been through this. I do not like change."

"Well then, if my lady hates change, allow me to just pack the man up and ship him back to Rome. We would not want to disrupt her life."

She tried to suppress her smile . . . and failed.

She always did.

◈

Morning sun gleamed off freshly polished helmets, swords, and buckles. It glinted off the sands, blinding, warm. The hundred men were as still as statues, their attention focused completely on Jason, their ranks unbroken, their lines as straight as the blades that hung still against their legs, ready for any commands that may issue from his mouth.

He walked the length of the ranks and back again, surveying his men. They were all in fine shape; they stood in perfect posture, their faces immobile even in the face of the star that taunted them with every inch it raised in the sky. He was satisfied. He knew he would be. Cleopas Visibullis had not gained his position by training his men to meet less than the highest standards.

His voice carried easily across the still field, reaching each of his men. "I am Jason Visibullis. I have spent six years in Rome. Some of you have lived there most of your lives, others among you have never seen it." He walked a few paces to his right, stopped again. "The one of you who has been here the longest has seen ten years in Jerusalem. I was born and raised here. Some of you may think that will make me weak in my duties, when those involve putting a heavy hand on this land. I will put that thought to rest now, and if you are still not convinced, then my performance will prove it as well.

"I was born to a mother who taught me the way of the Jews. But I am a Roman! I have studied many texts, books, and discourses. But I am a soldier! I was born in this country, raised in this dust. But Rome is the fatherland! Rome is the heart that beats in my chest. Rome is the force that guides me. And the one that wills me to guide you. I tell you now what I expect of you. Loyalty. Honor. Obedience. Bravery. Devotion. We may not be at war, but we are warriors still. And as the best of our kind before us, we will be ready for any rising that may come. You will not question who you are or who you serve, just as I will not, and by working together cohesively we will live up to the name that the great Caesar has given this legion. Our standards will fly high before us, wherever we may go."

He paused, surveyed the ranks yet again. "I will assume perfection. I will assume you capable of anything. And I forbid you to prove me wrong. Drill!"

They had been waiting for the command. The neat lines broke into perfect formations, the uniformly outfitted legs falling in uniformly sized strides and taking their men in motions that were, by now, second nature. Going through the exercises that kept their reflexes sharp and their skills at their maximum, each soldier ceased to be a man and became simply a part of the machine. Each one a member, none a whole on his own.

Jason watched them in pride. These were his men, now, his responsibility. His to command, his to lead, his to help in trouble, and his to punish in failings. Over the past years, he had on occasion wondered silently whether he had what it would take to control of the lives of a hundred men. But he had stopped asking that. Eventually, he had come to realize that he was no less fit than any of the others studying and working for their commissions. Better than most. His father had raised him well for this calling, and it had become a song in his ears.

This was what he had been born for.

SEVEN

Ester spent the day lounging with a painstakingly copied text of Aristotle, daydreaming more than she was actually reading anything about his version of *Ethics*. Cleopas was always encouraging her to read more and diverse things, and he had said he wished the Great Library at Alexandria had survived a few more years so that he could take her there. She smiled at the impossible dream. Abigail, too, would have loved to go, she knew.

Although, if Abigail married soon, even had it been possible that decision would not be hers to make. The thought caused Ester pause. She had, of course, realized that giving her maidservant in marriage to a good citizen would mean that she would no longer be at hand. But had she really stopped to realize that the new husband could chose to move away, taking Abigail with him? Or that he would not approve of his wife socializing often with her former mistress?

Ester sighed, turned a leaf absently. There was the other option, of course. She knew it would probably suit them all best. And she knew, too, that Cleopas would expect an answer from her soon. But she hesitated, for some reason, to agree. Perhaps it was just that she feared she would be making the decision for herself, and not for Abigail. Perhaps she thought it entirely too perfect to be perfect.

Perhaps she should simply raise the question to Abigail sometime and see what the young woman thought. It was, after all, her life. And since Cleopas had left the choice up to her, she was free to present it to her friend if she wished.

But she did not wish, not really. Abigail got so uncomfortable whenever her future marriage was brought up. It would not be a conversation. It would be a conformation of Abigail's will to Ester's. So before she brought anything up, Ester would have to know what her own will was.

And Cleopas would not keep her to his demand of one month, she knew. Not if she were truly struggling with the decision. He was a patient man. And he had, at the moment, more pressing concerns. His son.

Jason, in most ways, had calmed all of the fears she had been nurturing over the past ages. He had grown well, had gotten strong, and learned to hold his own in conversation and on the field without resorting to anger. He had gained a modicum of temperance to balance out his confidence and was no longer so judgmental of their people. He had actually expressed joy at being present for the Passover this year, for which she was grateful. It hurt her more than he could know when he rejected her faith, but he was making an effort. She had to credit him for that. And he had been so attentive. Each night he had spent with her and his father, in spite of the friends that she knew were busy roving the town, getting a feel for Jerusalem, settling in and cavorting. He would surely have preferred their company. But he had nonetheless chosen his parents'.

On the other hand, there were moments when she looked into his eyes and saw a stranger. She saw a man she did not know, one leagues removed from the boy she had raised, had agreed to send away. He was a Roman now. She knew that. He was interested in politics and battle and serving Caesar. Not in Israel. Not in Jehovah. Not in being one of God's chosen. What did it mean, after all, in this world? What was the importance of being chosen when the life one was chosen for was subjection?

But subjection was part of Israel's history. She knew that. How many times had the Lord pronounced them to be a stiff-necked people? Every gift he offered, they refused. Every time of peace was inevitably followed by war, and it was because they always strayed. Rebelled. Served false gods, worshiped idols, played the harlot. Israel was a nation seemingly incapable of being the steadfast people their God requested, required. It was no wonder he allowed them to fall again and again into despair, preserving only the remnant necessary to restore the faith eventually. The true question was why he had ever chosen them to begin with.

But he had, and she was grateful. She did not pretend to understand the mind of her God. All that mattered was that he accepted her as a child, gave her the commandments and statutes that would allow her to dwell in the bosom of Abraham with her fathers. And he had blessed her with a husband that served with her, a household that was proud to be Hebrew. Even if her son would not claim the heritage, it was his. All he had to do was reach for it. And all she could do was pray that he would.

She realized, after waking from a short nap after she had eaten, that her day was terribly lonely, and terribly quiet without Abigail beside her. But Dinah had needed her help in Passover preparations. Ester would have offered to help them with the cleaning, but she knew her loyal attendant would not allow it.

She smiled. That Abigail did not hesitate to put her foot down in some matters yet would never consider doing so in others never ceased to amuse her. Indeed, the girl would not allow Ester to lift a finger unnecessarily, but when the woman issued forth a command or even a request, she would never disobey. Whether it be one as simple as "Could you get me some water?" or as difficult as, "You must learn to read and speak Latin."

It was, of course, the harder ones that were most beneficial. It seemed to be the way of life.

Abigail entered the courtyard and knelt by Ester's knee. "The masters are returning, Mistress. Shall we get you ready for dinner at the general's?"

Ester looked down at the lovely young face with a smile. "Yes. The blue, I think. With my sapphires."

Abigail nodded and rose. Ester followed her into her bedchamber and slipped out of her everyday tunic while the girl brought in the finely woven wool. "Is it going well? Did you make as much progress as you had hoped?"

"Barely," Abigail replied, "but it will do. Dinah will finish the room we were on while we are away, and tomorrow we will clean the bed chambers. Then we will be ready for the celebration."

"Good." Ester lifted her hair so the jewels could be fastened, then sat down so her hair could be brushed. "Cleopas said Jason had expressed great satisfaction at being with us this year for Passover."

Abigail reflected smile shone in the polished metal of Ester's mirror. "He will remember all you taught him, lady. He will remember that our Lord does not forsake his chosen."

"But will he remember that he is one of those chosen?"

Abigail began brushing her hair. "He will remember."

Ester sighed. "I am glad you are so sure, Abigail. For I can never seem to remember to be so."

Abigail shook her head and motioned to the scroll Ester had brought in with her. "What do you think of the *Ethics*?"

That conversation sufficed them until Cleopas came in.

❧

"Would you take some warm water in to Jason, Abigail?"

She smiled at Cleopas and nodded her obedience. "Yes, Lord." Slipping out of the room silently, she headed for the kitchen.

Dinah looked up when she entered, smiled. "Are you taking the young lord his water?"

Abigail nodded. "I imagine Andrew is in more need of the time to clean up than I."

Dinah chuckled. "He is quite filthy today. I made him stay outside."

This made Abigail smile, and she had to peek out the door to verify that, indeed, he stood in the courtyard, sloshing water over his head. "What was he doing, rolling in the mud?"

"I believe so," Dinah replied seriously, sending Abigail into laughter. "Here you go." She poured a third of the water into a basin, then lifted her voice to carry outside. "Andrew, hurry."

"I am coming!"

Abigail left the room on that note, figuring it was best to be gone when Andrew started tracking mud onto their clean floor. She had a feeling Andrew would have liked to have missed it as well. She cradled the basin in her arms as she journeyed back the hall, the heavy clay keeping the heat from seeping through too much, and arrived at Jason's closed door a moment later. She rapped lightly.

"Enter."

She used her free hand to do so, slipping into the room. Her peripheral vision told her that Jason stood by the latticed window, but as her concern was the larger basin directly before her, she did not turn her head in that direction. Instead, she expertly poured the water, not spilling so much as a drop, and added enough from the cool pitcher sitting on the table to bring it to a reasonable level. Then she asked, "Do you need anything, Lord?"

Jason looked up from his task, his gaze heavy . . . lingering. "No." When his intense gaze refused to waiver, Abigail felt heat stain her cheeks. His grin did not help matters. "I have all I need."

She nodded and exited silently, easing the portal closed behind her. It would take a while to get used to the young master's presence, she knew. A small amount of awkwardness was to be expected until that happened, but that was nothing to concern herself with. She would simply take the next weeks to learn what he liked and be at hand to provide it. She was the servant with the most leisure, it was only reasonable that it fall to her. She would just have to cut back on her studies. Smiling to herself, she was fairly certain that Andrew would not mind fewer lessons.

✦

Abigail closed her eyes momentarily and drew in a deep breath of the cool night air. Elizabeth reclined beside her. "I think he is incredibly handsome."

Eyes open again, she looked curiously at her friend. "Who?"

"Jason."

Abigail sighed. "Elizabeth, you are married now."

"Married, yes. But I am not blind." Her friend bit her lip almost playfully and leaned against the wall of the house. "I can just imagine what it would feel like to have him kiss me."

"Elizabeth!"

Elizabeth laughed at her horror. "You should see yourself, Abigail. How can it be possible that you have never thought of such things? You are older than I. Even before I was given to Cleon, I wondered. And now that I am a wife, I realize how wonderful it can be to know a man. Although Cleon is not the most satisfying."

Abigail covered her ears with her hands and closed her eyes, more to get her point across than because she was truly shocked by the conversation. "I would retain my purity, Elizabeth. I am yet a maiden."

Elizabeth rolled her eyes, her impatience clear. "You cannot be that innocent. No one is. Every woman wonders. Who is the object of your dreams, if not Jason? Andrew?"

She moved her hands to cover her face, resting them on her elbows. "Elizabeth, I do not wish to speak of this."

"Why not? Come now. Which of them would you chose?"

She did not want to think about it. Thinking about it could only cause problems. Andrew was her friend, someone she had to work with everyday, and to have entertained such thoughts, however briefly, would cause tension. And the young master was a stranger—and the young master. She could not think of him like that, either. But Elizabeth was in a prodding mood, so she said, "I should hope that, if I am to marry, it will be to an established man of the city. An upstanding Israelite who loves our God and would appreciate the efforts Mistress has put into making me a good wife."

"Abigail, you are a boring girl. You *want* an old man? Well, then take mine. I'll take one of yours."

Abigail flushed. "They are not mine. And you cannot simply trade husbands."

"Pity."

Abigail studied her friend, wondering what had happened to the Elizabeth she had thought she knew. It seemed that one day, they were two girls talking about absolutely nothing and having fun doing it, and now they spent their time arguing over the proprieties of men and masters. Ever since that day almost two months ago, every time they had met, it had ended in this way. She wished for nothing more than a resurgence of their past comradery.

The door behind them opened at that moment, sparing Abigail response. Andrew came out and sat down on the other side of Abigail, blessedly oblivious to the conversation that had just passed. "How have you been faring, Elizabeth?"

Elizabeth's dark brows still had a bit of an ironic cock to them. "Well, thank you. But if you will excuse me, I should go attend my husband." She pushed herself to her feet and left them.

Abigail sighed.

"You look upset," Andrew observed in a soft voice, gaze on her profile.

She shook her head. "It is Elizabeth. I know not what to say to her anymore. Ever since she was given to Cleon, our conversations have been on topics of men."

Andrew breathed a laugh. "You are women now, Abigail. It is natural for conversational topics to change in that way."

But Abigail shook her head again. "It is not the topic in itself, Andrew. It is Elizabeth. I fear for her." She turned to meet her friend's eyes, certain her concern was obvious. "She is not content with her husband and does not mind telling me so. I fear that she will do something irresponsible. And I do not wish to watch my friend destroy her life."

Andrew arched his brows. "And?"

He knew her too well. "And," Abigail hesitated, finally drawing in a deep breath and letting it out again. "Do you think Master and Mistress will give me in marriage soon?"

"Yes." He did not so much as hesitate.

"I fear that as well." Her eyes focused on the middle distance. "I know Mistress thinks of me as a daughter. I know she wants what is best for me. But I do not wish to leave her. I am comfortable in my life, Andrew. I love her and Master and you and Dinah and Simon. I do not know how I could leave to start my own house."

He opened his mouth only to close it again and pick up her hand. "Dear one, you are stronger than you think yourself. And what is that saying about borrowing worries?"

She smiled at the familiar rebuke and squeezed his hand in appreciation of the reassurance. "You are a good friend. I have been blessed. How many women have such friends as I? Many of the men I see in the markets treat even free women as though they are slaves, shameful to be seen with."

"Many men are fools." He gave her a small smile. "They think that being head of the family makes them more superior than they are. They forget the virtues of Abigail, Ester, Ruth and think only of Delilah, Jezebel."

"You have been taught in the same synagogues as they. How is it you have gleaned the truth and they a falsehood from the teachings?"

His smile turned to a grin. "Perhaps I am just superior to them. What would Aristotle say to that?"

She had to laugh. "Nothing worth quoting. I believe Moses was right. The slave is not an inferior being, just one that has experienced misfortune. Joseph was a slave, after all, as were all the children of Israel to Egypt."

"And now to Rome." His words were softer even than before, his gaze on the ground. "The difference is only that Rome lets us *think* we are, if not free, not slaves. We pay them in taxes rather than labor, but the result is the same. But it is that delusion, I think, that has turned so many into fools. They think they can buy their advantage. But they, too, will pay."

Abigail could only look at him, her hand still in his, and wonder what exactly he meant.

"I was speaking with Vetimus today," he continued. "He has been following the teachings of the Nazarene. He says the rabbi was teaching recently of the desolation of Jerusalem."

Her brows knit. "Its destruction, you mean?"

He shook his head. "I think not. Simply its inability to accept Messiah. Vetimus said he expressed grief over the inhabitants of the city, for it was as if their house were left standing empty."

She was silent for a moment. "And do you believe this Nazarene that would have himself proclaimed Messiah?"

Andrew sighed, rubbed his thumb absently over her knuckles. The action made warmth steal up her arm. The influence of Elizabeth's questions, no doubt. "I do not know about Messiah being him. But that just makes me wonder if he is perhaps right. If perhaps I would not know what Messiah looked like when I saw him. He has performed amazing feats. Walking on water. Healing the sick. Casting out demons."

"Supposedly."

"He healed Claron."

That Abigail could not dispute. "Yes. He healed Claron. He has also gotten the Sanhedran so angry that they are ready to kill him themselves. He spoke in the temple, when he is not truly even a rabbi. He is a carpenter."

"As is Jehovah," Andrew replied quietly. "Look at all he has fashioned."

Abigail studied him, smiled. "I think you want to believe in him. I think these stories have struck something within you."

"It is not merely that." He shifted a bit before meeting her gaze. "They have hit something within Master. And if my lord would put his faith in a carpenter from Nazareth and proclaim him the Son of God, then I trust it is because his wisdom has shown him something I have not seen in full."

This gave her pause. "The master believes him?"

"The master wants to, I think. The master is searching for something that will bridge the gap between him, a Gentile, and the Law. Did not you yourself say that was the task of Messiah? Well, this Jesus is offering it."

"Yes, but anyone can offer it. *I* can offer it. That does not mean I have the authority to make it good."

Andrew turned to face her, his deep eyes reflecting all the thoughts that swarmed through his mind. "I have no answers, my friend, only questions. But it seems to me, if no one ever asked, they would never be taught. Perhaps this carpenter is Messiah. Perhaps he is not. Perhaps there *is* no Messiah foretold. All I know is that the Law, while good, is impossible to keep fully. I have sinned. You have sinned. Master has sinned. And how do we know if all the good we have done has been enough to outweigh the bad? How can anyone fallen hope to join his ancestors in the bosom of Abraham? Our God will forgive if we ask, yes, but how? Who takes the guilt?"

"Why would anyone have to?" she returned. "Why can it not just vanish? Omnipotence can surely accomplish that."

Andrew sighed. "I know not. I will wait, watch, listen to Master as he listens to Vetimus, who will keep following this would-be Christ. And in the meantime, we should go in. Mistress will wish your presence soon."

Abigail nodded and let him use the hand he still held to assist her to her feet. She would not worry about this Jesus of Nazareth. She had her own concerns. Best to leave the man to the discussions of the men for now and concentrate on her own life. There was no need to be borrowing troubles.

EIGHT

By the end of Passover, Jason was ready to go back to Rome. He had told himself countless times over the preceding months that his distaste for Hebrew traditions had been more imagination than fact. But after being thrown back into the gut of their beliefs, he realized he had not exaggerated in his memories at all. The same story told again, the same words recited, the same food on the table. The same celebrating in the streets, as if Israel had just escaped Egypt.

It had been centuries ago! he wanted to scream. It does not matter anymore!

But he kept it to himself, now. He would not insult his mother anymore. He would not make her fear for his immortal soul by expressing his doubt in her God. Besides, it was basically the same Hades that was offered to the Jews as to the Greeks. What did it matter? He would just bathe in the River Lethe, sweet waters of oblivion, and never be bothered again by these petty things of life.

Of course, Rome had their remembrances, too. Although Divine Augustus had deemed them not proud enough of their heritage so had ordered the poet Virgil to write his *Aeneid*, figuring that if the Greeks had the *Iliad* and *Odyssey* to proclaim their brilliant heritage, so should Romans. And if Jason preferred the original Greek stories to their more recent counterparts, it was probably because he had read them first, and Virgil's masterpiece had just seemed a copy. Either way, it was better than these ridiculous recitations of Law.

But it was over now. Passover would not come again for another year. That, indeed, was something to praise God for. At least he had only ordered the observation to be annual.

"Master Visibullis?"

Jason turned at the voice, his eyes falling on a man of greater girth than height. His skin was oily, sweat beaded on his brow, but his eyes looked honest enough. "Sido, I presume?"

The man nodded. "What news have you for our lord Asinius?"

Jason smiled. "Nothing much. His son has been adjusting well, staying out of trouble, getting to know his troops. He has been sober and abstinent, as far as I know."

Sido grinned. "We will see how long that lasts. My bet is on a month at the most."

Jason chuckled. "You give him much credit. I say another few days, and he will have located the most attractive harlot in Judea and convinced her to donate her services free of charge."

"I am certain our lord Asinius would expect nothing less. Titus is, after all, a man."

"Indeed." And a man had needs. He would have to do something about his own soon enough.

Sido reached into his money bag and pulled out a few coins of gold. "Your wage."

Jason shook his head. "It is too much for nothing of interest."

Sido shrugged. "It is what I was told to give you. If you do not want it, I will keep it myself."

Jason took the coins and dropped them into his own purse. "Tell your master that his generosity outweighs his wisdom, Sido."

The man barked a laugh. "I would rather live to see another day, Lord. I will see you in a month."

"Indeed. May I have no more to tell you then."

"Indeed. Farewell."

Jason nodded and left the meeting place, heading back into the walls of Jerusalem. It was his day off; this evening he would be on watch, the next day he would rest to be ready for his normal routine the following morning. For now, he was free, so he figured he would browse through the markets before going home. He had barely reached them when he heard a familiar voice hailing him.

"Jason!" Menelaus jogged his direction with a grin. "My friend, where have you been? I have not seen you since we arrived."

Jason smiled and turned to clasp his friend's wrist. "Menelaus. You look well. I have been with my family, letting my mother suffocate me to her heart's content."

Menelaus laughed and fell in beside the other man in the direction he had been headed. "When will you grow tired of it? Lentulus and I have been exploring, but your native eye would be welcome."

"You should have caught me yesterday, my friend. I am on watch tonight, so am off today. I could have taken you around last eve had I but known."

Menelaus sighed but was obviously not distressed. "Next week, perhaps. And have you seen Titus?"

"I see him every day, at least in passing. I would not be surprised if he were around now, actually, I believe our schedules are the same."

They both looked around, as if expecting the other to appear, but he was not within sight.

"I will keep an eye out for him," Menelaus said after a short inspection of the marketplace. "In the meantime, just point me in the direction of women. I cannot go another day without the pleasure of soft lips on mine, warm flesh under my hands—"

Jason cut him off with a chuckle. "No need to go into detail, Menelaus. I am aware of its delights. And I believe if you just follow this street—" He motioned to an avenue nearby— "until it intersects another, and follow that one to the right, you will find all you need to be satisfied at a fair price."

Menelaus looked that way as a starving man eyed a feast. "Perfect. What of you? Coming?"

Jason stood for a moment before shaking his head. "I would rather spend my money elsewhere. And I believe I can find my satisfaction in my own home. My mother has this slave, Abigail." He paused, turned up his lips. "Her beauty puts Titus's women to shame, Menelaus. She is young and fair and unspoiled. I shall greatly enjoy making her mine."

Menelaus's eyes narrowed. "This is unfair, Jason. You get to live in a house, with a cook and slaves to wait on you, and even one to warm your bed. I shall write Caesar with complaints of such blatant inequality among his officers."

Jason punched his friend lightly in the arm. "Go ahead. I would like to see his response."

Menelaus pushed Jason in return, then shifted once more to look in the direction he had been pointed. "Well, I will call on you next week, perhaps, if the invitation from your parents is still open."

"Indeed."

"And I would like to see this slave of yours. To make certain you are not exaggerating."

Jason laughed. "What cause would I have to exaggerate?"

Menelaus shrugged. "You are a wretch. For now, I will take my leave. I can hear sweet lips calling me–"

"And your wages," Jason finished for him with a smile. "Go on your way, my friend. I will see you soon."

Menelaus started walking away. "Give Titus my greetings. And Apidius, if you see him."

"I will. And you give Lentulus mine."

They parted with hands raised in farewell, but Jason did not long think on his friend. There was a particular pair of sweet lips he would like to hear calling him too.

Abigail stepped out of the small tub, humming the psalm she had heard Dinah singing minutes earlier. Morning stillness bathed her as surely as the water had and brought peace to her soul. In a few minutes, the day would truly begin. Breakfast preparations, helping Ester rise, seeing to the daily tasks. But for now, she was alone.

She wrung out the sopping mass of her hair, then straightened with a start when a creak disturbed her peace. It sounded almost like someone entering the house . . .

The young master–he would be returning from his night watch, and she had completely forgotten. Panicked, she grabbed her tunic and pulled it over her head. The hem settled into place just as the shuffles that had replaced the creak solidified into a tired-looking Jason.

He looked a bit surprised to find her in the empty kitchen, and the way his gaze trailed over her made her uncomfortably aware of the way her tunic clung to her still-wet figure. What must he think of her? She quickly veiled herself with her hair, face down.

"I have interrupted you, I think." A smile saturated his voice, but Abigail dared not look up to see it.

"My apologies, Lord. Dinah and I always–that is, we forgot . . . . You must be famished. May I bring you food in the triclinium?"

"I will await my parents, thank you."

He said no more, but still she felt his gaze on her. Hot, more intense than ever. Certain her cheeks had turned scarlet, Abigail averted her face and prayed he would leave.

Instead he motioned to the tub. "Shall I dispose of that for you?"

The offer, though more thoughtful than she would have expected of him, unsettled her all the more. Why did he not just dismiss her as usual and go to his chamber? "No, Master, but thank you. Simon always takes care of it after Dinah and I are through."

"Ah. I shall leave you to it, then. I trust you will bring fresh water to my room once you have . . . dried out a bit?"

Could her mortification increase any more? She thought not. "Of course, Lord."

Thankfully, he started toward the kitchen's exit, though he paused in the threshold. "Abigail?"

"Yes, Lord?"

Again, his voice was smiling, teasing. "You have lovely hair."

She covered her face with her hands as he left, groaned into them. A more humiliating experience she could not recall. Best not to dwell on it. She knocked on the door to Simon and Dinah's chamber to signal she was finished, then quickly dried off, changed. Her hair she left loose, otherwise it would still be wet this evening.

Back in the kitchen, she put water over the fire for the young master. Dinah entered with a smile. "Good morning, Abigail. Have you started the meal?"

"Not yet. This is for the young master."

Dinah paused with her hands on a stack of bowls, eyes wide. "We forgot! He did not walk in on you, did he?"

"No, but barely." Her heart stuttered again at the mere mention of it.

Dinah covered her mouth with her hand. "We shall not forget again, hm?"

"Certainly not."

Cleopas then stuck his head into the room. "Abigail, my wife did not sleep well last night, but she is finally resting. Let her sleep for another hour or two, if you would, before bringing her breakfast."

"Of course, Master." She nodded, though it made nerves light up in her stomach. She had hoped for an excuse to postpone tending to Jason, but now she had none.

When the water was hot, she poured it into a jar and headed for his chamber. He answered her knock with his usual "Enter," and she slipped inside. Perhaps he would spare her further embarrassment and ignore her.

She poured the water and headed to where he sat on the edge of his bed, working out a knot in his sandal. As she knelt, she wondered again why he had not replaced his personal slave. Surely a master did not enjoy such menial tasks as washing his own feet.

But since it fell to her for now, she went about it silently. Or would have, had he let her.

"Did my mother not need you yet?"

"She is still sleeping. Your father said she had a restless night."

"Does that happen often?" It was not concern that colored his tone. Curiosity perhaps, but more, it sounded as though he merely wanted to make conversation. A strange thing, given it was with her.

"Occasionally." One foot clean, she dried it off and guided the other into the basin. "Enough that it is not odd. Not enough to be alarming."

"You serve my mother well. She depends much on you."

She could smile at that. "It is no chore to serve her. All I do for her is out of love."

"The perfect slave." Was that amusement, now, in his voice? "Such virtue is usually only pretended. Though it does beg the question—were you taught it, or is it the condition of your soul?"

An answer sprang from her lips before she could censor it. "I suppose it depends on if you ask Meno or Protagorus."

His spine snapped into alignment. Calling herself a fool, she glanced up to see the shock on his face. He shook his head, incredulous. "You are familiar with Plato?"

How had she forgotten even momentarily her concerns about his opinion of her education? She set her gaze back on his feet. "Your parents often wish me to read his dialogues to them of an evening."

His finger hooked under chin and forced her head back up. Perhaps his touch was gentle, but his eyes were not. "You *read*?"

She would have preferred to nod, but he still held her face captive. "Yes."

"Greek?"

"Yes."

"Hebrew?"

"Yes."

His hand fell away, his eyes went blank. "Latin?"

She nodded now, and stifled the urge to apologize for the affirmative. "Your father willed it."

"My father willed it," he echoed. He shook his head, amusement sparking life back into his countenance. "I am realizing anew, fair one, was a strange family I was born into. A mother educated as the son of the high priest rather than the daughter, married to a Roman who has adopted Jewish law, both of whom educate their slaves better than most do their children."

"They are the best of people."

"They are arcane." At least he smiled. "But yes, very good. They have certainly done well by you. My mother has shaped you into the paradigm of womanhood. Beautiful, modest, humble."

And very uncomfortable. She dried off his foot and prayed she could make her escape without the need to respond.

He stayed her with a finger under her chin once again. "You are learned, apparently more so than most women I knew in Rome. Yet I wonder how knowledgeable you truly are. Have you known a man?"

Shame at the very suggestion fired her cheeks. "Of course not."

He grinned, even chuckled. "I assumed as much. Your eyes are innocent, for all their reading. You have no idea how alluring that is. I would wager you have never even been kissed."

She would have fled, had it been an option. But he had not dismissed her, and he still restrained her with his touch. Then his head inclined toward hers. She wanted to find some clever words to say to halt him, to deflect the intent in his eyes, but she felt frozen in place. It was the talk of Socrates, perhaps. The man, centuries dead, had managed to sting her with his torpedo fish venom just as he had his friends of the day. She could not think, could not move, was nothing but a paralyzed victim of rhetoric that had led her into a trap.

His lips touched hers. A stroke, a caress. Soft but nevertheless terrifying, especially when he slid his hand to the back of her head and anchored her there with his fingers woven through her hair. He parted her lips, deepened the kiss.

She did not respond. She knew not how, and would not have, even if she did. It felt so strange, that sensation of another's mouth on hers, nearly repulsive. It made an unwelcome heat singe her spine, spike down her legs. Her hands shook, but she dared not reach for support, as he was the only thing close enough to grip.

He urged her up, then to a seat beside him. She tried to reclaim her mouth, but he followed her in her retreat and pushed her down into the pillows. Overtaken by panic, she tore her lips away from his. "Master, please. I cannot do this."

Jason's smile was far too confident. "You will learn."

"No." She held him away as much as she could with hands pressed to his chest. "It is wrong. Your parents have not given me to you–"

"No fear." In another situation, the lopsided grin may have been charming. At the moment, if felt more like a threat. "I am perfectly capable of taking you without their assistance."

"Master–"

"That is right." His tone went hard, cold. "I am your master. You are a woman–and less, a slave. Will you object to me?"

She clamped her mouth closed, but a veil of tears blurred her vision.

He kissed away the drop that spilled over, but any tenderness inspired by that vanished when he slipped a hand onto her leg. "Hush now, beloved. I will not hurt you. This is a good and normal thing."

With a wild shake of her head, she struggled to slip away. An impossible goal, given the way his body pinned hers to the bed. "It is a sin."

"If so, it is mine, not yours." He sounded unconcerned by the possibility. "You have no choice in this, Abigail."

As if to prove it, he took her mouth again. It did not distract her from the hand he moved upward. Pain blinded her, but her whimpers earned no response. Then something else happened, a pleasure that underscored the pain.

It was wrong. She knew it was wrong, wanted nothing more than to find an escape. But she could not move, and confusion swirled inside her with each kiss he gave her. She did not want this . . . so why did her body respond of its own will to his touch? Torment and desire twined inside, one overtaking the other only to be overtaken in turn, until she gasped in shock at the sensations crashing through her, then sagged at their ebb.

Jason pulled away, victory in his eyes. "You see how I can please you? And I have more to offer than that."

She drew a deep breath in through her nose, trying to regain her composure. Tears stung her eyes again. She knew not what he had taken from her, but deep in her heart she knew she was no longer the chaste woman she had been when she awoke an hour earlier.

Jason pulled her tunic back down to cover her legs. "You will come to me tonight, after my parents have retired. We will finish this."

Turning her face away, she struggled to hold back the sobs begging release. "What have you done to me?"

He sat up, as if it hardly mattered. "I have been kind. I have chosen to ease you from your maidenhood instead of forcing it from you all at once. Had I done that, it would have been much more painful." The stroke of his thumb over her cheek felt like a brand. "You are already mine. There is no sense in fighting me."

The truth of that weighed heavily on her soul. She pushed herself up and stumbled off his bed. "Am I dismissed?"

"Until tonight. I will be waiting." She got a step away before his voice halted her again. "And Abigail? I think it would be wisest not to mention this to my mother."

As if she would uncover her shame to the eyes she most revered? With barely a nod, she left the room.

◆

"You seem bothered."

Andrew looked up quickly at the words, and if the familiar voice carried no reproval in itself, he inserted it in his own mind, as he was deserving of it. Even so, he knew his master did not make such observances unless he wished to know the cause of them. So he drew in a deep breath. "It is Abigail," he confessed. "She seemed upset at the meal this morning."

Cleopas nodded knowingly and handed his servant the waterskin to hold while he reached for his buckler. "Did you talk to her?"

"I did not have the chance."

Cleopas let out his breath, pausing to finish the conversation before heading onto the field. "She is most likely still adjusting to the changes, Andrew. Much of the burden of serving Jason has fallen to her. Combine that with her concern for Ester's health this morning, and I think that would account for her behavior."

Andrew nodded. "I was coming to the same conclusion myself." He watched his master's face gain its satisfied expression and gathered his courage before the elder could take the first step away. "Master. Have you spoken with Mistress about Abigail?"

Cleopas now nodded. "Directly after you asked me. I gave her a month to decide, but she has been distracted by her son's arrival; I think she has probably not even had time to think about it. But I will remind her tonight, Andrew." He smiled. "I do not wish to raise your hopes unduly, but I should think that soon Abigail will be your wife."

Andrew could not hold back a smile at the news. "It would be a blessing, Lord. I love her deeply."

"I know." Cleopas tapped his fingers against his belt. "Ester is just reticent to consign her to slavery forever, as you have chosen for yourself."

Andrew hesitated but decided to speak. "Perhaps she should speak to Abigail about it, Master. I think she will find that our young friend is not only willing to remain in your house, but unwilling to do anything but. She expressed to me just last week her desire to continue to serve our lady."

Cleopas appeared to give it thought for a moment, then nodded. "I will make the recommendation." Pausing, he smiled and clapped a friendly hand on Andrew's shoulder. "And I will stress your love. I think she will agree. It may, however, take her a while to come to that conclusion. I invite you to be patient."

Andrew returned the smile wholeheartedly. "Knowing the reward that could await me, that is the easiest task you have ever assigned."

NINE

Ester drew in a deep breath as her servant brushed through her hair in preparation for bed. She glanced into the polished metal surface of the mirror, more to see Abigail's reflection than her own. And what met her eyes both pleased and troubled her. Her beauty became more undeniable every day. And when a lovely face combined with eyes luminous in intelligence and a bearing gracefully underscored by modesty and humility, the result was a lady worthy of the best.

But on this particular day, Abigail's brows had been drawn more than not. Ester had to wonder if the girl had borrowed some of *her* distress. The decision on her mind weighed more heavily with each sun that dawned past the deadline her husband had set, and though she knew he assumed she had forgotten the question in the face of Jason's return, she knew from the way he had nodded to his manservant just minutes ago that he would not tarry long in reminding her of it.

She had not forgotten. She had just not decided.

Abigail did not deserve to be a servant for the rest of her life. She deserved a husband who had made a place for himself in the world, who was respected and would share that esteem with her. She could be the crowning jewel of any household, and it would be selfish to hide her away here. As much as she loved the one she thought of as a daughter, her desire to maintain that companionship could not outweigh her need to do right by her.

A long sigh escaped her lips.

Abigail's brows drew together for the countless time that day. "Are you quite certain you are not feeling ill, Mistress?"

Ester managed a smile bordering on sincere. "I am well, child. Though I am concerned that you are not. You have not seemed yourself today."

Abigail moved behind her and separated her hair into three sections to be braided. "It is nothing. I have just been tired."

"You have gained more responsibilities since Jason returned." Her displeasure crept out in her voice, she knew. "Cleopas insists that we will not provide him with another slave, that it is up to him to do so, but when it affects our own–"

"It is not that." Abigail accompanied the rare interruption with a reassuring hand on Ester's arm. "The extra duties have been light and few. I simply did not sleep well last night."

Not sure if she ought to be convinced, she sat quiet and still once more as Abigail braided her hair. She stood at the completion of the task and offered a smile. "Thank you, Abigail. Go ahead to bed."

♦

Abigail stood outside her mistress's chamber, stalling and trying desperately to think of a way out of the situation that had been chasing her thoughts all day. Panic clawed at her throat. There had to be an escape. The answer had to be there, just beyond her sight, just past her reach. All she had to do was stretch her fingers out a bit farther and there it would be.

But habit was a strong force, and even as her mind ricocheted about the possibilities, her feet carried her out into the hall, around the corner, and did not stop until they had put her in front of the closed door behind which lay her imminent destruction.

She could not go in. That was a simple answer. She could ask Andrew to see to Jason's needs from now on–but claiming what? That she could not handle it? He would know it was untrue, that she was hiding something, and she could not admit to him what. He would wonder if she had invited the attention, had done or said something to Jason to make him think her the sort to agree to such a tryst.

She could ignore it altogether, mention nothing. She could go to her room, to bed, and hope fervently that the young master would have forgotten his desires by morning.

Only he would not. She knew that. If she did not go into his chamber now, he would seek her out in her own. The look in his eyes that morning, the things he had done to her, had spoken strongly of his determination. He would come, and Andrew and Dinah and Simon would all hear him knock, would hear the angry voice he would undoubtedly raise at her audacity, would hear any protest she might make. And if one of them decided to intervene–something she could well imagine Andrew doing if it became clear that a man was forcing himself upon her–it would not be good.

A slave did not raise a hand against his master. If he did, he seldom lived long enough to see the results of his bravery. And though Cleopas would surely not *want* to punish him, he would have no choice when it came to his son or his servant.

No, if there would be shame, she would bear it alone. If there would be dishonor, better that it be on one than the whole house. And with luck, the young master would take her tonight and then be satisfied. She could work to forget the incident, salvage her innocence, and think up a way to explain to Ester why she could *not* be given in marriage. A man would not want a soiled woman as his wife. But the thought of confiding to her mistress what was about to take place–

She had to stop thinking about it. She raised her fist, her knuckles rapped against the wood, and her body was as rigid as granite as she waited with dreadful expectancy.

"Enter."

She opened the door enough to slip in, then closed it behind her. It was her usual way, always returning things to the way they had been before her arrival, but this time it carried significance. It was she who stepped into this, she who closed the portal on escape. Her nostrils flared as emotion surged through her again. She struggled against the tears and dug her fingernails into her palms to keep the shaking under control.

Jason lounged on the couch, a manuscript in his lap, and looked up only briefly at her entrance. "'Crito,'" he said in introduction to the papers in his hands. "The story of Socrates' last hours before his execution. Are you familiar with it?"

Her "Yes" was barely more than a movement of lips.

"I always liked this dialogue. It is one of the few times we see what Socrates actually believes, when he is not just repeating someone else's theories in his own rhetoric." He paused, crooked his head a bit, and glanced at her again. "Did you know that Cato read this through three times on the night he committed suicide? When Caesar's armies were approaching?"

She could only open her mouth this time without any sound coming forth. No, she did not know, and she did not care. She tried to swallow but found her throat suddenly parched and swollen.

Jason put the dialogue down carefully and sat up, his focus fully on her now. His gaze was surprisingly soft, as was his voice when next he spoke. "I am trying to help you relax, Abigail.To draw you out with conversation of things we share a common interest in." He smiled, his brows arching companionably. "I have never been able to discuss Plato with a woman before. I find myself intrigued by what it could result in."

Abigail focusing upon not looking as terrified as she felt, but suspected she failed miserably.

Jason fought a grin. "Come here, Abigail."

Disobedience would have required thought. Her feet acted on their own yet again and took her to stand directly in front of him. He stood, closing the distance between them even more. Then he reached out and brushed a few stray hairs off her cheek. She did not flinch at the touch, though she would have liked to.

"Kiss me," he demanded in a whisper, his hand at the back of her head.

Her eyes flew to his in surprise, her hands flying up protectively at the suggestion and landing on his chest when he drew her against him rather suddenly. "Master," she breathed in a voice near a squeak, "I cannot. Please, I do not know how–"

"Did I not teach you this morning?" Humor deepened both his tone and his eyes.

She flushed at the memory. "But Master–"

"I think," he interrupted thoughtfully, "that you should call me Jason when we are alone. Otherwise it will seem as though you are here only out of duty. And that is not the case, is it, Abigail? You are not here simply because I took the choice from you, are you?"

She had no response to such digs, such jests. She was uneducated in the proper way to dance around one's lover, had never heard nor experienced the right kind of wit to employ. So she did the only thing she could think to do to get him to stop such a conversation. She stood up on her toes and brushed her lips against his.

Once she made contact, he took over, eating through her mouth and running his hands over her until her tremors apparently grew too great for him to ignore. He drew away a bit, moved his hand to cup her face.

"Do you know how beautiful you are?" He gave her no time to answer. "I have never seen one so fair. There are many women in Rome, Abigail. Many women who vied for my attentions. But in spite of their stained lips and arranged hair, none of them can compare to what I see in you. You have really what they create in a facade. You are the paradigm that they all aspire to."

He ran a thumb across her cheek, the hand on her waist growing restless. His fingers clenched in a fist around a stretch of the fabric. "Take this off," his muttered hoarsely.

She stared at his chin. Did he really expected her to do such a thing herself? The haze she saw in a glance at his eyes told her he did indeed. Her breath caught in her throat and held; she reached down with unsteady hands and clasped at the cloth. She closed her eyes, forced air into her lungs. And moved her arms up.

It was hours later when Jason finally gave her leave to return to her own room, and she went with weak limbs and a bruised soul. She was exhausted, but what was more, she felt broken. As though she was no longer the self that she knew, no longer the Abigail that deserved even a morsel of love from those dearest her.

As she moved silently into her little chamber and slipped onto her pallet, hard now in comparison to the bed she had just occupied, but blessedly familiar, she felt the thread of bitterness that had been overshadowed by her mistress's faith surge to life again, squeezing her being in a vice of affliction.

"Jehovah," she whispered fiercely into the darkness as the tears flooded her eyes as the Nile did the plains, "why must you submit me to this? What have I done, what have I not done, that I deserve to be used so? Why does your supreme will see fit that your maidservant be forced to such a pass?"

No answer penetrated the darkness, and she had expected none. The Lord did not speak to those too weak to stand up for him. He did not deign to respond to those who obeyed men before him.

But it was he who had placed her in this home. It was he who had given her the face, the figure that had drawn the young master. It was he who instructed his servant's servants to obey their masters, who gave to men that inescapable right over women.

Unbidden, the story of Lot came into her mind, and the depravity of his city of choice. When the angels, the very messengers of God had visited him and the mobs had come knocking at his door to demand they be turned over for their carnal pleasure, Lot's response had been quick. "I have two virgin daughters–do with them what you want, but leave these men alone!"

"A noble defense indeed." Pain hardening into anger, she directed her mutter into her single pillow. "That one would sacrifice one's daughters was acceptable, even laudable. Certainly, he offered it to the salvation of the heavenly creatures, but what of his daughters? What of your daughters, Lord? Did you create us just to provide for the lusts of man?"

The answer seemed obvious, and the weight of the realization forced her breath out in a sigh. She closed her eyes, ignored the aches coursing through her lower body, and pushed herself resolutely into sleep.

TEN

Andrew's fears of one day were not assuaged the next by the circles he saw under Abigail's eyes. When he entered the kitchen she stood alone, going about her daily chores as absently as ever. But he did not like the exhaustion he saw on her face or the shuttered eyes she turned on him when he entered. It had been many years since she had looked at him with such lack of feeling, many years since he had seen that hollow spot within her. Looking at her now, he knew fear.

"Abigail." He moved to her side. She did not stop working at his approach, but he interrupted with a finger to lift her chin up, forcing her eyes to follow. He longed to be able to gather her into his arms, to kiss away the worry as he would hopefully soon have the right to do. Instead, he lowered his hand again, slightly reassured when he saw a flicker of familiar warmth in her eyes. "What is wrong, my friend? You look unwell."

Her lips turned up slightly. "Do not be concerned. It is just a lack of sleep."

"And what had caused such a lack? Is there something on your mind?"

She sighed, hands still. "There is much on my mind, Andrew. Too much to articulate, because so little amounts to anything on its own. You already know of my concerns."

A few knots loosened in his shoulders. "I did not realize, though, that your concerns would be so manifested. Perhaps you should speak with our mistress of your thoughts, let her know you do not wish a marriage that would take you away from her."

Abigail blushed and shook her head. "I cannot. I cannot broach such a thing myself. But if she asks, Andrew, I will tell her honestly of my desires."

He nodded, knowing that was all he could ask. "Our lady loves you, my friend. She will not be unfair."

Abigail opened her mouth as if to respond, but just closed it again and smiled a bit more genuinely. She turned back to her work.

Andrew did not interrupt her again, but rather grabbed some breakfast for himself before moving down the hall to assist his master.

◆

Abigail went through her day as she always did, putting one foot in front of the other, one hand over another, to complete her tasks. She was relieved when Ester bade her take up the lyre and sing, a task that required little physical effort.

But as her lips formed the words of the psalms she had known all of her life, her thoughts drifted of their own accord to the shepherd-king who had written them. David, the man said to be after God's own heart, yet who sinned again and again against the Lord. Why was he blessed? What was it about that ancient man's soul that made him worthy of a promise, a title, that no other ever received?

Abigail did not know. Indeed, she could not begin to understand the man he must have been. But in thinking of it, she thought as she often did of the woman after whom she was named. Abigail, first the wife of a man so foolish Jehovah himself struck him dead. Abigail, third wife to David, who received that honor because of wisdom and the courage to speak it.

Humbled, this Abigail's fingers strummed the lyre absently. She, too, had tried to warn her master of his sin, but he, unlike David, would not obey. Was she then blameworthy or excused for her actions? Unbidden, her mind wandered to another of David's wives, one far more notorious. Had Bathsheba consented to being taken to the chamber of her king, or had she felt herself helpless? Did she realize as she took that fateful step how her life would change? She lost her husband, her family, even her first child.

But she had been the mother of Solomon. And David had favored her as a queen. She had his love, and she had the touch of God.

Her fingers stilled, and her eyes stuck on nothingness before her. Could her God use this situation for good? If she repented of any sin and put her trust in Jehovah, would she be blessed in spite of this cursed existence?

If, then yes, perhaps. But that if. . . . She mustered up her soul, calling forth all the faith she had. A miserly amount indeed. For too long, she had been living on Ester's belief, on habit, on rote. She knew all the words, but they were empty in her being. She knew the Law, but she did not believe it could be upheld. She knew her God was One and All, that she was one of his children, and she wanted only to escape from his gaze and be free.

Even the thought of freedom reminded her of her chains. Her eyes refocused and moved to Ester, who slept peacefully upon her couch. Emotion flooded Abigail's heart. To Ester, she was not bound by slavery, but by love. It was to God she was a slave, because of his will that she was brought to such ruin. Ester had always loved her, always provided, always cherished.

But Ester, when all was said and done, was only a woman. She held no power in her hands.

&

Jason neared the edge of the market, eyes seeking out familiar forms. It took little effort to spot Titus and Menelaus in their brilliant red capes and arrogant expressions. He approached them with a grin . . . and perhaps a bit of a swagger, given the way their brows arched. "Where are the others?"

"Unable to join us." Menelaus folded his arms over his chest, amusement evident. "So. The slave girl? Or did you find another?"

Though he arched a brow, he knew his mirth would be clear. "I know not of what you speak, my friend."

Titus choked down a laugh. "How stupid do you think us? No man saunters around like that unless he has come from the bed of a beautiful woman. Come now, you would not dare hold back from us, would you? After I shared my women, my house–"

Jason cut him off with a playful shove in the shoulder and motioned with his head toward the markets. "My mother's slave," he admitted after a few steps. "And there will be no sharing, so do not even ask. Abigail would probably die of shame if another ever approached her. She is the paradigm of modesty, my friends, and purity. You will all writhe in envy when you see what I have taken for myself."

"And when will that be? When do I get to see this symbol of beauty? Until my own eyes behold this girl you speak of, I will not believe she is so perfect."

Jason chuckled and slapped a hand to Menelaus's shoulder. "You will believe. I spoke with my mother this morning, actually. You are both invited to dine with us tomorrow evening."

"I cannot," Titus said. "I have a woman of my own to meet tomorrow"

"I will be there." Menelaus nodded, smiled, and chuckled a bit. "Shall I invite Lentulus and Apidius?"

Jason debated a moment, then gave a lopsided smile. "Not this time. Best to introduce my parents to the beasts I call friends in small doses."

They shared a laugh and continued their exploration through the markets. They browsed through the stalls, generally ignoring the words that the merchants spoke to try to convince them to buy their wares. The scents warred for place in their nostrils, just as the voices did in their ears. Fruits mixed with perfumes mixed with spices. Merchants mixed with haggling purchasers mixed with laughing children.

A necklace caught Jason's eye. It was Egyptian, he could see from the colorful beading and bold lines. It would suit Abigail. He could already imagine how her skin would lend it light, how the beads would sparkle and wink at him as he slid her clothing off and kissed her. Nonchalantly, he leaned against the counter of the stall.

He tapped another necklace, one heavier, with precious stones. "How much?"

Eyeing him up, the merchant named a price ridiculously high. Jason arched a brow, smiled. He cut the price in half.

The merchant blustered. "You insult me! It is worth three times as much! I give you a bargain!"

"Bargain! You are blind, old man. Your wares are cheap!"

"They are not!" The man's eyes gleamed with the bickering he undoubtedly enjoyed.

"They are. Look at this awful craftsmanship." Jason disgustedly flicked at the necklace of his choice. "It would fall apart with a breath. The other is probably no stronger."

"No, I assure you, this is the best piece I have! The others are nothing, it is true. But this one–this one is a rare piece of art."

"On the contrary, you are a thief." He grinned to soften his words. "Even for that other you would try to rob me. For this one, you would have me pay with my limbs."

"For nothing, I charge you nothing. For something, I charge you something. It is fair."

"And I will be generous." He took a coin out of his purse, put it on the table, and picked up the necklace he had just insulted. "For nothing I will give you something. Have a good afternoon."

The merchant stood agape for a moment, then let loose a laugh as Jason sauntered away.

"He is buying her gifts," Titus said in a mock whisper to Menelaus once Jason was close to them again. "This is getting out of hand. Before long, he will be sighing as much as Apidius."

Jason sent him a teasing scowl. "I have seen the way you dress your women, Titus, and yet never have I heard you sigh. Would you give me less credit than yourself?"

Titus's grin was wicked. "Naturally. I am better with women. They fall at my feet. If I adorn them, it is to please my eyes before I feast. If you adorn them, how can I know it is not from affection? You have never had your own woman."

Jason did not mind the poke, since he intended to return it. "And now, my friend, it is I with my own woman, and you who must borrow from the common supply. And if I choose to adorn her, it is to please my eyes before I feast. If you adorn them, it is to pay for their services so they do not cry out against you in the streets and keep their friends from taking you into their rooms."

They shared a smile, and Jason tucked the necklace into the pouch at his belt, tallying the hours before he could hold that woman in his arms again. With any luck, she would welcome him with fresh water for his feet as she often did, and he would have a few moments in which to sate his appetite until later.

Once again Abigail stood before Jason's door, praying her tasks in there would be innocent. Praying he would ask her only to fetch him something, or give her some task, or just dismiss her for the evening, as he had until all nights before the last. She raised her hand and knocked lightly on the door.

"Enter."

She did so, slipping the door closed behind her.

Jason stood from his couch with a smile when she came in and went to her, not pausing until he had pulled her into his arms and crushed his mouth against hers. Any hope of escaping another night in his bed vanished. If only she could have continued avoiding him as she done throughout the day.

"I was waiting for you." He murmured the words against her mouth and untied the end of her braid. His fingers ran through the locks to set them free.

"Were you?" Her voice came out unsteady and quiet.

"Were you not certain I would want you again? I hunger for you, Abigail. I thought of you all day. That will not change soon. If it does, if I tire of you, I will give you leave not to come. In the meantime, nights I am home, you will be with me."

She had no response to that command. She could only shut her eyes and resign herself to the lot she seemed to have drawn.

"I have something for you." He put a finger under her chin to tilt her face up to his, and drew his body away from hers enough to hold something between them.

The sparkle of the necklace ignited a fire in Abigail she had not thought herself capable of. Pure, raw anger made her voice shake. "You have already shamed me enough. Must you now turn me into a harlot as well?"

He had the audacity to smile. "It is a gift, Abigail. It is not payment. I thought of you when I saw it, and it is my pleasure to see you wear it."

"And where would I?" Her eyes met his for only a moment before latching onto the ground. "Such gifts are useless, Lord. I would have no explanation for your mother as to where I got such a thing."

He ignored her protests and fastened it around her neck. "You may wear it with me, for now. I trust you have someplace to store it when you are not in my chamber?"

She sighed and nodded. Why argue more?

"Good." He leaned back to survey her. "You are so beautiful, beloved." As he moved closer once more and aimed his mouth for hers, he uttered again, "So beautiful."

Beautiful . . . she thought it the most hateful word in the world.

             ◆

"She is a Venus."

Jason watched as Menelaus outlined alluring female curves in the air. "More beautiful than your women, Titus, with a modesty the likes of which you cannot find in Rome. Jason was not deceiving us."

The others laughed, but Jason let his gaze wander to the stalls of wares they meandered by. He listened with only half an ear as Menelaus continued to expound on Abigail's charms. It had been a week since he dined with them, but this was the first the whole group had been together.

He had expected to feel a rush of pride when his friends realized what was his. Instead, he felt only the same frustration he had felt when he left that morning.

Apparently Titus noticed the clenching of his jaw. He leaned close with a knowing smirk. "Something amiss in paradise, Jason? Has your chaste goddess turned into a shrew?"

This was one of those times when the Roman was utterly intolerable. He knew well Titus would not stop poking until he hit a tender spot. So he might as well present something. "It is not as you think, Titus. It is just this annoying Jewish tradition."

Titus's brows inched up. "Which tradition would that be?"

Jason shrugged, grateful the other three had ambled ahead a few steps. "She will not let me touch her. At all. Because it is the time of her monthly impurity. I understand that she would not wish to come to my bed, but she objected when I tried to *kiss* her! Blasted Jewish law!"

Titus's eyes dimmed with lack of interest. Good. "It will not last long," he said lazily. "You have no cause to complain. One week, and she will be yours again."

"Indeed." He closed the distance between him and Menelaus, who still painted Abigail's portrait to Lentulus and Apidius.

But it was not the physical distance Abigail was insisting upon right now that bothered him; it was the fact that she made it clear every night that no matter how often he took her body, she still was not his. She would not call him by his name, she would not so much as touch him unless he demanded it, and she continually avoided him whenever possible. She did her duty as a slave and as his lover, but no more. When she served him, no matter the task, it was without that dedication with which she waited on his parents.

Even though her love for them had sparked their first conversation, Jason had not given it that much thought. But now, having this cold and rigid Abigail in his arms whenever he wished, he realized it had been her warmth that had drawn him. When she was with his mother, she was all soft curves and gentle femininity. With him, she had turned to marble. Exquisit and unyielding.

Well, that would have to change. He would force her to realize that her body's reactions were nothing to be ashamed of, but rather to be embraced. He would teach her that their relationship could please them both. He would make her feel for him the same love and devotion she felt for the rest of his family. Or at least solidify the bonds between them until denying them was no longer useful. Only then, when she was a pliant and loyal servant to him, could she be useful in more than giving him his pleasure. He had learned in the Asinius house how well a beautiful face could be used with one's peers. And Abigail's countenance was fair enough that any man would melt in her presence as ice in a summer's sun.

At last, he relaxed. He knew what he had to do.

ELEVEN

Abigail opened up the crude wooden chest that held her personal belongings and fingered the growing stack of items from Jason. Over the past month he had continued to give her gifts, though it was all she could do to acknowledge them. Each piece of jewelry felt like chains of bondage, and the clothing he had slipped to her made her burn in shame. Never had she dressed provocatively, but the garments he asked her to wear for him turned her into a Jezebel. She despised them.

She despised him for giving them to her.

The sound of Andrew's door told her it was time to stir herself and go serve the evening meal. She stepped out into the hall just as he shut the portal to his room again.

He smiled. No matter the mood she was in, Andrew always smiled at her. And Abigail always smiled back, though it felt incongruous to the pain inside.

"How was your day?" He fell into step beside her as they headed for the kitchen.

"Uneventful." Abigail sighed and surprised herself by saying, "I miss our lessons, Andrew. It would seem they are over, though, would it not?"

"It would." He sounded genuinely saddened, though she knew the studies had never been enjoyable for him. The time together, though, had always left them both laughing. Perhaps he missed that as much as she did. "It seems the master has decided our educations are satisfactory."

"Mm." Pausing before the entrance to the kitchen, she turned to face Andrew and offered him a sweet smile. "You were a poor pupil, anyway."

It had been a long while since she had teased him, and the quickness of his grin told her he had noticed the lack and missed it. He tugged on her braid playfully. "Perhaps it was my teacher who was poor."

For the first time in a month, Abigail entered the kitchen laughing.

As if responding to her mood, dinner conversation was light and easy that evening. It was not until they carried out the sweet pastry for dessert that Cleopas's expression grew a bit tight and his eyes focused on neither son nor wife, but addressed them both at large.

"I have been giving much thought to what I have heard about this teacher, the Nazarene."

A silence fell over the table. Abigail focued on Cleopas just as his family did, awaiting what that comment would introduce.

Cleopas cut off a bite of his dessert but did not raise it to his mouth. "The stories are jumbled. But I cannot deny what I have seen. Jairus's daughter lives again, though she had died. Vetimus's son walks, though he was lame. I cannot judge of the other tales, but I hear of what he teaches, and I feel a stirring within me." Now his eyes met Ester's, then Jason's. Both mother and son looked away uncomfortably. "I wish to know what he has to say about his place according to the Law," he said to his wife.

"And I wish to know what it means to those of us who are Gentiles," he said to his son.

As if those two statements transcribed the entire situation into stone, he took the first bite of his pastry. "The next time he is near, we will journey to hear him speak."

Ester nodded, obviously at a loss, and Jason made no response at all.

Abigail and Andrew left the room, knowing they would not be needed until the end of the meal.

"Does this surprise you?" Andrew asked quietly while Abigail dished up food for the two of them.

Abigail took a moment to collect her thoughts; given what she and Andrew had talked about when Jason first arrived, of the interest Cleopas was showing, she could not say she was truly shocked. But at the same time, she had never expected her master to actually *pursue* the teachings of this Jesus. It was one thing to listen to the stories, another to take part in them. "I know not what to think."

"None of us do." Andrew accepted the plate that she handed him and sat down at the table with a short sigh. "That is why the master wishes to investigate."

"That is reasonable. And it is consistent with the way he taught us to acquire knowledge; listen, then ask, then investigate." She attempted a small smile and managed to forget for a moment her own tribulations. "Our master is a wise man. And as you said before, if this man has gotten his interest, I am not one to question it."

Andrew smiled. It was soft, contemplative, matched the expression in his eyes. She expected him to say more, but he did not.

When the moment grew too long for her comfort, she arched a brow. "What?"

He grinned and tore off a piece of bread. "Nothing, Abigail. I was just thinking how proud I am to call you my friend."

For several heartbeats she let herself feel the warmth of the compliment before remembering that she did not deserve it.

The lamp had been extinguished hours ago, and darkness lay as heavily over her as Jason's arm. Her eyes were opened, staring sightlessly up at the ceiling and imagining now the hairline cracks and marks that she had long ago memorized. She was waiting for the three words on which her nights had come to rely: "You may go." But Jason kept putting them off tonight.

He had settled beside her and continued to trace his fingers slowly over her arm, a feather light caress that she deliberately kept from thinking about. She was tired but had grown accustomed to getting less sleep. Still, her eyes grew heavy, and she wanted nothing more than to return to the tiny little room that was hers.

Beside her Jason shifted, and she felt him move to lean over her, though she knew he could not see her any better than she could see him. The moon was hidden tonight behind a bank of clouds, the stars eclipsed, and there was nothing to reveal to her the expression on his face.

"Abigail?" His whisper pierced the night.

"Yes, Master?"

"Why do you still resist me?"

She froze at the question, each muscle going taut until she could have passed for a work of stone. "I do not, Master."

He brushed the tips of his fingers over her cheek. "You still call me Master, when I asked you to call me Jason. You still get tense every time I touch you. You still enter my chamber every night as though you hope I will send you away."

To that truth she had no answer.

"I give you pleasure, Abigail. You know it is true, as much as you may wish to deny it. Your body responds to my touch, even if your mind does not."

Yes, her body was traitorous. It was a sin as dark as the night around her, but she would not make it worse by welcoming it.

His fingers stroked over her eyes, forcing them closed, then settled lightly there to keep them that way. "I want you to relax, beloved. I want you to be comfortable with me." He paused a moment, and she tried to open her eyes, but he would not let her. "You will stay with me. I want you to sleep in my arms. I want you to wake up to my face. I want to consume your thoughts as you do mine."

Her muscles sagged, but he surely knew it was more in defeat than acceptance. He would take from her the only time of privacy she had, and he would do so knowing very well what it was he was demanding. He would control her in what ways he could until he controlled her in what ways he wanted.

He ran his lips softly over hers. "Go to sleep now, sweet one. You can rise at your normal hour, and no one will know the difference."

No one but her.

†

"I know." Ester released a resigned sigh. "I will put it off no longer. First thing in the morning, Cleopas, I swear to you I will ask Abigail if she wishes to marry Andrew. I will not even wait for the meal. I will rise when you do and ask her immediately."

Cleopas smiled and drew her close to his chest. "I know this has been hard on you, my love."

"You have been so patient, my husband." Ester snuggled against him. "And generous to even give me this choice, then to allow me to give it to Abigail. Most women have no such say in their marriages."

Cleopas squeezed her shoulders and pressed a kiss to her forehead. "And we could have done the same with Abigail, binding her to a man of the city. I am sure you are right, that there would be many eager to take such a beautiful woman into their house, in spite of being an orphan and then a slave. But you do realize by now, do you not, that Abigail deserves more than a stranger?"

Ester let out her breath slowly and nodded. "When I told her of how you and I met and were married, of how we had come so quickly to love each other, she said she wished for that. I hope that you are right, and that with Andrew she will find it. Abigail deserves happiness."

"She does. And Andrew knows as no one else could exactly how precious she is. He understands her, and he loves her. I think he has proven how much in his patience."

Ester smiled, even chuckled a bit. "He has. The poor man, he probably despises me for making him wait so long."

Cleopas laughed too, and kissed her. "Impossible. No one could despise you.

There is no one in the world so lovable."

Content with her decision for the first time, Ester settled in to wait for morning. But of course, her temperament was not of the type to allow for a solid night's rest when she knew there was an exciting task ahead of her. She tossed and turned for hours, dozed on and off, and at the first light of dawn, decided it was ridiculous to try to stay in bed any longer. She would go to Abigail's chamber now and discuss the marriage, waking her if need be. Abigail would forgive her. Indeed, she would be glad to receive the news as soon as possible! That determination made, she dressed and hurried to her maid's chamber.

She knocked quietly because she did not want to wake the other servants, but she soon discovered it was also too quiet to wake Abigail. So she opened the door and stepped in, lamp in hand.

What she saw was an empty bed, straightened and neat. Ester sighed, wondering what Abigail was doing up already. She did not usually rise so early, did she? Then again, if she were having trouble sleeping, she was not the kind to wile away the time in bed. She would be up getting something done. So Ester left the room as silently as she had entered it and moved to the kitchen.

That room was empty and asleep, the fire still banked from the night before. At a loss as to where to look next, Ester headed back through the servant's hallway.

Andrew was just emerging as she came through, and she stopped with a smile. "Andrew. I am looking for Abigail, but she is not in her room or the kitchen. Do you know where she could be?"

Andrew did not seem surprised by his friend's absence, which told Ester that she was probably up early more often than she suspected. "She often attends your son before you awake," he murmured, "so that she can be there to assist you at her usual time."

"Of course." Ester rewarded him with another smile. "Thank you, Andrew. Well, I am certain you want me to find her as quickly as possible, so I will go check Jason's room."

She left Andrew with a nervous grin on his face and moved toward her son's chamber with a light step. She did not think Jason would be awake yet on his day off but knew that Abigail moved silently and was likely refreshing his water and straightening up while he slept.

She knocked lightly on the door but did not wait for a response before easing it open. She would just motion for Abigail to join her, and then take her elsewhere for the conversation.

"Mother!"

Ester's eyes had been scanning the room for her maid, but they now flew in the direction of the startled voice. Her eyes went wide when she looked over and saw her son in his bed, leaning over a woman. Ester did not need to see the averted face to know that it was Abigail.

"Jason!" She sputtered for a moment, horrified, then snapped her spine into rigid alignement. "You have one minute. I suggest you utilize it to make yourself decent."

She whirled away and slammed the door behind her.

Jason heard his mother bellowing out his father's name and winced. He thought to look down at Abigail. A tear coursed down her cheek, still turned into his chest. He brushed it away gently.

The contact seemed to spur Abigail into motion. Without so much as a word, she jumped up and stumbled over to where her clothes still lay on the floor. Her hands shook as she slipped the tunic on over her head.

"Abigail." Jason reached for his clothing as well. "I will handle this."

She was not given an opportunity to respond The door burst open again, and this time an enraged Cleopas entered, Ester in tow.

His mother met Abigail's gaze. "Abigail, go begin breakfast."

Abigail averted her gaze, color staining her face. She hurried past her masters without attempting to look at either of them and fled the scene.

His parents turned their gazes on him. Jason sat on the edge of his bed and awaited the lecture.

It did not take long for it to begin, though the twiching muscle of his father's jaw was the only visible sign of his anger. "Jason, what in the world were you thinking, taking your mother's slave into your bed?"

The indolence he had lived in as an adolescent flooded him, and he shrugged without concern. "Satisfying my needs."

Cleopas clenched and then unclenched his fist. "You do not *satisfy your needs* with a maid that your mother thinks of as a daughter."

"She is just a slave."

"She is *not*." The hot tears flowing down his mother's cheeks caused him more dismay than he cared to admit. "Abigail is my dearest companion. You know how much she means to me, and yet you would defile her–"

"Mother," Jason broke in, voice harsh to cover his guilt, "you are overreacting. She is still your companion."

"You miss your mother's point. You have made Abigail *your* companion, and now we cannot give her to another. And it so happens that she was looking for her this morning to ask her if she would agree to becoming Andrew's wife."

"Andrew!" Jason could not have explained why he was shocked, but the outrage of it brought him to his feet. "You would give her to a slave? Father, she is too good for him!"

"Not anymore," Ester spat.

Cleopas silenced her outburst with a glance, then turned back to Jason. "If you wanted her, you had only to speak, Jason. I am certain your mother would have had no objections to making Abigail your wife."

"Wife?" Jason could only stare at his father. Had he lost his logical mind after so many years emersed in the stifling Law? "I did not want a *wife*, father. I wanted a lover, and that is what I took."

"That is not how things are done here!" His mother slashed a hand through the air. "You are not in Rome anymore."

"Your mother is right," Cleopas agreed solemnly. "When you desire your parent's slave in Israel, you let him give her to you in marriage, you do not just take her to your bed. This is not Rome."

"And I will not be here forever. I will go back to Rome, and I will not do that with a

Hebrew wife."

"Son, you must marry Abigail." His father's face was hard, uncompromising. "You have dishonored her, and now she can never be given to another man."

"Do you expect me to apologize for that?" Jason sneered. "She is mine, and she will stay mine, but I will not marry her. You cannot force me to, and I will not do it."

"Then you will not have her!" Ester took a step forward, rage coming off her in waves.

Jason's gaze, probably looking as cynical as he felt, had her taking a step back. "Would you rather I frequent the beds of harlots, Mother? Because either way, I will see that my needs are satisfied. If you choose to take Abigail from me, I will go elsewhere. Is that what you want?"

Cleopas held up a hand, his expression saying his word would be law. "Jason, you are our son. And whether or not we condone your behavior, it is our duty to love you and respect you above anyone we have brought into our household. Know that we do not wish for this to continue. But I would rather you keep Abigail as your lover than turn to the prostitutes and their diseases." He drew up to his full height. "But that means that she is yours. You will see to the care of her well being, and you will be honored by her as her master. But when you tire of her, you will give her back to your mother. Is this understood? That means that according to Hebrew law, as her master, you have the rights to her body. But according to Roman law, she is not your wife."

Jason nodded. His mother stifled a sob.

"And," Cleopas continued, "she will continue as your mother's companion, performing all the duties she has until now. Is that satisfactory?"

Again, Jason nodded. Ester stalked from the room, leaving him and his father to stare at one another. Jason did not like the look that entered his eyes.

"Before your mother, I have taken your side." His voice was low, strained. "She will not easily forgive that. But before you alone, I will say this very clearly. You have dishonored your mother, and you have disappointed me. You have refused your heritage, and you have scorned what she holds dear. You have destroyed the life of a young woman who could have been happy. And if any chance of her happiness is salvaged, it will only be because Andrew loves her more than you could possibly understand and is willing to take what you cast off."

He, too, turned toward the door but paused before exiting. "I wanted to think you had matured into a man of wisdom, Jason. But if you had, you would realize as my slave does that you just rejected a treasure."

❧

Abigail had fled to the kitchen as was demanded, but she found it impossible to carry out the task assigned. Her hands would not work. They shook too much, and the tears that clouded her eyes kept her from focusing on anything. She could hear the dim sound of raised voices in the far end of the house, and she shuddered. She heard quick footsteps coming her way and quickly dashed at the brine in her eyes.

Andrew barreled into the room and did not stop until he was a breath away from Abigail. He framed her face in his hands, and she looked up to see his countenance contorted with pain.

"It is true?"

The only answer she could manage was a quivering lip.

Andrew moaned and drew her against him, wrapping his arms around her. She was too upset to object and held on tightly as a few errant sobs escaped her throat.

"I am so sorry." He buried his hand in her hair. "Why did you not come to me? I would have protected you. I would have–"

"I know." She turned her face up and saw his emotion raw and unhindered. It pleased her as much as it terrified her. "I could not let you, though, Andrew. He would not have stood for it, and you would have gotten hurt or worse."

"Oh, dear one," Andrew mumbled, resting his forehead on hers. "If only the mistress had not waited so long. She was coming this morning to speak with you. I asked for you, Abigail. I asked to have you as my wife, and the master said it was up to the mistress, and she said she wanted to make sure it was what you wanted before she agreed."

Her eyes went wide and filled with tears again.

Andrew stroked a thumb over her cheek to catch the drop before it could make its track. "What would you have said?"

"Oh, Andrew." She reached up and tentatively touched a finger to his cheek. "Nothing could have made me happier. I never suspected that you thought of me like that."

His smile was sad and small. "How could I not? You have grown into such a lovely woman. I love you, Abigail. I have always loved you, and now it has become so strong that it absorbs me."

Her eyes slid closed, and she settled against him. "I, too, wish our lady had not waited so long. Perhaps if I had already been your wife, Jason would not have approached me."

"Even if we were only betrothed, I would have had the right to do something about this." His voice was hard now, as if he barely had control over his anger.

"Or if we were betrothed and he did not care, I could be stoned."

"No." Andrew pulled back a little, face set. "You would have called out."

"Would I? I do not know if that is true. Jason is not an easy man, Andrew, nor a weak one. If I had called out, you would have come, and if you had come, you would have fought him. But if you had raised a hand against your master, he would have killed you."

The way his lips parted proved he understood it was not only of the hypothetical problem she spoke, but what she had actually done. "So you gave up your life to preserve mine? You would not let me protect you so that you could protect me?"

Abigail bit her lip and glanced up at him. "It would seem that I love you as much as you say you love me."

He swallowed hard, but still his voice came out low and rough. "I will wait for you, Abigail. I want no other. I do not care that he has had you. I love you, and you will be my wife. I heard him refuse to marry you; but he will grow tired of the pressure his parents put on him to do that, and he will be done with you soon. And when he is, I will be here waiting."

She opened her mouth to respond but was halted by the sudden noise of more quick footsteps, heavy and hurried. Andrew barely had time to drop his arms from her before Jason burst into the room. He halted just inside the kitchen and surveyed the situation with a frozen gaze. His face was impenetrable.

With a few quick movements, he had advanced on them and shoved Andrew into the worktable, holding Abigail back with one hand while the other gripped the front of Andrew's garment.

"You will never have her," he swore in a hiss. "I will see to that." He released him and turned to Abigail, pulling her against him and covering her mouth with his in a show of possession and force. Breaking the embrace, he demanded quietly, in Latin, "Do not disappoint me, Abigail."

A moment later, he had let go of her, too, and had stormed from the house altogether.

Shaken and dazed, Abigail stood where he left her. She jumped when Andrew put a gentle hand on her shoulder.

"Go to our mistress. She will need you."

TWELVE

Abigail entered Ester's chamber silently. She watched her mistress for a moment as the early sunlight caught the tears streaming down her cheeks and turned them to liquid diamonds. Abigail's heart clenched up and pounded so forcefully that she thought it would burst from her chest. This was the woman who had nurtured her most of her life, who had taught her and helped her grow, who had shown her what it meant to be a woman of virtue and strength.

And she had failed her. The one person in the world she never wanted to disappoint, and she had.

Feeling more base than she had the day she was sold into slavery, Abigail moved forward and fell to her knees at Ester's feet, bending over until her forehead touched the ground in supplication.

A gentle hand settled on her head. "Rise, my child. I know you are not at fault. My son is not the kind of man to give you a choice."

Abigail sat up and did not object when Ester eased her head into her lap and stroked her hair.

Ester sighed. "I would ask you why you did not come to me, but I already know the answer. You were ashamed and afraid, and I cannot blame you. I would not have confided in anyone, either. I only hope that you can forgive me."

"Forgive you?" Amazed, Abigail raised her head and looked with confusion at her lady. "You have done nothing to need forgiveness, Mistress."

"I have failed you. I was so busy trying to decide what to do about your marriage that I failed to see that my son would share the interest I knew you would evoke in others. I did not realize that just because I thought of you as a daughter, he would not see you a sister. I should have."

Abigail kept her eyes on Ester's only because she knew the woman willed them there. "You could not have seen, my lady. He has been careful to hide his interest. He knew you would not approve, so he kept it from you."

Ester pressed her lips together and let her eyes slide shut. "How long?"

She wished she had an answer Ester would like more than the truth. "A month."

Her mistress groaned. "If I had answered Cleopas about Andrew when he first brought it up, you would not be in this situation."

"You only did what you thought best, Mistress."

Ester cupped her cheek and managed a small smile. "You are precious, my daughter. You deserve better than this. Cleopas demanded Jason wed you, but he refused. He also would not give you up. So my husband has given you to him. According to our law, that makes you his wife in action, if not on paper. According to Roman tradition, it also makes him free to give you back to me when—when he wishes it."

Abigail tilted her chin up. "If my master has chosen this course, then I trust it is best. I will honor your son as my husband, and I will serve him faithfully in all he asks. What he calls me will not affect that."

Ester nodded. "And Andrew?"

"He told me this morning why you were looking for me. He said he still wishes to have me as his wife when Jason tires of me." Meeting Ester's gaze, she added, "This is what I wish, too. I love Andrew, and I want to remain at your side."

Ester nodded, but her eyes were still clouded. "Will you sing to me?" She moved to her couch and reclined, closing her eyes, while Abigail got out her lute and began a psalm.

"'To you I will cry, O lord my Rock:
Do not be silent to me.
Lest, if You are silent to me,
I become like those who go down to the pit.
Hear the voice of my supplications
When I cry to you,
When I lift up my hands toward Your holy sanctuary.'"

Her voice was pure and true, but the words were only words in her ears. She sang the song because she knew Ester liked it and would appreciate it, but it was in her mind alone and did not come from her heart. Even as she uttered the words, she knew she would not cry out to the Lord. He *was* silent to her. She was not David. She was not any man. She was just a slave woman, and exactly what that meant had been demonstrated today yet again. She could be given, she could be refused, she could be dishonored without consequence, all because her master crooked a finger.

Well, so be it. She had been left with at least one thing she loved: Ester. And Ester she would continue to serve with a whole heart.

She moved from one psalm into another, singing of supplication, praise, and prayer. Then after an hour Ester held up a hand. "I will take some camomile, my child. And have Dinah prepare me some food."

With a respectful nod, Abigail put down her instrument and went to the kitchen, but she did not miss the way Ester blinked back tears as she left. Dinah was busy as always, but she halted her work the moment Abigail entered and came to wrap her arms around her.

"I heard. I wish you had told me. I thought you were just going through moods, when really you were going through a terrible trial. Are you all right, my friend? Do you need anything?"

Abigail smiled and pulled away. "Camomile for the mistress. And she wishes breakfast."

Dinah scowled. "That is not what I meant."

"I know." Abigail put a hand on Dinah's cheek. "I am fine, Dinah, thank you."

Dinah nodded. "We are out of camomile."

"Then I will get some." She drew in a deep breath and wasted no time, but grabbed a few coins and headed for the door.

⚜

Jason wished not for the first time that Menelaus, rather than Titus, had the same schedule he did. This was *not* one of the days when he was in the mood to listen to the Roman's arrogance; and what was more, Titus always seemed to pick up on his moods and force the reasons out of him, and he also did not want to talk about it. Not with Titus. But Titus was the only one around, was indeed waiting for him at the edge of the markets when Jason finally wandered in that direction.

After storming from his parents' house, he had wandered around for a while with no goal, then had rendezvoused with the merchant in Caius's employ to receive his monthly allotment and give the latest news on Titus–not that there was much.

Though it was another reason Jason did not desire his company that day. He always felt slightly guilty for spying on his friend, even if he *did* never have much to share.

They met on the fringes of the marketplace, and Titus nodded a greeting. Jason returned it and hoped that his friend would be uncharacteristically oblivious today.

Naturally, the first thing Titus said was, "I saw your father this morning. He looked to be in a rage over something. Trouble at home, my friend?"

Jason sighed and debated for a moment how much he should say. He decided it would save them both much time and effort if he just admitted the situation now. Not looking at him, he replied, "He and my mother discovered this morning that I had taken Abigail."

Titus let out a laugh that at first irritated him, but then strangely made him relax. "They only just found out? Amazing! I assume they did not approve?"

To that Jason rolled his eyes. "They insist that things are not done that way in Israel, that I should have taken her as my wife if I wanted her so badly."

Titus scoffed, even waved his hand to dismiss the possibility. "Are they insane? You cannot take a Hebrew slave as your wife if you desire a political career in Rome."

"They did not like it when I said that, either." Jason put on a lopsided grin as they meandered between the stalls aimlessly. "I believe my parents hope I will remain here for the rest of my days. And they tried to insist that now I simply *must* wed Abigail."

"Of course, you refused."

"Yes." Jason let his breath out in a slow gush. "But my father came up with a sort of compromise to appease my mother. He gave me Abigail as my slave, which means that I can do what I will with her. But that also means I must see to her welfare. And part of the arrangement is that I still allow her to serve my mother, of course. And that when I tire of her, I will not sell her, but return her to them."

The arch of Titus's black brow showed that he thought that unnecessary. "She was already yours. What difference does it make if she is *more* yours?"

"Hebrew law is a complicated thing."

Titus slapped an encouraging hand to his shoulder. "It seems to me, at least, that what you need is to forget about this blasted Hebrew law for a while. Forget about this slave. You have been thinking of her too much, and it is not healthy. She is only a woman, and a servant at that. My advice," he said lightly, "is to broaden your horizons. Find yourself another woman today; that will help you put her into the proper place in your mind."

Jason felt the money that was stored in his belt and wondered at the counsel. It may have the effect Titus claimed it would, but he was not so certain he wanted to waste his money on what he could have for free at home. And he remembered, too, that his father had relented in order to keep him away from the harlots. He could not bring himself to disrespect that.

"But the prostitutes seem tasteless now."

"So do not take a prostitute." Titus swept an arm outward to encompass the swarms of people flocking the stalls. "There are women everywhere, and more are willing than you would suppose, if you ask them right." His smile showed that he had been successful in that often enough.

"Let us pick out a beauty for you. There." He pointing to a woman at a stall nearby. "Perfect. She is youth, she is grace, she is beauty, she is appeal. I would take her myself, but I am feeling generous. Just walk up . . ."

Jason strode her way, setting his jaw in determination. He waited until he was near enough to keep his voice at a normal level before speaking. "Abigail. What are you doing out here?" His eyes moved over her dress; it was the fine linen garment she wore within the house but seldom without.

Abigail spun around, her eyes wide for an instant. When she realized it was him, she relaxed and held up a measure of herbs. "We were out of camomile, and your mother wished some."

Jason studied her for a moment, then took her elbow and steered her toward an alley. Her face was drawn, her eyes sparkling with worry. Once they were out of the stream of shoppers, he turned toward her. "Are you angry with me for how I acted with you this morning?"

"No." Her tone was calm, and she even looked him in the eye. "You are my master. You may do with me as you will. I have neither the call nor the right to be angry about it."

She looked as though she meant it–but anxiety still lit her eyes. "What, then?"

Abigail searched his gaze. After a moment she made a quiet answer. "Your mother was very upset, Jason. I know not what you said to her, but it has hurt her greatly."

It was the first time she had called him Jason. He rewarded her with a smile. "I will apologize, beloved. I know I caused her pain, and I will make it right." His smile grew when he saw some of the worry fade from her eyes. "Believe it or not, I love my mother as much as you do."

She took a moment to apparently gauge the truth of those words, then smiled genuinely. "Perhaps, then, you should tell her that."

"Perhaps I should." He ran his thumb over her cheek. "Was she angry with you?" She shook her head, and he nodded. "Good. Did she tell you of what my father said?" A nod. Seeing she would not volunteer her reaction, he pushed for one. "And what did you have to say to it?"

Abigail drew herself up much as Cleopas had done earlier before handing down the law. "I said the truth. That as long as I am yours, I will honor you as my master and my husband. Even if I am not to be your wife."

How could he help but admire her articulated courage? Not any woman would declare a loyalty that so obviously opposed her own desires. This was the Abigail that had been so irresistible, and he hoped that this change in their lives would inspire her to remain that way. Perhaps now that she was more firmly his, she would not be caught by those ridiculous inhibitions.

"I must return to your mother," Abigail softly interrupted his musings. "She will be waiting for her tea."

"Of course." Jason stepped away with a fond smile. "Tell Mother that you saw me, reprimanded me, and that I will soon be home to beg her pardon."

Abigail opened her mouth, undoubtedly to assure him that she had not intended a reprimand, but as he moved to her side, her face froze.

Jason turned to see what she had rendered her speechless. Spotting Titus, who was leaning against a wall and making no attempt to hide his interest in her or the situation, Jason grinned. He knew very well that this friend of his who had maintained for so long that he had no desire to see Abigail was now suffering the pangs of jealous lust. Oh the delights of a turned table.

"Titus. This is Abigail."

"So I assumed." His eyes still roved over her, and he smirked when she flushed under his perusal. "And now I see the modesty that has been so acclaimed. I admit it, Jason. Your woman is enticing. Are you quite certain you will not share her?"

Abigail's offended gaze flew to the ground, and she stepped closer to Jason's side. The unconcious trust warmed him. Putting a reassuring hand on her back, he sent his friend a reproving gaze. "Titus, must you be a total reprobate? Come, Abigail, I will walk with you back to the edge of the markets."

Titus fell in beside them, too, and the three walked the short distance in silence. Jason murmured a farewell to Abigail, who said something similar and hurried off toward home. He and Titus stood and watched her.

"And Titus?" Jason said as she rounded a building and disappeared from sight. "You most certainly would *not* have taken her yourself."

Titus laughed. "I suppose we shall never know."

They turned together and headed back into the crowd.

THIRTEEN

Abigail knew something was wrong when it was not Elizabeth waiting on Julia, but another woman, older and obviously unfamiliar with her mistress's needs. Abigail had to forcibly keep from wincing when the woman almost spilled red wine on Julia's white stola.

"Leave me, you clumsy fool!" Julia waved the slave from her presence with a slash of her hand. She widened her eyes and inclined her head toward Abigail, as if in silent commiseration. "Abigail, I am certain Elizabeth would like to see you, if you wish to leave."

Ester gave a nod of acquiescence, so Abigail dipped her head and slipped from the room. Not knowing where else to look for the friend she had not seen in weeks, Abigail headed to the room she knew she shared with her husband. Arriving at the crudely hewn door, she knocked.

The door opened, and Elizabeth stood silhouetted there. Upon seeing Abigail, she smiled and drew her into an embrace. "My friend! I am so glad you are here."

"What is wrong?" Abigail let herself be drawn into the room. A small latticed window allowed some light in, and she glanced around to find the space disheveled.

"Cleon died," Elizabeth stated casually.

Abigail's jaw dropped, and she immediately looked her friend up and down. "I am so sorry, Elizabeth. I did not guess. You are not in mourning."

Elizabeth wrinkled up her nose in distaste. "I despise those awful, course things. I wear them when I leave my room, of course, but I just cannot force myself into them for the entire day." She sat and invited Abigail to join her, curling her legs up underneath her as if preparing for a cozy little chat. "But Julia has granted me a week with no duties, so I can stay in here as much as I want, anyway. Was that not kind of her?"

"Very." Abigail settled as questions pushed their way forward. "Elizabeth, when did he pass away?"

"Two days ago."

"And you did not send for me?" Abigail did not know if she was offended or grateful. Two days ago, she was still trying to smooth out relations between her new master and his parents, a task that had proven beyond her skills. Jason had apologized to his mother, but taking back the words he had spoken did nothing to erase the sting they had caused.

Elizabeth looked surprised at the suggestion. "Of course not, dear. He was given a Roman ceremony, and you would not have felt comfortable."

"But I would have come for you." She picked up her friend's hand and tried desperately to feel now the attachment to this girl that she had felt not so long ago.

Elizabeth rolled her eyes. "I did not need any support, Abigail. Really, it was quite a relief. He had been ill and weak for a fortnight, and I was exhausted from tending him.

He was old and ready to die."

Abigail had never felt such utter appal. She gazed for several long, deathly silent moments at this creature she could not quite feel any love for. "Elizabeth, he was your *husband*."

"I knew you would lecture me." Far from looking uncomfortable, she smiled. "And I wonder that you have the gall. I heard that Jason has taken you to his bed. Not quite the virtuous little maid any longer, are you?"

Abigail flushed with heat. "It was not my choice. But even so, I am his now, so I will honor him. You would do well to learn loyalty for yourself."

"I have." Elizabeth practically purred with self-satisfaction, it seemed to Abigail, and she could not begin to imagine what caused it. "It is just that my loyalty does not lie with a corpse. I pledge myself only to the living."

Abigail's eyes slid shut in dismay. "What have you done, Elizabeth?"

"Followed your example, of course." Her sweet tone bit like acid. "I gave myself to my master."

"Elizabeth! When did you do this? When you were married, or after, when you should have been cloistered in mourning?"

Elizabeth rolled her eyes again and pushed herself up to pace the close space of her room. "Yesterday, Abigail. I was not still married. And it was not as though I threw myself at him. It just–well, he called me in to offer his condolences, and–you know how quickly it can happen!"

Abigail met her glare cooly. "No. You have shamed yourself, Elizabeth."

"I have not!" Elizabeth cried. Her breast heaved at the outburst, and she stood there, the sun gleaming in behind her, and looked like a wrathful madwoman. "*I* at least have the honor of widowhood. What do *you* have? You will never even be a wife, now."

Abigail's spine stiffened. She would be humble with her betters, with her masters, she would never argue with them about her worth. But with this slave, she would not let herself be slandered. "I will. Andrew has already asked for me."

Elizabeth seethed in exasperation. "Perhaps before he knew how you had been spoiled."

"And after. He promised to wait for Jason to release me."

That seemed to deflate Elizabeth. Her shoulders sagged, and she turned her back on Abigail. "Then you have a man who loves you, as well as one who wants you. As always, Abigail, you prove yourself to be followed by good fortune."

"Good?" Too irritated to sit, Abigail surged to her feet. "I have a man I love whom I cannot marry because of the claims of a man I despise! How is that good?" Immediately regretting her words, she covered her mouth with her hand and squeezed her eyes shut against sudden tears of disapprobation, for herself and her companion. She knew beyond doubt that she should not have said such things in Elizabeth's presence.

Elizabeth's hand landed on her shoulder, and it was gentle. She opened her eyes to find her friend's gaze on her, as soft as her touch, and tears burning there, too.

"I am sorry," Elizabeth whispered. "I have been jealous of you for so long, Abigail. Your mistress loves you, mine barely tolerates me. Your master has educated you, mine never even noticed me except to realize that I was an attractive option for his favorite slave, and now perhaps for himself. You are more beautiful, you are more loved, and I know there is nothing I can do about either. But I should not have tried to cause you pain." She pulled Abigail close and held her there fiercely. "I am sorry you were forced into this situation, Abigail. I am sorry I did not want to see how it would hurt you."

Abigail returned the embrace, and for the first time, she let the tears truly come.

Cleopas had not brought up the subject for a month. He knew very well that both his wife and son hoped he had forgotten about the spiritual lessons of the Galilean, and he did not correct them. He had no intention of bringing up the subject before anything could be done about it.

He knew his family did not understand his need. Ester was still afraid to contradict her father's rhetoric, and her father had scoffed if anyone mentioned the possibility of a messiah, apparently. Well, it was not as though Cleopas was ready to declare the Nazarene the savior of mankind; but that did not mean it was not worthy of investigation. Every story he heard, even the ones so outrageous that logic told him they *must* be false, pulled on something within him.

The fact was, he was not a Jew. The Israelites would never accept him, a Roman, into their sanctum. He could never obey all the Laws, because they would not let him. How, then, was he to gain his place in Paradise? But at the same time, he loved the one God, Jehovah, with all of his heart. He wanted to serve him, he wanted to be counted as one of his children. Perhaps he was wrong to expect the messiah, the King of the Jews, to be able to intervene for him; perhaps popular opinion was correct, and the true messiah would be a great warrior to wage battle against Rome. But just maybe he was a teacher instead, and maybe the lessons this Jesus taught were true–maybe it was the love in a man's heart that counted with the Lord, not the number of sacrifices he made or how the Sanhedran viewed him.

How was it that neither wife nor son realized how crucially they needed something to bridge the gap between Jew and Gentile, to tear down that boundary, and to make them all equally clean before God? But Ester clung to the traditional interpretation of the Law, and Jason refused to acknowledge them at all. Of his household, only his slaves were willing to accept his word that this man deserved some attention. That brought a melancholy sigh to his lips on more than one occasion during that month that he remained silent about the topic festering within his chest.

But then he learned that Jesus of Nazareth was near again.

That night at dinner, Cleopas again waited until the dessert had been brought out before speaking his mind. Ester sat, smiling at Jason over something, her face beginning to age, but still more beautiful than any other in his eyes. Her expression was soft, as it so often was, and he knew that if he gave the word, she would obey him whether she agreed or not. Jason, on the other hand, sat even now in a pose that spoke of arrogance and independence. There would be no leading his son where he did not wish to go. From there, his gaze flicked to Andrew, standing tall and still and awaiting a movement to tell him where he was next needed. Andrew served with his whole heart and trusted him with his whole heart, as well, but would otherwise take no interest in the subject. And Abigail, mirroring Andrew in pose. She stood nearer Jason than Ester now, but it was still her mistress that she kept her eyes trained on. She, too, trusted him with a blindness that his family did not. But behind that quiet mask, he knew she had an inquisitive mind that would at once force her to question these things herself and make her hesitant to accept any answer.

Realizing he was on his own in this desire, he cleared his throat. Best to keep his words straightforward. "Jesus is teaching a few miles outside the city. Tomorrow at first light, we will journey to hear him. We will stay tomorrow night with my relative, Drusus, and return the following day."

The clatter of utensils against dishes stilled, and he could feel four sets of eyes on him.

"Very well," Ester said after a moment's hesitation. He knew she did not like Drusus, a third cousin of his who had moved to Israel a decade ago, where he served as a physician. She returned studiously to the food before her.

Jason mirrored Cleopas's calm. "I cannot, Father. I have the watch tomorrow night."

Cleopas wanted to tell him to request it off but remembered that another centurion had been ill and would likely not have returned to duty by his scheduled shift the next night; they would need Jason. So he only nodded. He then looked at the slaves. "You will go, too. Go inform Dinah and Simon that they will also journey with us. I wish my entire house to hear what this man has to say."

"Abigail will stay with me." Jason's smile looked forced when Ester's gaze flew to him. "I am sorry, Mother, but if Dinah is gone, there will be no one else to get my meals."

Cleopas knew he was right, but still he had to sigh in dissatisfaction. He would have liked to have Abigail form opinions that he could discuss with her. "Very well. Everyone else should be ready to leave first thing in the morning. I have already informed the general of my absence."

Andrew did his best to tease and cajole Abigail into smiles as they packed for the master and mistress, but then it struck him. In the middle of a laugh, he sobered. His hands halted in their tasks. "I do not like it."

Abigail looked at him with curiosity. "You do not like what? The trip?"

"I do not like that you are staying here with *him*."

"Come, my friend." She carefully folded one of Ester's tunics. "Why does it bother you any more than any other day would? I will be doing nothing but my usual chores."

"Every day bothers me. I hate to think of you in his arms." He saw her blush at his words and pursed his lips. "I am sorry to embarrass you, my love, but it is the truth. I would have liked a day's reprieve from the torment your master puts me through."

He shook his head and went back to packing. "He goads me deliberately. I fear that his need to keep you from me is counteracting his need to rebel against his father's subtle hints that marriage would be best." He stopped working again and turned to face her.

Abigail was still looking at him, her gaiety gone and replaced with sympathy. "I am sorry, Andrew."

"It is not of your doing." Andrew sighed. "I know not why I expected otherwise. Why should I assume that he will lose interest in what I desire wholeheartedly? Is it wrong of me to hope that he does not see in you all that you are worth?"

Abigail reached over and lay soft fingers on his arm.

Andrew covered her hand with his. "Promise me one thing, beloved. I know you must serve and honor him–but promise me that you will make it end at duty, that you will not encourage him. I will be as patient as necessary, but I need to be assured that you–"

"I will do all I can to discourage him. It will not take long, my love. Jason constantly demands an emotion I cannot give, and he will decide I am unworthy of his attentions."

Andrew gently squeezed her fingers. The smile they shared felt intimate, but he could not help but notice that hers was tinged with guilt.

Abigail moved about Jason's chamber, her focus on the chores she had not yet gotten to thanks to the packing for his mother. Jason had disappeared shortly after dinner, which was not unusual. She expected him back soon and determined to have his chamber neat for him.

Perhaps it would alleviate some of the disquiet her conversation with Andrew had caused her.

Arms circled her waist from behind, making her jump.

Jason's chuckle filled her ear as he kissed her neck. "You have been busy tonight. I imagine you are tired."

Actually, she was energized from the activity but did not dare to mention that lest he take it as an invitation to help her expel that energy.

Jason settled his hands on her shoulders and massaged them gently. "Tomorrow will be more relaxing. We will sleep late and lounge around all morning. My friends are coming for lunch, but that will not take much preparation, and I will help you."

"Your friends?" He must have invited them when he went out.

"Mm." He nudged her toward the bed, smiling when she sat down. He sat beside her, then eased her back onto the pillows. "There will be five of us. Menelaus and Titus, whom you have met, as well as Lentulus and Apidius, whom you have not yet. It has been a long while since we have all gotten to dine together." His ran his lips over her jaw. Her eyes slid closed in uninvited pleasure. "It will be a good day, Abigail."

For him, perhaps. But she was not looking forward to facing more of his lecherous friends.

Abigail had never in her life lain in bed so far past dawn. Her eyes would not stay closed, and she had to keep herself from tossing restlessly; but Jason had given his orders, and she knew she would disturb him if she rose.

She had listened to the hushed commotion as the others set off and had wondered at the strange pang she felt at their leaving. She would miss Ester, it was true; in the many years since she had been in this house, she had never spent a day away from her mistress. And it would be strange to go into the kitchen and know that Dinah would not bustle in at any moment, or walk around and not run into Simon or see Andrew trudging in dusty and tired after a day at his master's side.

But today would bring its own tasks. She would have to serve a group of men she did not know and knew already she would not like. It would be far removed from the meals she was used to, with Ester and Julia or Vetimus and Phoebe and sweet little Claron.

Thoughts of the boy, and hence his miraculous recovery, reminded her again of the reason her family had left. What did they expect to hear from this teacher? What lessons could he possibly teach that would help them where the Law could not? And what was it about the rabbi that had attracted Cleopas so thoroughly that he would be willing to take time away from his busy life as prefect to make this journey?

"How long have you been awake?"

The voice, groggy and smiling, startled her. She turned to see Jason's deep eyes on her, a sleepy smile on his lips.

"Since dawn. Habit."

"Mm." He pulled her closer and kissed her jaw. "You are not a creature of leisure, beloved. I know many slaves would have taken advantage of the day off to sleep until noon." He chuckled. "But I suppose we have already discussed your virtue, have we not? I forget which dialogue we sided with."

Abigail found herself slightly amused, which caught her off guard. She could not quite keep the humor from her tone. "I believe, Jason, you were too shocked that I knew what you were talking about to actually discuss the dialogues."

Jason chuckled again. "Perhaps you are right. Well then, Abigail, with which do you agree? The opinions Socrates brings up with Meno, or with Protagorus? Can virtue be taught, or not?"

Finally, a subject she could hold her own on with him. "Virtue *must* be taught, but that does not guarantee that it will be learned. Without instruction, however, the best of men would still be groping in the dark for the morality they may seek. Just as even with it, few will choose the path of righteousness."

Jason levered himself up with his elbow to look into her face. "And you, my precious one? Have you found this righteous path?"

"I know where it is. But sometimes I fear its toll is too high." She bit her lip, wishing back the honest words, and lowered her lashes to cover her eyes.

She felt Jason's steady regard on her for a moment before he brushed his lips against hers. "Let us rise, fair one. I will select the wine for the meal and help you prepare it. Some bread and cheese and fruit will suffice."

"I can do it," Abigail assured him, set on proving to herself that she served him as selflessly as she did his mother. "It is your day off. Rest and enjoy it."

"Nonsense." Jason was already climbing over her and reaching for clothes. "It will be too boring. I usually go out on these days, but since my friends will be coming here, it seems pointless." Standing on the floor beside the bed, he looked down at her with pursed lips, as if evaluating what he saw. "Wear one of the garments I bought you, Abigail. The red one, perhaps."

Her cheeks flushed to the color of the cloth he referred to, and she took one of her rare stands. "I cannot, my lord. Not before other men, strangers!"

Jason's grin was lopsided and boyish, and he suddenly reminded her of Cleopas in his teasing moments; the resemblance did little to ease her discomfort. "I suppose it leaves little to the imagination. And I suppose that I do not want my friends thinking I am offering you to them. What about the blue?"

She considered for a moment, then nodded. It fit her more closely than she would have liked, but it at least covered her. And she had to admit that the fine Egyptian cloth felt soothing against her skin.

"And the Egyptian necklace, too," Jason added. "It will match well."

"Master," she began, though he held up a hand to halt her.

He was still grinning. "How often do you get to wear nice things, beloved? Take this opportunity."

She gave in, but with a sigh. For some reason, her reticence made Jason laugh.

The morning, already half gone, flew by. They got out some wine, sliced bread and cheese and fruit. Only after everything was ready would Abigail change into the beautiful garment, unwilling to risk spilling anything on it.

Dressed, adorned, and incredibly nervous, Abigail emerged from her room mere minutes before the guests should arrive. She fingered the ends of a lock of hair, wanting to pull it back so that it would be out of her way; but Jason had said she should leave it down, so it hung free and long and thick down her back, nearly brushing her waist.

"You are enchanting," Jason proclaimed in a voice almost reverent. He reached out to run his fingers through a tendril of her hair, smiling with pride.

She had no time to answer, as at that moment a knock sounded on the front door. Abigail hurried toward it, habit and training kicking in. As she gripped the solid iron ring, she told herself that she had no reason to suppose this visit would be anything out of her ordinary routine. She would serve, refill cups, and otherwise blend into the decor. She tugged on the handle and pulled the door open, moving with it so that it blocked her from view and presented Jason, who had followed a few steps behind her.

Jason smiled and greeted his four friends as they entered.

Abigail watched as they look around, felt their gazes on her when she closed the door behind them. The shortest spoke first. "Very nice. My compliments, Jason." Did he mean the house or her?

Jason just snorted a laugh, which answered her question, and turned to the others. "Come, let us dine." He led the way into the triclinium with a smile. "I am still slightly amazed we all have time off today. Please, make yourselves comfortable."

The four filed in, and Abigail took the opportunity to appraise these friends of her master as he greeted them by name. Lentulus, the first behind Jason, was a bit shorter than he, with hair of a lighter brown. He was light of build but had a look of agility about him, reminding Abigail of a feline able to bound onto a wall. Apidius, next in line, was the tallest in the group, but also looked to be uncomfortable with that fact. His shoulders were rolled forward, his head inclined slightly. His hair hung in curls over his head, and his face had a gentility the others' did not. Menelaus, closest to Jason in both height and build, also seemed to be the most jovial. He was smiling now, as he had been since she opened the door, and the other features of his face faded away in the light of his gleaming white teeth. Titus, the last one through the door, moved with long, strong strides that accentuated his muscled frame. He was taller than Jason but shorter than Apidius and had those strong features that the Romans were wont to worship. Abigail could not readily imagine what his face would look like with an honest smile cracking the chiseled countenance.

They all took seats, several speaking at once to explain how they had come by the day off. It was Titus who said, "And your father? I heard he would be absent for two days, but not why. There is no problem, is there?"

Jason waved the subject away. "Nothing like that. He and my mother were just going out to visit some friends." He smiled at Abigail as she filled his goblet full of the sweet red wine and then moved around the room to do the same for the guests.

Apidius, still smiling his thanks at Abigail, ventured to say, "Is he not headed for Ephraim?"

"I believe he is."

"Perhaps he will run into the Galilean rebel. We heard he was moving in that direction. The governor is not certain he is a threat, but still, one can never be too certain about these dissidents. All reports of his actions are heard along with the rest."

Jason smiled. "From what I have heard, this man is but a teacher. A rabbi. He upsets the religious leaders but stays far from politics."

"I have heard," Apidius said with a sparkle in his eye that warned of a joke and a matching curve to his lips, "that some are calling him the son of a god."

They all laughed. Abigail, hefting the tray of food, tried to ignore the conversation.

"But what god?" Titus put some bread, cheese, and fruit on a plate when she offered it to him. "If he is the son of Volcan, I do not think that will earn him much of a reputation."

The others laughed again, though this time Jason just smiled and swirled his wine. Abigail had already given him his food, but he did not touch it.

Lentulus reclined on his couch. "Well, if he is a teacher, he must the be the son of a wise god. Minerva, perhaps?"

The laughter continued at the suggestion that the virginal goddess had created a child.

"I believe the idea," Jason interrupted, "is that there is only *one* God. And his Son, therefore, would be something special."

Menelaus cocked a brow. "Are not all gods' sons?"

Jason opened his mouth but then just shook his head and looked at Abigail. She had stopped by his side, waiting to be needed. "Abigail, I suspect you are more adept at handling these questions. I am afraid I ignored much of the teachings on the Law. Can you explain the difference to my dear pagan friends?"

He had softened his words with a grin for those pagan friends, but they were probably all wondering what he meant by drawing her into the conversation.

Abigail looked into his eyes and realized he was not putting her on the spot; he wanted his friends put in their places. She was warmed by the knowledge that though he was not ready to embrace his mother's religion, he was also not willing to let it be insulted within his father's house. Bolstered by the trust he obviously put in her to be able to defend the faith, she directed her gaze to Menelaus, since he had asked the question.

"The sons of your gods," she said, "are merely demigods. Or heros such as Heracles and Achilles, men with supernatural strength, but men still. They were mortal, they were flawed, and they inevitably bargained their life for glory." Her lips turned up. "In many ways, I suppose they are not unlike your gods: petty, self-interested, and bickering with their fellows."

She switched her language to Latin, finding the formality suited her words. "My God is none of those things. He is omnipresent, omnipotent, omniscient." In Greek again, "If he, therefore, were to have a Son, that Son would share those qualities, and yet be fully man. Which means he would bleed when cut, suffer pain both physically and emotionally, and face temptation as every other man. But unlike them, he would not give in to human sins, as even your *gods* purport to do."

The four guests stared at her in complete amazement. It was Titus who regained his tongue first. "Then this god-man would look at you, want you like every other man, have the power to take you, but turn away?" He gave a scoffing laugh and looked at his friends. "Then he is not a man."

Abigail raised her chin a notch. "My God, and hence his Son, would look at me and see my heart rather than my face. As only the *best* of men can ever do."

Apidius gave a smile that was warm rather than hot. "I think we have been chastised for our roaming eyes."

Titus waved that off. "It is a point not worthy of debate anyway. There is no *one* god with those qualities. Israel is the only nation backward enough to dare think there is. Look around you." His cold gaze bore through her as he held out a hand in demonstration. "How could one being have created this world, and how could one being maintain it?"

Abigail picked up her wine pitcher and moved around the room to refresh their cups as she answered. "Perhaps you should ask how *more* than one could do such things, Lord. Your gods–" She poured the fruit of the vine into his cup and glanced briefly into his face "–their powers are divided. You have Jove, with power over the heavens, Neptune over the sea, and Pluto over the underworld. The earth was available to them all. Juno, goddess over women. Apollo, the sun. Diana, the moon. Mars, war, and Cupid, love."

She had moved to Apidius as she spoke and was at Lentulus's elbow when she paused to shake her head. "If these gods were harmonious, perhaps it would be conceivable that they could keep the fabric of the universe from fraying. But their natures are more tempestuous than the sea. They disagree on everything. They imprisoned their own family, cuckold one another, and undermine the other gods for a bid at more power." She was at Menelaus now and offered him a smile. "If your soldiers behaved that way, Lord, what would the legion look like?"

"Not like a legion." Menelaus turned his grin toward Titus. "The woman has a point. If one being could have all the power of our gods, but without the multiplicity of wills, he would be much better able to control the world and all within it."

"And Odysseus would not have been ten years returning to Ithaca," Abigail added dryly.

Titus's lips itched upward but did not break into a full smile. "I daresay your righteous god would not have made his way any easier than Menelaus's did."

Apidius had pursed his lips in thought. "Going back to a Son, then. How would this not make that multiplicity? If such a man was a man but with the powers of a god, how would that not make him another god?"

Abigail had to give a moment's thought to that one and looked over at Jason to see if perhaps he wanted to handle it. But Jason looked at her as expectantly as the others, his mouth curved to show that he was enjoying the discussion. She put down her pitcher carefully to give herself time to think. "Perhaps it would help to think of God not as one thinks of a man," she began. "Think of him as–Rome. Rome is an entity in itself, one thing bound together into a cohesive whole that lets it be called Rome. But there is also the Roman Empire. Corinth is not Rome. But it is under Roman control. If a map of the empire were drawn, it would include Corinth. Now, Corinth can act on its own interests, can indulge in the lives of its private citizens, and that makes it no more or less Roman. But if Corinth aligns itself with its capital, if it were ruled by a man whose will was dictated by the will of Caesar–well then, it would be but a limb of Rome, would it not? Separate, but part of the whole. Having its own wills, but choosing the greater good instead. A Son of my God would be like Corinth, I think. Individual, but inseparable. He would have the authority of Rome, let us say, without the location."

Lentulus sent his eyes to his host, brows raised and impressed. "Jason, your woman is as articulate as our professor at the academy."

Jason smiled. "You should hear her talk of Plato."

It was Titus, this time, who maintained the serious subject. "So then this Son of the one God would have all of this God's powers, a will of his own that he deliberately subjected to his Father's, and a place of his own." He shook his head. "Then if such a man ever existed, he would indeed be a threat to us. He would come and set up rule of the world with a snap of his fingers."

But Abigail smiled. "Jehovah would not will that, though. The God of the Jews wants alone to reign in our hearts, and if he does that successfully, we will all treat each other with love and respect. There would be no need for a king, just a prophet to hear the words of God. So his Son would not come to rule nations. He would come to direct the people's hearts back to the Father."

Menelaus arched his brows. "So I suppose you think this Jesus is not threatening, then."

Abigail shrugged. "I think I do not know who this man is. I can speak of a hypothetical Son and what he would necessarily be. But I will not ascribe that office to a man just because he teaches well. He may turn out to be a sophist rather than a philosopher."

Laughter rang out again, and Abigail bowed out of the conversation under the guise of going to the kitchen to replenish the food. By the time she returned, talk was on other topics, and their eyes were back to assessing her very much as a woman and not at all as a source of knowledge.

Her goals of blending into the walls were impossible to meet.

FOURTEEN

"You made me proud today, Abigail."

Abigail glanced over to where Jason was helping clear the room of the evidence of his friends.

He should not be doing such work, but he smiled into the scowl she sent him. "Romans tend to be a bit–arrogant. Sometimes I feel the need to assure them the other half of my heritage is every bit as admirable as theirs. You certainly did that today, proving the Hebrews can be as articulate as they can be beautiful."

Abigail smiled now too. Ester would love to hear him uttering his pride. "They seem to accept you readily, Master, for all you are. They respect you."

Jason rolled his eyes. "They respect me because they think of me as a Roman. And while I am that, it certainly does not mean that what my mother gave me is worthless. Just because I favor my father's traditions does not negate the other half of my heritage. Indeed," he added dryly, "with my father embracing my mother's religion as he does, it seems I *must* defend it to them. I fear, though, I have been ignoring it too long in their presence to adequately do so. But you did well speaking for the Hebrews, Abigail."

She ducked her head at the compliment.

"Well." He looked around him with satisfaction. "That seems to be the last of it. We have the next day to relax, beloved. I will not even make you cook. There is enough here already to feed us until Dinah returns."

"Surely you will want dinner tonight before your shift begins." As she spoke, she realized for the first time that she would be left alone all the night long. The idea did not settle well. She would not mind a night in her own chamber, but with *no one* else around? An uneasiness began to claw its way up her throat.

"Oh, did I not tell you?" Surprise shone on his face. "Another centurion is covering for me tonight, repaying a favor he owed. I will not have to go anywhere." He grinned with a hint of mischief. "Although I see no reason to tell my father this little bit of news. He will be angry that I did not then take the opportunity to go hear the Nazarene teach."

Relieved at not being alone, Abigail could not drum up any aversion for the deception. She nodded.

They spent the remainder of the afternoon and evening in normal activities for Abigail; for a while she sang, lute in hand, and then she read aloud to Jason from Aristotle's *Politics*, a manuscript he had just recently acquired. As dusk settled, they engaged in a lively debate on the subjects brought up in the treatise, and on more than one occasion Jason looked at her with complete disbelief.

"I am beginning to understand the decisions my father made on your education," he said at one point. "To *not* instruct you in these subjects would be to deprive oneself of hours of entertaining argument."

She rolled her eyes and turned to another point in the treatise.

After the moon had risen and the stars made their appearance, they settled into bed for the night. Jason ran his fingers lightly over her back as she rested against his chest. "I think you would like Rome, Abigail. In Israel, so much emphasis is put on the Law that other literature is hard to come by. But there, there are libraries, academies—everywhere you turn, there is the opportunity to read and learn."

Abigail studied his profile in the moonlight, unable to miss the love in his voice for that city he had left so recently. Surely it was a vain hope on her mistress's part that he might remain in Jerusalem forever. "When do you plan to return?"

Jason took a deep breath, then let it back out slowly. "I do not know, really. I hope within five years. Caius Asinius, Titus's father, has promised to help me launch a political career when I return. Hopefully when that happens Father will gift me with the land he still owns outside the city."

This was news to Abigail, and she wondered why she had not heard of it in six years. "Your father owns land in Rome?"

"Yes. Titus and I went out to look at it before we left for Israel. The steward is a trustworthy man, one Father knew since he was a child. He takes excellent care of it, and he corresponds with Father regularly. But I cannot imagine my parents ever going to Rome to live."

"No. I cannot either."

"It is a beautiful place." A smile colored his voice. "The estate is large, probably about five miles outside of the walls of Rome, and absolutely breathtaking. The house is three times the size of this one, at least. Not exactly the largest in the area, but nothing to scoff at. Titus was impressed, and that must say *something*."

He glanced down at Abigail. "Perhaps I will take you back with me."

Abigail stiffened with panic at the suggestion. "Five years is a long time, Jason."

To her surprise, he chuckled. "Indeed it is, beloved. That is why I make no firm promises to you. But many things could happen in that time. We could have children. If that happened, I would naturally take you wherever I went."

The possibility of becoming pregnant had not been one that Abigail wanted to entertain. "Would you?" She squeezed her eyes closed to try to force the idea from her mind.

"Of course. You are my responsibility, Abigail. And if children come, they will be too. I would never ignore the existence of my own child, and I would also never separate him from his mother. You would therefore both come with me."

"Of course." She said no more and was glad when he, too, kept silent. The possibility of being taken from the home she had grown up in, away from the only people who had loved her since the death of her own mother . . . . She would not think about it. Surely he would tire of her soon. She would be content with today's troubles and not borrow any from tomorrow. That was what Andrew would have told her to do.

              ◈

Ester did not attempt to hide her turmoil from her maid. Instead, as the daily routine was reinstated after the short reprieve and the men were off to the day's work, she drew her friend onto the couch beside her and let out a laborious sigh.

"I simply know not what to think of it all." She focused her eyes on the ceiling. "I watched him heal a blind man, Abigail. Just a simple touch, and the man could see. And this Jesus himself." She interrupted herself with another sigh. "He looked like any other man. But his words, Abigail–his lessons were sound, but then a man asked him a question obviously meant to make him stumble, and do you know what he did?"

Abigail arched her brows in question.

"He said, 'Beware the poison of the Pharisees, for they seek glory for themselves at the cost of their souls. They speak the Law and live for their own whims.'"

Abigail made no reply, but Ester shook her head. Resentment clouded her vision. "My father was a Pharisee. Does that necessarily make him a bad man? A selfish one?"

"No, my lady." Abigail's quiet voice cut through her temper. "But he is a perfect example of a man who thought more of his own position and the reflections upon it than of love for his child, is he not?"

Ester froze, shocked that the girl would stick up for her even against her own words. "Perhaps. But many men would do the same."

"And perhaps that is so because men see their leaders doing it. If a man's heart is not obedient to the Law, does it matter that his lips are?"

"'Love the Lord your God with all your heart, mind, and strength,'" Ester quoted softly. "You are right. But who is he to see into the hearts of man? To judge whether they are obeying in deeds only, or also in their souls?" She shook her head almost mournfully. "It is easy to condemn those who despise you."

Abigail smiled, took and squeezed Ester's hand. "Yes, my lady. Just as it is easy to despise those who condemn you. Perhaps we should judge neither side."

Ester returned the smile. But in her mind, the question was far from settled.

◈

The walk home felt long, given how Cleopas's thoughts thudded with each step. The teacher's words still echoed inside him. They appealed to him in a place within himself that had never been touched before. He *wanted* to believe. But doing so would mean setting himself apart from his friends, his colleagues, and possibly his family.

But he knew. Deep within, he knew that he *did* believe, he was just unwilling to profess that right now. He would contemplate more, he would weigh his options, he would speak gently and at length to his wife and son.

He glanced over to Jason, then behind him to Andrew. The younger men had made a study of ignoring one another as much as possible, and Cleopas was alternately amused and irritated by the obvious displays of possession of Abigail. He often wondered how they would both react if he simply informed them that *neither* would ever have her as completely as they both wished. But he knew it was true. With Jason, she would never have a complete trust or equality, and with Andrew she would always feel a shame for having been with Jason first. Neither could win. Neither would want to hear him say it, either, so he would not waste his breath.

They neared the house, and the sound of two sweet voices floated to them on the breeze. Cleopas looked discreetly at his companions, searching for something he was distressed at not finding. Both had an expression of rapt desire in their eyes, but in neither was it the selfless joy that he felt when he heard Ester's voice. In neither did he see a willingness to sacrifice his own wishes in order to make the woman he wished for happy.

Suddenly weary, Cleopas sighed and let the music wash over him. No matter what he did now or could have done in the past, he could not make these people he cared about happy. It was not within him, it was not his place. He may have been the father, the master, but he had no control anymore over the contentment of those who lived under his roof. It was not his fault, and it was unchangeable. But still, it made him feel a bit less worthwhile than he was accustomed to feeling.

Drawing in a deep breath and willing the peaceful words of the psalm into his soul, he decided to put it from his mind. His son was a man who had and would make his own decisions. Andrew, even if a slave, was also a man, who resented when his were taken from him. Trying to interfere would be futile. He blinked in decision and resigned himself to that fact.

Abigail looked over at Dinah, who chuckled when the three men tromped through the kitchen and left it again after warm greetings all around. "What is humorous?"

Dinah shook her head, her brown eyes alight with knowledge. "You, my humble little Abigail. You, who have never sought anything but your own place, you who have protested when Mistress raised you above it, you who feared so much being married away from this house–do you not realize that you have become the axis around which it turns?"

Abigail widened her eyes. "What do you mean, Dinah? I am nothing more than I ever was."

"Exactly." Dinah's nod looked satisfied. "But now, everyone realizes what that is. My daughter, the two young men desire you. The two elder think of you as their own child, as do both the mistress and I. Sweet one, you are the love of us all." She offered a smile as honeyed as her famous cakes and lifted a hand to rest on Abigail's cheek. "You are the only one who does not know it."

Touched, Abigail blinked away a few tears and covered Dinah's hand with her own. "My mother, if I am loved even a fraction as much as I love you all, then I am blessed indeed. But even so, I am no more than a slave girl. I have no more influence than a slave girl."

Dinah laughed and turned back to her work with a shake of her head. "Go attend your master. He will want to freshen up before the meal. I can handle the rest of the preparations here."

With a nod, Abigail took some of the heated water and headed for the room that was swiftly becoming more familiar to her than her own. When she entered, Jason turned to her with a smile.

"Summer is upon us, I believe," he said in greeting, wiping the perspiration from his forehead. Once she had mixed the warm water with the tepid already in the room, he caught her around the waist and pressed a kiss to her lips. "Of course, beloved, the sun dims in comparison to your beauty. You are the loveliest thing I have seen all the day long." He kissed her again, then pulled away with a smile. "And how was your day?"

"Uneventful." She gave him a muted grin. "And yours?"

He shrugged. "Typical."

They fell into their own usual routine. They spoke casually as she bathed his feet, he teased her softly before he kissed her again, then sent her back to her other duties with a gentle swat.

Abigail paused outside his door, sucked in a breath. She knew not when it had happened, but habit had taken over. She did not dread his company as she used to, even looked forward to those moments together. Unintentional as it had been, they had formed a relationship.

FIFTEEN

Ester had retired early, leaving Abigail with a blessed hour of solitude before she would be expected to join Jason. She went to her chamber with heavy lids, wondering if she would wake up if she took a brief nap before going to her master. She doubted it. After giving Andrew a weary smile when she passed him, she slipped into her room and closed the door behind her.

She set her lamp on the chest and surveyed the room that felt nearly unfamiliar to her now. The small room was washed in the gentle golden glow from the flame, the soft light soothing her.

She settled onto her pallet in a sitting position, afraid to lie down lest she fall asleep. Figuring she should get some studying done, she picked up a packet of letters Cleopas had asked her to review for him, and tried to convince her mind to keep working for an hour more.

It could not have been more than five minutes, however, before a knock sounded on her door. She let out a fatigued breath. "Enter." She was more than a little surprised when it was Jason who slipped into her room, closing the door behind him.

"Jason! I thought you were out."

"I just returned." Jason smiled and looked around him. "Do you know I have never been in here? It is rather close, is it not?"

She had to assume her cynicism was a result of exhaustion. "Would you expect anything different for a slave? I have been blessed to have the space to myself."

Jason settled down beside her, his gaze steady on her face. "Are you tired, fair one?"

She contemplated her answer for a long enough moment to prove she was. "A bit."

"Well, then." Jason took the papers from her hand and put them aside. He pulled her into his arms and slid them both down on the pallet. "You should rest. Go to sleep." He kissed her forehead.

Abigail looked into his face in confusion. "Lord?"

He chuckled. "I can go one night without the pleasures of your body, beloved. You are clearly exhausted. Sleep, in your own bed. If you do not mind, I shall just hold you."

She opened her mouth but could think of no reply. Before she had much of a chance to develop one, another knock sounded on the door. Because she had no desire to invite another person in, she hauled herself up and opened it herself, stepping out when she saw Andrew in the hall.

His eyes, of course, were quick to scan the interior, and his brows furrowed. "He is invading even your private chamber now?"

Abigail just sighed. "What is it, Andrew?"

He was not so easily distracted. "He should leave you at least one place where you can go and not be threatened by his presence."

"You are overreacting. And moreover, if you wish to discuss this, choose a time when my master is not awaiting me. What is it you need?"

Anger and hurt flickered in his eyes, and he lifted a hand that revealed a necklace of pearls. "For Mistress. Master wishes you to put it on her casually in the morning when she dresses."

She nodded, took the jewels from his hand, and said a brisk good night. She then opened her door once more and slipped inside.

"What is that?" Jason asked when he saw her putting the pearls onto the top of her chest.

"A gift for your mother, from your father."

Jason nodded. When she looked at him, she found his face to have the same expression Andrew's had a minute before. "Does he often come to your room?"

Abigail suddenly wished that all young men would disappear from the earth for just a day. Perhaps then she would get a little peace. "Only when duty requires it, Jason. Slaves do not have the luxury of waiting until morning to carry out their tasks."

He ignored the last part altogether. "I do not like him coming here. See to it that you do not invite him in when it is *not* part of duty."

"Yes, Master." She clipped each syllable.

He met her gaze, his own unyielding. Lifting a finger, he pointed at her, then at the place beside him. She spun to extinguish the lamp, then obeyed.

"I know he is your friend," he said softly into her ear once she was settled against him, "and that I am not. You enjoy his company. Perhaps I resent that, just as he resents that I am your lover and *he* is not. But that is the way it is, Abigail. You must convince him that it is also the way it will remain."

When had anger become such a dear friend? And from where came the courage to voice it? "And how, Master, am I to convince him he will never be my lover, when I cannot convince *you* that he will always be my friend?"

"Call me a selfish man if you will, Abigail, it would be accurate. But even so, I will have what I want. You should know that by now."

"Indeed," she said through a clenched jaw, "I have figured that out." The arms that were holding her were tense with frustration, but they made no move away.

In fact, he pulled her closer. "Tomorrow night I will be with my friends. I will most likely return quite late. There is no need for you to wait for me, Abigail, you will need your rest for the next day's work."

"Very well." But she felt no relief, given the irritation coursing through her.

He tucked her head under his chin. "Go to sleep."

It was quite a while before she had calmed down enough to obey.

⚜

It felt as though the day were repeating when the next night Abigail once again entered her own chamber, lit the lamp, and settled down with the packet of letters and was once again interrupted by the sound of a knock upon her door. Tonight, she was not so tired. She had slept well the night before, once she had convinced her mind to let her, and the day had been restful and fun. She had accompanied Ester to lunch at Julia's and had enjoyed her visit with Elizabeth. Her friend was warmer toward her now than ever before, and they found a new closeness in shared circumstances. So it was not with the same irritation that she called out, "Enter."

When Andrew opened the door and stepped through, a determined look on his face, Abigail's good mood wavered. "Andrew. You should not be in here. Jason—"

"Is out." He stood for a moment just inside the doorway, gazing down at her. Abigail could not discern what his expression meant. He had never looked at her with so much displeasure, so much anger.

She waited a full minute for him to state his purpose, then she refolded the parchment so that he would see he had her undivided attention.

Eventually, he let out his breath, let his countenance relax, and moved to sit beside her. "I am sorry, my love." His voice was not at all repentant. "I just find myself growing impatient. Your master is constantly doing all in his power to remind me that you are not mine. I am but a man!" He ran a hand over his face, rested his arms on his knees. "Are you trying, Abigail? Are you trying to put him off? It has been a month since I last spoke to you of it, yet still he is relentless."

Abigail was not surprised that his promise of limitless patience was not so limitless. She felt a sinking in her heart—Andrew would tire of waiting. And even if he did wait as long as it took, would his feelings remain unchanged, or would it be his pride that kept him to his promise, much as Jason's kept him from relinquishing her?

"What am I to do, Andrew?" she asked quietly. "I cannot refuse him, and I have never encouraged him. If he persists, it is not because of anything I have done. Please, believe that."

"I do!" he proclaimed, then belied his words by adding, "But surely you must be able to do *something*, Abigail. He is a man of strong temper, you could—"

"Argue with him?" Abigail suggested. The irony in her tone drew Andrew's gaze to her eyes. "I do. He enjoys it. I can mindlessly obey, refusing to argue, and he will just smile and remain satisfied. The only time he gets upset with me is when it is about you. And I cannot do anything that would dishonor him, you know that, so—"

Andrew silenced her by capturing her face in his hands and pressing his lips against hers. He drew away a fraction, enough to look into her wide eyes. "He is not my master. I will not cater to him." He covered her mouth with his again, and this time the kiss was not just to stop her from speaking, but to engage her.

For a moment, Abigail was too surprised and confused to know how she *should* respond, so she did not. In that heartbeat, a battle raged within her. She knew that, as Jason's, she should push Andrew away. But in her heart, was she not more Andrew's than Jason's? To what should she be true, the claim that Jason never should have made, or the one forged within her?

Andrew's embrace grew insistent enough that she responded without thought. She wrapped her arms around his neck and returned the kiss, waiting for either guilt or passion to take her over. Neither did. She was too unwilling for anything but complacency. His kiss was enjoyable, but she kept comparing it to Jason's too much to lose herself in it.

Andrew, apparently, had no such distractions. She knew very well that he was not thinking this through, otherwise he never would have pulled her down to the pillows, never would have let his hand travel down her torso to rest on her hip. His touch, a feather light brush and nothing more, sent a tendril of pleasure curling up her spine. It was that which made her realize she had to put a stop to this. If she did not do so now, she may not, and he would hate them both.

It was not until he took his mouth from hers and set it roaming over her jaw that she could manage to speak. Even then, she could only croak out, "Andrew!"

But that was all it took to push him back into sanity. He retreated a few feet, his eyes bright with shame and apology. "I . . ." He shook his head. "I am sorry, Abigail. I should not–forgive me."

He pushed himself up and fled the room. And left her lying where he had put her, tears burning her eyes and hands gripping the blanket beneath her.

She had not thought it possible that she sink further, but here she was. Did she have *any* virtue left? If so, she could not find it within herself. All she saw there was a pitiful creature unable to resist a temptation because of its sin, but rather only because of its consequences. She saw a woman undeserving of respect or love.

Even Andrew had proven himself as interested in her body an he was in *her*. Had he not mentioned before that he was bothered by the thought of her being in Jason's arms? Did he ever say he was bothered by the pain she must be going through? No. It dismayed him that she was not his. Even with Andrew, it had become about possession.

Perhaps she was no more than that, in the end. Perhaps she had forfeited any other worth when she went to Jason's bed, or perhaps she never had any to begin with. Woman was created to be a companion for man, after all. Women were raised to be naught but a wife, a mother. She was not even suited for that, so what did that leave her? A future as a man's consort, not given the dignity of marriage, only a step above a harlot. She closed her eyes against the tears, glad her mother was not there to see what she had become. Wishing she could be blind to it, as well.

She stayed in that same position for many long minutes, then stirred herself and stood. Andrew's touch and kiss had ignited a desire in her, one that had grown accustomed to being sated. Why should she bother denying any longer that she enjoyed the touch of a man? It seemed to be what she had been made for anyway, so she might as well.

Stooping before her trunk, she moved the lamp to the floor and opened it. She pulled out the red garment that she had refused to wear in front of Jason's friends, some complementing accessories, then closed the lid once more and replaced the light. She extinguished the flame, tucked her possessions under her arm, and slipped soundlessly out of her room, down the hall, and into Jason's chamber.

It only took her a minute to change out of her everyday tunic and into the soft, sheer fabric that fell over her curves seductively. She fastened a necklace around her neck, brushed out her hair, and surveyed herself in the polished brass of the mirror.

A stranger looked back at her. A very beautiful, very sensual stranger with eyes turned to warm cinnamon thanks to the scarlet cloth, hair flowing down her back a river of jet, and a body slender even in its curves. She closed her eyes against the image and turned to the soft bed. She would wait there for her master to return.

◆

Jason bade farewell to his friends with a laugh, wondering if Menelaus would make it back to his quarters in one piece. The man was swaying considerably, the wine of the evening taking its toll. But Titus had put a supporting arm around him, so the others had decided to go on their own ways. Jason headed back to his father's house, the quiet of the still night encircling him. An edge of dissatisfaction cut through his mind. He knew that Lentulus was headed for a woman to take away his own hunger, and Jason briefly considered finding one himself.

But no, if he decided he was in that great a need, he would simply go to Abigail. She was more beautiful than any of the women whose doors would be open, far healthier, and what she lacked in experience she made up for with that sweet modesty. His friends may say he was too consumed by her, but he could not agree–they were all that preoccupied with the fairer sex, he just happened to have one woman who comprised all he needed instead of having to find a new one each night. That made him fortunate, not consumed.

He approached the house as quietly as possible, let himself in, and headed for his room. He could see from under the door that a lamp was lit inside. Curious, he stepped in and shut the door behind him.

The scarlet of her dress immediately caught his eye. She had apparently been asleep and was just blinking awake, stretching in a way that made him forget he had been tired at all. "Abigail? Did you forget that you did not need to wait for me?"

Giving him a sleepy, simmering smile that made his blood race, she moved gracefully from the bed in a way he imagined Venus may have done. "I did not forget." She slid her hands up his chest and eased against him, pulling his head down so that her lips could caress his.

Had he just been thinking about how much he liked her modesty? That was strange, because at that moment, nothing had ever pleased him as much as her forwardness. His arms came around her, and he reveled in the joy that came from returning *her* kiss instead of forcing her to return his. He felt his conscious thought slipping away as her mouth moved down his neck. He barely even noticed when she led him to the bed. He was in a daze when she helped him from his clothes and gave him the attention he had been demanding for the past three months. Even so, he knew very well he would remember this night for the rest of his life.

SIXTEEN

Ester lounged on her chaise, laughing with Abigail over the comedy they had just read together. Over the past weeks she had been watching her young friend change, and it showed now in the light in her eyes. The play they were reading was not quite indecent, but about as close as it could get and still make it past Cleopas's censure. In the past, the girl would have flushed even as she read some of the lines. Today, she laughed at them with the appreciation of a woman who was familiar enough with the world to find the humor in it.

Ester was not certain what she thought of this new face of Abigail. She missed the girl that was afraid to leave childhood, but at the same time, she liked the woman that was suddenly able to talk as an equal on subjects the child had just listened to silently. But mostly, Ester wondered what had happened in the past three weeks to make that possible when the previous three months had only seemed to tire Abigail without giving her any benefit. It took no genius to realize it had something to do with her relationship with Jason. But exactly how *that* was going, Ester was afraid to ask. Possibly because, yet again, she was not sure of her own thoughts.

What she truly wanted was for everyone involved to be happy; but could that happen? She would personally be satisfied if her son married Abigail, but whether that would achieve the desired results for the two of them was something she was not comfortable speculating on just yet.

Apparently, though, she had been doing just that, for Abigail's laughter drew her from her reverie, and she smiled at getting caught in another world. "I am sorry, my child. Did I miss something?"

"No, Mistress. Nothing of importance. Do you wish anything?"

"Nothing I know how to ask for. You have changed lately."

She expected Abigail to give a vague reply, or perhaps evade the statement altogether. Instead, the younger met her eyes. "Yes, I suppose so. I have come to realize your son is not quite as horrible as I had wished to make him. Of course, Andrew helped me come to that conclusion by refusing to speak to me for the past fortnight."

The news was shocking, and the dry tone of voice unfamiliar. "Andrew? But why?"

Abigail's smile was somewhat reassuring. "Oh, I think he is just frustrated with the situation. And to keep from revealing how much, he has been avoiding it." Abigail covered Ester's hand with hers and gave it a gentle squeeze. "It is all right, Mistress. It will smooth out soon enough."

Ester nodded, not fully convinced but willing to let it pass. Especially since she saw a familiar servant coming toward the house from the direction of the general and Julia's house. "Is that Laertus?"

When the boy neared the house, Abigail stood and called down from the rooftop. "Good day, Laertus."

The boy halted far enough away that he could look up and see her clearly. "Abigail, it is Elizabeth. She is terribly ill, and she has been asking for you. She will let no one else near her. The mistress knows not what to do to, so she sent me to fetch you. Can you come?"

Abigail looked to Ester, who was quick to jump up. "Of course! I will go with you, Abigail, and comfort Julia. I am sure she is upset; she is really quite fond of Elizabeth."

Abigail nodded and dashed down, then inside to grab a few things for the walk. They were on their way in just a few minutes. "Do you know what is wrong with her?" Abigail questioned Laertus as they walked.

The slave shook his head. "She had gone into the markets to fetch something for the mistress. She must have fallen ill there. Someone carried her back to the house but then just left her on the doorstep. She was unconscious and has been in terrible pain ever since she awoke. She has been retching violently, but she will not let us attend her."

She picked up her pace. Surely now, when she and Elizabeth had finally reached that pinnacle of openness that made them true friends, Jehovah would not take her confidant through illness.

Except that he would. He had taken her parents, had he not?

When they entered the general's house, Laertus took Ester to Julia while Abigail sped straight for her friend's small chamber. She knocked lightly on the door but did not wait for permission to enter. When she stepped inside, the first thing her eyes fell on was Elizabeth.

The young woman was as pale as the moon, frightened eyes open and glazed over with pain. Perspiration stood out on her forehead, and her hands shook. She had her knees drawn up toward her chest, telling Abigail it was her stomach in pain. The room smelled overwhelmingly of vomit.

"Abigail!" Tears gathered in Elizabeth's eyes and spilled over. She held out a wavering hand, which Abigail grasped.

She settled carefully beside her, looking down into her ashen face. "My friend, I came as soon as they sent for me. What is it?"

Elizabeth's answer was to roll slightly to the side, revealing a dark stain of blood under her. Abigail did not have to have any experience in this sort of thing to know what had happened. "Oh, Elizabeth. You were with child."

Elizabeth gave a small nod. "They cannot know." Agony saturated her voice.

"They would think it was Cleon's. Let them attend you."

But Elizabeth just shook her head. "I would have begun to show if it were Cleon's. Abigail." She gripping her hand harder and struggled to sit up. Abigail put a restraining hand on her shoulder to keep her down. Elizabeth relented with a groan. "Abigail, I did this on purpose." Her voice broke, the tears streaming faster now. "I could not have a child."

Abigail gaped. "But–how? Elizabeth, even I have heard of how this works. The only way to–to *be rid* of an unwanted child is to wait until you are far enough along to induce labor."

"I could not wait that long," Elizabeth declared fervently, eyes ablaze. "It could not have been Cleon's, and if anyone found out, I would be killed. Julia would see to it. Or even if not, the general would not want me if I were large with child. I could not be pregnant, Abigail. I could not."

Abigail could see that saying anything to the contrary would not only be irrelevant, but unheard. She just smoothed her friend's hair away from her head and waited for her to go on.

"I went to my mother," Elizabeth continued in a muted voice. "I knew that if there were a way, she would know it. She did not want to help me, but she saw as I did that I had no choice. She gave me the poison. It could kill me too, but it is a risk worth taking." She clenched her teeth, obviously in pain. "I am dead otherwise. I had nothing to lose."

Tears gathered in Abigail's eyes, tears of sympathy and compassion. She hated to see her friend like this, in the clutches of pain and despair. And worst of all, she was right. She had nothing to lose. Cleon had been gone almost four months, had been ill a fortnight before that. No one would believe it was his child, and it would not take much consideration to figure out whose it was. And Julia would have been furious, not so much that her maid had gotten pregnant, but that it was by her husband. Elizabeth would have been stoned, at the least.

She gripped her hand tightly and whispered, "I will tell no one, Elizabeth. I swear to you. I will stay with you until the bleeding stops, and I will see that the clothes are destroyed. And you will not die. Tell me how to treat you, my friend. What was it you took? What can I give you to ease the pain?"

Elizabeth feebly tugged on a ribbon tied around her neck, which was enough to tell Abigail to pull it from under her robe. Attached at the bottom was a small sack that opened to reveal some herbs that Abigail did not recognize.

"Brew," Elizabeth muttered faintly.

Abigail nodded, stepped out into the hall, and flagged a servant woman. "I need hot water for a tea, and more to clean up in here. Get me some rags that can be thrown away, as well."

The woman did not seem to mind being ordered around by her; she wasted no time in carrying out the mission. Abigail slipped back into the room while she waited for the supplies, murmuring meaningless, soothing phrases to her friend as she ran her fingertips over her forehead. When the tap sounded on the door ten minutes later, she hurried to fetch the things from the servant, remembering to offer a smile of gratitude.

She brewed the herbs in the water and helped Elizabeth sip it; if her grimace was any indication, it was not a tasty concoction, but she downed it all slowly, with determination. Once that was done, Abigail set about cleaning up the vomit, scrubbing everything as best she could and putting the soiled rags in the hall. Then, she sat down to wait.

She had never been on a death watch before. She prayed she would never be on one again. With each hour that ticked by, she wondered if it would be her friend's last, and with each minute in that hour she alternately supplicated and cursed her God for letting such things befall his children. For the next day, she got very little rest, and she did not leave Elizabeth's room for more than five minutes at a time. She knew that Ester returned home, assumed that she would tell Jason what kept her here, and otherwise kept to her vigil.

By sunset the following day, Elizabeth was out of danger. Her sleep was steady and her fever gone. The bleeding had stopped. Abigail dutifully took the stained clothes from bed and woman, hiding them so that she could get them on her way out, then destroy them. She dressed Elizabeth in a clean garment, put fresh sheets beneath her, and woke her long enough to tell her she was leaving.

Elizabeth smiled softly and pressed her friend's hand. "Thank you, Abigail." Her eyes said far more than her words.

Abigail kissed her brow, then stood. "I will send others in to see to you, now. You will be well soon. Go back to sleep."

Elizabeth nodded and was drifting off again by the time Abigail could open the door.

When Abigail returned Andrew was the first to greet her; he was outside cleaning some of Cleopas's equipment and rose when he saw her approaching.

"Abigail," he greeted, his voice tight. "How is Elizabeth?"

Abigail nodded once. "Better. She will recover."

"You look exhausted." He put a hand on her shoulder. "Let us hope you do not get ill, as well."

She gave him a small, distant smile. "I have no need to worry, my friend. What struck her is not catching. She ate something she should not have and reacted very violently, that is all."

Andrew studied her for a long minute. "That is good," he said at last, his tone telling her it was but an introduction to what he truly wanted to say. "I was worried, Abigail. You are a good friend, and you would not think of your own health. It made me think, dear one, of how terrible it would be to lose you. And that made me realize that I have been acting very poorly. I have been treating you as though you are no longer that friend I so love, as though I have already lost you. Forgive me."

She covered his hand with her own. "Of course, Andrew. It has been a trying time for us all."

"But I have only made it harder." His eyes were apologetic and contrite. "I should be supporting you. I will do better, my love. I will be the friend I have always been."

She had no doubt that he meant it. What she doubted was his ability to make it so.

It started as a suspicion. Abigail thought nothing of it at first, but then thought again when not a day passed without nausea. It was true that she was never regular; Dinah had assured her that was normal for someone her age. So when her monthly impurity did not begin on time, she gave it no mind. Two weeks moved by before she thought of it again, and at that point she was too busy worrying about Elizabeth to actually think about it. But in the weeks of her friend's recovery, she could not keep the thoughts at bay any longer.

When an entire month passed without the bleedings that should have hit her twice, she knew. She was pregnant. And as she looked at Elizabeth's too-thin face one day, she knew she could not share her burden with anyone. Elizabeth had enough concern of her own and did not need Abigail's thrown onto her fragile shoulders.

She could have talked to Dinah or Ester, but the thought of telling one of her mother figures that she, unwed and unwilling, was with child was too much for her to consider. Andrew and Simon were out of the question. And besides, if she were going to tell anyone, it should be Jason.

But the thought of telling Jason was even more terrifying. Why, she was not sure. She suspected he would be rather pleased with the news, proud to be the first of his friends to plant his seed and reap an offspring. But by law, her child would be a slave. Even if Jason loved his son or daughter, it would be his belonging more than his child.

She never realized how much that would bother her. If she were married to Andrew and having *his* child, it would also be born a slave; Cleopas's. But that, somehow, did not seem so bad, perhaps because to the father the baby would be more than that.

Not that such a situation was at all pertinent. She was not having Andrew's child, and now she never would. She knew that. She remembered clearly what Jason had said: if they had a child, he would never give her up. She would have to follow him wherever he went. He would force her to leave Israel, Jerusalem, Ester, her friends. She would be his and only his. Their child would be, too.

She held her secret close to her chest, where she could worry it like the tassel of a prayer shawl. As long as no one else knew, every option was still available.

One night when she lay beside Jason, listening to his even, deep breathing, the war raged so hot within her that she thought she would burst. She knew not what to do, and her time for deciding was running out. Soon, her figure would start to change. Not drastically perhaps, but Jason would notice.

She closed her eyes, deciding that the following morning she would act. It was market day, and she would be sent to shop. It would give her several hours alone, away from home, when she could go to Elizabeth's mother and ask her exactly what the risks of the poison were, what was in it, how it worked.

If she did not like what she heard, then she would go home and tell Jason the supposedly-joyous news.

❧

Abigail pulled her head covering as low over her forehead as she dared, cast her gaze upon the ground. Every step made her heart thud, fear and queasiness swamping her. She had made this trek once before, a week ago. It had been difficult then, but not like this.

In most of the doorways, scantily clad women lurked, either shouting to each other or to the few men out and interested at this early hour. Abigail suppressed a shudder. Never had she envisioned herself walking the same streets as these harlots. She had braved it last week only to give Elizabeth's mother an update on her daughter's condition.

If only her reasons today justified her presence so well. If only she did not feel as base as the women selling themselves.

She spotted Lydia in her doorway. Though no longer a young woman, she was still beautiful. Her hair still shone with luster, her skin was still smooth. But her eyes . . . as Abigail drew near, she saw again that Lydia's eyes were older than the earth underneath her feet.

"Good morning." The harlot offered a smile. "I am afraid I have forgotten your name."

"Abigail."

Lydia nodded. "And how is my daughter?"

"Improving every day." Abigail drew her lip between her teeth for a moment, forced a swallow. "That is not why I have come."

Lydia straightened, drilling her with those hard eyes. "What is it, then? Have you followed my daughter's example and taken up with a married man?"

"No." Eyes on the ground, she felt her cheeks burning. "He is not married, but that does not make the situation any easier. I cannot have his child."

Lydia's gaze was unforgiving. "Why not? Will your mistress have you stoned? Your master? Will the man hurt you?"

"No." This was a mistake, surely. Why had she come here? "That is not the point. If I have this child, our lives will be his forever."

A bitter laugh slipped between Lydia's painted lips. "Welcome to the world, beautiful one. Your life is never your own when you look as you do. It is best to belong to someone who will take care of you." She shook her head, and her curtain of curls swayed with mesmerizing regularity. "I will not help you." She even turned to walk inside.

"Wait!" Abigail exclaimed, anger taking the place of shame. "You cannot just dismiss me like that! I can pay you. I have jewelry–"

"I do not care." Lydia spun to face her again. "Your life is not a bad one, Abigail. You are not in danger if you have this child, so any solution I can offer you would be a risk you should not take. You could die."

"I do not care!" Abigail echoed, but with more fervor. Tears of rage gathered in her eyes. "I feel as though I am already dead. I have no hope anymore."

"You are a child and a fool." Disdain dripped from the downturned corners of her mouth. "You do not endanger your life because of a lack of *hope*. You do not risk sterility because you do not like your master. You have years ahead of you, possibly good years. Do not throw them away."

"That is what I am trying to keep from doing." Fire swept up her spine. She did not pause to think that she was suddenly convinced to an action she had been unsure of simply because someone told her not do it. She did not want to examine her own rebellious spirit. "You do not know me or my situation. Why do you question me? Is it your place to decide my future?"

Lydia cocked her head, examined her steadily. At length, she nodded. "Wait here."

Abigail's eyes slid closed as the fire blew out of her spirit. What had she done? Nothing, not yet. Buying the poison did not necessitate taking it.

But she would have the option.

❖

Jason and Lentulus plodded down the street. He knew his friend did not want to be spending his day off engaged in this particular enterprise any more than he did, but they both recognized that they had no choice. They all took their friendships more seriously than they would ever admit.

"If he does this again," Lentulus said from between clenched teeth, "I will personally turn him into a eunuch."

Jason laughed, but he was almost convinced it was a good idea. This was not the first time they had had to fetch a drunken and unconscious Menelaus from the home of a harlot. At least the woman knew to find them, rather than turning to an officer that could punish him. But one of these days it might serve him right if they left him or dumped him on the steps to the governor's palace to see what fate dished out.

"There it is." Lentulus nodded toward the crumbling building where they would find their friend.

"So it is." Jason scanned the street without interest. "I cannot say as I regret my absence from this area. I–" he cut off abruptly, halted in his steps.

"Jason?" Lentulus turned with question in his eyes.

"Go on without me." Jason took off across the street. It did not occur to him to wonder how he could spot her so quickly in a place he never expected to find her. He was far too busy wondering what exactly Abigail was doing in this part of town. He knew whatever the answer was, it would not satisfy him. It was too dangerous for someone as beautiful as she to wander these streets–the men who frequented them had a tendency to take first and ask the price later.

"Abigail!" Her eyes flew to him, and he did not miss the panic and the guilt in them. He stopped a foot away, his face taut with anger. "What are you doing here?"

"I–" Abigail shifted from foot to foot. "I mean–this is Elizabeth's mother's. I have been keeping her updated on her daughter's condition."

Jason's eyes narrowed in unveiled suspicion. If that was the simple truth, why the flush, why the averted gaze? "I do not like you here. Go home and do not come to this part of town again."

A harlot filled the doorway, vial in hand and curiosity on her face. She regarded them for half a second before smiling. "Good morning, officer." She took up position against the post of her door. Her gaze flitted dryly to Abigail. "You have a handsome one here, love. Of course, if I had known the father agreed with your decision, I would not have been so disagreeable. Here you go." She helt out the vial to Abigail, who, mouth agape, made no move to take it. "This should take care of your little problem. Although, it really is a shame. It would be a beautiful child."

"_Child_?" Jason turned his gaze, hard and unblinking, on Abigail. Her lips were still parted, but she seemed to have nothing to say. When she forced her eyes up to his, there was fear in them. She looked as though she expected a blow. He just grabbed her arm. "Home. Now."

"Master, I–"

"Quiet!" He would not even look at her. He kept his gaze on the path before them, his jaw clenched as tightly as his fingers were around her arm. He said nothing more, just kept propelling her forward so quickly she was forced to break into a run once in a while to keep up with his long strides.

It had been a long time since he had been so angry. It bubbled inside him, boiling just under the surface, making his vision blur and his veins rush with the power of it. He was not absolutely certain he could keep a hold on it, and he was not absolutely certain he wanted to. The deception enraged him, the betrayal cut deeply. The poison she had been about to ingest pumped through him.

Was he that distasteful to her? Did she detest him so much that she would kill his child? Kill herself? Was life with him that terrible? He was not cruel. He did not abuse her. Never had he raised a hand in violence against her, nor so much as denied her anything she asked. He gave her gifts, he touched her gently, he did not insist upon taking his pleasure if she was tired or unwell. He was not only fair, he was kind. He thought he was treating her as she deserved.

Now he wondered if she deserved anything better than the harlots his friends frequented. She had acted no better than one. With no more loyalty. What happened to her promise to honor him as she would a husband? Would she have tried to kill the child of her husband? No. A woman without a son to see after her in her old age faced poverty and despair. What had she been thinking?

He barely noticed when they reached the house. Simon opened the door for them, confusion on his face. Jason merely took the full basket from Abigail's grasp and shoved it into the servant's arms on his way past. He did not so much as pause, however, until he had pulled her into his chamber and slammed the door. He tossed her onto the bed, then paced the floor silently for a moment more.

When he stopped and turned to face her, Abigail visibly braced herself. He opened his mouth, raised a hand in gesticulation, then paused. Closed his eyes, made an effort to calm himself, and tried again. "Abigail." His voice was at a normal volume, if still too tight. "What in Jove's name were you doing?"

She swallowed. "I am pregnant, Jason."

"So I gathered." He let out a growl, raked his hand through his hair, and paced again. When he turned to her, his control was once again slipping. "Were you going to tell me, Abigail? Or were you just going to poison yourself so that you lost it, probably killing yourself in the process?"

"I had not decided," Abigail admitted quietly.

"There should have been no decision!" He cursed, wanting desperately to throw something to a shattering death. Nothing was handy, so he settled for cursing again. "It was that friend of yours, right? That slave of Julia's. That was what was wrong with her. She was getting rid of a pregnancy. What, is she sleeping with the general?"

"Yes. To all of it."

He cursed her this time, and she flinched at the words he used. Then he was deathly silent for a moment. When he spoke again, the fury was calmer, but not abated. "She had a reason. You did not. You are in no danger of stoning, Abigail. The worst that can happen to you is remaining mine. Why is that so dreadful to you? Am I not fair? Am I not kind? Do I not treat you well?"

"You are fair and kind." Abigail quaked. He heard the tears in her throat, but she wisely held them back. They would not help her. "You treat me well. It is only–I do not want to go to Rome."

It took him a moment to register what the murmurs meant. "You do not wish to go to Rome?" he repeated hollowly. "*That* is what this is about? A possible decision *five years away?*" His wrath suddenly snapped, sizzled, erupted. "I would have let you stay if you asked! But not now, Abigail. Now you have proven yourself undeserving of such regard. You are my *slave*, and you will remain so for the rest of your life. You will have my child."

He approached her so quickly and forcefully that she recoiled. He loomed over her, pushing her into the mattress by the pure power of his anger. Putting an arm on either side of her to support himself, he glowered down into her terrified face. "You will have my child," he said again. "You will do whatever you must to be sure it is healthy. There will be no more deception. You will not attempt to harm it again. If you do, I will have you stoned. Do you understand me, Abigail? There will be no excuses, there will be no second chances. There will be no more mercy. When I want you, I will take you, and I when I do not, you will stay out of my way."

He pushed himself away and up as quickly as he had come down on her, then pulled her up with him, tacitly ignoring the shaking in her limbs. "You will tell no one how you have shamed me. Not even my mother. You will rejoice at this blessing as a woman should, and if the other servants ask you why I dragged you in here so angrily, you will tell them it was because I found you visiting your friend's mother, that you were just going to inform her of her welfare. To make me forget my anger, you just informed me that you are with child. I am overjoyed!"

He pasted on a bright smile that probably still simmered with rage, holding out his arms in demonstration. "I am going to rush to share the news with my friends. *You*," he said, grabbing her by the hand and pulling her toward the door, "are going to tell my mother that you will be giving her a grandchild. Come."

⬥

Once more Abigail followed.

Jason's mother, perhaps stirred by the commotion of their entrance, came into the hall just as they reached her chamber. "Jason." Confusion etched her countenance. "I did not expect you back so soon."

"I am going out again." He sounded remarkably cheerful, even smiled convincingly. He kissed his mother on the cheek. "We are having a baby, Mother. You will soon have a grandchild. Is it not a blessing?"

Ester beamed, her joy genuine and evident. "Jason! Abigail!" She hugged first one, then the other, framing Abigail's face with her hands. "Dear one, you do not look well. Is it making you ill? That is normal enough, especially so early in the day."

"I will be all right," Abigail said meekly.

"See that she eats." Jason's tone brooked no argument. "I suspect she has not yet done so this morning. Am I right, beloved?"

The endearment sounded like wormwood, but Abigail kept by a hair from wincing. "You are right. I was waiting for my stomach to settle."

He nodded, still smiling. Before leaving, he kissed Abigail's forehead, then Ester's cheek once more. "I will be back soon."

To Abigail's ears, it sounded like a threat. She closed her eyes, the tears welling up again. Was this how it would be now? A loving face before others, and hatred when they were alone? She was not sure she could bear it.

A gentle arm came around her, and Abigail opened her bleary eyes to see Ester's compassionate smile. "It is much for you to adjust to." Her mistress led her into her chamber and sat with her on the luxurious chaise. "I remember that much. The nausea, the fluctuating emotions. You will be crying one minute, then laughing the next. It is a blessed time, Abigail. And Jason is so pleased. Perhaps now he will marry you."

"Perhaps." She could hold the tears at bay no longer. As they squeezed through her shuttered eyes, Ester urged her to lie down.

"Rest, child. I will have Dinah make you something to eat. You must take it easy now," she said cheerfully. "No more waiting on me hand and foot. You have my grandchild to think of."

Abigail wished she could fall asleep and never wake up. Ester's joy would be as hard to handle and Jason's ire.

SEVENTEEN

She was waiting for him. Jason saw her standing outside her door, arms crossed over her chest, lazily scanning those meandering nearby. He could tell by the way she straightened but did not move upon spotting him that it was he she was waiting for. Which was fine with him. He intended to get a few answers. Before he could head in her direction, though, he heard Lentulus hailing him rather desperately.

"Jason! By Jupiter, man, give me a hand! Where did you go?"

The sight of his friend trying to haul Menelaus up the street, the latter draped over him like a child's rag doll, was enough to bring a smile to Jason's lips. Lentulus had apparently had a difficult time rousting Menelaus at all, for even now he was so drunk that he could not stand on his own.

"One moment!" Jason called back, then headed for the harlot.

The harlot did not so much as push off from the frame, just regarded him with those old, cynical eyes. She held out the vial to him. "Before you chastise me for assisting your little woman in her dark task, why do you not see what I put in here?"

Curious enough to put aside his anger, Jason accepted the small pot and removed the cork. He dipped a finger into it, then stuck it on his tongue. His brows shot up. "Honeyed water?"

She shrugged, tamping down a smile. "Fear and expectations can go far. She would have felt ill, but she would have truly suffered only the pangs of conscience. By the time she realized I tricked her, she would have panicked herself into realizing she wanted the babe."

His eyes narrowed, and he handed the harmless potion back to her. "Why?"

"Because she is just a confused child. She saw that Elizabeth was recovering and thought it would be an easy way out of what seemed like a problem." Her face grew serious, intense. "But she does not understand, Lord. Elizabeth was lucky. I have given this poison to six women now, my daughter included. She is the third to survive. Your girl–she did not realize the risks, she was too scared to recognize that her problems were not big enough to justify them. I could not reason with her. So I thought to fool her."

Jason measured the woman for a while. She was still attractive, though age was creeping in, the kind of woman that a man took in the night and forgot the next day. The kind that no one ever thought to attribute feelings or sense to. But he saw in a heartbeat that her life had taught her many lessons. He nodded. "Thank you."

She returned the nod, smiled. "Be easy on your woman, Lord. She is young and disappointed. And now the rest of her life is not her own."

His smile was wry. "I shall keep that in mind."

She obviously did not believe him. "I know she is your slave. But I have recalled some of the things Elizabeth told me about her. She was born free, and a soul does not ever forget that feeling."

His felt his face harden, and he took a step away. "She would have married a slave. She cannot mind it so much."

She folded her arms over her chest. "But being the wife of a slave is very different from being the slave of a rich man. I am technically free. But I would trade every vestige of freedom I have to be a wife of any man. Abigail is probably not so different."

He left then and headed for his friends, telling himself a whore knew nothing that was relevant to his life. But still, her words tunneled into his mind.

"It is about time," Lentulus said testily when Jason joined him and put an arm around Menelaus from the other side. "This idiot is not light."

He could not resist a tease. "But you are strong, Lentulus. Wiry, is that not what you call yourself? Able to run faster, jump farther, leap higher–"

"But drag less. We each have our talents. You should have brought Titus for this task."

Jason laughed, and they began hauling the lolling Menelaus up the street. "Titus has no patience for Menelaus when he is like this. He may have tossed him in a gutter."

"As would I, if I could heft him high enough."

Menelaus, blinking against the bright sun, muttered something incoherent and nearly convinced Jason to assist in the effort. Instead, he half-carried him back to his quarters, doused him in water, and told him in no uncertain terms that next time, they would leave him to his vices.

It was after midday by the time Jason returned home. His mother greeted him with bright eyes and a ready smile.

"She is sleeping. I have noticed that she has been tired lately, and now I have an excuse for making her rest." She clasped her hands together, then gave him an impulsive hug. "I am so happy, Jason."

"I am still not going to marry her, Mother." He ignored the look of disappointment that flooded his mother's eyes before she could blink it away. He kissed her forehead to soften the blow, then moved into the hallway. "Where is she?"

"On my chaise."

He nodded. "I will put her to bed. Did you get her to eat?"

"Yes." She followed him into her room, watching as he gently lifted the sleeping Abigail, settling her against him. She then moved in front of him so that she could open his door. As he settled her on the bed, she said, "She was crying for a good while. Did you upset her?"

"It was a misunderstanding." The lie came easily. "She was visiting her friend's mother to tell her she was better; I did not know why she was in that part of town, and I was unhappy enough that I did not give her much time to explain before forcing her home."

"Oh." Ester nodded, but she was obviously concerned. "Elizabeth's mother is a harlot. She should *not* be in that section of town."

"Then we agree." He smiled, then turned back to Abigail. "I will stay with her a while."

Ester took her cue to leave.

Jason just stared down at Abigail. Her face was peaceful in sleep, picturesque and perfect, but so very young. He wondered briefly how old she really was. Old enough, clearly, but when her intelligent eyes were not open and scanning the world, when she wore no belt to show off her figure, she could pass for a child. She had that smooth, even complexion, the soft curve of facial bones still not fully developed.

Jason slowly let out his breath and forced the compassionate thoughts away. She was *not* a child. She was old enough to be given in marriage, she was old enough to have a babe of her own. She was learned and intelligent. She was alluring. She had the face and figure to draw any man, the kind of beauty that had been a siren song in many an ear. So he had given in to the temptation–who would not have? Any of his friends would have taken her if they could have, even Apidius, professedly in love with his Roman Drusilla.

What a hopeless situation. He would have liked to be able to keep his distance from her, to punish her for her deception by forcing her to be nothing but a servant for the rest of her life. But he could not. He was not strong enough to resist the promises her sleeping mouth made or the invitation of her still arms. It gave her a power over him that he resented, but one he could not escape. He did not understand why this Hebrew girl had gotten into his blood so fully when no other woman ever had, but he could not argue its fact. When he looked upon her, the rest of the world receded; his responsibilities in the legion seemed unimportant, his dreams of Rome too distant to be concerned with. His only comfort was the thought that she was only a diversion for this transitional time of his life, that when Rome loomed nearer in his future, it would gain his full attention once more.

Her eyes fluttered open under his steady gaze, blinking away the sleep. He did not avert his eyes, but rather just whispered, "What am I to do with you, Abigail?"

He watched sorrow flood her eyes. "Forgive me."

Her sincerity struck something within him that made the pain resonate all the more. She gripped his hand, and he raised it to his lips and kissed the tips of her fingers. "I do not know if I can, fair one. I do not know if I want to."

Her lips quivered, but she bit her bottom one until it stopped. "I would not have done it, Jason. I could not."

"That is not the point, beloved. You deceived me. You dishonored me. Relenting in one decision does not change those things."

"I know." Her eyes slid shut in agony. She opened them again when he settled beside her, a breath away from her face.

"I wish I did not want you," he said fervently. He kissed her.

"So do I." She kissed him back.

◆

Jason was on watch that night, so Abigail was headed for her closet to sleep when Andrew stopped her. It only took one glance at his face to realize the news had spread throughout the household.

"You are having his child."

Abigail nodded, unable to think why his eyes suddenly lit.

"This could be good, dear one." He took her hands in his. "Your body will change. He will lose interest. But my love is deeper than that, you know that. I will always want you. If he dismisses you, I will gladly wed you; I will be a father to the babe, too."

She sighed, squeezing his hands in return. She was too tired to argue, to tell him he could not be more wrong. She did not want to say the truth aloud, that he would never release her now, even if he *did* lose interest. That he would never relinquish the rights to his child. So instead, she took the easy way out. "Perhaps so, Andrew. It is good to know how much you care."

He gave her a sweet, promising smile and released her fingers. "You were going to bed. I will not hinder you. Rest well, my love, and take care of yourself; though I suspect everyone in the house will see that you do. We all love you, Abigail. We are all prepared to share in your joy."

Share in her joy? How could they all love her, yet not realize this was not a joyous occasion for her? How could they think that bringing a child into this situation could be anything but a curse? But she smiled. "Thank you, my friend. I will see you in the morning."

She turned into her little room, not bothering with a lamp. She crawled onto her pallet, closed her eyes, and was asleep within minutes.

It did not last long. The floor was too hard for her after spending most of her nights in a soft bed, and her stomach would not settle. She dozed off only to wake again before an hour had passed, then tossed and turned for twice as long again. She waited not so patiently for her internal clock to tell her it was time to rise. When she finally lost patience and dressed for the day, she left her room to find dawn barely streaking the horizon.

She barely made it outside before she lost her dinner from the evening before. Retching, she knew true misery. She was standing outside in the pre-day chill, trying to hold back her hair, knees stinging from when she fell onto the ground with the violence of her sickness, tears streaming unhindered down her face. She was completely alone, only the distant call of a bird telling her a world existed outside of her circle of pain. When her stomach was empty, she struggled to her feet and moved slowly to rinse out her mouth and wash her face. She pressed a hand against the flat of her stomach.

Soon enough, it would not be so flat. Everyone would be able to look at her and know. The vendors in the marketplace, the townspeople, Elizabeth and the rest of the general's household. Some would look at her with a smile, others with pity, still others with derision, depending on how much they knew about her.

By the time she called up enough energy to make it back inside, Dinah was up and stirring the fire in the kitchen. When Abigail came in, probably not looking much better than she felt, the woman put aside her tasks and enveloped her in her matronly arms instead.

"It will be all right." Dinah rubbed her capable hands over Abigail's back. "I know you are not happy right now, but trust me, child, it is good for you to have a babe of your own. Jason will welcome a son and care for you because of it. And if he does not, then Andrew will. Either way, a baby is a blessing."

Because it was one Dinah had been denied, Abigail would not allow herself to disagree. Instead, she smiled blearily and pulled away to help her with the morning's work. Jason returned when she was elbow high in bread dough, so he just placed a dutiful kiss on her cheek and informed her that he would see to his own cleansing and join his parents for breakfast. She could only nod.

She had cleaned herself up in time to assist Ester in dressing, then plodded through breakfast. The minute Jason finished his meal, he stood and took Abigail's hand. "You look exhausted."

Her eyes sought the ground. "I did not sleep well."

"Did you try to stay in your own room?"

"Yes, Lord."

He gave her a fondly irritated look and shook his head. "Do not attempt it again, sweet one. You need better rest than your pallet will grant you. Come. We shall sleep."

He led her from the room.

Titus drummed his fingers on his knee as he sat waiting not so patiently for Jason to come. They had agreed to meet half an hour ago, and Titus was not a patient man. Especially since he knew very well what would be keeping his friend at home: a lovely set of curves and large brown eyes. He grunted and shook the thought from his head. There would come a day soon enough when he would go home, and then he, too, would have women at his disposal every hour of the day. More of them than Jason had.

In fact, he had just received word from his father. It was this news that made him anxious for Jason to arrive; he needed to tell someone, and no one else would want to hear it. Actually, Jason may not, either, but he was friend enough to listen anyway, and reliant enough on the graces of the Asiniuses not to grumble too loudly. A knowing smile pulled at Titus's lips. Six more months in this wretched place, and he would be back in Rome, running his father's companies for him. He was not sure how Caius had arranged it, but he would not complain. He may not like being under his father's rule, but it was better than the military. Similarly, he may resent that one of his best friends was that largely for political reasons, but he would not complain; it was nice to have some pull over the self-confident Jason Visibullis.

He finally saw him approaching and stood, prepared to offer some snide comment about his lack of punctuality. It died on his lips, however, when he saw the look in Jason's eyes. Titus drew in a deep breath. Why was it that *he* was always the one around when Jason was troubled? He was getting tired of dealing with his friend's petty concerns. They were always about the girl, anyway, and Jason was never sensible enough to take good advice and not give her so much of his attentions.

"Jason," he merely said in greeting.

"Titus." Jason managed to put irritation into the word. "I am sorry I am late. My mother insisted I dine with her before leaving."

They fell in together and headed for the markets.

He would not ask. He did not want to know. But the silence stretched all the way into uncomfortable and left him little choice. "So how is your Venus faring?"

Jason speared him with a scalding look. "She is pregnant."

Titus made no response for a moment. He knew not which to make. He was certainly not surprised by the news; these things had a tendency to happen when one frequently engaged in activities of a certain nature. It was Jason's tone that baffled him. When he did speak again, he made sure his own accent was neutral. "Is this a bad thing?"

"She seems to think so," Jason returned testily. Then he spewed a few choice expletives that made Titus grin. "What is wrong with her? I do not *pretend* to understand the workings of a woman's mind. They are impossible, incomprehensible, utterly forsaken of all reason–"

"Are you just figuring this out?"

Jason glared at him, but his humor was improving visibly. "Have any of your women been pregnant, Titus?"

"Yes." Titus glanced at the stalls they passed but saw nothing of interest. "Although one was sold to us because she was barren. And another became so when she aborted a child well into her term. Yet another miscarried accidentally early on; that was not so long ago. Too soon to know if there was permanent damage. And Caelia," he said with a small smile, picturing the curves of his favorite, "has no excuse, and has long been ashamed of it. You see, my friend, when a woman knows she is competing for your attentions and affections, she will deem it a matter of pride to carry your child."

Jason grunted. "Diversity is your answer to everything."

"It works." He shrugged. "You waste too much energy on your slave. The benefit to having such a woman is that she is there when you want her but without the claim to you a wife would have. But if you forsake other women, you might as well marry."

His grimace led Titus to think that had yet again been the topic with his mother. Then he nodded. Finally. "You are right. I have been too occupied with Abigail."

Titus clapped a victorious hand to Jason's shoulder. "Remedy it, my friend. Take out a few coins and treat yourself to an evening on the town."

Jason moistened his lips. "I suppose I can spare the coins."

Titus grunted. "You seem to have enough lately. Though where you get it is a mystery."

He seemed to consider a moment, then pasted on a lopsided smile. "Your father."

Titus stopped midstep and turned questioning eyes on his friend. Jason's amusement was catching, but he kept it at bay. "My father?"

Jason chuckled. "He is paying me to report anything compromising you may do."

Titus knew dual emotions; he wanted to strangle his father and laugh with his friend. "Compromising? But Jason, we both know that when not around him, I am the epitome of responsibility."

"And I tried to tell him it was a waste of his money. He insisted."

"He would, the fool. Well, then, that settles it. Since it my father's money, you must take my advice in spending it." Then, in a mock whisper, "Just do not tell him what we do with it. He may be forced to admit you are just as human as I."

Jason laughed along with him and followed him down his avenue of choice.

❦

Abigail had expected Jason to return in time for the evening meal; when he did not, she figured he must have decided to eat with his friends, so she went about the evening as usual, catching up on some of the translation Cleopas asked of her and seeing to Ester's needs. By dusk, when the city glimmered gold, he still had not returned, but Ester dismissed her firmly for the night.

She went to his chamber and looked around her without interest. At length she settled into a sitting position on the bed, legs curled up underneath her, and waited for Jason to return.

When the door finally opened, Jason looked over at her as if surprised to see her there. He was well on his way to drunk, if not quite there yet. Abigail sighed. He would not be very pleasant on the morrow when he had to haul himself out of bed at dawn.

"I do not want you tonight, Abigail." He waved toward the door. "Go."

Despondency mixed with confusion. She spoke because she was not sure he remembered, in his current condition, his commands of only that morning. "But Master, you told me not to try to sleep on my pallet anymore."

Jason glared at her emptily for a moment. "I changed my mind. You can always sleep in here tomorrow when I have gone."

Her emotions settled on depression. "Yes, Lord." She slid off the bed, moving automatically to help him off with his sandals. She stopped short of him, though, her eyes widening. The scent of perfume was overpowering, decidedly feminine, and strong enough that she had to take a step back again to keep the bile down.

"What?" he asked when she recoiled.

The depression sprouted and blossomed in anger. "You smell of a woman. A cheap one."

"And why would you care?" He yanked off his own shoes and tossed them unceremoniously to the floor.

"Why would I care?" She heard the shock in her voice, perfectly mirroring her heart. "I do not want to share my lover, the father of my child, with a disease-ridden whore!"

"And *I* do not want your opinion on how I should live my life. You are just a slave."

"Yes, I am just a slave." Her words were bitter. She spun away from him, but then turned back again, in the mood for a fight, regardless of the consequences. "But you are the one who told me I must think of your child, do all in my power to see to its health. Well, *Master*, how can I do that if you are passing diseases to me that you acquire from the filthy streets you have forbidden me to enter?"

He took a menacing step toward her. "Perhaps I just will not touch you anymore, Abigail. That would make you happy, would it not?"

Sudden tears sprang to life in her eyes, and they were too unexpected for her to control. She clenched her fists together and let them fall onto her legs. "No! It would not. Can you not see? Can you not understand? That is what makes me a monster. What makes me so deserving of this punishment. I want your touches, I want everything you do to me, but still I cannot give you my heart. I am no better than your harlots!" Her knees buckled, and she sagged to the floor sobbing. She pounded the floor with her fists, declaring herself a wretch with every breath.

Jason's knees hit the floor beside her, and he hauled her into his arms. "Hush, beloved. You are no monster."

"I am a sinful beast." She curled her fingers around the cloth of his tunic to anchor her against the comforting solidity of his chest. "Jehovah is punishing me for my sins."

"Jehovah is the one who made man in such a way, able to enjoy such pleasures. How can it be a sin to do so? You are not sinful just because you respond as a woman should."

"I have profaned what he made holy." Her tears slowed, bringing resignation. "I have enjoyed the means he gave us without desiring, and in fact resenting, the purpose." A hand on her abdomen illustrated what that purpose was.

Jason drew in a deep breath and rocked her. "Perhaps it is not a punishment for your sins, dear one. Perhaps it is a blessing in spite of them. Look at it that way, please. Do not hate our child."

"I could hate no child." Hopefully her voice did not sound as hollow as it felt.

"Then try to *want* this one." He put a finger under her chin to force her face up. She must look a fright, but he just kissed her trembling lip, a light caress that soothed more than she wanted it to.

She rested against him. "I apologize for my outburst."

"It was deserved. I apologize for my behavior. I will not repeat it, I swear to you. You will be the only one I turn to, beloved." He kissed her forehead, then gathered her into his arms and stood, placed her gently on the bed. He smiled down at her. "You need your sleep."

She accepted it as the peace offering it was.

EIGHTEEN

The cold certainty of death sent a perpetual snake of dread up Abigail's spine. She saw it in Ester's gaze that morning, taking the form of concern. She felt it in the continual ache of her back. There it darted in the worried exchange that Dinah and Simon didn't think she heard.

She was not as well as she should be. Four months along, and still the sickness gripped her, still exhaustion ruled every limb. She was too weak. Too ill.

She would miscarry. And Jason would think she did it on purpose and have her stoned.

Clenching her fingers against the trembling, Abigail carefully set down Ester's plate and took up her place between her and Jason. She dared not look at her master. His eyes would land on her abdomen, fill with that hope that could condemn her. If she lost his child, he would never forgive her. That fragile peace negotiated through anger and tears would crumble around her.

She squeezed her eyes shut, soul yearning to pray for the deliverance of the babe within her. But Jehovah would not hear. She had sinned against him. His punishment was deserved.

Nausea swamped her, churned her stomach. She opened her eyes again, but her vision swam. She had better sit down. Better . . .

Darkness fell over her like a blanket. For a moment, she indulged in the sweet relief of no feeling. But there in the black of her mind, she found no rest. Once again her soul yearned toward God. She snatched herself back and struggled to shrug off the night.

Blinking, she saw the ceiling of Jason's room. His face, so close. And beyond him, Ester, Cleopas, Andrew, even Dinah and Simon.

Jason's face shifted under her glance, from worry to determination. "That is enough. Abigail, you have been pushing yourself too hard. You will stop. No more physical labor. You will not help in the kitchen, and you will not wait at the table. You may keep my mother company, but that is the extent of your service." He shifted his gaze to his father, who Abigail noted looked shaken. "If the others cannot keep up with the work without her, I will get another slave to help, but Abigail will not put herself at risk any longer."

Cleopas, Ester, and Andrew were all nodding solemnly at his wisdom. Abigail was apparently the only one who did not agree. "I am fine." Her voice came out too faint. They would never believe her. "The sickness is always at its worst in the mornings, but even that should be passing soon." Seeing that Jason was not at all convinced by her argument, she added, "Women have been carrying children for eons, Jason, and still managing their labors."

"And mine will not be one of the ones who dies of the effort." Jason looked back to his companions, who all looked as determined as he. "I trust we will all see to it?"

The others nodded of one accord, and Abigail let out a sigh of defeat.

"I need to get back to the kitchen." Dinah smiled at her, then she and Simon left.

"And we must set off for the Praetorium." Cleopas motioned Andrew to precede him from the room.

"I believe I shall send a note to Julia asking them to join us here," Ester declared gaily.

"And I," Jason said, sitting beside Abigail and taking her hand when his mother exited, "shall stay right here and make sure you rest." He smoothed a few strands of hair away from her face.

"It is your day off."

"So it is." He gave her a tender smile.

Abigail sent him a reproving look. "Do you not have plans with your friends?"

"They will not miss me." Sliding down beside her, he pressed his lips to her temple. "Rest now, beloved. When you awake, I will bring you some food. What would you like?"

She gave a half-hearted push at his chest. "I would like you to remember that you are the master and should not start waiting on your slaves."

Jason grinned and captured her hands. "And I would like my slave to remember that I am the master and shall do as I will. And I will to spend my free day making sure she rests."

Too tired to resist the comfort he offered, she let it wash away some of the fear and slid into sleep.

◆

Jason put in his night shift without much enthusiasm. He ran into Titus, who asked outright where he had been that day and frowned at the answer. Menelaus and Apidius dropped in just to say hello shortly after dark, and they, too, seemed rather put out that he had chosen to spend the day with his mother instead of them.

"It is the girl." Menelaus shot him an accusatory glare.

Jason sighed. "She was ill."

"She is pregnant," Titus retorted, "of course she was ill. That is no reason to coddle her."

"They are merely concerned for you." Apidius spoke in his customary soft tone, but his eyes offered no sympathy. "Your involvement with the slave keeps growing, Jason, and it is not healthy."

"It is unhealthy to be concerned for the welfare of my child?" Jason brushed past them all to continue his circuit around the wall. "How novel."

Menelaus jogged to catch up with him. "You should not get attached to this child, though. It will be a slave like its mother. You will marry someday and have legitimate children to carry on your name. This one will not be one of them. Prepare yourself for that."

"Why?" Jason stopped in front of a dozing soldier. He ought to make note of it, but instead he just delivered a sound thump to his helmet. It sufficed. "The divine Tiberius was not the legitimate son of Augustus, and he is emperor. Brutus is rumored to have been the son of Julius. Why can I not recognize my child as my child?"

When the soldier rose to his feet, Titus shoved him back down so he could step past. "You are not an emperor. You cannot make your own rules."

"Jason, listen to yourself," Apidius pleaded. "You lobby for an illegitimate child born by a slave whom you have yourself admitted is unworthy of your promise. If you favor her child, she will claim rights over you."

Jason stared at his three friends, realizing at once that they were right and they were wrong. Realizing that Abigail already held those claims, even if she never used them. Realizing that his parents' convictions were rooted more deeply in him than he had realized. He could simply not look at it all as his friends did, without any involvement. He could no longer focus on a distant ambition when there was a tangible promise in his hands.

What could Rome give him? What could politics do for his soul? Perhaps his father had been right. A boy had the right to leave home and find his way in the world, but a man . . . a man had to focus on deeper matters. Family. Faith.

He turned to his friends, lifted a hand. "I do not need you following me on my rounds, pushing around my men. If you have anything more to say, say it to each other. I have my duties."

By the time dawn had arrived, his mind had mulled over the situation until it spun. He strode home in a sour temper, ate quickly in the kitchen without waiting for his parents, and went to bed. Abigail was still sleeping when he climbed in, and the very sight of her brought a sigh to his lips. As he put his arms around her warm body and drew her close, he forgot all about the problems. They did not matter. She was his to hold, and that did.

◈

Abigail arose late, surprised she had managed to get so many solid hours of sleep. She moved quietly so as not to disturb Jason, slipping into her garment and noting that soon she would need something looser to hide her stomach. She left the bedchamber silently and went to find Ester.

She was reading in her room and smiled when Abigail entered. "You are looking better. How do you feel?"

"A bit queasy, but not as bad as yesterday."

"Have some breakfast." Ester motioned to the tray of food sitting on the table. It looked fresh, untouched. Ester had probably had it brought solely for Abigail's sake. "I will be leaving shortly with Julia, Abigail. We are paying a visit to the governor's wife today. My husband and son both agree you should stay here. As do I."

Abigail nodded, unable to feel offended by the decision. She had no desire to walk across town to the governor's palace, and she had even less desire to present herself to all the people in between. Besides, the wife of Pilot was strange, always claiming prophetic dreams and mystic abilities. Abigail was in no mood to listen to her.

They chatted aimlessly until Julia called, then she walked with her mistress to the door to see her off, lifting a hand in greeting to Elizabeth before shutting the door. She then turned, absently rubbing at the ache in the small of her back as she tried to decide what to do. She could go talk to Dinah for a while, or perhaps assist Simon with the accounts until Jason woke up. The outer room could really use a dusting, but she knew better than to attempt the chore with her master nearby and able at any moment to surprise her.

She stifled a smile and took a few steps in the direction that would lead her to Simon. She felt a stirring in her stomach and froze for a moment, making sure it was not nausea. But it was different. It came again. Movement, true movement. Her baby had quickened.

Excitement exploded within her. This was her baby. Her child. Her life, moving around inside her as if to proclaim itself real, true, and undeniable. She sped through the house and burst into the chamber Jason still slept in, throwing the door first open and then closed without any thought to the level of noise.

"Jason!" She leapt on the bed at him. "Jason!"

He blinked and jerked up. "What? What is it?"

"The baby!" She grabbed his hand and rested it on her stomach just in time to catch the next little burst of movement. She giggled. "Did you feel it? He is moving, Jason. Our baby is moving."

He sat very still for a moment, contemplation on his face. A grin bloomed when another little motion came through the wall of her abdomen. "He is, indeed. He will probably keep doing so, too, keeping you up at all hours, bruising your insides."

"Of course he will," Abigail agreed with pride. "He will be strong like his father."

Jason pulled her closer and watched her as she stared down at her rounded middle. She spread both of her hands over her stomach and smiled. "It is amazing. What do you think he is doing?"

"Getting his exercise."

"Yes, he will want to be the fastest boy in the streets."

"Of course." He pulled her closer still, adjusted his hands lower when another flutter moved that way. "Or if it is a daughter, she will be as beautiful as her mother and will want to be faster than all the boys, too, to escape them."

Abigail laughed. It faded away, down to a smile, then into seriousness. She looked into his eyes for a moment, then shifted her gaze down.

He kissed her temple with more tenderness than she would have thought possible a few months before. "What is it, beloved?"

"Nothing. It is just–I had not thought."

He lifted her chin up so that she would look at him again, and she saw his brows drawn together. "What had you not thought?"

Abigail shook her head, but he probably still caught the gleam of moisture in her eyes. "You may not want your first son to be–with me."

Jason's laughter caught her off guard. "My love, you mistook me completely." He moved his hands to cup her face. "I was trying to assure you that I would love a daughter as much as a son. That I would not consider it a failing if you were to give me a girl." He punctuated his assurances with a long kiss. "I would treasure a son. I would cherish a daughter."

Abigail held his gaze for a long while, basking in whatever it was that he was offering her. She was not sure what the name for it was. Approval? Acceptance? Affection? Whatever its name, it brought her a measure of peace. "Truly?" she queried softly, just so she could hear him say it again. "You will love our child, even though–"

He stopped her with a finger over her lips. "I will love our child." His touch turned to a caress over her cheeks, his firmness into gentleness. "How could I not?"

Abigail was afraid to relinquish herself completely to the mood, but there was something in his eyes that inspired her. Her lips turned up in a smile that felt unfamiliar to them, more mature, more mysterious, more knowing. "Because I am only a slave, Jason."

His lips soon moved to mirror hers, and he shook his head lightly. "You were never only a slave, Abigail. You were born free. A soul never forgets that."

As he kissed her, she was almost convinced.

NINETEEN

Jason strode through the winter chill toward the guards' barracks at the palace of the governor. Menelaus had invited them all to dine with him there, and he had agreed to come. With every step, however, he wished he were home. Good as it would be to see his friends, it would be better still to lounge beside Abigail and watch their babe move under his hand. To talk with his father, listen to the stories his mother told.

His friends did not appreciate his dedication to his home life, he knew. Perhaps they saw what he had come to realize: that affection for Abigail had turned into love. They did not approve. But how could he resist? He had been fond of her to begin with, but seeing her smiling, laughing, beaming with adoration for the child he had planted within her . . . it proved an irresistible tug on his heart. She loved their babe. Surely love for him would follow.

He pulled open the door to the barracks and was greeted with a blast of heat and raucous laughter. No, he did not miss the revelries of his companions. Did not miss Rome. Would it be so bad to give up those dreams? If he stayed here in Jerusalem, married Abigail, then perhaps she would finally let him past the last barrier of her heart. Perhaps she would forgive him for all he had taken from her if he gave her that.

"There he is!" Menelaus sloshed wine into a chalice and thrust it at him the moment he closed the door behind him. "Sit, drink away the chill. I only wish I had a few wenches to help keep us warm."

The others laughed and raised their cups in salute. Apidius downed his in a single gulp that made him shiver in what looked like pleasure. "It has grown colder than I would like. But perhaps it will grow colder still and freeze the rebels out of the hills, eh?"

Titus snorted from his couch near the fire. "Do not bet on it, my friend. Desperate men feel no cold."

"I do not like what I have been hearing about Barabbas's band." Jason set his cup down so he could shrug out of his cloak, then took a seat beside Lentulus. "If Oedipus and the Cyclops taught me anything, it was that a man with no name cannot be trusted. Come now–'Son of a father'? How are we to call out for help and claim it is such a man tormenting us? Our fellows would laugh."

Lentulus's smile held no amusement. "It is a clever name. And he has proven himself to be a clever man, always evading us though everyone knows he is a murderer, a rebel, and a thief."

"He will be caught," Menelaus declared. "And that is the final word on him. This is an eve for *forgetting* our duties, my friends. If we are going to speak of unpleasantries, let us speak of our own." He turned smiling eyes on Apidius. "Have you heard from Drusilla?"

Apidius sent his friend a mock scowl. "Yes, and your lack of faith in my betrothed is appalling. She is well and anxious to be reunited. If I am not transferred closer to

Rome within a year, her parents have agreed to bring her here, and we will be married."

"Well then." Titus raised his drink once more. "To Drusilla the faithful! May she bear our friend many sons!" The others echoed the toast, making Apidius blush.

"And how is your woman, Jason?" Lentulus turned to him with a hint of smile. "I imagine she grows larger by the day."

Jason swirled his wine without taking a drink. Her smile flashed before his mind's eye. "She is in good spirits."

Meleaus laughed. "He speaks of spirits because it is all she has left at this point. Her figure is gone, likely never to return. Let us see how he brags of his Venus when she is fat and stooping and nursing a babe."

"Yes, Jason, we should all go into town later. You are surely in need of a woman you can get your arms around." Titus flashed a wicked grin.

"Abigail satisfies me." Jason put his cup aside altogether.

His simple certitude called a halt to the laughter. The other four fell silent and all stared at him.

"By the gods," Titus muttered, "he has fallen in love with her."

"Jason." Menelaus leaned forward, face intent. "I thought we had agreed that it was unwise to take so much interest in the slave and her child."

He folded his arms across his chest "You all did. I did not."

Apidius tossed his hand into the air. "It is hopeless, though. The child is a bastard."

Jason steepled his fingers and met none of their gazes. "Not if I marry her."

A silence, swirling with undercurrents of fire, rushed the room in a gust, then fled again in the face of the explosion.

"You cannot!" Menelaus and Titus roared together.

"Think of your career," the Roman demanded.

"And your future," the Greek added.

"It is unthinkable, Jason." Titus was so agitated he thrust himself from his seat and took to pacing. "You are accepted in Rome only because your father is Roman. If you went through with this—"

"My son would be a Roman citizen by birth." Jason kept his tone placid.

"He would be despised." Menelaus corrected. "He would be more Hebrew than Roman, and the Hebrews grow more and more rebellious, more apt to be crushed. Mark my words, Jason, the day is not far off when your mother's people are forced from Rome altogether, labeled as the miscreants they are proving themselves to be. If you married this Jewess—"

"This *slave!*" Titus spat.

"Your future would be ruined. And you would not be benefitting the child, either. He would be an outcast in Rome."

Jason regarded his friends, sending his gaze around the room slowly, calmly. Menelaus was distraught, Titus enraged, Apidius imploring, Lentulus withdrawn. Strangely, the decision he could not make before was suddenly resolved completely in his mind in the face of his adversity. He stood smoothly, without concern. "There is much to this world outside of Rome, my friends. I realize my wife and my children would not find a welcoming home there. That is why I will stay in Israel."

Menelaus groaned. Titus looked ready to pummel him. "For the love of the gods, Jason!"

"*God*, Titus." He picked his cloak up again and headed for the door. "There is only one. And I am beginning to realize the love of him goes deeper within me than I thought."

"Jason." Apidius stood in his way of the exit, the only one still calm. Even Lentulus appeared to be agitated more than Jason had ever seen. "Do not act rashly, my friend. Think of the consequences. Consider what you are about to do."

Jason made his words soft as he looked up into his companion's gaze. "I have been doing so for many weeks, Apidius. You love a woman. Surely you can understand. Would you not forsake all this," he said with an outstretched arm, "for her? The parties? The politics? And really, what else will I be missing from Rome?"

"Your friends," Lentulus answered.

Jason turned to face him, feeling nothing but calm. "If my friends would forsake me because of whom I take to wife, then they are not my friends." He gave them a moment to let that sink in. "You will all be invited to the wedding feast. If you cast your loyalties away from me, I will not blame you." With that, he brushed past Apidius and left the room, the building, and the grounds. He headed back to his father's house without a backward glance.

A peace settle over him. It was the first time he could ever remember when he actually knew, knew from deep within, knew from sight, from hearing, and from heaven, that he was *right*. It put a decided bounce in his step.

Andrew took his master's weapon and sheathed it as Jason approached them. He was smiling. It seemed he was always smiling these days, and his joy only made Andrew's heart sink.

"Are you ready to leave, my son?" Cleopas clapped a hand to Jason's shoulder.

"I am." They set off, Andrew falling in a step behind. They had barely cleared the gates of the compound when Jason turned his head toward his father. "I need to speak with you. About Abigail."

Cleopas chuckled. "Much is about Abigail these days. I have discovered that is not a very telling introduction. You will have to elaborate."

Jason smiled but still managed to look serious. "I have been giving it much thought and last night I came to my decision. I wish to marry her, Father."

Andrew's breath came out in a strangled gasp.

His master glanced back at him but then focused on his son. "You are certain?"

Jason nodded, his ardor evident on his face. "I love her."

"So I have come to see. But if I may ask, have you given any thought to all this will change?"

"Yes, Father, I have. I will stay in Jerusalem, serving under you as long as they allow me; I assume you can help me in that goal. I do not wish to take her from Mother. I know how attached they are to one another."

"Indeed." Cleopas's smile was indulgent. And far too warm to exist in the same world as the cold that had overtaken Andrew's heart. "I need not tell you how ecstatic your mother will be at this news. You will finally be giving her the daughter she has always desired."

"Yes."

Silence fell. Perhaps it was filled only with happy contemplation for the other two, but Andrew fisted his hands together and wished for a moment of privacy to rebuild the fortress of his emotions.

Cleopas turned to Jason again as they neared the house. "What of your plans of Rome, Jason? I thought you wished to take possession of our property there and manage that estate."

Jason sighed, but it was with satisfaction. "I did, Father. But what is the point, if I do not have a family to manage it for? Abigail would not be happy in Rome, and I will not force her to go. And because I love her, I could never leave her behind. It became a question of Rome or Abigail, and I have made my choice."

Cleopas put a firm hand on his son's shoulder and smiled. "I think you have made a wise one, Jason."

Jason nodded brightly. "I know I have. I will talk with Abigail as soon as we get home, if you will tell Mother. Then I am sure the rest of the evening will be spent in plans."

"I shall go in and share the news with Ester, then try to keep her from pouncing on Abigail until you have had a chance to tell her yourself."

"Good luck." Jason laughed. He hung back as his father stepped inside, turning to Andrew. "A moment, Andrew."

Andrew stopped, his burdens hanging down at his sides, not impressed with the unusual note of humility in Jason's voice. "Yes, Master?"

Jason drew in a careful breath, and sent a searching gaze over him. What did he see? They boy he had tormented once? Or the fact that he grown into a man just as tall, just as strong as he? When his gaze touched on the ring in his ear, did it remind him anew of his dominion over him?

"I know you love her," he said at last. "I have long punished you for it, and I apologize. No man is the master of his heart. Andrew." He drew himself up a bit taller. "I know you despise me. You probably would rather hear of my death than my decision to wed her. But know that even if I have not known her as long as you have, I love her still. I will treat her well, and I will honor her."

Andrew made no response for a long moment. A few words could not erase all he had done. A promise did not guarantee that Abigail would be happy. "You will indeed. Or you will pay."

Jason's lips curved up. "You are good man, Andrew. We have never liked one another, even when we were boys. But I can admit now that my father was always right about you. I am sorry."

Andrew stood still in his place as Jason turned and followed after his father into the house. He felt his life slipping away, seeping into the unforgiving ground, and he could do nothing to stop it. For the first time in almost two decades of servitude, he wished he had never stepped foot in the Visibullis house.

◈

Abigail left the room with a smile when Cleopas asked to speak with Ester. She headed to Jason's chamber, assuming he would be in shortly to clean up. With one hand supporting her back and the other resting on the ever-growing curve of her stomach, she said a silent prayer for the babe stirring within her.

Ester and Dinah still occasionally whispered that the pregnancy was hard on her, but the fear had receded. Love covered it, hers and Jasons. Perhaps it would be enough to take her all the way through birth in another couple months. Perhaps Jehovah would be merciful after all. It was worth the hope. Worth the prayers.

She opened the door to his room and left it in that position when she saw he was not inside. A moment later she heard his footfalls and turned with a welcoming smile.

Jason walked directly up to her, gathered her in his arms, and kissed her soundly. "How do you feel today?"

"Well enough." If she ignored the pain spiking down her hips.

"Good." She watched his face shift into an expression at once serious and blithe. He took her hands in his. "Abigail, I have something to speak with you about. Let us sit."

They moved to the couch since it was closest, then he left her momentarily to grab a box, one that sent a waft of memory through her. Setting it closed on the other side of him, he took her hands again and looked into her eyes. "Abigail," he began once more, then halted for breath. When he spoke again, it was in Hebrew. "I have come to love you greatly. There is not an hour that passes when you are not in my thoughts. Your name is honey on my tongue. Abigail. I want you to be my wife."

She felt her eyes go wide as he settled a gentle hand on her cheek. Could he possibly be serious? For so long now he had been refusing to even accept it as an option, and did he now volunteer it as a solution? What of his objections, his plans? What of her ruinous effect on his future? "Jason–"

"I have given it much thought," he assured her solemnly, once more in Greek. "Beloved, I have made my choice. We will stay here, in Jerusalem, and I will serve under my father. Dear one, you will be my wife." He opened the box and lifted out a length of gold, attached to which was a large ruby pendant.

Suddenly Abigail remembered the box from her first day in this house; Jason's inheritance. "'Who can find a virtuous woman?'" he quoted as his mother had done so many years ago, "'for her price is far above rubies. . . Favour is deceitful and beauty is vain, but a woman that feareth the Lord, she shall be praised.'"

Tears filled Abigail's eyes as he slipped the jewel over her head and brought it to a rest between her breasts. "I am undeserving of those words, Jason."

He kissed her hands. "You are more than you think yourself, Abigail."

The sound of hurried footsteps reached them, and a moment later his parents burst into the room. Abigail had never seen such rapture on Ester's face, and Jason smiled brightly into it.

"My children." Ester did not stop until she could put an arm around each of them, hugging them at once. "The Lord has blessed us this day. Blessed be the name of the Lord! I am so happy."

Jason laughed. "I praise him with you, Mother. Though there are a few things I will insist on. You must keep the wedding feast small, and make it soon. And now that Abigail is my betrothed, soon to be my wife, there will be no more eating in the kitchen; she will not be a servant. She will sit with us."

"Of course!"

Abigail looked in dismay at their matching grins, landing her imploring gaze on Cleopas, too, though he would only smile at her. "I cannot! Jason, I cannot be served at the table where I served."

"You can," Cleopas pronounced firmly. "Abigail, the others adore you and would serve you gladly. You are the only one whom it would bother."

She saw quickly that they would not be convinced; the Visibullises had decided that she would be one of them, and nothing she could say would dissuade them.

That evening, she sat at the table and was treated as though she had never been a slave.

TWENTY

Menelaus tapped the hilt of his knife against the table's edge and glanced over at Titus, who drummed his fingers on it. Lentulus sighed, a hand covering his face and the tips of his fingers buried in his hair. Apidius hacked without skill at a block of wood with his own knife. Their silence had covered the room for almost ten minutes.

"This is ridiculous," Menelaus finally grumbled. "We must decide."

Silence again. It ground on for another two minutes. Lentulus finally showed his face. "The general is going, and his wife. Pilate is considering it, too."

"Pilate is going." Menelaus had received the news only an hour before.

Apidius tossed his mutilated wood onto the table. "That is irrelevant. The general and Pontius go for Cleopas's sake. They do not care who his son weds. But if we go, it will be for Jason. If we go, he will expect us to stand without shame beside him. We go now, and we profess ourselves his friends regardless of any decision he makes. We do not go, and we tell him clearly we are through with him."

Menelaus considered for a moment, running his tongue over his teeth. Then he threw down his knife and stood, the clatter drawing all eyes his way. He set his face into the steely determination he imagined had been on his namesake's countenance when he declared that he would not leave Ilium until he had his fair Helen at his side once more. "Jason is my friend. In Rome, he was higher in class and should not have graced me with his presence. But he did. Who am I to do otherwise in return?" He picked up his cloak and put it around his shoulders. "I am going to the wedding feast."

Titus nodded, but by his grim expression Menelaus was not sure whether it was in agreement or resignation of another lost friend. Until he spoke. "I am going as well."

Lentulus and Apidius looked at each other in relief and stood; their thoughts were obvious. If the mighty Titus Asinius would go with dignity to watch their friend wed a Hebrew slave, then they could, too.

By the time they arrived at the prefect's dwelling, the feast was already underway. Music spilled onto the dusk-hued street, blending with the rays of the old sun. Laughter reached Menelaus's ears, and many voices talking at once. When they arrived at the door, it was opened by the old, smiling slave he had seen a handful of times before.

"Welcome." He motioned them indoors.

They all took off their cloaks and handed them to him, looking around and at each other as he led them in to where the feast was taking place. The aroma of food reminded Menelaus that they had not eaten in their haste to sit around and contemplate all afternoon.

They were not noticed as soon as they entered, which was unsurprising given the number of people within, and it gave them a moment to look around them, taking in the other guests and the bride and bridegroom. Jason was looking his best, decked out in wedding array and smiling with a light Menelaus had never seen in him before.

"He is happy." Awe with that probably colored his tone.

"So it seems." Titus hummed, but it sounded more like a growl as he looked toward the corner of the room. Menelaus turned to see what had snagged his disapproval and saw Abigail. She, too, was smiling, but the glow on her face was not that of complete happiness as Jason's was, but rather of peace. The corner's of Titus's mouth turned up. "I am not so certain his bride is as content."

"Do not be absurd." Apidius grinned as he stepped up beside them. "She is still lovely, even with the extra curve. Have you ever seen such a face?"

At that point Jason spotted them, and his smile grew even broader as he left his father's side to greet them. "My friends!" He clasped each of their wrists in turn. "I am glad you came. Come, get something to eat. Dinah's dishes could be put on the emperor's table, and she has been busy with the preparations for days."

"Thank you." Menelaus let himself be ushered to the tables of food. Jason's mother soon joined them, her smile as bright as her son's. It was no wonder the Visibullis men were so taken with the Hebrew women. These two were perfect examples of feminine beauty.

"Welcome. Jason has spoken much of you. Thank you for joining us on this joyous day."

He replied politely if without enthusiasm and focused on the food; Cleopas had apparently spared no expense, proving his approval of the marriage. The wine was strong and fine and free-flowing, the house was dressed in festivity, and Menelaus felt like an island of depression in the midst of a sea of gaiety.

"I hope his lovely wench appreciates what he has given up for her," he muttered to Titus once he had cleaned off his plate and gotten some drink into his stomach.

A menacing gleam entered Titus's eyes. "Perhaps we should make sure of it." He began to maneuver toward the bride, Menelaus a step behind him. Titus managed the hunt as though it was unintentional, greeting his other acquaintances in the room, and managing to look almost surprised when he found himself before Abigail, who was at the moment standing at the edge of the room, surveying her wedding celebration calmly. Menelaus drew even with Titus, effectively blocking her path in case she chose to flee.

"Congratulations, Abigail." Titus took her hand as all the other guests had and bowed over it.

She straightened her spine and tugged her hand free. Menelaus claimed it and gave her a feral smile. Perhaps, if it were anyone but Jason she had ruined, he could have admired the determination in her eyes.

"Thank you for coming." She reclaiming her hand again. "Jason was not sure you would."

"Neither were we." Titus made the admission sound like an accusation as he ran his eyes deliberately down her.

"It is hard to watch one's friend sacrifice a brilliant career," Menelaus practically growled, "for a *woman*."

Abigail's shoulders moved back, and her chin came up to reveal eyes throwing sparks that illuminated her whole face. She changed in a moment from Venus to Juno, angry and prepared to shift the world because of it. "I did not ask for the sacrifice."

Menelaus lifted a brow. "Did you oppose it?"

She let out a breath of a laugh. "Oppose it? As I am sure you have not forgotten, I was a slave. I had no say. He loves me and decided to marry me, so here we are."

"You do not love him." Titus stated it, but it was obviously a challenge.

She turned on the Roman with all of her fury, somehow managing to keep it quiet and focused on its target. "He was my master, and now he is my husband. I will honor him and respect him and serve him."

"But you do not love him." Titus sounded smug now.

A hand settled protectively over her babe. "He is my life. Please excuse me." She did not wait for their permission but slipped quickly between them and disappeared in the crowd.

"Well, she has spirit." Menelaus watched her go with a hint of a smile. He knew few men who would dare stand up to Titus Asinius as she had. "I must grant her that."

Titus just shook his head. "Such women are a bane to men. They possess and conquer."

"And bear sons who can do the same. Jason's son will be strong and well taught, at the least."

"In what culture, though?" Titus crossed his arms forbiddingly over his chest. "If she prevails with her Hebrew traditions, the child will be caught and crushed by them."

Menelaus shrugged. "Jason will not allow it. He is Roman in his thoughts, Titus, on that we all agree. He will see that his sons are, too."

"He is off to a great beginning, marrying his Jewess slave in the Hebrew fashion."

Menelaus could only laugh at his friend's obvious abhorrence and clap a hand to his shoulder. "Forget it, Titus. Let us eat and drink and enjoy the friends present. It is our only role now."

Titus sent one last scathing glance at the bride before following him back into the crowd.

※

For days, Abigail shuddered each time she thought of the loathing Jason's friends had for her. She did not like them, either, and had not since the first time she met them all when Cleopas had journeyed to hear the rabbi speak. Then, they had all looked at her with enough lust to make her want to hide. Now, they looked at her with such hatred she wanted to scream.

It was not her fault! She had done nothing to try to convince Jason to marry her. She had never mentioned the word to him, never hinted that she would wish it. At the last, it had been inevitable; he had come to care for her, to love their unborn child, and he could not tolerate the idea of it being illegitimate. He had weighed his options and made his choice.

It had not been hers. She would never have chosen to force him from the life he had wanted for so long. But now she would bear the consequences of his decisions, she would be the focus of the wrath of his friends. They probably thought they were concerned for his best interest; well, so was she, but she had never accused them of being unfavorable influences, had she? She never pointed her finger at their pagan habits, had never admonished their heavy drinking or their contempt for her people. She had never once insulted the Roman people or the Roman culture, and as payment for her fairness she was being reviled.

So be it. It was Jason's opinions that mattered, and he had proven where his loyalties lay, ultimately. They had been married by the authority of the one God, in the Hebrew tradition. By his choice. And she was glad. It warmed her to hear him begin to talk of Jehovah as one of his children would, to pray to and praise him. She would not be ashamed of her pleasure in her husband's renewing faith, and she would make no excuses to the friends who would just as soon stone her as speak to her.

Yes, for days she simmered, hiding it as best as she could, refusing to let her smile slacken when her husband was home. It was easy enough to cover any unhappiness; there was the excitement of marriage, the plans for the coming child. Soon enough, she could put the Romans' disapproval from her mind completely.

Naturally, it was when she had come to her internal peace that Jason drew her close one evening and said, "I have been thinking, Abigail, about how we shall raise our children. How will we reconcile the two worlds of which they will be a part?"

Abigail sighed wearily. Was this where he would renege on his previous acceptance of the Hebrew Law and declare that to raise them as Romans was the only way to ensure their positions in the world? Would he say that he had spoken to his friends, and they had made a good case for returning to Rome, after all?

Jason chuckled as if he could read her thoughts and found them preposterous. "Do not look so woebegone, my wife. I am merely going to suggest we mirror my parents' choices. You do not find that so awful, do you?"

"No." She smiled at her own doubts. "I find that perfect."

He spread his palm over the mass of her stomach. "Good. The particulars, of course, we will have to figure out for ourselves. For instance, a name. My parents compromised by choosing a Greek one for me, but I am not so certain that is my desire. I have been thinking that since the baby will have the Roman surname, we should choose a Hebrew first name."

For a moment, all Abigail could do was stare at him. "That is what you wish?"

His smile could not have been more sincere. "I do. Something traditional, although I have not really thought of one I prefer over another. Daniel, perhaps, or David."

"Or Jonathan, or Joshua," she suggested warmly.

Jason grimaced at the last. "Joshua is too popular these days. Especially with all the changes you can make translating into Greek and Latin. But Jonathan I like."

"Or Micah, Jeremiah, Zacharias." Her brows drew together. "What are the names from your mother's family?"

Jason shook his head. "She does not talk about them much, I do not know. What of yours?"

"My father was Michael, and his father Aaron."

He considered for a moment. "We will decide; there is no rush. I believe the name is given eight days after birth, correct? At the time of circumcision if it is a son."

"Yes." She covered Jason's hand with her own. "And you would wish that, too?"

Jason pressed his lips to her temple. "It is the sign of the covenant between God and our people. If we have a son, I would not want to deprive him of that. If he chooses another path, that is his decision; but I will not take it from him, just as my parents decided with me. And I am finding that it is a difficult covenant to put aside. All of my life I have struggled against the Law, Abigail. And now I find myself praying that

Jehovah can forgive my negligence. I finally see that my father was right in embracing my mother's faith."

Abigail pressed on his hand, her words soft. "You have grown into a good man, my husband." She returned the smile he offered, wondering if the changes they had made in their lives would be enough for their demanding, jealous God. To be safe, when they went to the synagogue that Sabbath she would suggest he purchase a sin offering for them. And then she would pray it sufficed.

🜔

Cleopas sharpened his knife, his eyes on the horizon where the sun was setting in a glorious wash of colors, splashing the earth beneath it with regal hues of fire that burnished the city gold. He heard his son climbing the ladder onto the roof and soon saw him appear.

"A beautiful evening." Jason filled his lungs with the crisp air, then let it out again as he sat beside Cleopas. "Abigail is sitting at a window watching the sunset, but she did not wish to leave the warmth of the hearth."

Cleopas chuckled. "That is best. Soon, my son, you will be a father. Ester tells me Abigail has another month, perhaps six weeks to go until the child is ready to join us."

"I believe Abigail is beginning to wish it were sooner." A smile filled his voice. "I, too, am anxious, though for different reasons. It will be such a blessing to hold my child. And we have decided to name it after Mother's parents. Benjamin if it is a boy, Hannah if it is a girl."

Cleopas's lips turned up in peaceful appreciation. "Your mother will be pleased. Of course, she is always pleased these days. You have made her heart glad, my son, in the ways you have grown."

Jason chuckled. "I cannot say that was my intention, but I value her approval."

"There was a day you did all you could to avoid it. And another not so long ago when you would be spending your evenings out in the city with your friends."

"My friends are less than pleased with me. And I with them. Moreover, I would rather spend my few free hours with my wife. Hence, I suppose, why they are less than pleased. Which is, in turn, why *I* am so with them."

Cleopas chuckled again. "You will all resolve it, I am certain. In spite of the many things in which we differ, I have a respect for those you call friends. They strike me as loyal and dedicated. Those qualities are difficult to find in men these days."

"And they feel I have defected by marrying Abigail." Jason shook his head. "They almost did not come to my wedding, Father. And apparently Menelaus and Titus cornered Abigail and told her in no uncertain terms that she was ruining my life."

Cleopas raised a brow. "Two grown men to battle one small, pregnant woman? I hope they emerged unscathed."

Jason let out a roar of laughter. "Knowing my wife, she put them in their places. The men would not say, and Abigail refused to discuss the episode, but her wit is quick and her tongue sharp. You did well to educate her."

"She had the mind for it. She knows Latin now better than I, I think."

"She certainly knows the Law better than I. It is rather embarrassing to have to ask one's wife to explain the customs of one's people."

Cleopas smiled. His heart swelled at the thought that his son was actually asking the questions. "You have much more knowledge of it than I had when I married your mother. But it has the benefit of making sense, and of genuinely working for the good of the citizens. I believe you have come to realize that of late, have you not?"

His eyes went contemplative. "Indeed. But my concern is that it is impossible to keep all the laws, Father, no matter how hard I strive. Remembering them all is difficult enough, remembering to do them–and how am I to know that the sacrifices I offer are enough? How can I tell if Jehovah is pleased with my efforts or if he is still holding my failings against me? I have a fear of turning out like Cain, offering what I have, but not being accepted, then losing it all in a moment of anger."

Cleopas was silent for a moment as he considered. He put his knife back in its sheath and set it aside, and only then spoke. "The Lord looks at the heart, my son. He will forgive you your sins if you truly repent of them. But if you offer a sacrifice without truly being remorseful for the actions, why should he accept it? Saying the words, doing the motions is not enough. He requires devotion. He ordered his people to write the Law upon their hearts; that means he wishes us to love them, to obey because we believe they are good and right. Perhaps Cain was not sincere; perhaps he offered the spoiled vegetables, or did it only for recognition, not to the glory of Jehovah. The only way to be sure you are forgiven is to realize you need to be, and to truly desire it, being prepared to put aside the part of you that sins. I believe the failing of many men today is that they do not recognize their own imperfections."

Jason mirrored his contemplative silence. When he spoke, it was hushed, as if the coming night and its time of rest was already sneaking in. "Mother did not teach you that."

"No." Which made him sigh. "Your mother is still battling with the idea that the performance of traditions may not be enough. And it pains me, because she has always served with her heart, yet still she refuses to acknowledge that as being the important part, rather than her words or the amount she gives to the synagogue." He shook his head in dismay. "So many people have scorned her, have proven again and again that their faith ends at their lips, yet she defends them as being righteous."

Cleopas felt Jason's gaze on his profile, steady and measuring. "Father . . . not all that long ago, you baffled me. But since living under your roof again, I have seen the authority you hold. The kind I once thought came from position or title. But watching you . . . I think perhaps it is your goodness that makes you stand so straight. Yet still you are humble." He chuckled, shook his head. "You are a blend of contradictions. The Roman who is such a dedicated Hebrew. The soldier who promotes peace. The master who teaches his slaves they are his equals. I can only pray that someday I can be the kind of man you are."

The words warmed him all the way to his core. And lit a hope he had all but given up on. "Jason . . . months ago, you would not have heard me if I spoke of this. I pray now that you will. Another thing your mother will not accept is Messiah; but he has come. I have heard this teacher they call Jesus the Christ, and I have felt in my heart that he holds the keys to our salvation."

"The Son of God." There was a strange note in his voice, as if he remembered something Cleopas was not privy to. "But how do you know he is not just another man speaking empty words? Many have claimed to perform miracles, Father. Many can speak the same claims."

"But no other follows his own lessons as this man does, and no other man has ever chastised the people so much without ever compromising the Law. The man John whom was titled the Baptist recognized this Jesus as the messiah prophesied in the Word. Even Herod feared that man."

"Before or after he had him beheaded?" Jason shook his head. "I thought his contention with this John was that he accused Herod of adultery."

"So he did," Cleopas conceded, amused. "As well he should have. He took Phillip's wife into his bed, dishonoring his own brother. But that is not the issue, Jason. Jesus of Nazareth speaks the truth. I know this. What I do not know is how to convince my family."

Jason held his gaze for a long moment. "You cannot, Father," he said at length. "If his lessons are the truth, then judging by what I have heard of them, each person must come to the conclusions within his own heart. All you can do is be an example; and at that, you have never failed. Watching you has taught me how to be a man, a soldier, a husband, and hopefully now a father. Watching you has taught me that a man need not be weak to have a faith, but is made strong by it. So watching you will undoubtedly convince us all that a teacher to whom you give such credence, you, a man of such wisdom, must be right."

Cleopas reached out and clasped his son's arm. "Thank you for your trust in me, Jason."

Jason's smile held wisdom where once there had only been self. "I am only returning the favor."

TWENTY-ONE

Abigail was bored. Her headaches kept her from reading, her swollen hands from playing the lute, and her otherwise altered shape from any other form of employment. She spent most of her days lounging around, going on the one walk her protective family allowed her, and talking or listening to Ester and Dinah. When Jason and Cleopas returned, she was subjected to a session of questioning in which they demanded how she had felt during every minute, then had to bear their demands that she get more rest, eat the food Dinah offered her, or perhaps jump over the moon. . . .

What she needed was a distraction. Like a baby. If she would just have the baby, all would be well, and they could all stop fussing over her and focus on someone else, instead. But if she dared mention her hope that the newest Visibullis would come early, she was admonished by Ester, who claimed that such a thing would be unhealthy for the child.

In her brooding mood, she found herself thinking much about the words Jason had told her he had had with his father, about the Nazarene. But she would inevitably decide she did not have enough information to form an opinion so just frustrated herself more. It did not help that both her husband and his father talked of little else for the days following their initial conversation. She was getting very weary of it.

This was Jason's day off, and Abigail knew he would be returning soon from the markets, where he had gone with his friends at their insistence. He had promised to share the midday meal with her, though, so she expected it when she heard the sounds of his approach. What she did not expect was the sound of someone else's with his.

By the time she managed to stand to go investigate whom he had brought him with him, Jason had appeared in the doorway to the room, hand-in-hand with a small boy. Abigail's brows flew up of their own accord, and her eyes shifted from the beautiful, terrified child to the man who stood before her smiling.

The boy could not be more than six. His eyes were wide, flecked with gold, his hair burnished curls that fell over his forehead. His features were remarkable, finely chiseled and arranged, though he looked as though he had not had a decent meal in quite a while. He stared up at her, soulful and forlorn.

Abigail tore her gaze away from the child and focused it on her husband.

"His name is Samuel," Jason said by means of introduction. "I just purchased him. I thought we would need the extra help when the baby comes."

Abigail replied in Latin because she knew the boy would not understand her. "Jason, we do not need a slave."

Jason kept his countenance neutral and his words in Latin. "His mother was desperate, my love. She would have sold him as a catamite to another if I had not stepped in."

Her questions turned to sympathy, softening into pride for her husband. When had he become so gentle and considerate?

The boy spoke in Hebrew, drawing their attention back to him. "I am strong. I will work hard."

Abigail lowered herself slowly to her knees so she was on a level with him. His eyes, so serious and intense, reminded her of herself as a child, when she was sold by her supposed family. She tried to keep her face serious, though she wanted to smile. She suspected, however, that this tiny child would be wary of mercy.

"Do you speak Greek?" she inquired in her native tongue.

"Yes," he replied in the language he spoke of.

"And have you begun your lessons on the Law?"

Samuel hesitated. "I have learned of Passover, and the commandments."

Abigail nodded solemnly. "It is a start. You will be expected to study with me, Samuel. I will not have an uneducated boy in my house. You will have to learn how to read and write, in both Hebrew and Greek, and then we will have lessons on Latin as well."

Samuel seemed to fluctuate between confusion and acceptance. "My mother said I would be a slave, that I must do as my masters bade me in all things."

She smiled. "Well, I bid that you learn."

He hesitated a heartbeat more, then nodded.

Her heart broke. It had not been so long ago when she had been in his place, a waif of a child with too much knowledge of the cruelties of the world and not enough faith in its goodness. A tear slipped from her eye, and she put her small hand on his smaller shoulder. "Samuel, you will be well taken care of. I am glad you have come."

Samuel solemnly reached out and wiped away her tear. "Have I made you cry, Mistress?"

"No." It was true enough. Nothing he had done, nothing he had any control over elicited her tears. It was his situation, her own, and the kindness this house offered. It was unbelievable to her that she had come full circle, that there was now someone who called her what she still tried to call Ester.

Seeing that his eyes had fallen to her abdomen, she took his hand and put it where the baby was moving, watching the wonder that moved over his face. "There is a babe in there, Samuel. He will be born soon, in just a few weeks. Have you ever been around a baby?"

Samuel shook his head, curls bouncing.

Abigail smiled. "Neither have I. But you will aid me, will you not? I may need you to help me care for him. I have heard it said," she continued, pitching her voice down in conspiracy, "that every new child needs someone to be his older brother. Can you do that, Samuel?"

Samuel, eyes wide with the seriousness of his promise, nodded once more. Then paused. His golden brows drew together. "What will I have to do?"

Abigail's smile only grew. "Well, you may have to sit beside him sometimes and make sure he stays where he needs to. Perhaps sing to him. And as he gets older, he will need to know how to play games."

The little boy studied her intently. "I will do all I can to help you, Mistress."

"I believe you will, Samuel." She brushed the curls from his forehead, though they fell onto it again the instant her fingers moved away. She smiled at the errant locks, wondering how any mother could part with such a child. "Come, I shall show you to your room."

Getting up proved to be more of a challenge than going down, however, and Jason ended up practically lifting her from the floor. She rewarded him with a sweet smile, trying to let him know he had done the right thing in bringing the boy home. She held out her hand to Samuel, who put his in hers with perfect trust.

She led him down the hall and into the room that had been hers until a few months before. The wooden chest was empty now, her belongings all in Jason's room, and the pallet was clean and freshly made up. All evidence of her term there had been erased.

She kept her tone gentle. "This is where you will stay. This next door belongs to Andrew, who is my father's slave. He will gladly help you in anything you need at any time. And across the hall is Dinah, who cooks for us, and her husband Simon, who manages the house. In fact, we should go meet Dinah now. She may need you to taste some of the foods she had prepared, to see if they are satisfactory."

"Clever," Jason muttered in Latin into her ear. She jabbed him playfully in the ribs.

When the three entered the kitchen, Dinah did not even look over her shoulder. "Abigail, I thought you were resting. I promised to bring your meal in to you when the young master returned."

"The young master returned with a surprise." Jason's tone was bright with humor.

She turned now, and her face lit when she saw the boy. She immediately crouched down, with far more ease than Abigail had, and said, "And who are you, child? A young prince come to stay with us?"

Samuel did not smile as Dinah did, but his lips at least hinted at it as he shook his head. "I am Samuel. My mother sold me, and he," he said, indicating Jason, "bought me so that the fat man could not." His brows drew together once more. "The fat man looked at me strangely."

Dinah's eyes flew to Jason, who nodded once, his face serious. She was quick to put another smile on. "Well, no one will look at you strangely here, Samuel. Now. My mistress is dining with a friend today, so I only have to prepare the food for your master and mistress. If they allow it, you can help me."

Abigail nodded. "I suggested he help you with the tastings, Dinah."

Dinah caught her meaning and smiled. "An important job, indeed." With a flourish, she scooped up the boy and deposited him on the top of the table. "There. You sit and I will give you a sampling of the meal. Anything you do not like, tell me." She turned to Abigail with a pointed look and a matching finger. "Go rest."

Abigail scowled because Dinah would expect it, but then let Jason lead her off. "Where did you find him?" she asked as soon as they were out of earshot, as they headed for the main room where Dinah would expect to find them.

"In the markets." All amusement left his voice. "Right there on a street corner, Abigail, his mother was hocking him along with baskets and palms. I could not let that man take him home."

"Of course not." She sighed. "He is a beautiful boy. It is a dangerous thing to be when one is unprotected."

Jason stopped in the threshold and turned to look at her, then drew her against him. "I am sorry, Abigail."

Only then realizing how he would take her words, she rushed to say, "I did not mean–"

"I know. But it is true nonetheless. You were helpless against me, and I showed no mercy because I wanted you." He drew in a deep breath, his eyes averted.

"You have changed, my husband." She leaned into his embrace. "And I cannot wish away what gave us our child."

Gazing into her eyes, he was apparently convinced. He smiled, then drew her the rest of the way into the room and made her sit. "I realize that Samuel will not actually be of much use right now; but I also thought you could use a companion, my love. Not to mention a distraction until the baby comes."

She returned his knowing grin. "True enough. I will have to see to some clothing for him. And he is so thin! Dinah will remedy that quickly, I think. And your mother will fall in love with the child." She chuckled. "She will probably spoil him as she did me."

"And you will not?" His smile made her flush. "You have a soft heart and a long memory. I imagine you will treat all of your slaves as you were treated."

Abigail's face reflected her disconcert. "I cannot imagine having slaves at all. I will always think of such people as my equals."

"I believe that is the point," Jason said, shocking her. "Does the Law not say that slaves are not slaves because of any lack of worth, but rather because of a lack of fortune? Was not Joseph a slave, and the entire Hebrew peoples?"

She felt a slow smile sneak onto her mouth. "They were, husband, and it does. Although Aristotle and Plato would surely disagree."

He picked up her hand and held it tenderly. "But Plato and Aristotle were only men, beloved. We must forgive them for their false opinions."

Abigail laughed, full and bright. She looked over to the doorway before her mirth had been spent, saw Dinah and Samuel there. She held out a hand in invitation.

Samuel ran into her open arms and clung.

Abigail pulled the boy up into what remained of her lap and held him. He shed no tears; indeed, as he draped himself over her round stomach and rested his head against her breast, his perfect face reflected perfect contentment.

Within two minutes, he was asleep, and Abigail refused to let him be moved. Jason, smiling indulgently, simply shook his head and smiled at Dinah.

"It seems," he said to the elder woman, who was beholding the scene with sparkling eyes, "that we will soon have *two* children, Dinah."

"It seems you will." She suddenly shifted back into her stern expression and glared at Abigail. "But he will be no cause for excuses. Eat."

Abigail chuckled softly and picked up some bread.

◆

Jason left for his night shift with a shake of his head, a fond smile on his lips. As he walked, he reflected on the differences between his family and his friends. He had left Menelaus and Titus and Apidius by the time he happened across Samuel, but he had a feeling his friends would mock him for the purchase of the boy. They would look at his beautiful face and tease him as a lover of boys, or else would deride him for having too soft a heart and wasting money on one who was useless. His family, on the other hand, lauded his quick judgement and acted as though he had just bestowed a gift on them all.

And Abigail–Abigail had become the sole being in Samuel's eyes already. He never looked away from her and was perfectly content to rest at her side all evening. He may have called her "Mistress," but Jason knew well she would be his mother. And hopefully the excitement of the evening had worn her out enough that she would rest well tonight. Too often for his peace of mind, she tossed restlessly until dawn. It did not seem healthy.

He entered the garrison and greeted a few acquaintances, then began his rounds along the wall. As usual, the city was quiet as he gazed out across it, and the activity outside the walls was at a minimum. They had to be careful these days, with the threat of rebellion so strong, but still his night watches were usually peaceful and uneventful.

This night, however, it was not to be. It was not an external disturbance that called him from his position, though, but rather a familiar face.

"I am to relieve you," the centurion said wearily. "The general wishes to speak with you."

Curious, Jason nodded and wasted no time in going to his superior. He found the general pacing the confines of the room, hands clasped behind his back. Jason had never seen the man look old before, but at that moment his face was haggard.

"Jason." He stopped, his eyes bright with–what? It was not just anxiety, but it was not fear. Guilt? "I need to speak to your wife."

Jason stood agape. "Abigail? When?"

"Now!" the general shouted, then drew in a calming breath. "It is imperative, Jason, or I would not ask you to wake her. It is Elizabeth, her friend, Julia's slave."

His lover, Jason thought but did not say. He merely nodded. "I will bring Abigail at once."

It did not take him long to reach the house, and he entered quietly so as not to wake everyone else. He slipped into their chamber, where Abigail slept soundly. Sitting on the bed beside her, he gently shook her shoulder until he could see in the moon's rays that her eyes opened.

"Abigail, you must come with me to the general. It is about Elizabeth."

He needed to say no more. Abigail pushed herself up, using him as leverage, and hurriedly dressed. She surely had a million questions sprinting through her mind, but she asked none of them. Jason was glad, since he had no answers. He grasped her hand and led her silently from the house and across the compound to his superior.

The general was once again pacing, and he once again stopped when his solitude was interrupted. He motioned without words to the chairs sitting before his table, and Jason helped Abigail into one, then stood behind her with his hands on her shoulders.

"What is wrong, General?" Abigail asked after a moment of silence.

"Elizabeth." The general sat across from her. "She went out this afternoon at Julia's request; we have just discovered that my wife is with child, and she has not been well. She wished some food, or–" He visibly stiffened, became the stern commander. "Once before Elizabeth was carried back from the markets so ill she could not stand. You attended her. This time, Elizabeth was carried back dead. I want to know why."

Abigail pressed a hand to her mouth. Jason felt the tension coil into her shoulders, would have sworn he heard the scream that sounded only in her mind. What must she be feeling? Her only friend . . . but his Abigail did not crumble. She threw up her chin and seethed instead.

"I shall tell you why. She is dead because you took her to your bed. Because she had to hide it to keep from being stoned at the command of your wife. She was pregnant, General, and poisoned herself to be rid of it. The first time, she was fortunate; she survived. This time, she was obviously not so lucky."

Once again, his commander looked old. "She never told me."

"Of course she did not tell you!" Her voice vibrated with rage. "It was your favor she lived for! If she lost that, what would she have? She was a woman without a husband, a slave without any hope."

The general was obviously not accustomed to being chastised by anyone, especially a woman. His face mottled in rage, and the pressure of Jason's hands on his wife's shoulders intensified in warning. She took the advice and closed her mouth.

The general clenched his fist for a moment without saying anything, then burst out with, "Who gave her the poison? If you know, you will tell me!"

The prostitute's face flooded Jason's mind. The old eyes. . . bitter, but not so uncaring that she would let a young woman ruin her life.

Abigail drew in a breath. "I do not know."

Jason skimmed his thumb over her neck softly to let her know that he approved of her deception.

The general brooded for a long moment, obviously debating whether or not to believe her. But eventually his eyes fell to the swollen abdomen on which her hands rested, to her face, undoubtedly etched with exhaustion, and then to Jason. He nodded. "Very well. I do not know what I shall tell Julia. She should not be distressed right now, and this will surely upset her. She was fond of Elizabeth. And what reason can I give? The truth is out of the question, but what lie would be acceptable? If I say it was disease, she will be terrified of succumbing to it herself."

Abigail stood, somehow managing to do so with a modicum of grace. Her eyes were hard, though Jason knew the tears would come soon. "That is your problem to solve, General. But if you want to honor the memory of she whom you have destroyed, you will bury her in the way of her people."

Once again, he looked shocked by her forwardness. But he nodded. "It will be done. You may go home with your wife, Jason, Statius will take the rest of your shift."

"Thank you, General." He put an arm around Abigail and led her back outside. She was shaking, and he knew it was from emotions and not the wind. Still, he rubbed a hand up her arm for comfort and warmth.

She managed to make it back into the familiarity of their bed before losing her composure. Jason held her as the brine flowed. "Jehovah, give her your comfort," he whispered into the night. Had it grown darker while they were out? It felt it. "My sweet Abigail should not have had to lose another she loved, but still we know you hold us in your hand. Help her grieve, our father in heaven. And please, lift the darkness. Lift the darkness."

He held her until a halfhearted dawn stained the sky.

TWENTY-TWO

The alarm sounded, jerking Abigail awake. The call to arms, for all the soldiers in Jerusalem. Dread poisoned her blood. She had heard that sound twice before in her years here, and it always meant the same thing. Decisions, mixed loyalties, and fear.

Heart thundering in mutiny, Abigail did not bother to speak. She just helped her husband on with his breastplate, cloak, shoes, and weapons.

By the time they reached the hall, the rest of the household was also up, Cleopas armed and ready to leave, Ester clutching a robe around her shoulders. Andrew stood a step behind, Samuel hiding in confusion behind him, Simon and Dinah just rushing from their room sleepily. The boy, upon spotting Abigail, made a dash for her, attaching himself to her legs. She murmured something consoling without having any idea what words she used. She put a hand on his head.

"Andrew," Cleopas was saying, "Simon. You will both stay here and protect the women. I do not expect any trouble here, but bar all the doors after we leave, and do not open them to anyone you do not know. Are you ready, Jason?"

"I am." He leaned down and kissed Abigail, then tugged playfully on one of Samuel's curls. "I will be back as soon as I can. Try to get some rest, beloved. Samuel, you will take care of your mistress, will you not?"

The boy's shoulders moved back, and he nodded seriously. Jason smiled. "Good. Mother, you rest, too." He kissed her cheek.

That ridiculous demand was not worthy of response, so Abigail just moved over to Ester as the two men tossed farewells over their shoulders and rushed out the door. Simon barred it after them, and Andrew turned to survey his charges. He apparently decided that rest would be out of the question so did not order them back to bed.

"Come." He motioned them into the main room. "There is no sense in standing there. They will not be gone long, I am sure."

"I hate this," Ester muttered, taking Abigail's hand and clinging to it.

"I know." She tried to will comfort into Ester as they sat, but it was hard to do, given the fear that saturated her being. The previous times she had sat here with her mistress, it had only been her master whose safe return she prayed for. Now it was her father. Her husband.

When Samuel took his usual place in her lap, she wrapped grateful arms around him. He had ony been with them for two weeks, but he felt as much a part of her world as the others in this room.

"I am getting too old for this kind of excitement," Ester said. "These are the moments when I wish I had married a merchant, a scholar, a workman–anything but a soldier. I cannot imagine what it would be like if we were at war! I would not know a moment of peace."

"They are capable soldiers. They will return soon, as they always do." The words came easily to Abigail's lips, but they felt empty

"I know." Ester sighed. "But it makes the wait no easier."

Abigail said nothing. But silently, she agreed.

♠

Jason heard the name run through the ranks like Bacchical drink, turning expectation into desire for blood. Barabbas. The rumored attacks were finally taking place. The rebel had acted, staged his mighty coup. And now they would get to raze his ambitions as the walls of Thermopylae. Tonight, he would be crushed. The "Son of a Father" would leave his parents childless; they would kill the thief and be rid of his poisonous influence once and for all.

They did not tarry long. The officers gave their commands to their men and they all took off at a trot in various directions. This particular uprising appeared to be well planned. There were reports from all around the city of different attacks being waged on the soldiers' positions, and the demand for reinforcements was intense.

Jason took the time to mutter a prayer of thanksgiving that he had not been on duty that night. Injured men were being carried past them, and they were the ones who had been assaulted first, when their guards were down.

Now, everyone was alert and ready for battle. Even Cleopas, who would usually have been expected to stay at the garrison and supervise activity there, took command of the men whose centurion had been wounded already and headed into the streets.

Jason and Cleopas headed off in the same general direction, and a glance around showed Jason that Titus and his group of soldiers were nearby as well. The look on the Roman's face was fearsome, and it made him smile. Any rebel to get in Titus's way would know true terror before he was cut down.

Shouts echoed through the streets, furious cries of pain and rage. Behind the barred doors of the residences, all was silent. The people were probably awake, but they huddled inside without even lighting a lamp. Still, Jason imagined their fear seeping out into the roadways, sliding over soldiers and forming puddles of darkness on the ground, where the moonlight could not reach.

The sound of metal clashing against metal reached Jason's ears; it was familiar enough. For years, he had watched and taken part in drills, perfecting his swordsmanship, learning how to fight well and win. But he could not deceive himself into thinking of this as an exercise; this was a test, the ultimate kind. He had never been in the frenzy of a battle before, but it was unmistakable. The panting of men pushing themselves to their limits in the effort to be victorious blended into the incessant pounding of soldier's shoes upon the stones that paved the way to the action.

"Attack!" The cry came from above them, and Jason and his men all coiled in anticipation of their enemies' obedience. Before he could blink, there was a roar of barbaric voices, and a cloud of men bore down from the walls, hitting them on all sides. They had obviously been training for this moment a long time.

The Romans had been training longer. His men did not panic, they did not run. They held their formation until the rebels began to scatter, and then pursued as Jason called out the command to regroup at the corner in a few moments.

Without fail, the mutineers were routed and quelled. Without fail, more came to take their places. The battle raged on, taking the form of small skirmishes that Jason kept thinking would be over quickly. But every time one group fled and the Romans pursued, they ran into more of the Hebrew rebels.

By his count, all of Jason's men were unharmed but growing weary. He was, too, but it was irrelevant. He was not sure if he had been lucky enough to fall into an area with a high concentration of the outlaws, or if they had recruited so many that their numbers allowed them to attack the soldiers all over the city in such force. But the question did not matter. All that mattered was bringing peace back to Jerusalem.

He was chasing down a man who was fleet of foot and was quickly losing him. Breathing hard, Jason decided not to pursue too far from his position, so turned back. His body moved just in time to freeze at the horrible vision that met his eyes.

Cleopas, strong, able, good Cleopas had been engaged by a bear of a man whose every blow had forced his father back until he was against the wall. His attacker was merciless. Jason realized in a flash that Cleopas would fall under that man's brutal sword.

He did not hesitate. He let out a roar that filled the air and charged. It was his place to save his father.

Too late. Before the sound ever pierced the air, the sword had pierced Cleopas's chest. As Jason flew up, the life drained out of his father's eyes and he sagged, empty, to the ground. Instead of paralyzing pain, it was lightning rage that burned through Jason, and he headed for the man who was even now taking flight.

The pursuit did not last long; they ran into an alley with no outlet, and the rebel apparently realized he would get no reprieve, so turned and headed back for Jason, sword raised.

He knew it was Barabbas. He did not know how he knew; he had never seen the face, but he had heard the description of the man. His beard was unkempt, his hair wild, but his eyes, even when lit with the taste for blood, were intelligent. He did not attack frantically, but rationally. Each thrust was calculated, each parry practiced. If he retreated a few steps, it was to better strike. Jason knew within seconds that his skill was at least matched. He would not let himself think that it may be outdone.

Somewhere in the background, he heard a shout that was his name, but it did not so much as distract him. Somewhere inside, he recognized the voice, recognized the warning within it, but he could not spare it any attention. He was fighting for his life, and he knew it. His every thought was on his movement, on what he could do next to direct death to the man across from him instead of inviting it to himself.

He was gaining the upper hand when a skirmish from the wall above them sent a piece of stone shattering to the ground behind him. The sound of splintering rock barely made it into his consciousness before it proved his destruction. Barabbas saw his opportunity and took it. He went on the offensive again and forced Jason back just one step.

Just one.

Jason stumbled, unable to find solid footing, and in that moment, his enemy's sword struck.

For a second, the metal shaft that entered his stomach suspended him, kept him on his feet. He stared down at it before the pain had time to be felt, wondering if all the blood on the sword were his, or if his father's were mixing in, too. Then the sword withdrew, and gravity took hold. He stumbled backward, fell, and the pain soared into his perception.

It was then that the shouts came into focus, the shouts that he realized only then had never ceased. It was Titus, and he was near. He heard him give the command to pursue and capture, he heard the sound of many feet obeying. But all he could see was the black sky above him, a few stars glittering very far away. He could feel a throbbing and did not know if it was the cadence of the soldier's feet as they ran or his own heart rushing blood to the wound that would only ooze out and take his life with it.

Then a face blocked his vision. It was contorted in pain, but it was familiar and therefore welcome. "Titus."

Titus knelt down, pressing a hand against the wound to try to stop the bleeding. "Jason. Be calm. I will get you help. My men are even now laying hold of the man who did this."

"He killed my father," Jason wheezed, that emotional pain now joining the physical one that was slowly forcing all other awareness away.

"Yes," Titus admitted, "but he will be avenged. I swear that, Jason."

Jason nodded, letting his eyes slide shut for a moment, then opening them again. Abigail, his poor Abigail. She had already lost so much, so many she loved. And with his father gone . . . "They will be alone." His voice came out as little more than a gasp. "Mother and Abigail will be alone. Titus, swear to me they will be cared for."

His friend gripped his hand. "Of course they will be. Jason, you will not die."

The night had felt so heavy ever since he had taken Abigail to the general. Now it closed in, pressing down on his chest. Stifling his vision. "Tell my mother that Father died quickly, without suffering. Tell her I love her. And tell Abigail I am sorry that I will not meet our child. Tell her she is my sun, moon, and stars."

"Jason . . ." Titus glanced down at the hand he had pressed to the wound, and something shifted in his face. "I will tell them. They will be protected. I swear to you, my friend, that your family will be cared for."

"Ring." Jason moved a finger within Titus's hand. The Roman looked down at the heavy gold that encircled his middle finger, the one he had put on the day he left for Rome. The day he first met Abigail. "Tell Abigail to give it to Samuel. Tell him . . . tell him he is my son. I would have adopted him. I would have . . ."

The night weighted his chest, forced his eyes closed. The sweetest face he had ever seen filled his vision, words fought for a place on his lips. They emerged in Hebrew, no more than a breath. "Protect her, Jehovah. Sustain her. Show her your truth, your Son . . . my father, I give her to you."

The darkness, once sluggish, pounced.

◆

Titus slipped the ring off his friend's hand as Jason's eyes closed again. He watched as he coughed, gurgled, a stream of blood leaking out of the corner of his mouth. He watched as the one true friend he had ever hand, the one man never to be put off by his moods, struggled for another breath. He watched as the chest stopped heaving, as the soul fled the body on its way to wherever it went, leaving nothing but a corpse behind it.

Titus stood. His men were returning, the murderer in hand. The man was unconscious, but alive. "Marcus, Dominus, bring the bodies of the Visibullises. The city is ours again, and we are returning to the Praetorium."

No one argued. No one ever argued with him. They merely fell in behind him obediently as he stormed off in search of the general.

He found him, but the news he delivered seemed to go unbelieved.

The general blinked, as if expecting him to change his story. "Both of them? How can it be that two of the three men that are dead are the Visibullises? Losing one of them would be bad enough–to lose both in one night?"

Titus nodded toward the two lifeless figures his men lowered to the ground. "It was Barabbas. We caught him moments after he took Jason's life. He had rushed to the defense of his father."

The general sighed and raked a hand over his hair. "This will not be an enjoyable task, but I must go inform the women."

"I am coming with you." Titus stepped forward, his fist still closed around the ring. "I spoke with Jason before he died, and he made me swear to give them his messages, and that they would be taken care of."

"Of course they will." The general's voice sounded absent. "The house will remain theirs; they have enough wealth amassed to pay their taxes. And if Abigail has a son, it will be made all the easier."

Titus only nodded silently and started walking. The general fell in beside him. After a moment of silence, the elder said, "You did well in apprehending Barabbas, Titus. You and your men will receive commendation."

"I will see him crucified for this. Allow me to be there when he is executed, Lord."

"Of course. But you are leaving in a few weeks–"

"I would stay another six months in this infested pit if it was to see that barbarian meet justice." Emotions crowded his mind, but he pushed them away. He was granite. He was ice. "He will pay for what he has done this night."

"Indeed."

They arrived at the Visibullis house and approached the front entrance, pounded on the door. A voice called out from within asking who it was.

"The general and Titus Asinius," Titus answered.

He heard the bar being removed, and a moment later the heavy door opened. Cleopas's man stood before them then, his face unyielding, as though already knowing what news they brought and refusing it. He stepped aside to let them in.

The commotion had brought the others out into the vestibule, and Titus looked around uncomfortably at the collection of Hebrews that remained of the Visibullises. The general cleared his throat and turned to Ester.

"Which one?" Her lips already trembled, her eyes already filled.

He reached out and took her hand. "Both of them, Ester." Before he could say more, she fell against him sobbing.

When Titus glanced at Abigail, however, he found her frozen. Her eyes turned toward him. "No. It cannot be."

He stepped toward her, wondering if she would crumble as her mother had and what he would do if she did. "I am sorry, Abigail. Cleopas was struck down, and Jason rushed to his rescue. He would have killed the man, but a stone crumbled in his path, and he fell. I was not near enough to save him, but I spoke to him. He said to tell you both that he loved you, that Cleopas did not suffer, and that–" he found he had to swallow before he could go on. The intense gaze from her unblinking eyes was unnerving. "He said to tell you he was sorry he would not meet your babe. That you were the sun, moon, and stars to him. And to give this," he said, holding out the ring, "to a boy. That he is his son, and he would have adopted him. I know not what that means."

"I do." Calmly, she crouched down. It was only then that Titus spotted the child behind her. Too beautiful to be innocent, surely . . . what was he doing in Jason's home? "Samuel," he heard her say to the child as she handed him the gold, "this is for you, from Jason. He wishes you to have it, because he loves you and wishes you to be his son."

The boy did not ask where Jason was now. He did not ask about the ring. He simply took it silently, clutching it in tiny hands, and wrapped his arms around Abigail's neck. Titus stood by all the while feeling out of place and dissatisfied with these proceedings. But then Abigail released the boy, struggled back onto her feet, and turned with the same calm back to him.

Now her eyes looked to burn, but with fire instead of water. Suddenly, he understood her. She would not crumble. She would force others to. "Who killed my husband?" she demanded quietly.

"Barabbas. We have him in custody, and he will be punished."

"You will tell me when he is scheduled to die." Her voice would have sent a shiver down a spine made of weaker stuff than Titus's.

He just nodded. "I will. Abigail, you will be taken care of. Know that."

Abigail met his gaze. "You promised him, or you would not care what became of me. Do not pretend it is otherwise."

Titus could not explain why the truth offended him so much. "You carry his son. Of course I care what becomes of you."

"No, you care what becomes of his son, and only because now it is the only child he will have. You said I would ruin his life." She lifted her chin and gazed coldly at him. "It would seem Rome did that without any help from me."

"It was the rebels who did it." Titus kept his voice quiet, so that only she would hear. "Jason died honorably."

"He was living honorably," she hissed back, "which is what is of import."

Titus was silent for a moment, watching her eyes as a storm moved through them. He found it echoed with him. Seeing that the general was pulling away from Ester, he drew in a breath. "These past months Jason was happy. I saw that. And now, knowing they were his last, I do not begrudge him what made him so content. I–I am glad he married you."

She made no acknowledgment of the difficult words, did not look at him again. He seemed to have lost her somewhere, to some mist that swirled in her eyes and obscured any light within. He took the opportunity to leave her.

He went to Ester, took her hand in his. "Your husband did not suffer, and he died with honor. As did Jason, in Cleopas's defense. He said to tell you he loved you."

Ester nodded, but he was not certain she actually heard him. She looked ready to collapse.

"We have much to attend to." The general encompassed Abigail in his glance, though he had not said anything to her. "I will have someone bring you their bodies. And Ester, I will see that Julia comes to you in the morning."

Ester made no response, just turned into Abigail and started crying anew. Titus turned and fled the house, in need of fresh air.

"She will not recover easily from this," the general said from beside him, presumably of Ester. He sighed. "At least Abigail did not fall apart. She will be able to support her mistress–mother. Whichever she calls her now."

Titus did not reply. He had nothing left to say.

TWENTY-THREE

Abigail sat by the bed, eyes on Ester without seeing her still form. Ten days after their world fell apart, and yet another loss loomed. For a week Ester had merely sat, listless and disinterested in life. Then the fever had come. These last three days had been a blur of delirium and thrashing limbs. They had called in several physicians already and had even sent for Cleopas's cousin Drusus.

Abigail closed her eyes and let out a shuddering breath. What more would Jehovah take? He had already snatched a father, a mother, a best friend. And now another father, a husband. Would he take another mother as well? Then what? Her babe? Would he strip her of all that mattered before finally ending her misery?

The others went about their duties, prepared for Passover. As if anything mattered. As if anything existed but this yawning emptiness inside.

A glance outside at the angle of the sun told her that Dinah would be in soon to urge some broth past Ester's lips. She did not feel like speaking to her friend, hearing yet another reprimand about how she needed to rest more, eat more, preserve the Visibullis child in her womb. Abigail lived only for the babe, but she was tired of the constant hovering. She stood, intending to escape.

A wave of dizziness washed over her, and she gripped the door post. So many images swam before her eyes. Jason, in the last moments she ever saw him, armed in his centurion's garb with a sober expression on his face. The shattering in Ester's eyes as she heard that the two most precious beings in the world to her had been slain. Titus, standing there so cold and unfeeling while he delivered the news that ripped them apart.

Raw emotion bubbled up and nearly choked her. She should not be so angry with him for being the one to tell her. She knew that. But still it boiled within her.

"Abigail?"

She opened her eyes again at the familiar voice and blinked at Andrew. Part of her wanted to feel the warmth of friendship when she looked at him, perhaps even love. But the bigger part wanted to look away. Seeing him reminded her only of her guilt.

He sighed. "You need to rest."

Everyone seemed to think resting would solve everything. No one stopped to consider the demons that haunted her sleep.

◊

Andrew watched Abigail wobble and did not hesitate. He scooped her up in his arms, then carried her to the room where Jason's presence was still so palpable. She had not removed any of his things, and Andrew had to stifle the desire to scream when he entered. Controlling the urge, he put her gently on the bed. "You must rest, dear one.

You have the babe to think of. It will not be long now before your child is born, and you are in no condition to go through a birth."

"I cannot think of that right now." Her features were sunken, her frame shrunken so that her large stomach stood out and made her look fragile beneath it. "Andrew, how did this happen? How, in a single night, did the entire fabric of our universe unravel?" Her eyes were staring straight up at the ceiling as she spoke. Then she squeezed them shut and lifted a hand to rub at them. "I cannot believe they are gone."

Andrew beheld her silently for a moment, sitting beside her. "Did you come to love him so much, Abigail?"

"No." Her voice was choked. "And that is wormwood to me. I wanted to love him. He had changed so, turned into such a good man, Andrew. He loved me very much, and he did so much to earn my affections." She shook her head, looking miserable. "If we had had more time–perhaps he would have overcome my last reserve."

That was not what he wanted to hear. He took her hand in one of his and ran the knuckles of the other softly over her cheek. "Abigail, I must know: do you still love me?"

She looked at him at last. He searched her eyes for the Abigail he knew, the Abigail full of life and intelligence and wonder. In her place, he saw a woman with no hope, no feeling, no desires at all. But then she smiled at him, and though it was but an echo as from afar off, he saw a sparkle of his old Abigail there. It was enough for him. "I will always love you, Andrew. How can you ask?"

"These past months we have lived separate lives. You are a mistress now, a wife, now a widow. I am still a slave."

"You are still my friend."

He lifted her hand to his lips. "I wish I had the right to ask you to be mine, dear one. But it is surely not possible now. You cannot marry a slave when you are mother to the heir to the Visibullis wealth."

"If it is a girl, then this physician cousin will gain it all, anyway." Her eyes moved to his once more, and she squeezed his hand. "Let us see, Andrew. My mourning has many days left, and I need them. Perhaps. . . ."

"Yes, perhaps." Andrew smiled sincerely for the first time since he was told of her impending wedding.

&

Menelaus walked into the barracks where the centurions resided, scanning the selection of men until he found the one he wanted. He approached Titus with squared shoulders. It seemed as though they had nothing in common now that Jason was gone. Lentulus and Apidius had made no attempt to spend time with them. It was as though, even when not around them much, Jason had been the element that bound them together.

To Menelaus, it felt like an affront to his friend's memory to tolerate the distance between those of them remaining. Still, he suspected it was hopeless. Titus would be leaving in a fortnight, heading back to Rome. Apidius would be transferred to Corinth within six months. A chapter of his life was over permanently, and he had a feeling those to follow would never be as carefree as this past one.

"Titus."

The man looked up, his expression softening slightly. "Menelaus."

"I am going to offer my condolences to Abigail and Ester. I did not want to go too soon, but I have heard that Ester is ill."

Titus nodded. "Tell Abigail about the crucifixion."

Menelaus nearly growled. "Tell her yourself. You are coming with me. Apidius and Lentulus refused, and it is shameful. We were his friends, and we have shown no respect."

Titus did not even look up. "I put in an appearance at the burial. But it is a bit hard to go and talk to someone about how nicely the weather is warming up when the last time one spoke to said person was in telling her that her husband is dead."

"Jason would expect it."

Titus cursed and threw down the piece of leather he had been working. "Jason would understand. It was his greatest virtue. He never pushed points."

"Of course he did! He manipulated you more than anyone, Titus. In the name of Jove, he was getting paid by your father."

"You think I do not know that?" Titus spread his palms flat against the table. "You think I do not realize my father thought of Jason as the perfect son? I need no reminders of his charms. Just as I do not need you to tell me what he would expect of me. I have gone to the authorities to make sure the house would not be taken away from them. *That* is what he asked me to see to."

Menelaus pointed a finger."No, he asked you to be sure they were taken care of, and that includes more than the roof over their heads. Ester could be dying. Will you live with the guilt if she dies, and you have done nothing to be sure she was getting the proper care?"

Titus cursed again, but this time it rang with defeat. He stood. "Let us go." He pushed past Menelaus and stomped from the room. The others smartly moved out of his way, and Menelaus followed in his wake.

Outside, they discovered quickly that the streets leading from the northern gate were not sympathetic to their plan. They were clogged with people, townspeople who usually moved far out of their way to avoid the Roman soldiers. Today, they ignored their existence.

"Are those palm branches?" Menelaus looked in disbelief at the street over a woman's shoulder. "What, is there some prince visiting today that we have not heard of?"

"It is Messiah!" a woman proclaimed as if in answer to his question, pointing in the distance at a point he could not make out. "Hosanna! Hosanna! Blessed be the name of the Lord! Hosanna!"

She was not the only one calling out, shouting with joy at the approach of whomever it was they called Messiah.

"Jesus!" another cried nearby.

Menelaus rolled his eyes. "Not him again. Come, let us take the alley."

Titus made no argument. They bypassed the congestion and made their way silently to the house. From the outside, it looked as it always had. But he approached it with the knowledge that within it had become a tomb.

Their knock was answered by the old manservant, who let them in without erasing the concern from his face. "My mistress is unwell and unable to receive visitors. But if you care to sit down, I will fetch Abigail."

Menelaus took the lead with a nod. "Please. How is Ester? The governor mentioned his concerns for her."

He hesitated. "She grows worse, then improves, only to grow worse again. From one hour to the next, we do not know how she will be. But Mistress Julia has been a most faithful friend, coming every afternoon to sit with her and give Abigail a chance to rest."

"The general is fortunate to have such a wife," Menelaus said absently. He had had few causes to interact with Julia.

They were shown into the room where ten months before they had come to dine with Jason. He looked around at where the five of them had sat, where Abigail had served them, dressed in the beautiful garments Jason had bought. Tempting them all, astonishing them all with her conversation. He should have realized then that it was more than a simple affair for Jason. His looks had mixed lust with pride with respect; and that last ingredient guaranteed involvement.

Agitated, he and Titus sat down. Hopefully Abigail would arrive soon so that they could say what needed to be said and leave. Menelaus folded one leg over his knee, then drummed his fingers on it. Titus glared at him and sat completely still, arms crossed over his chest in a way that clearly labeled his reticence.

His attention was snagged when a blur of movement entered the room from the far door, skidding to a halt a few feet within to reveal a boy with eyes wide in shock at their presence.

Menelaus leaned forward with a crooked smile. "Hello, boy. Who are you?"

"Samuel." His voice was not meek, but he advanced no further into the room.

Menelaus's smile grew a bit. "And where did you come from?"

"The tribe of Judah," the boy answered.

Menelaus glanced over at his companion. Titus was looking at the child with a complete lack of humor. It was obvious he had no desire to participate in the inquisition. Menelaus turned back to the child. "Are you a servant here?"

Samuel nodded, sending curls scattering momentarily, then coming to rest in the exact places they had been. "I serve my mistress, Abigail. She is having a baby. My master Jason bought me, but then he went away. It made me sad because he was kind and brought me here, and now my mistress does not smile." His golden brows drew together. "That is very sad. She smiles very nicely."

"Samuel." Abigail's voice came from the other entrance. She was smiling now, or at least hinting at it. She held out a hand, and Samuel rushed to close the distance between them. He attached himself to her side.

Abigail turned her attention to Menelaus and Titus only when Samuel was with her. "I am sorry Ester is not able to receive you. She is finally sleeping peacefully, and I could not disturb her, though she would certainly be glad to know you have come."

Menelaus decided to ignore the ice in her voice. "We heard she was ill. Is there anything we can do? We could send over the Roman physician–"

Abigail raised a hand to halt his offer. "The general already offered, and the physician has come and gone. There is nothing he can do; he says the illness comes from her desire for it and will not leave until she wills it. We have sent for Cleopas's cousin, who is also a physician, in the hopes that a familiar face will stir her. He should be here in a week."

Menelaus could only nod. Titus unfolded his arms, his face still expressionless, impassable. "I hope she recovers. Have you heard the news of Barabbas?"

Abigail shook her head, eyes going sharp. "The general will not speak of such things to Julia, and she is the only one who has come recently."

Titus looked proud when he said, "He will be crucified. The last day of next week, during your Passover. The general thought it–appropriate."

"And Titus gets to stand and watch him die from beneath the cross." All kinds of envy sprang up in Menelaus at the reminder. "As his last official duty before heading back to Rome. He receives all the blessings."

He expected her to pale at the mention of such a thirst for blood, but she did not. She simply nodded and said, "May your return to Rome be safe, Titus. Menelaus, you will of course always be welcome here. Jason always named you as his closest friend."

Menelaus darted a glance at Titus to see if the words, obviously meant to prick him, had any effect. There was none to be seen, of course, but he still wondered if she simply held a grudge against his friend for being the bearer of the evil news. If not, she should have disliked him just as much; he had been as much her enemy as Titus.

Abigail was apparently thinking the same thing, for she continued, "Which is why it grieved him so much, at the end, that you withdrew from him to the extent that you did." She drew herself up. "If there is nothing else, I should return to my mother. Thank you for coming."

He stood, not really wanting to stay, but offended nonetheless at the dismissal.

Titus must have agreed. With his most Stoic mask in place, he rose to his feet. "Abigail. Why did Jason buy the boy?"

Abigail stopped in her retreat from the room, spun, and speared him with her gaze. "Because Samuel needed a home, and Jason was a good man. Why would *you* buy a boy?"

Titus did not so much as look down at the child who still stood protected in the folds of Abigail's garment. "I would not."

"No." Abigail searched his face as though for a hidden wellspring that she found not there, or dry. She sounded vaguely disappointed when she said, "You would not. Good day, Titus. Menelaus."

This time, they let her go. Menelaus moved closer to his friend. "He is a beautiful child. He looks like a catamite."

Titus snorted. "I suspect that was Abigail's point in mentioning that Jason was a good man. I would wager that our friend bought the child to keep him from such a fate." He shook his head. "His heart had become soft."

"I know." Menelaus sighed. "He became a better man than I can ever hope to be."

Titus glared at him for a moment, then just rolled his eyes and strode toward the door.

TWENTY-FOUR

They had never gotten to finish their conversation. It was her fault, and it ate at her. He had looked so sincere as he spoke of the man he called Christ, so genuine in his desire that she listen. And Ester had ignored him. The topic made her uneasy, and she had stated that she was tired. He was always such a gentle man. He had looked at her, knowing she lied, but he had not forced the issue. He knew it would do no good, that the more he pushed, the farther she would flee from his words.

She had thought, as she lay in bed beside him that night, falling into the realm of slumber, that someday she would have to listen. To keep putting him off when he brought up the teacher would eventually anger him. So the next time, she would at least hear him out.

Now there was no next time at all. How cruel was God to snatch her husband away when there remained something unfinished between them? And to take as well her son, the only other one who had heard Cleopas's words and would be able to explain them to her? She did not want to live without Cleopas. She *could* not live, knowing in his last moments he was disappointed in her. Jehovah was supposed to be merciful as well as just–where was his mercy when he stripped a woman of both husband and son in one fell blow, leaving her alone, forsaken, and unforgiven?

She wanted to escape it, needed to escape it, but could not. She tried to do so by turning inward, forgetting the presence of the world in which those dearest to her were no more. But inside, it was no better. Her mind was tormented.

She could hear Abigail's voice continually, calling her back, begging her to return. But she could not. For her daughter's sake she would, but there was so much else to be battled. And how could she look at Abigail, large with child, and know that the babe's father would never again smile at them? How could she look at the boy Jason had brought home and not see the compassion that had been shining in her son's eyes, now extinguished?

Why did God take two men who were strong and good, who were working for righteousness and pursuing His precepts, and leave the murderous, traitorous wretches unharmed? It was not fair. And was it wise? The more good men he took, the fewer there would be to teach the rest of them. Now there was no one to lead her, no one to love her.

She wanted to die. But on the other hand, she feared death as she feared nothing else. Was she good enough, clean enough, righteous enough to enter Paradise, or would she be thrown into the pit of weeping and gnashing of teeth?

She wanted Cleopas. She wanted Jason. She wanted Abigail's sweet voice to tell her it had all been a cruel joke, that they were well and sitting beside her. Then she would return. She would open her eyes. She would live again. Only then.

Abigail sighed when Ester moaned. There had been so many days with no changes in her. Abigail felt the tears of frustration welling up. She wanted to lash out, at the world, at Ester, at anyone. She wanted to demand that the woman she loved so much love her in return, love her enough to fight. She wanted to demand that Ester give her babe a chance to know her.

But nothing worked. No pleas, no words, nothing could touch the widow who through sickness of heart and body now looked so old and weak. And though Abigail knew it was selfish, she hurt to realize she did not mean enough to Ester to call her back. She was angry with the woman for taking the easy path when she herself did not have that option. She had to live for her child. Should not Ester have to live for *her*?

But she was not Ester's child. That became very clear. No matter how many times Ester claimed she was a daughter, no matter how much she rejoiced when the marriage to Jason made it legally so, she very simply was not. Ester's love for her did not run so deep. It was not enough to combat the pain of her loss.

Perhaps it would have been better for them all if Cleopas had never come to Silas's house, had never bought her. Then she would not have been compelled to love again, to open her heart to these people that would only leave her, as her father had done, as her mother. If she had just remained closed off, this would not hurt so much. It would be better to be a simple slave, working in a kitchen somewhere with no other cares. Then she would not be educated enough to recognize her own inadequacy, she would not be praying so fervently that her child was a son to carry on the Visibullis legacy.

She prayed more too–she prayed a curse upon the man who had done this to her. Barabbas. Every time she thought the name, new rage boiled up inside her. Barabbas. The Son of a Father had taken away both a father and a son, had left her son fatherless, had left her mother sonless. And for what? Did he actually expect to liberate Jerusalem from Rome? Was he fool enough not to realize that even if he gained control of the walls, of the Praetorium, there would be more soldiers that came to win them back? Rome was too large, too mighty, and too prideful to let a band of outlaws take over one of their legions. Fighting was useless. Until God gave them their nation back, it could not be won.

She took a modicum of comfort in knowing that Barabbas would meet the penalty for his murders. And on the dawn of the day when the execution was scheduled, Abigail awoke knowing she would find a way to be there. No one would want to let her, but she would not be stopped. She would go outside the walls of the city, climb the hill to Golgotha, and be there when the destroyer hanged.

When she entered the kitchen, the others were there already, talking among themselves. After the Passover meal the night before, for which she could not stay awake, she expected them to all be solemn and introspective. Instead, there was an air of anticipation in the room. When she entered, Andrew turned to her with a smile.

"Drusus is at the gates. I must go meet him and lead him here. And it seems there is some excitement in the city today: Jesus whom they call Christ has been arrested."

Abigail sighed. "Why do they arrest a teacher?"

Dinah gave a dry laugh. "Because he offends the Sanhedran and proclaims himself Messiah. The difficult part will be finding something to convict him of before the court of Pilate. Simon was out in the markets today and heard the talk. He will be brought to the Fortress of Antonia soon, where Pilate will pass judgement on him, as well as the other criminals who are to be crucified today."

Barabbas. Abigail straightened, suddenly determined. "I am going."

Her announcement was met with a moment of silence followed by an explosion. Andrew's arguments were the loudest. "You cannot go out into the crowds in your condition, Abigail, it is absurd! And besides, I have to meet Drusus, and Simon is needed here."

She leveled a gaze at him filled with all the defiance that filled her. "I do not need an escort. And I do not need your approval. I have not left this house in a fortnight, and I am about to go mad. You have heard Ester in her delirium–she is troubled by Cleopas's opinions about this rabbi. I will go and find out what becomes of him; perhaps some new information will settle her mind. Have you thought of that?"

They apparently had not, as it silenced them momentarily. Then Dinah insisted, "You still cannot go alone, dear one. It is not safe. Simon said a mob is growing–"

"Then no one will take notice of one small woman with child, will they?" Abigail grabbed her head covering from where it sat nearby and draped it over her hair. Not waiting for a response, she headed for the door. "Dinah, you will watch Samuel for me, will you not?"

Andrew was only a step behind her. "Abigail, this is foolish. Go back inside."

"No." She inclined her head a bit so she could look over at him but kept walking. "You can walk with me until our paths separate, if it will make you feel better."

"Why are you so determined?" He put a restraining hand on her arm that she simply shrugged away from.

She knew that to give him her real reasons would result in being physically forced back to the house. He would not approve of her lust for revenge. "I already told you."

"Abigail, be reasonable."

She turned on him, spinning around and letting him see the rage she had been so careful to hide. "I have been reasonable all of my life, Andrew. I was reasonable when I was sold. I was reasonable when my master insisted I learn. I was reasonable when their son took me to his bed. I was reasonable when I was given to him, I was reasonable when I married him. I have had to be reasonable in the face of his death. What has reason ever done for me? I am educated enough to know how miserable I am, but too weak to do anything about it. Well today I will act like the mistress Jason made me. I will go where I please." She spun around again and stalked off.

She got only a few steps away before Andrew was back at her side. "I am sorry for pushing you," he said quietly. "But I am only concerned for you, my friend. Be careful, keep yourself safe, and leave if things get volatile. Promise me."

"Of course I will." She placed a hand on her unborn child. "I have the babe to think of. I am merely stifled and curious."

"I understand." He smiled and lightly touched her shoulder. "I must part from you here. Be cautious, and do not be long. Ester will miss you, and Drusus may wish to speak with you about her, as you have attended her the most."

"I will not be long." She gave him what she hoped was a reassuring smile. When he headed for the gate where the cousin would be, she turned toward the Fortress of Antonia. Her thoughts were not long on Andrew or the traveler he would meet.

The closer she got to her destination, the thicker the crowds became. As she made her way to the court of the building, she heard a roar go up from the mob gathered outside, and she increased her pace. She ended up on the edges of the assembly, near one of the entries into the fortress. She asked a man near her what was happening.

"Jesus of Nazareth was tried before the Sanhedran this morning." His face betrayed his agitation. She could not tell if he approved or disapproved. "He was convicted of blasphemy and brought here. Pilate sent him away once already, to Herod, who sent him back. He has only just arrived again. He is there." He pointed to the balcony overlooking the crowd, where she recognized Pilate seated. Guards held a man nearby; the prisoner had been beaten badly and could barely stand. From the distance, she could not see the rabbi's features.

Pilate appeared to be putting a question to Jesus, but the man just turned his head away, refusing to answer. Abigail's brows came together. She had met Pilate several times and knew him to be a man eager to please. The question today would be which group he wanted to placate.

"Rumor has it," someone said from the other side of her, obviously to whomever would listen, "that Pilate's wife had a dream last night warning him not to get involved with this man's sentence."

"She would," Abigail said under her breath. "She has dreams about everything." Someone nearby chuckled.

Pilate rose at that moment, moving to face the crowd. "I find no guilt in this man!" he proclaimed, loudly enough to gain the attention of the masses, who hushed to hear him. "But your courts have found him guilty. Shall I release him to you for the Passover?"

A deafening roar went up, and Abigail could not make out what they were calling for. Her head began its customary throb behind her eyes at the noise.

Pilate could apparently hear better from his position than she could from hers, for his face adopted a look of confusion at what met his ears. "Shall I release the teacher," he inquired again, "or Barabbas?"

She felt her face freeze. Surely he would not, could not release the leader of the rebellion against Rome. It could not even be an option. But she watched as another man was thrust forward by the centurions, one of which she recognized as Titus, even from this distance.

This time, the crowd was silent for a heartbeat before responding, and this time, their pleas were intelligible even to Abigail. It started in many places throughout the crowd. She could hear the voices, hissing around her. One man spoke from right behind her, commanding over her head, "Call for Barabbas!"

"No!" She wheeled around even as the people took up the chant.

"Give us Barabbas!"

Pilate looked as uncomfortable as Abigail felt, obviously not anticipating this response. He glanced over his shoulder at Jesus. "What shall I do with the man they call the King of the Jews?"

Again, it was a hiss of prompting that preceded the crowd's shouts of "Crucify him!"

Abigail could feel her hatred curling up within her, pounding with every beat of blood through her veins, rising and rising until she had no choice but to scream. "No! Kill Barabbas! Spare the teacher!"

Her voice was lost in the continuing thundering from the people, but the prompter behind her must have heard her. "Quiet, woman!"

She turned to face him and saw a man whose dress labeled him as a religious leader. Her fury now had a focal point. "I will not! What has the teacher done to deserve death? Nothing!"

The man was aged, but robust. His gray hair and beard were still full, and his face was hard and unforgiving. "The decision has been made, woman. Barabbas is being released, and Jesus will be crucified."

"No!" Her voice choked on the sob of rage in her throat.

The religious leader looked disgusted with her. "Stay out of politics, wench. Go home to your husband."

A heated gush of breath brought words spewing forth. "My husband is dead. And the man you just insisted be released so that your political agenda could be met is the man who killed him."

The man's cold eyes narrowed. "Barabbas killed no one but Roman wretches."

"He killed my husband! He killed his father! They were the best men I knew–"

"Roman whore!" The man recoiled from her as if from a serpent. His eyes flew to her stomach. "Is it a Roman whelp, too?"

She was shocked enough by his words to be rendered speechless for a moment. In her second of inaction, the man seized her by the arm and began pulling her toward the doorway that would lead into the fortress. "I will show you what traitors deserve." He dragged her unwilling form where he wanted it. No one took any notice, just cleared out of the leader's way and then filled the gap when he went by.

"Let me go! You are hurting me!" His hand was in a death lock on her arm, and the more she struggled against his grip, the more bruising it became. He ignored her appeals.

He stopped in front of the exit from the fortress and gave her a jarring shake. "Hold your tongue." Turning with expectation to the opening, they waited only a few seconds before the pounding of footsteps was heard.

Abigail's heart leapt into her throat. She knew now why he had dragged her over here. Barabbas was being released, and this was where the guards would leave him. The murderer would come, and the man beside her would offer her to him, telling him to finish what he started so well during the uprising. For some reason this stranger, this man supposed to lead her people, hated her enough to want her and her child dead. Was it because Jason was Roman? Or because she had objected when he told the crowd to crucify Jesus?

She was inflamed enough to ask but was not given the chance. The commotion within grew louder, and three figures emerged. Her focus was drawn to the central man. He was still dressed as a prisoner. His clothing was old and threadbare, his hair wild and unwashed, and his body bent from hunger and abuse. His face was dazed, and he blinked in the sunlight, the expression he wore one of confusion and astonishment.

"Barabbas," the man holding her said as if he knew the man, "congratulations on your release. Did I not tell you it would work this way?"

Barabbas just looked at the man before him, slumping when the soldiers who had led him out let go of his arms.

The leader pushed Abigail forward, hatred burning in his eyes. "This is what we are all fighting to avoid! A Hebrew wench bearing a Roman whelp. The men you killed were her husband and father."

She expected Barabbas to leer, to lunge, to do something in keeping with the rage that had fueled an uprising. Instead, he looked at her with absent pity. "I am . . ." His voice faded as though he forgot he was speaking. He looked around, his eyes brightening with life and filling with a strange sort of terror.

When they fell on Abigail again, she could not bring herself to throw upon him the hatred she had felt half a minute ago. All she could feel now was the same unbridled panic, the sudden alarm of finding oneself in a situation foreign and unpredicted.

Even before he moved his gaze away from her, Barabbas's feet started moving. Soon, his whole body followed, and he was running away from them and the crowd behind them as quickly as possible. The religious leader snorted in disgust and strode back into the crowd. Abigail stood where she was left, staring after the retreating figure of her husband's killer.

"Go home, Abigail." The voice was cold and angry, and its familiarity did not register until she looked over to find Titus only a few feet away, his face a thunderhead of wrath. She could understand it. He wanted to watch the death of a man and instead had been ordered to set him free. Yes, she could understand it. But quite suddenly her soul was an empty chasm in which such emotions vanished in their endless search for a resting place. She stared at him as if not comprehending his words.

"Go home. This is no place for you." When still she stood immobile, he growled. "Now! I have no time to see you to safety. I must supervise the crucifixions."

She nodded, even turned away from him, put one foot in front of the other. But she knew not where she was going. Home lay somewhere in that direction, but it was on the other side of a sea of people who would not part for her and was still cheering.

"Crucify Jesus!" she heard them shouting.

"His blood will not be on my hands." Pilate dipped his hands in a basin of water.

"Let his blood be on us and our children!" someone called out loudly. The new chant was taken up.

Abigail closed her eyes. Why would they wish the blood of an innocent man upon their people? She did not want her child to suffer for their desires. *She* did not want to suffer for their unwise choices. For centuries, her people had been paying the prices of their fathers' sins. It had to end. She did not wish the death of the teacher. She did not know him, she could not judge him. Why did these people decide they could?

Tired, drained of her anger, all she wanted was to go home. She wanted to sit beside Ester, she wanted Dinah to force her to eat, she wanted Andrew to admonish her for her foolish foray that had come to nothing. She would tell the sad news, and they would sit together quietly, wondering what Cleopas would have said, what Jason may have thought of it. What did it mean, that their Christ stood defeated?

But nowhere in the Holy Scriptures themselves have I heard or read of a king come to triumph over nations. I have heard only of a savior come to be defeated. . . It would not be an absolute defeat, friend, just an apparent one.

Her own words from over a year ago echoed now through her mind. Giving up her endless struggle through the masses, she paused in thought. What was it the Scriptures said of the messiah? She did not remember so clearly anymore. She had not studied the Law much in the past year, she had thought about it no more often. Could it be that her master was right? Could this possibly be the fulfillment of the prophesied victorious defeat?

She could not know. She was no interpreter of prophecies, and there was no one to teach her now. Overwhelming helplessness welled up in her then, and her shoulders sagged.

The crowd surged. Caught in their midst, Abigail had no choice but to follow or be trampled. She did not know where they were going and could not bring herself to ask anyone. Each face she looked into was unconscious of all but the excitement. Cries still leapt from throats, arms were thrown up as if in celebration, and everyone pushed forward at once.

She was smaller than most of those around her, men who ignored her presence, and she could see nothing of where she was going. Soon, though, she knew. She had come out this morning intending to make this journey, and her plans were to be fulfilled after all. They were headed out of the city, to Calvary. There, the holes were already dug for the crosses. There, more people were already gathered for the day's spectacle. She began to feel sick.

The journey seemed to last for hours, though it could not have been very long at all before they all arrived at their destination. Once there, the mob dispersed, everyone going to find a good place to watch the executions. What was it about the grisly display that drew men so? It was a well documented phenomena–even Plato had discussed it in Socrates' voice, speaking of the raging battle within a being that inspired him to watch the horror even while another part shrunk from it.

Abigail shrank entirely. She did not want to be here. Maybe now that the crowd had loosened, she would be able to go home. She turned back quickly toward Jerusalem to pursue that theory and ran headlong into a solid body. The man reached out to steady her.

"Careful," he said in a voice far softer than the others she had been hearing all morning.

Abigail looked up into his face. It was familiar, though it took her a long moment to place him. "Jairus?"

The man's brows drew together even as his hands dropped from her arms. "Do I know you?"

She shook her head. "I met you once, a year ago. I am Ester's companion. You told us of your daughter."

"Ah!" He smiled, the expression looking out of place with the milling mob as a backdrop. "I remember you now. You have changed."

She flushed, her hands moving automatically to her abdomen. "I married her son. He and Cleopas were both killed in the uprising."

Jairus looked shocked by the news. "I had not heard. I knew Roman soldiers were killed, I knew that one was a high official. If I had known, I would have come. How is Ester?"

"Not well." She shook her head "She has no will to live. I fear for her. Perhaps it would do her good to see a face from her past."

"Of course. I will try to come this afternoon. If I cannot make it, then the first of the week, after the Sabbath." Then his brows drew together again as he surveyed her condition. "You should not be here, my friend."

The reminder of where she was brought the agitation back. "I know. I was caught in the crowd. I am on my way back now."

But Jairus shook his head and pointed to the road leading back into Jerusalem.

There were figures on it marching with military precision, and the sound of a drum could be heard faintly over the many voices around her. "They are coming with the prisoners. There will be no escaping now. I would take you home, but I . . ." He hesitated, looking distraught. "This man changed my life. I must be here. So many are here in hate, I want to try to balance it. I want to see what becomes of Jesus."

Abigail nodded wearily. "Cleopas believed he was the messiah."

"I would have gotten along well with Cleopas," Jairus mused, as if to himself. Then he shook himself. "Stay by my side, my friend. This mob is unpredictable, and I would not forgive myself if something happened to Ester's daughter."

"Thank you." Tears sprang to her eyes. She blinked them away and swallowed with difficulty.

Jairus put a hand on the small of her back to guide her in the direction he had been going before their collision. "We will stand there," he said, pointing. "I know the routes they take, and it will put us on the edge of where they will walk. We will be near when they pass by, and I will be able to see my savior once more before they–the crosses will go there," he interrupted himself, pointing at the top of the hill, uncomfortably near where they stopped.

Abigail nodded numbly, staring with revulsion at the spot where in a few minutes men would hang. Right now it was empty but somehow ominous, much like the dark clouds gathering on the horizon.

The drums grew louder as the procession neared, and a deadly hush fell over the crowd. It parted around the path, and Abigail realized with horror that Jairus had been right in his predictions–they were suddenly on the very edge of the mass of onlookers, standing with toes on the road. She wanted to close her eyes against the coming visions but knew she could not. She was here, so she must watch. She must watch so she could tell of the event to her family. They would be worried about her, and she would give them the full explanation. Eyes wide and aware, Abigail turned with her protector to catch sight of the soldiers and the prisoners in their midst.

TWENTY-FIVE

Andrew had met Drusus only a handful of times over the years he had served Cleopas; the cousins had never been friends but had kept up a hint of the connection for the sake of their family name. Now, he expected the man to arrive with a swagger–if Abigail's child was a girl, Drusus would stand to inherit the entire Visibullis estate, a property considerable and expansive, including not only the house and land in Jerusalem, but also all that in Rome.

But Drusus arrived with no knowing smile, with no strut in his step. He arrived tired and obviously worried, a man quite different from the one Andrew had met before.

"I am sorry I was so long in coming," the physician said as he and Andrew hurried through the city, taking back alleys to avoid the crowds flocking the government buildings. "I planned to set out the day I received your first missive, but my wife fell ill. She, too, passed away only a week ago."

Shame mounted fast. "Lord, we did not realize. We would not have sent for you–"

Drusus halted his apology with a raised hand. "She was a bitter and tired woman. I would be lying if I said it were not a relief. But I had to see to the arrangements, the funeral. I set out for Jerusalem as soon as I decently could. How does your mistress fare?"

"Not well, Lord. Some hours, she is peaceful and her fever lets up, others she tosses in delirium and burns to the touch. The doctor who has already come says it is her mind causing the affliction, and that treating her body is useless. I fear he is right."

Drusus sighed, raking a hand through his gray hair. He looked weary. "Let us pray if it is the case, we can find a way to treat her soul." They walked a few steps in silence. "And Jason's wife? How is she and the child?"

Andrew listened carefully to the tone of voice and found no fault in his concern. "Both are healthy as far as we can tell. Abigail has been very tired throughout these months, and the worry of our mistress has only made it worse this past fortnight. She should deliver soon."

Drusus nodded. "Let us pray it is a son. Cleopas deserves an heir. I have none, and if the estates were to come to me, they would also end with me. I do not want the Visibullis name to perish along with this generation."

Andrew nodded in understanding, pleased that the man realized it was more a matter of family than self.

They were near the house, then, and entered quickly, with no ado. Drusus insisted that he be shown to Ester at once.

He sat with her for ten minutes; she was in one of her incoherent phases of delirium. Andrew stood with Simon and Dinah outside in the hallway while he questioned her, felt the pulse in her wrist, and tested her forehead with a knowing hand. Then he was silent and still, obviously contemplating. At last, he stood and moved into the hall.

"I dare to agree with the other physician," he told them. "She is troubled and sick of heart. We need to get her away from this house for a while. Every time she opens her eyes, she sees what Cleopas gave her, the room she delivered her son in. Simon, make arrangements to leave here. The sooner the better. I would like to start today, before the Sabbath. I have a friend with an inn outside the city. It is pleasant and quiet, and very peaceful. I think it would be a good place for her to go for a while."

No one objected. In fact, they all sprang into action. Simon headed out to make the travel arrangements, Dinah set about getting food for the short trip and otherwise closing the kitchen, and Andrew began to pack for Ester, since Abigail had not yet returned.

"Where is her daughter?" Drusus asked after a half an hour had gone by. Andrew had finished his self-assigned task and was ready to head to his own chamber to pack for himself.

He sighed and shook his head. "She was going to watch the trial of the teacher we heard while visiting you in Ephraim. She would not listen when we told her it was unwise. But she should be returning soon."

"Good. We need to leave soon. I do not like the look of that storm moving in. It will only take us an hour to reach the inn, but the clouds say that may be barely enough time." He turned to Ester once more, and his brows flew up. "Who is that?"

Andrew turned to see Samuel had joined Ester on the bed and was caressing her temple with a small hand. He smiled. "Abigail's servant, Samuel. Though he is more her son now. The young master purchased him not long before the uprising. He has been an amazing comfort to us all."

Drusus smiled for the first time, erasing some of the tension in his visage. "He appears to have a gift for soothing. Ester has quieted." He chuckled. "A future physician if ever I saw one."

Andrew surveyed the peaceful scene for a moment, then began to worry once more. Abigail had been gone too long already.

Titus awoke that morning hungry for revenge. It was not sated because of the command of a fickle crowd. It only shifted in its focus. When Barabbas was set free, when he was given the order to see the man outside, he knew he would still have his lust fulfilled, even if he had to track to him down like a deer and kill him himself. And then he would see that Pilate, that Herod, that the religious leaders, that Jerusalem itself felt the force of his rage. When he returned to Rome, he would play in politics as his father wished, and he would set the entire force of the empire on the proud little nation that thought it just to crucify a teacher who taught lessons they did not like.

Had the fools never read Plato? Did they think they were the first to execute a man for saying things that offended the elect? What did it do to Socrates but make him a martyr, a symbol for centuries to come? If they wanted a man to be forgotten, they should not deal with him publicly. The fact that these rulers of the synagogue could not figure that out did not speak well of them to Titus.

But he released Barabbas because to do otherwise would result in punishment. He went back in to see to the one who took his place. But inside, he wanted nothing to do with the man they called King of the Jews.

It was his job to lead the man to the Praetorium. He did so hollowly, his face never portraying any emotion. But when the rest of the garrison gathered around and mocked the man, forcing a twisted crown of thorns into his head until the blood dripped down into sorrowful eyes, Titus averted his gaze. It was not the sight of blood that bothered him. It was the sight of blood that should have been Barabbas's.

"Hail, King of the Jews!" One of the soldiers beside him laughed at the ridiculous form the prisoner made, wearing one of the general's scarlet robes that would forever be ruined by the crimson blood. A centurion spat on him, another took up a reed and struck him on the head. Titus listened to the crack of the crown and knew that the blow would have driven the thorns even deeper into the man's head. But the captive only groaned, never fighting back or lashing out like most of the prisoners would have.

"Enough!" Titus stepped forward, hand held up. "Get those off him," he ordered, motioning toward the scarlet robes, "and put his clothes back on. We have a crucifixion to see to."

The men jumped to carry out his words. One soldier pulled off the red cloth, another threw on his original garment. Everyone else prepared for the procession to Golgotha. Within minutes, they were on their way. Outside the Praetorium, they thrust the crosses at the three prisoners being led to execution. Only the third had been so beaten that he could not manage his own cross.

"You." Titus grabbed a man as he walked by. The citizen looked terrified when he looked up into his face, but Titus just tossed him in the general direction of the third cross. "Bear the cross for your king."

The man looked timidly around him, then his gaze rested on Jesus. Instead of uttering a protest, he shouldered the burden and fell into the line. Titus watched with a hint of amazement. He knew it was not his authority that made the man offer no objection. Perhaps he had just taken pity on the creature doubled up in pain.

"March!" The drums began to beat their cadence.

They were just outside the city when the Nazarene stumbled and fell, unable to get up no matter how many prodded him with unmerciful feet.

"Stop it!" Titus roared when one of his men kicked him in the ribs. "He will die on his own soon enough. Pick him up."

But the soldier hesitated. Titus did not give the order again. He merely glared at his comrade and reached down himself to haul the abused man to his feet.

"Forgive him."

Titus froze when he heard the whisper. He looked into the face of his prisoner. One eye was swollen closed, the other bruised but open. The iris that looked at him was a deep brown, filled with improbable compassion. "What?" Titus sucked in a quick breath, unable to believe the man would dare to speak and say something so absurd.

"He knows not what he did." Jesus's words obviously took effort. His lips were broken open.

Titus turned from the face because he could not stand to see the mercy within it. What place did mercy have in this world, where good men were killed while criminals ran free? Why should this condemned teacher tell him to forgive his soldier for something that was not even worth forgiving?

"Forgive him," Jesus whispered again. "He did not wish to be set free."

Titus lifted the man, put an arm around him to support him, and fell back into line. Barabbas–he spoke of Barabbas. But such an order was impossible. And how would he even know to make it? Had he spoken to Barabbas while they were being held? Had the murderer told the teacher that Titus had been the one to drag him into custody?

No. He had been there the whole time. The two had not spoken, though their gazes had held for a long moment. Was it possible. . . ? No. No man read minds. This one must have just been very perceptive. He must have seen how Titus felt toward Barabbas, how angry he had been to have to release him.

Titus felt a burning on his hand, the one that gripped his prisoner. Looking over in mixed irritation and alarm, he wondered what could be causing it. What he saw was a trickle of the man's blood running over his own flesh. Strange. He did not feel the tickle of the fluid, or the bodily heat. No, what he felt was an intense sensation that began at the point of contact and slowly coursed through him. He began to shake.

Jesus looked over at him. They were climbing the hill to Golgotha now, approaching the final scene of his life. He knew it. His one good eye said clearly that he knew it, that there was no escape. But still, those split and broken lips turned up into an expression too pained to be called a smile but nevertheless meant to give comfort.

"It is as they say," he whispered.

Titus did not have to ask what it was they said. The thought had crossed his mind a heartbeat before the man spoke.

Abigail watched the first to pass by. Soldiers, those who would stand guard to be sure the masses did not swarm forward during the execution. They were followed by one of the prisoners. He staggered under the load of the cross that was on his shoulder, but the soldiers that followed had no mercy. The whip lashed out, and curses were hurled in Greek and Latin. The crowd roared out a chorus of derogatory epithets in Hebrew and Greek.

"A thief," Jairus said to Abigail. "He was caught stealing from the tax money bound for Rome."

Abigail nodded, absently rubbing at the ache forming in her lower back. She watched the second group of Romans march by, then the second criminal. He stumbled before them under the burden. One centurion kicked him, another grabbed the cross long enough for the man to stand, then put it back on his shoulders.

Jairus nodded. "One of the rebels caught in the uprising. Caught, I might add, with a considerable amount of gold stolen from a wealthy citizen I know."

"Barabbas would have been in his regular company." Her eyes moved down the row of people marching by in search of the one who had taken his place.

"Indeed. And Jesus, too, though very differently. He spoke to the wretched to give them hope. Now he will die as though one of them."

The third cross came into view, but the man carrying it was obviously not the convicted. He wore clean garments, and he bore the burden with strength. His face, however, betrayed his turmoil. The reason for it soon became clear. Before him staggered the Nazarene, so beaten that he could not walk under his own power, so weakened he would have dropped under the weight of the cross. Abigail could not tear her gaze from the pitiful man. His hair was tangled and matted with dried blood, fresh life oozing from wounds on his face. From the side, Abigail could see that his lips were cracked, his nose bleeding, his eyes swollen. Nausea burst in her stomach, but still she could not look away.

She had never seen the man in person before, certainly never so close. The stories she had heard, the image she had drawn was a far cry from this reality before her. What she saw was a man broken, battered, abused. What she had expected was someone with shoulders thrown back in strength, laughing in the face of the world. From what she could see as he stumbled nearer to her, he was weak—but still, a breath at the back of her neck told her there was more than merely what she could see. Even as he was half dragged along, there was a power in him. A strength that she saw in his silence, something that went deeper than anything she had within herself.

He was close now, only a step away, and Abigail had a horrible fear that he would look at her. Quite suddenly, that thought struck her as unbearable. She knew, knew with every portion of her being, that if he looked at her, he would see her in her completeness. He would see how black her soul had become with sin and hatred and bitterness. He would see all she had done and thought to do and wished herself capable of. He would see that though she wished him spared, it was only so that another could die in his place.

Something within her drew back the closer he got, pulled at her until she wanted to turn and flee to escape his approaching presence. But Jairus was still at her side, gazing silently now at the man before him.

Jesus stumbled on a rock and would have fallen if it had not been for the centurion holding him up. All of her focus, all of her concentration was on the man who was falling toward his knees. Then an arm caught him, and he jerked against gravity. Jesus's head flew back, his eyes turning to heaven and his mouth opening as if to speak.

The action broke open one of his wounds, and his crimson life dripped onto the ground. He was pulled to his feet, and his head was once again jarred. A stray drop of blood arched through the air and landed on the round of Abigail's stomach.

Immediately, she felt a burning on the flesh beneath her garment. It was so quick, so debilitating that she could not even respond. A fire spread through her, devouring her, leaving in its wake a relief that brought tears to her eyes. She looked down at the stain on her clothes in disbelief. It was so small, so insignificant. One little drop of red, a perfect starburst against the faded blue of her woolen tunic.

One little drop to soil her garment.

One little drop to cleanse her soul.

It was gone. The sin, the bitterness, the darkness, the hatred. It was gone, and it did not leave her empty as the disappointment had. It left her filled. Filled with life, filled with hope, filled with *him*.

She sagged against Jairus, willing now that Jesus would look her way. She wanted to look into his eyes, she wanted to cry out her epiphany, she wanted to fall at his feet and worship him. He was the Christ! He was Messiah! He could see her sins, he could see her ugliness, and he could forgive her. The questions of how she would know if he were what he said were suddenly irrelevant. How could anyone not know? How could anyone feel the power of *him* and not realize he was not only *of* God, but that he *was* God?

"Hosanna," Abigail whispered, tears streaming down her cheeks.

"Hosanna," Jairus echoed, behind her now, since he had turned to follow Jesus's progress with his eyes. "Blessed is he who comes in the name of the Lord. Hosanna in the highest!"

"Hallelujah." Abigail sobbed quietly. "It is he. Blessed be the Lord, for he has heard the cries of his children and has answered! Father, forgive my doubt. It is he. It is he!" She fell to her knees with the force of her sudden emotion, and Jairus did not seem to notice. Indeed, he seemed to forget her presence; he wandered away, toward the place where the men would be attached to their crosses. It was a place to which Abigail did not wish to follow.

They stripped the prisoners, dividing their clothes among the centurions that attended them; it was part of the reward for supervising a crucifixion, this piece of clothing that one could keep and take home.

"It is without seam!" One of the three centurions with Titus held up the tunic that Jesus had been wearing. He eyed his companions warily. "It would be a shame to divide it."

Titus growled, shaking his head. "So cast lots. Later. We have a job to do." He motioned toward the crosses.

The other soldiers dropped the clothes and all set about the task. The crosses were laid on the ground, the writhing men held down onto them. Getting the first one into position was not very difficult, but the screams that were torn from his throat as they hammered the spikes through his wrists, then his feet, were enough to throw the second criminal into a fevered pitch of panic. It took four of them to hold him down.

"Just knock him out," Titus suggested from where he stood, hammer and spikes in hand, waiting for them to subdue him.

"And deprive the masses of his cries?" One of the soldiers sneered. "Never. There, we have him. Hurry."

Titus bent down, looking only at the hand in front of him. It was clenched tightly, still trying to turn away from the soldier who grasped him. As soon as Titus touched the spike to his flesh, he let out a blood curdling wail. Titus raised the hammer and drove it with a single blow into the wood of the cross. One more secured it, then he moved to the other side and the other hand. Within moments, the thief was fixed. As two of them lifted the second cross into the second hole, the rest of them moved to the last convict.

"What was he saying to you on the road?" one of his companions asked Titus as they walked the few steps.

"Nothing." Titus knew better than to say the truth to this man. He would not understand that his flesh still burned from where Jesus's blood had touched it, he would not understand the knowledge that had been in that one-eyed gaze. He would not understand that Titus's stomach turned at the thought of having to drive stakes into the wrists of one man when he had not hesitated a minute before.

As it was, another already stood ready with the tools. Titus approached Jesus, who was being stretched out on the wooden beams of the cross. He made no objections, no opposition. He let his arms be extended, his feet put one on top of the other. His good eye moved to Titus, then, when he felt the cold tip of metal against him, he closed his eyes. When the stake pierced, his body jerked with the pain and he emitted a low groan. None of them knew if he was too weary to manage more, or if it was a last show of quiet strength. He was raised, and the cross slid to its place in the ground.

"Let us cast the lots," a soldier proclaimed.

Titus turned from them in disgust.

"We can wait no longer."

Andrew turned to see anxiety written on Drusus's face. "The sky grows darker, and aside from the storm, night will overtake us if we do not leave soon. We have given her hours."

Simon and Andrew looked at each other, exchanging a silent message. Simon nodded. "You are right, Lord, we need to get the mistress moved soon. I will stay and wait for Abigail."

Andrew threw back his shoulders. "I will stay."

Drusus sighed. "Neither of you can stay. You will both be needed to carry Ester's litter."

Andrew ran his tongue over his teeth in thought. "Then we shall just leave her a note. The general promised he would help in any way he could; we will tell her to go to his house and ask one of his servants to accompany her to the inn."

Simon nodded, Drusus looked at him curiously. "A note? She reads?"

Andrew and Simon's gazes met again, and they laughed. "She reads," Simon verified. "I shall fetch some parchment and ink. Andrew, tell the others that we will be going."

"No!"

They all turned to the doorway, where Samuel had approached unheard. "I cannot leave her! I will not!"

"Samuel, she will join us by nightfall." Andrew reached for the boy.

He dodged Andrew's grasp, his eyes wide and frightened. "No. You cannot make me leave! I will not! *I will not!*"

He dashed from the room before any of them could so much as take a step. Andrew took off after him, calling his name, but the child had headed straight for the door. By the time Andrew reached the threshold, he had disappeared from sight. He shouted and slammed a fist against the post.

"I do not have time for this!"

"He will return," Dinah said calmly from behind him. "Probably not in time to come with us, but he will wait for Abigail. He will be all right, Andrew. Come, we are ready."

Andrew had no choice but to turn back inside. Within ten minutes, the note was sitting on the worktable in the kitchen, weighted down by a bowl, and the group of five had left the house laden down and headed out of the city.

TWENTY-SIX

Abigail heard the people mock him. The criminal on his left. The soldiers beneath him. But Jesus would not fight back. He would hurl no insults. He would acknowledge no demands. Their cries of "Save yourself if you are the Son of God!" went ignored and unanswered.

By that time, the clouds on the horizon had obscured the sun, lending the entire event an ominous current. The electricity in the air must have had everyone on edge; the masses erupted in shouting, cursing, and insults aimed not only at those hanging before them, but at each other.

Abigail barely paid it heed. Her attention was riveted on the face that she could see on top of the middle cross, where Jesus listened in agony to the mockery that was hurled his way. She had gotten back to her feet at some point; she could not have said when. She kept her eyes on one point only, and had only blinked when necessary. When they offered him vinegar on a sponge, she was watching when he refused it. When they hung the sign Pilate had made, she read "This is Jesus, King of the Jews" in all three languages. The words stung with equal force in each one.

No one understood what it meant to be king of the Jews. The Hebrews thought it should be a position of honor and resented that such a wretch would call himself by such a name. Did they not remember that Israel should have had no king but God? That even the wise and successful kings like David and Solomon had faltered, failed, and been torn by bloodshed and sin? To be Israel's king was not so much an honor as an allotment. And Rome—Rome thought Israel was a broken nation. They appointed their leaders, changed their titles on a whim . . . all according the will of Caesar, not of God.

But Jesus, as he looked out over the swarms of angry people, arms stretched wide and chest heaving, reigned supreme in ways none of them could ever know. Abigail wished he *would* call down his legions of angels, just to show this faithless generation that he *was* the Son of God. But she knew he would not. The man whose face held her gaze was humble, low, and weighed down by the sins of them all. As his eyes brushed over the faces in the crowd, brushed over hers, her heart swelled up. He knew them all. He saw their souls. And even as he loved them, he mourned for their failings. The longer he hanged, the more she could see its weight upon him.

The other criminals still spoke, probably numb to the pain. One cursed Jesus, the other cursed the first and begged Christ to make a place for him in his kingdom.

Jesus looked over at the dying man on his right and offered a bruised smile. Abigail saw his mouth move and could hear just enough to make out his words. "You will surely be with me in Paradise."

Then the darkness grew more pronounced. Some of the crowd began to disperse, but Abigail remained where she was. She could not leave. What it was that riveted her to her spot she could not have said, but she knew she would see it through to its end.

Titus watched, listened. He kept his face in the same impassable expression as always, but something had shifted within him. He did not participate in the wagers his fellow soldiers were making, nor did he say so much as a word after the crosses were raised.

His mind traced over his life. That one open eye had seen more than Titus ever had in any introspection, and that was unacceptable. He remembered his stubbornness as a child, his willfulness as an adolescent. He recalled the many angry words he had tossed at his father, the fits of rage that had usually ended in a beaten servant or days of moody silence. He remembered the women, the revelries, the drunkenness. He remembered judging everyone for every fault without ever seeing his own.

How had he missed his shortcomings all of these years? How had he convinced himself that beating a slave for no reason was acceptable simple *because* he was master over the creature? Had he truly said not so long ago that the more women one could take, the better off one would be?

His stomach burned with the faults. A month ago, he never would have labeled them as such, but now he knew, in that place deep within that he had forced into dormancy long ago. It had finally reawakened in a spurt of destruction to rival Troy. His carefully constructed life was lying in tatters around him, all of his glories suddenly filthy parasites he wanted only to be rid of.

But how?

Forgive him. The words echoed again within his mind. Which "him" was it now? His father, for never understanding him, never trusting him, for teaching him that the way to get what he wanted was to take it by force? Jason, for being better than he without ever trying, for getting killed before Titus could ever apologize for his misjudgments? Barabbas, for killing his one true friend? Abigail, for taking that friend away? Cleopas, for raising him so well? Did he need to forgive Menelaus for never being what he wanted him to be, Apidius and Lentulus for never being more than what they were? Did he truly have to forgive Pilate for giving in to the crowds, the crowds for their fickle will, the religious men for their jealousies, Jerusalem for its weakness?

He looked up into the face of the man on the center cross, and the King of the Jews looked to heaven.

"Forgive them, Father," the dying man said barely loudly enough to be heard, "for they know not what they do."

A shudder ran down Titus's spine. How could a man hanging on a cross, innocent of every crime but offending a few, be begging for forgiveness for his foes? How could he cast his face up to the heavens and expect a response when he found himself in such a situation? If he were what some said, if he were the Son of God, why did he not do as the crowd suggested and save himself? Why did he let his body weaken and die, why did he let his spirit shake? How could he still love a Father who let this happen to him?

"*Eli, Eli.*" Jesus' cry sent a murmur through the crowds.

"He is calling for Elijah!" one citizen shouted nearby.

"Fool," another reproached, "it is Hebrew."

"*Eli!*" Jesus called again. "*Lama sabachthani?*"

Titus needed no interpreter to tell him what the words meant. He could feel them in his soul, feel them in the form of a tremor that started in his stomach and shook him all the way through. Why had God forsaken him? Even the man they called Christ did not know, he had to ask, he felt the loneliness that was man's punishment for imperfection.

"Into your hands I commit my spirit." Titus watched the serenity descend upon the man's countenance, watched him seize in pain and cry out, "It is finished!"

The shaking this time was not in Titus. The earth beneath him trembled as he watched Jesus breathe his last, the skies split open into a terrible peal of thunder that echoed over the land as if it were protesting the absence of this man's soul. Titus watched half the crowd take flight and run, the other half shifting uncomfortably, as if ashamed to leave but afraid to stay. The tremors in the ground did not last long, were not intense, but were enough to put fear into every face.

"He truly is the Son of God." Titus looked in awe at the corpse that hung above him, closed his eyes when tears surged into them. When he opened them again, his fellow soldiers were staring at him with the same look of disbelief on their faces that he felt on his. They all knew him, though not well. The not well was because he was known to be unapproachable, unfeeling, and unfriendly. He could barely imagine what they must be thinking now. If anything close to what was going through his mind, it was unbelievable.

Their eyes followed his to where the Christ was hanging. He heard them all murmuring. One proclaimed Jesus a righteous man, another agreed, a third said he had never seen a man so perfect.

"Who is in charge?"

Titus turned to the man who had spoken. His garb said he was one of the elders of the synagogue. "I am."

The man motioned anxiously to the three on the crosses. "Sundown in approaching, and it will be our Sabbath. They cannot be hanging then. Break their legs and take them down."

Titus nodded. "It will be done. Musianus, Luke." He pointed them to either side, then motioned to Jesus. "This one is already dead."

"Dead?" The man's brows lifted. "So soon? Impossible."

"Tell him that." Titus spun away. He was anxious to be away from this scene, to leave his companions and the crowds and have time to think through what he had seen, what he had felt. He had to decide what to do about it.

The crowd was thin now, only a handful remaining on the hillside where before hundreds had been gathered. Titus looked at them for the first time, wondering what had brought them and what kept them. Were some of them the relatives of the criminals? Were some of them the followers of the King of the Jews? If he shouted out his questions, would there be anyone to answer them?

As if this mysterious God was directing him, his eyes fell on one figure, who was curled up in a small ball of pain. He set his jaw in resignation and determination.

⚜

When the skies opened, when the earth shook, something tore within Abigail too. The pain was unbelievable, coiling at the small of her back and then springing forward. Her entire body responded, stumbling to the ground. She knew that it was her baby, ready to make his appearance. But the pain of the contraction was so great she could not move, she could not get up, she could only moan and bite down until her jaw hurt.

Her eyes searched for the face of Jesus, but she saw that it was lifeless now, and her heart wrenched. Her gaze fell. The people who had been in front of her had left, and she could see the activity at the foot of the cross. The centurions were there, three of them looking at the other as he mouthed a few words, his eyes on the cross.

She knew the man. She knew what he said. She felt the echo of the statement within herself. Jesus was the Son of God, Christ, the messiah, and she had just watched him give up his life. The thrill, the terrifying panic, and the underlying peace all settled within her. She still lay where she had fallen, but as the contraction passed, she relaxed, closed her eyes, and took a deep breath.

When she looked again, Titus strode toward her. She was still too weak to so much as sit up when he knelt down at her side.

"What did you see today?" He brushed an escaped lock of hair back from her face.

The question did not seem odd to Abigail. She smiled peacefully, and the evening sun broke through the clouds in a mirror of her expression. "I have seen the messiah, sacrificed for the sins of the world. I have seen God made man."

Titus nodded, then sent his gaze over her. "You are in pain."

"It is passing." The ache in her back was so bad she could not straighten it out.

"The baby?"

"He is coming." She pressed a hand to where the child had dropped and squeezed her eyes shut. "I need to get home. I tried to leave when you told me to, but the crowds—"

"I understand. I will help you home."

When she struggled to sit up, Titus saw that she needed more than a little assistance. He scooped her up. Over his shoulder, he said to his fellows, "I am leaving."

"But there is still work to attend to!"

He turned so that Abigail was visible to them, her face turned into his shoulder in pain, her stomach looking large against her slight frame. "Jason's child is on its way." He knew the name of their fallen friend would carry weight. Jason had been known and loved by most of the members of the garrison. "I am taking her home."

This time, he was met with nods instead of objection. Titus turned again and headed for the city.

"Thank you." Abigail tried to stifle a whimper in his shoulder. "Why does the pain not ebb?"

He did not know, and the question ignited another trace of fear within him. Many women died in childbirth, many children with them. He knew that, but he could not believe it would happen to her, or to Jason's child. "Your and your babe will be well. By tomorrow, you will be a mother, and you will have a child to inherit Jason's legacy."

"Jason believed." She raised her head a few inches to look up into his face. She undoubtedly saw the way his eyes widened. "He listened to Cleopas, about the stories of Jesus. When no one else heard him, Jason did. I did not understand, but I do now. There is so much I wish I had paid attention to."

Something clenched up inside. A strange pride, perhaps even relief. It coupled with determination. Once again, Jason had led the way. This time, he would follow. "We will learn. We will both find someone to tell us of this Christ. When he looked at me, when he touched me—I will never be the same, Abigail. Only now do I realize how much I needed to change. But I know not how."

"He did not come to change the commands of Jehovah, but to fulfill them. That is what Cleopas said. The Laws are still our guides."

Titus, still walking forward as quickly as possible, looked down into the beautiful face that was pinched with anguish. Even with her added burden, she was light in his arms, looking fragile and delicate. But in her mind was the knowledge he lacked, the wisdom he had heard from her before but dismissed. She was a woman, she was a Jew, she had been a slave. But she had the advantage over him. "Will you teach me? I cannot obey laws I do not know. And I need to obey them, Abigail, I know that."

Abigail studied him for a moment, and he remembered the time only a few days before when she looked at him like that and found him wanting. This time, he was relieved to see her face soften as she nodded.

"I will share what I know, in the time we have. You leave for Rome in a week?"

"I do." Suddenly he was loath to board the ship that would return him to a world away from this one, far from all teaching and Messiah and peace.

Abigail's muscles tensed, her face echoing pain though her teeth were clenched against it. Titus picked up his pace.

She panted as the tension eased. "They come too quickly. It should take hours for them to be so close, and I had no pains until minutes ago. Pray nothing is wrong, Titus. Pray for Jason's child."

Titus had never uttered a prayer in his life. He had always performed lip service to the Roman gods, enough to appease his mother and keep away the wrath if the deities happened to exist. He did not know how one should go about earnestly beseeching a God who held all power, who was above all reproach, who held justice in his hand. But then he remembered the merciful visage of Jesus, and a calm descended on him.

"In the name of your Son," Titus whispered, "I ask you, God, to touch Abigail and her child. Keep them well, Lord."

"Amen." Abigail sighed and buried her face in his shoulder to try hide her tears of pain.

Something surged inside him, unfurling. Had he ever protected anyone before? He did not think so. No one had depended on him for anything but a nice evening, no one had put trust in him to see them to safety. It humbled him even as it made him aware of his strength.

By the time they reached her home, Abigail was unable to hold back the moans. Titus approached the kitchen door because it was closest, and it was open. He walked in expecting to find a slave to tell the situation to, but there was no on there, no fire in the hearth, no sounds of life. He walked through the house, going in the direction he knew Jason's room to be in. That door, too, was open but empty.

"Here we are." He placed her on the soft mattress of the bed. "I will go find help." He left her again, moving through the rest of the house. There was broken pottery in the kitchen, but nothing of value was missing, so he assumed it to be a result of the earthquake rather than thieves. The curious thing, though, was why there was no one else in the house, and no sign of where they could be.

He was headed back to the bed chamber when he heard the shrieking drawing nearer. The word was in Hebrew, the voice obviously a child's, and within seconds he saw a growingly familiar blur moving down the hall. It came to a halt in front of him. Samuel, with tears streaming down his cheeks and trembling lips.

"Where is she?"

Even this was new, this warmth that mounted when he saw the boy's love of his mistress. He motioned to the room. Samuel flew past him and into the chamber, throwing himself onto the bed even as Titus cautioned, "Careful! She is in pain."

He need not have spoken. Samuel did not jump on Abigail; he merely curled up adjacent to her, his head touching hers, and ran tiny fingers over her face, crooning the same word he had been shouting moments before, then translating it into Greek. "Mother. Mother. You left me."

Abigail opened her eyes and pulled him near, running a hand over his curls. "I am here. I am home, my son. I will not leave you again."

"Samuel." Titus tried to make his voice gentle. He had no experience with children and could not remember ever being so small himself. So he imitated Abigail. "Do you know where the others are?"

"They left," Samuel said between his sobs, his face buried in Abigail's bosom. "I would not go! Not without you. They could not make me!"

"Do you know where they went?"

Samuel shook his head. "The doctor took them away. They would not wait."

Abigail's features constricted again. She would be concerned for Ester, he knew, but she got out no words. Her back arched against another pain, and she held her breath until it passed.

Titus looked around in consternation, willing a solution to materialize. All he received was the certainty that he alone could help. "I am going for a midwife. Will you be all right for a while, Abigail? I will not be long."

Abigail nodded wearily. Samuel proclaimed, "I will take care of my mother."

Titus nodded. "I believe you will. I will hurry."

The streets were chaotic, a combination of usual pre-Sabbath rush and the added excitement of Passover, an execution, and a small but startling natural disaster. And what made it worse was that he had no idea where to go to find a midwife. He attempted to ask a citizen, but they all went out of their way to avoid him; it was the first time he really noticed or cared, and Titus knew prodigious frustration. He was about to just grab someone and demand an answer when a familiar movement caught his eye, the flash of a cloak, the bounce of a step.

Titus froze. He stared. He beheld with complete disbelief the figure in the distance, knowing he must be going mad. Jason was dead. He had seen his death with his own eyes, he had watched them entomb him, he knew for a fact it could not be his friend that was standing on the end of the street and watching him.

But it was. Every sense and every fiber told him it was. The man looked like Jason, was dressed in the garments he had been buried in. He smiled like Jason had smiled and lifted a hand in the very way that Jason had beckoned.

Titus knew he was going mad, yes. But still, he followed. After all, if his mind was conjuring up images of the dead, perhaps it would have said image lead him somewhere useful.

Jason led him, but Titus found it impossible to draw near. If he ran, so did Jason. When he stopped, the figment did as well and would turn and wait and gesture again for him to follow. Titus did so, wondering where they were going, and wondering too why it was that the others in the street got out of the way of *his* vision. He was led down a street he had never had cause to visit before, and then the man before him was gone. Titus looked around in confusion, ran the length of the street to look for him on the other side, and found nothing. Giving an exasperated growl, he turned again.

"You are a long way from the garrison, soldier."

Titus turned to find a woman standing in a doorway, wiping her hands on a faded piece of cloth. She looked amused, pleasant. She was probably in her mid thirties, attractive, but had that worn and tired look in her eye that seemed habitual to so many in the city.

Titus sighed. "I am looking for a midwife."

The woman smiled. "You have found one. Though who would have given you my name, I cannot imagine."

Titus shook his head. "No one told me. Please, can you come? My friend's widow is in labor, and she is in great pain. I fear something is wrong, and her family cannot be found."

The woman nodded, disappearing inside for a moment and reemerging a moment later with a satchel under her arm. She closed the door behind her. "Lead me to her." They fell into step together, Titus setting a brisk pace. The woman matched it. "I am Tabitha," she volunteered when they had journeyed a while in silence. "This woman—is she Hebrew or Roman?"

Titus sent her a suspicious glance. "Will that affect your decision to come?"

Tabitha smiled again, indulgently this time. "Mine, it will not. For many others of my profession, it would indeed. That is why I ask. I was wondering if I was your last resort. It is the only time I am ever called now."

Titus knew he was in no position to question her credentials. He merely nodded. "She is Hebrew. Her husband was a centurion, his father the prefect."

Tabitha did not slow, but she turned her face up to his with heightened interest. "I heard of their deaths. It saddened me. The father was a follower of Jesus."

He was beyond shock at that point, so he could not have such a reaction to her knowledge of Cleopas's beliefs. "His son had become one, too."

Tabitha nodded slowly. "And you, soldier?"

Titus looked over at her, his mind suddenly at rest. He could tell by the look in her eyes, that faded echo of what he had seen in Jesus's not so long ago, that she was a follower of the rabbi's teachings. Someone who would know what he had said and would be able to share it. If his vision of Jason had been his own madness, then his madness had led him right where he needed to be. He still could not smile. "Today I saw things that have changed me. Things I do not understand. But I know that Jesus of Nazareth was more than a man. I know that his blood made me see my own sins and wish them away. And I know that I need to learn much in order to be the man this Christ would have me be."

Tabitha put an encouraging hand on his arm. "There is hope. Jesus the Messiah judges with mercy. He spared my life when others would have stoned me, convincing the crowd to walk away. He knows we all sin and commanded the one without such a blemish to cast the first stone–there is no one who is righteous though, my friend. Your failings cannot be so great that you cannot overcome them with faith in our Lord; he forgave me mine, he will forgive you yours. You have but to desire it."

Titus would have responded, but they at that moment came within sight of the Visibullis house.

"Titus!" It was the voice of one of his men, running for him from the direction of the garrison. "Where have you been? Pilate wishes to see you!"

Titus exhaled forcefully. He turned to Tabitha, pointing to the house. "Abigail is within that house. The servants are all gone with the mistress of the house; let yourself in, go to the rear bed chamber. There will be a boy with her, who will probably meet you when he hears you enter; he is very protective of her. I will return as quickly as I can."

Tabitha nodded, even as Titus turned and strode impatiently toward his soldier. "What does Pilate want?"

The man stepped out of his way. "He would not believe the criminal called Jesus was already dead, but a man has come asking for his body, to bury it before sundown."

Titus made no response, just took off at a run in the direction of the governor's palace. He arrived in short order and entered.

Menelaus greeted him at the entrance and turned to lead the way to the governor. "Titus, they could not find you; I was beginning to think you had already headed for your ship."

"It does not sail for another week," Titus reminded him. "Why did you not just fetch one of the others to verify Jesus's death?"

Menelaus shrugged. "You were in charge. Pilate will trust no one else. Where did you disappear to, my friend?"

Titus looked at Menelaus. He seemed the same as he had been days before. How was it the entire world had not changed as he had? How could anyone still be so obviously interested in the things of everyday life, when the Son of God had just been killed upon a cross? "Abigail was at the crucifixion, and her labor began. I took her home, then went in search of a midwife; Ester and her slaves have disappeared, and I know not where to find them."

Menelaus looked surprised, if not overly concerned. "Curious. Well, you have done your good deed. I am heading into the city. Shall I wait for you?"

Titus worked hard to keep his disgust from his face. It was not Menelaus's fault that he had no idea what had happened that day. He shook his head. "I must check on Abigail. She was in terrible pain, and I fear something is not right."

"Titus." Menelaus paused outside the door that would open to Pilate. "You cannot do anything. I certainly understand your concern for Jason's child, but be reasonable. You cannot deliver the babe yourself, and your presence would not be welcome. Abigail despises you."

Titus was in no mood to argue. "We have reached a truce. I will return to her once Pilate is convinced."

Even as Titus reached for the door, Menelaus was saying, "Titus, do not. She is Jason's widow."

Titus glanced back at him with a brow raised in condescension. "I am not taking her to my bed, Menelaus. I am merely making sure she is not alone. Would Jason not want that? Or would he prefer I leave her to die with no one but a midwife with her?"

Menelaus looked ready to rebut, but Titus had the door open, and the governor called him in.

"Lord," Titus said, bowing his head in greeting. "You summoned me?"

"Yes." Pilate's nerves were obvious. He darted a glance at another man in the room, one whose wealth was worn openly. "This man has come for the body of the one they call the King of the Jews. I knew he could not be dead yet."

Titus had no qualms contradicting the governor. "He is dead. He died seconds before the earthquake."

Pilate looked even more anxious at that news. "But how? It is too soon."

Titus replied just so he could be the quicker out of there. "He was beaten badly, Lord. He could not even walk unaided to Golgotha. The blood he lost from the stakes was undoubtedly too much for him to survive long. He probably would have died even had we not crucified him."

The explanation seemed to satisfy Pilate. He nodded, then said to the other man, "Take his body, do what you will."

"Lord." Another man stepped forward from the shadows where Titus had not even noticed him. He was vaguely familiar, but it was not until he spoke that Titus remembered him as the man who had spoken to Barabbas what seemed like years ago, when the murderer was released. He was the man who had pulled a terrified Abigail along and offered her to the criminal. "We remember that while this man was alive, the deceiver said, 'After three days I will rise.' Therefore command that guards be posted at this tomb, lest his disciples come and steal him away and say he has risen. That deception would be even worse than what he has already done."

Titus rolled his eyes, partly because this man's foolishness was so great, partly because he knew Pilate would agree.

"You have a guard. This centurion," Pilate said with a nod toward Titus, "will select one himself. Go, make it as secure as you can."

"Thank you, sir." The religious leader left the room with a smug smile.

Titus, after bowing to Pilate, followed him out.

The Pharisee waited. "I want your best men. Nothing is beneath these deceivers, and they would steal the body from beneath our noses."

Titus was out of patience. He stepped close, close enough so that the man had to tilt his head back to look up into his face. "Patience, man. You said it was the third day he said he would rise, so for the third day, you will have your guard. Not tonight. Go to your house and prepare for your Sabbath, and leave the dead alone."

He turned and strode away before he could see what response his command got. He found his way out of the palace and headed straight for the house where he could find others who understood the sudden realignment of his world.

TWENTY-SEVEN

The groans had led Tabitha where she needed to go once she was in the house. It was a common enough sound for one used to attending child births, but even so the pain in the voice was obvious. Tabitha entered the bed chamber and looked over to see the pregnant woman lying on the bed, a small boy stroking her brow as she gripped the sheets as though her life depended on it.

She made her presence known with a small cough. When the two looked up, she smiled. "I am Tabitha, a midwife." She sat down on the side of the bed and took one of the young woman's hands. "What is your name, child?"

"Abigail." Even the one word was strained with agony. "Something's wrong with my baby."

Tabitha made no comment, just took a hand and ran it over her abdomen. It took little probing to realize the expectant mother was right. But she smiled. "Pain is normal, Abigail. When was your last contraction?"

Abigail shook her head. "They are close. Too close, I think."

Tabitha nodded, but again kept her silence. She looked to the boy with a smile. "And what is your name?"

"Samuel," he replied. "Will my mother be all right?"

Tabitha knew well that the woman before her could not have possibly given birth to the boy, but she was not about to argue with the title. She just stroked his hair gently. "Of course she will, Samuel. Now, I need you to help me. Do you know where they store the linens?"

He nodded.

"Good. Go get the oldest things. When you come back, I will go make my preparations. Hurry, now. Your mother will want you back here soon."

He scurried away, and Tabitha looked back to Abigail, whose eyes had not left her face. "The centurion said he would return soon, but he was called to the governor. He mentioned he was your husband's friend, and he seemed very concerned for you. But if you are not comfortable with his presence–"

"No, please." Abigail gripped her hand tighter. "I need to thank him." She broke off with another moan, but resolutely finished her thought between clenched teeth. "For bringing me home."

Tabitha nodded. "Before he gets back, I need to check your progress, child."

She was not dilated very far, and Tabitha knew that the labor would be long and hard. When Samuel returned with the old cloth, she put it nearby to be handy and informed them that she would be in the kitchen for just a few minutes.

She was there still when Titus returned.

"How is she?" the Roman asked immediately upon entering the room. Tabitha was pouring some water into a wooden cup.

She shook her head. "The babe is breached."

Titus's brows furrowed. "What does that mean?"

"It means that the child dropped before he turned. His head should come first, but he is not positioned correctly. He cannot be born as he is."

Titus beheld her a moment in silence, then asked, "What can be done?" in such a way that stated the answer had better not be nothing.

Tabitha sighed. "Right now, we can pray that the babe will turn on his own. I have seen it happen. If he does not, then once she is opened enough, I will reach up and try to maneuver him myself." Seeing his features pale, she drew her breath back in. "It is painful, yes, but it is the only other option. If the child is not turned, they will both die."

"That cannot happen. I swore to him she would be taken care of."

She gave him a smile that she prayed would comfort him. "There is nothing you can do to protect her now. You brought her safely home, you brought someone to attend her. Speak to her, then go home. There is nothing more for you to do."

❧

Titus headed for the room where Abigail was curled up on the bed. Every muscle was so tense that he could feel some of her pain just by drawing near. He sat on the edge of the bed and put a hand on her shoulder to let her know he was there.

Abigail opened her eyes, turned her head to look at him. "Titus. Thank you."

"I have done nothing." He took her hand, measured himself. Only compassion flowed through him, a feeling so unfamiliar he was unsure if that was even the proper name. "But I pray for you. I know not if your God even knows who I am, but I am beseeching him on your behalf."

She managed a smile and squeezed his hand. "My God knows everyone. He will hear you. Titus," she then intoned in a way that made him brace himself for whatever might follow, "I have said things to you recently I regret. You were a good friend to Jason. You stood beside him in spite of your disapproval."

Forgiveness . . . he had not even wanted it before, but now it bathed him in peace. "And I was wrong to disapprove. Forgive me for all I have said to you, Abigail, and concerning you. You had no ill intents. Jason made his decisions, and he made them well. I should not have judged him so harshly."

"Different standards." Titus let her grip his hand as another pain hit her, wondering at the amount of force her tiny fingers could exude. When she could, she breathed, "But no more. There does not have to be Roman and Hebrew now, Titus. We can all be held to the same standard that the Christ has given us."

"Yes." He looked up, to where Tabitha had entered the room. "And this woman was his follower. Perhaps she can tell us more of what he taught."

Tabitha looked at each of them, at the boy, then gave a serene smile. "I will tell you." She put the cup of water on a table where Abigail could reach it, then moved to the other side of the bed and took a seat beside Samuel.

"It began," she said with sparkling eyes, "over thirty years ago, when a virgin was discovered to be with child, though she had never intimately known a man. . . ."

❧

Andrew stood in the doorway of the inn, looking out into the approaching night.

"It grows dark." Simon put a hand on Andrew's shoulder. "She will undoubtedly remain at home for the night, where it is safe."

"But tomorrow is Sabbath. She cannot come then, and we cannot return for her. We must wait for the first of the week." His frowned his distaste for that necessity. "I am worried for her, Simon. She could deliver the babe at any time. And that earthquake–"

"We must trust. We must believe she is well, just detained by the commotion, the storm, the darkness. She is fine, she is probably staying with Julia for the night, she has Samuel with her. If they do not arrive an hour after first light the day after the morrow, we will go ourselves to find her."

Andrew nodded, turned back inside. But he was less than satisfied.

⸙

"I am not leaving." Titus stated it firmly from the chair he had pulled up to the bed, using the tone of voice his men knew they had better not cross.

Tabitha crossed it anyway. "It is inappropriate. You are not even a relative, and you are a man. This room is no place for you during a birth. Go back to the garrison."

"No." He leaned forward to pick up Abigail's hand when she moaned. His determination turned to concern. "She grows weaker."

Tabitha sat beside Abigail with a sigh and gently massaged her abdomen. For hours, she had told them what she knew of Jesus the Messiah, and as she spoke, Abigail had been alert, attentive, and her pain seemed to ease. But within moments of her conclusion, the woman had started thrashing in agony once again. Titus had helped hold her down so that she did not injure herself.

Now, as dawn streaked the eastern sky, Abigail had calmed all the way into unconsciousness. Samuel slept too, curled up beside Abigail. He had looked to be in equal amounts of torment as she those past hours, and he needed the rest. They all did.

Titus gazed at the exhausted midwife. "Sleep for a while. She will need you at your best later, and I will wake you if she stirs."

She nodded, placed her hands on Abigail's stomach for a moment as if to will strength into her, and then stood. She moved over to the chaise and lay down.

Titus was left looking down on the laboring woman, her face drawn even in slumber. His mind was a muddle, but one thing was clear: he could not just leave her alone. Because of the loss they shared, because of the things they had seen that day, because of the lessons they had learned, and because she had no one else, a bond had been forged between them. He did not understand it, but he knew it was there. And as he studied her, protectiveness overcame him.

The hand he held was small, so delicate that it seemed he could crush it without effort, yet so strong when it gripped his in pain. He put their palms together, and her fingers barely reached his second knuckle. She was no bigger than a child, yet here she lay giving birth to one of her own. He drew in a deep breath and thought back to the first times he had seen her. Her frailty had not struck him then, nor had her strength. All he had been able to see was a beautiful face, an alluring body, and the modest reserve that ensured he would never know either but from a distance.

Days ago, he had seen only his friend's widow, large with his friend's child.

Today, he saw a person. A being with a soul, with a mind, with a heart seeking the same things his suddenly was. He saw a life completely separate from his, yet somehow linked to it.

His world had always been just that: his. But now suddenly he was aware of the minuteness of his own existence, of the infinite God above him, of the aching woman beside him. He heard the soft, childlike breathing of the small slave boy, the restless sighs of the midwife, and he realized for the first time that he was not a world unto himself. He was not so superior, nor so alone. He was but a man, one who had spent so much of his life following his own senseless wills that he had not even known he was capable of thinking of another's. But that day a hand far larger than his had settled over him, and he felt its soothing touch.

He sat immobile for an hour, then Abigail blinked awake, her eyes hazy with discomfort. "Titus. Why are you still here?"

Titus's smile was as soft as her voice. "Because this is where I belong."

She lifted her palm from his and reached up to touch his lips with the tips of her fingers, her mouth curving up in disbelief. "I did not think you could smile." The teasing note in her voice sounded like music in contrast to the edge that had been there just a moment before. "I was certain that finely carved sculpture you call your face would crack and crumble if you ever attempted it."

Titus chuckled, his smile only growing. When her hand lowered, he took it again in his. "I have not had much cause in the past, I admit."

"You should remedy that. It only improves your features. Of course," she continued, pitching her voice even lower, "if you did so, you may not evoke quite so much fear."

"Well, we cannot have that, can we?" Then he sobered. "You were never afraid of me, Abigail."

She squeezed his hand weakly. "You were nothing but an arrogant heathen, after all. And you always respected Jason. I had nothing to fear from you. Though I admit I knew a moment of it that first time I saw you in the alley."

He nodded at those truths, tensing when she did. He watched her features contract, her back arch, and let her grip his hand as the pain rolled through her. By the time it ebbed, Samuel had come awake, and Tabitha too had left her bed in favor of seeing the cause of Abigail's groans.

The midwife felt her abdomen again. Her gaze met Titus's, and she shook her head just a bit. He sighed heavily enough for both of them.

As midday drew near, Titus had no choice but to leave Abigail's side for a while. He had tasks he had to attend to at the Praetorium, loose ends to tie up before he left in six more days. First, oddly, was arranging for the guard that the Pharisee had requested. The man had apparently shown up at daybreak to begin pestering the general about it.

"Asinius!" the general shouted when Titus entered. He motioned to the well-dressed religious leader. "This man says Pilate promised him a guard and put you in charge of it."

"Marcus!" Titus shouted in turn when his underling happened by. The man froze at the sound of his voice, snapping into attention. "For the next day, ten of you will be guarding the teacher's tomb."

"The *deceiver*," the Pharisee corrected.

Titus speared him with an unimpressed glare. He turned back to his soldier. "Go in shifts, two at a time. You and Dominus have first shift, then Trannis and Theophilus, Caius and Julius, Valerius and Lucio, and Subrius and Marcus Annaeus." He motioned to the Pharisee much as the general had. "He will show you the way."

The general looked none too pleased. "Those are some of our best men."

"Pilate's order." His soldier was already running to find his fellows. Titus sent a withering gaze over their guest. "This man apparently thinks the teacher's disciples are very clever, that they could steal a body from a sealed tomb without anyone knowing."

The general breathed a laugh. "He has obviously not seen the stone they sealed it with, then. It takes two men just to budge it and makes a terrible noise. There will be no sneaking."

Either offended or annoyed, the Pharisee turned and walked away a few steps.

"Titus," the general said more softly, drawing the younger's gaze back to him, "I heard that you took Abigail home, that her labor has begun. Have you heard any more? Did she have a son?"

The mention of it made him weary anew. "She is still in labor. The babe is breached, and the midwife is beginning to get anxious."

The general sighed. "They need an heir. Julia has been praying, lighting incense to Juno."

Titus felt his spine stiffen but knew not how to explain to his superior that such an act would only be offensive to the woman in labor. Instead, he said, "When I arrived with Abigail, the others were gone. Do you know where they went?"

"Gone? What do you mean, gone?"

"The only one remaining was a slave boy who said the doctor made them all leave. I would have thought they would have contacted you."

The general shook his head, his brows drawn. "I am certain it was Drusus, we knew he was coming. But we received no missive. Did the boy not know where they went?"

"No." Titus sighed. "And they have not returned. I cannot imagine them simply leaving Abigail unless the situation was dire."

"I will ask Julia. Perhaps she knows something I do not."

Titus nodded. "If so, send word. I will be at the Visibullis house with Abigail."

The general did not question his determination as Menelaus had. He merely nodded in return and went back to his duties. Titus hurried through the rest of his tasks, and when he walked out of the garrison an hour after entering it, it was as a civilian.

But strangely enough, being no longer a part of the military did not make him feel free, as he had anticipated. Instead, he felt a weight of responsibility that he had never before known. It settled over him heavily . . . yet rather than bearing him down, it bolstered him up. He returned to the house of his late friend and decided he would not leave it again until either the child was born or. . . not.

TWENTY-EIGHT

The pain grew steadily worse, but Abigail stopped noticing it. Her eyes, strained and tired, were focused on the window, watching as darkness stole over the land.

A day. It had been a whole day since the pains began, and she had nothing to show for it. No baby, very little progress; her hope was wearing thin.

"Jehovah, please," she whispered into the empty room–Tabitha and Titus and Samuel were all eating, and she knew they would be back in a matter of moments. Her voice wavered as her heart inclined toward heaven. "I ask you to spare my child. I know he was conceived in sin, and I know your justice demands punishment for that. But please, my Lord, I have lost Jason, Cleopas, I know not where Ester is. I ask your mercy, not for me, but for the men who loved you so much. They deserve for their name to live on."

A particularly sharp pain gripped her, and she squeezed her eyes shut. "*Eli!*" she called out, then panted. "My God, I beg you. Spare Jason's child. Take me if you will, but not the babe. Please, not the babe."

Her words had faded to little more than a breath by the time she finished her plea. She opened weary eyes into the dismal room, then choked on her own air when a shadow fell over her.

He stood tall, almost regal beside the bed, his best clothes hanging on him as she had seen them do so many times. His hair looked clean, his skin glowing in health. And his eyes–his eyes had that ever-soft quality that deepened in love as he looked at her.

"Jason!" She squeaked more than spoke, trembling at the vision.

He sat beside her, and though she could feel the warmth of his body seeping into her legs, the mattress did not sink under his weight. He reached up and brushed a damp, limp lock of hair away from her face. "Faith," he whispered.

It was the same voice she had heard for the past year, but not. Though nearly silent, the one word echoed through the chamber, resonating in every crevice.

"Jason . . ."

He put a finger over her lips. All she could feel of the touch was a warmth, like the heat of a candle.

"You believe," Jason said in the same resounding quiet. "It is enough. Your faith will see you through."

He put his warm hand on her stomach, and it covered the splatter of blood that had fallen there the day before. The same searing cut through her again, the same burning ignited in her blood and traveled through her. She felt the child turning within her, and she cried out at the glorious hurt it caused.

Within seconds, her shout brought footsteps flying down the hall, and a moment later the door sprang opened. All three stopped in the threshold when they saw the man sitting on the bed. She saw their eyes widen.

Jason stood again and smiled first at Abigail, then the others. "Thank you." He inclined his head in gratitude, and turned to walk away. As Abigail looked on, he glided through the wall and disappeared.

"I believe I am going mad," Tabitha murmured.

"If so, then we all are." Titus looked to Abigail, whose gaze was still on the wall through which her husband had gone. "I saw him earlier, too. He led me to Tabitha."

"A miracle," the midwife said in awe.

"The babe." Abigail rested her hand on her stomach. "He shifted."

That was enough to grab everyone's attention. Titus took his chair, Tabitha her spot sitting beside Abigail, and the boy climbed up uninvited into Titus's lap. She half expected the man to push him off again, but he surprised her by smiling at him.

As Tabitha began her probe, her face lit with victory. "It is well now. The labor may still take a while, but the child will be born."

Joyous tears ran down Abigail's cheeks as she whispered her gratitude to her God.

Samuel grabbed her attention when he turned a sober face toward Titus. "Lord, is my father an angel?"

Abigail buried a smile, wondering how he would respond. Titus shrugged. "I know not, Samuel. But what I *do* know is that he is of God."

It seemed to satisfy the boy. He snuggled closer to Titus, resting his head against the man's solid chest, and looked perfectly content. Titus looked down on the golden curls for a moment in seeming stupefaction, then slowly put an arm around him to anchor him.

Another miracle. She reached out and grasped his free hand. "The pain is easing. Praise Jehovah."

True to Tabitha's word, the labor was still not quick. But it progressed steadily, and as the night waned, the excitement grew. With the first light of dawn, the mew of new life sounded, followed by shouts of joy.

"It is a son!" Tabitha held the uncleaned babe up for the others to see.

Abigail laughed in exhausted contentment and reached out to hold her baby. Still squalling beautifully, the newborn came to a rest in her arms. His face was red, his cap of black hair going every possible direction, but Abigail was very certain that she had never seen a more perfect creature in all of her life.

After a moment of study, she opened her other arm. "Come, Samuel, meet your little brother."

Samuel scurried from his place in Titus's lap onto the bed, crawling to Abigail's side. He looked in awe at the tiny infant. "He is even littler than I."

Abigail grinned. "He will grow, just as you will."

Tabitha reached to take the baby back. "I will clean him. Titus, Samuel, you should leave now. Abigail and the child will need to rest."

This time, Titus did not argue. He picked up Samuel and stood over her bed. "You did well, Abigail. The Visibullises live on."

Abigail smiled at him in gratitude, then watched the two leave. She looked back to Tabitha. "Thank you. I do not know what I would have done without you."

Tabitha smiled in return, bathing the baby gently in a basin of warm water. "Our Father in Heaven brought us together, Abigail. I am just as grateful to him for it as you. I witnessed a miracle."

Abigail nodded, drawing in a deep breath. She could not take her eyes from the tiny, squirming form her new friend held. "He is perfect."

"Indeed he is."

They let silence remain after that as Tabitha finished cleaning the baby, then was ready to assist her patient with the afterbirth.

After all was taken care of, the baby suckling happily, Tabitha took her hand. "My child, you cannot stay here. There is no food in the house, very little oil, and you would be alone. Titus would probably insist upon staying with you, but he has much to do to prepare for his voyage back to Rome. You and the babe and Samuel will need someone to help you these next few days." She smiled. "I want you to come home with me."

"Tabitha," Abigail said, touched, "that is very kind. But if I leave, and then the others return. . ."

"Do any of them read? We could have Titus write a note, or leave a message with a friend."

Abigail smiled in spite of her concerns. "They read. We all do, except Dinah." She contemplated for a moment, then nodded. "We will write them, and I will go with you. I thank you for your generosity."

Tabitha's smile was bright as she stood. "I will go inform Titus and see if he can find a mule for you to ride. You are too weak to walk, but as I said, there is no more food, and you need to eat. The sooner we get you settled, the better."

Within an hour, Titus had brought over his horse and helped Abigail and the baby onto it, and they had packed all she would need for the next few days. Abigail penned a note explaining that her son had been born and she had gone with the midwife, detailing how to find her. She put it on the kitchen table as was the habit in their house, securing it with one of their many pottery bowls.

They set off. Before the day was more than two hours underway, Abigail was settled comfortably in a cozy room in Tabitha's house.

◆

Simon was needed at the inn, so Andrew set off with Dinah to find Abigail when she had not shown up by the appointed time on the first day of the week. They headed straight for their house, finding it as they had left it, secure and empty. Entering through the front door with a sigh, Andrew shook his head.

"It feels abandoned." He motioned toward the hall with the bedrooms. "But I will check the rooms."

"And I the kitchen."

They went in their separate directions, though the search did not take long. Andrew found Dinah again moments later.

Sorrow lined her face. "The note was still on the table."

Andrew sighed. "And the beds all made and unslept on. Where could she be?"

A knock sounded then, and both jumped, then rushed to the door. Andrew opened it to a familiar slave boy. "Laertus."

"Julia sent me to see how everyone fares."

"Abigail is missing," Andrew replied. "Have you seen her?"

Laertus shook his head, face pinched in concern. "She has not come to our house.

I am to see if I could be of service here, though."

Dinah sighed. "There is no one here. We had to move our mistress, and we cannot find Abigail."

"How is your lady?"

Andrew shrugged. "Unchanged. But Drusus has hope that a change of scenes will see her improving."

"If Abigail comes to you, tell her to find us. We left a note with directions." Dinah's anxiety laced every word.

Laertus nodded, but he was obviously concerned as well.

They followed him out the door. "We will look where we can think to," Andrew muttered to his friend, "but if we do not find her by midday, we will have no choice. Drusus said we should not tarry long."

"Where could she be?" Dinah looked around as if expecting an answer to sprout up. "She knew so few people in the city. Only the general's family, Vetimus. I am worried, Andrew. Why would she not come home? What if something happened to her?"

Andrew had no response.

⬩

"I have news."

Abigail looked up when Titus burst into the small house and headed straight for where she sat with Tabitha.

His face was alight, and he took a seat among them with a smile. "He is risen! They are saying his followers stole his body, but I know it cannot be. I posted the guard myself, and they were our best men. But this morning, the tomb was found empty, the stone rolled away."

Abigail exchanged a glance with Tabitha, then looked back to Titus. She did not need to ask about whom he was speaking.

"But, how?" Tabitha asked. "How could the stone be rolled away if there was a guard?"

Titus shook his head but still smiled. "I spoke with Subrius and Marcus, the men on watch. They said that as dawn broke this morning, they were seized by a terrible fright and were unable to move. The said that they saw a figure clothed in light walk out of the tomb, straight through the rock. He looked at them and smiled, then another man came up and rolled the stone away. Only then could they move again, and they ran to tell the general. Of course, they were not believed, and they were told rather sternly that they had been drunk, had passed out, and that it was during their disgraceful stupor that the followers did their evil deed. But I know those men. They do not drink excessively, and certainly not on duty. He is risen, my friends. Our Christ is alive!"

Abigail stared for a moment as the words sank in.

Tabitha rubbed at her temple. "He said he would rebuild the temple in three days. The temple of his body. Today is the third day." Her eyes lit up. "The prophesies have come true. There is no question now, if ever there was. Jesus is Savior, Christ, Messiah!" She reached over with a joyous laugh and caught up each of their hands. "We serve a risen savior, my friends! Christ is Lord!"

Abigail embraced her friends, laughing all the while as the miraculous truth flowed through her veins. Already she had seen the graves opened, one who was dead walking among them. It was not so hard to grasp the Son of God capable of resurrecting himself.

"No matter what else happens," Abigail said fervently, looking at the others, "there will always be hope for us. As I watched him die, I knew it was for our sins. I knew he was paying the price I should pay. But now he has triumphed over death, over sin. Now we can all live, free and saved and new."

They all smiled at one another, and all looked over to the basket in the corner when the newest life set up a cry.

It was Titus who stood, went over to the baby, and gently picked him up. "Little one, you chose a miraculous day to be born. And as you grow, you will be fed on the stories of this man whose blood has cleansed us all."

Abigail smiled and accepted the babe when he brought him to her. As she did so, she remembered the shouts her people had made when Jesus was being tried. *Let his blood be on us and our children.* Suddenly, what had seemed to her a threat was now a promise. On them his blood rested, indeed, and as the centuries of sacrifices that had come before him, it washed them clean of sin. Only this time, it would remain enough, she knew. He was not just a pure and spotless lamb to be offered anew each year; he was the pure and spotless Son of God, whose sacrifice would serve forever.

TWENTY-NINE

His vessel was scheduled to sail in two days' time—it was late as it was, but Titus was beginning to wish it had been even later to port. He was not ready to leave for Rome.

In his hand was a missive that inspired many thoughts, none of them particularly well defined. He would have to speak to Abigail. But first, he had to stop at the general's house and pay his last visit.

"Have you heard from Ester?" he asked the couple.

"In a way." Julia's strong voice belied her reclined position. "I sent one of my boys over a few days ago, and Andrew and Dinah were there, but they left again soon after. They were looking for Abigail, but Laertus did not know where to tell them to find her. They said they left a note with directions to where they were staying."

Titus sighed in frustration. "I was just there. The only note anywhere in the house is the one that Abigail left for *them.*"

"Well, Dinah cannot read. She would hardly know the difference if she saw one sitting there. At any rate, Laertus got no more information from them, except that Ester is unchanged. They should not be too far, though."

The general nodded his agreement. "Yes, I imagine they will return soon, and when they do, they will undoubtedly stop here to see if we have heard from Abigail. When you leave, just bring her to us. We will see that she and Ester are reunited."

Titus nodded without any intention of following that advice. "I will speak with you before I leave and let you know what Abigail decides to do. I am sure she will appreciate your generous offer."

His hosts nodded, and the general rose to see him out. He returned contemplatively to Tabitha's house, where Abigail was finally up and moving around, Samuel dogging her every step.

When he entered, he did not waste time with preliminaries. He sat down near where Abigail was cutting up vegetables and put the letter he still carried before her.

She eyed it with lifted brows. "What is that?"

"Correspondence from the steward at the Visibullis estate outside of Rome. They just received word of the deaths of Cleopas and Jason. If someone does not step forward soon to claim the property, it will revert back to the state. Abigail." He reached out to still her hands. "You must make the claim for Benjamin."

"Of course. I will write this steward."

Titus shook his head. "I fear it will not be enough. Word has gotten out about the lack of an heir, and Arminius, the steward, has already received several letters from people claiming to be Jason's wife, or another relative. He wrote me because he knew I would be personally acquainted with you. He recommended that if your child were a son, you come to Rome to offer the proof of that."

Abigail turned to face him fully. "Rome?" she echoed, sounding panicked. "*Proof?*"

"If you come with me, I can vouch for you and the child. You have the ruby Jason gave you, and the ring he always wore. It will be enough."

"But *Rome*? Titus, I have never been more than ten miles outside of Jerusalem!"

He smiled at her distress. "Then it is high time you had."

"But Ester—"

"One of Julia's slaves spoke with Andrew and Dinah a few days ago. Ester is unchanged, and not far off, but they did not know where she had been taken; they had apparently left you a note telling you this, but it has somehow gotten lost. Dinah saw your note, assumed it to be their note. . ."

Abigail groaned. "This should not be so difficult. If I had just stayed there—"

"You would have been alone and hungry," Titus finished for her. "They will probably check with them again in a few days' time. They now know where to tell them to find us. But Abigail, my ship sails for Rome in two days. If we do not find them by then, I suggest you come with me."

She regarded him hollowly. "With you?"

He nodded, certain she saw in his face how serious his considered this matter. "You cannot waste much time. And if Ester is unwell, she would be unable to travel with you even if you found her today. If you do not go with me, you will go alone, and that would not be wise. It is the only viable recourse."

Abigail drew in a deep breath, her eyes distant.

"You would not have to stay there for long." He squeezed the hand under his. "Just long enough to make your claim. Then you can return and be with your mother. While there, you can stay with my family. I can see no other option, Abigail. Tabitha cannot support all of you, and though the general offered to open his home to you, I do not trust him, and it would not solve the dilemma of the property."

"I know." She met his gaze once more. Hers had grown soft, almost reminiscent. "I never wished to go to Rome, but I obviously have no choice. Thank you for your offer, Titus. I suppose I must accept."

Titus gave her a small smile and stood. "I will see to the arrangements for your passage. Is there anything I should pick up for you from your house before we leave?"

"My trunk. It is in Jason's chamber. All I own is in it. Two days." She sighed. "Poor Benjamin will be fussy. His circumcision is tomorrow."

Titus felt the blood rush from his head at mere mention of the procedure, and Abigail laughed. "You are certain you wish to subject your son to that?"

"Jason willed it." Innocently, she tacked on, "And if you are going to learn the Law, Titus Asinius, perhaps *you* should consider it as well."

The suggestion was enough to send Titus quickly out the door, shouting over his shoulder that he would return soon.

From behind him he heard Samuel's voice. "Mother, may I go with him? Please? Please?"

"Very well."

Titus held up, bracing himself for the impact. As expected, Samuel barreled outside and launched himself at Titus's legs, shouting, "I am coming! Take me with you! I want to see the boat!"

Titus laughed and picked him up and swung him onto his shoulders. "We will not see the boat today, Samuel. It is at Joppa. I am going to tell one of my father's servants to book passage for you and your mother, though, and then, the day after tomorrow, we will go to see it."

"Is it big?" the boy asked, bending over to see Titus's face.

Titus grinned at the curls that fell down when Samuel put his head upside down. "It is big. With sails larger than your house and poles as tall as the fortress. And Rome is many times larger than Jerusalem, too."

Samuel gasped in amazement. "Bigger that Jerusalem? Benjamin will be frightened." His voice hinted at some trepidation of his own. "I will have to protect him."

Titus chuckled and tickled one of the feet dangling over his shoulder. "You will indeed."

"What is your house like, Titus?"

"Large," Titus said, considering. "Luxurious. But not very warm."

"I shall bring a blanket." That proclamation made Titus laugh again. "Will there be any boys to play with?"

"A few, perhaps."

"And the place Mother is claiming for Benjamin? Is it big?"

"Very big," Titus said. "Very nice. And very much more welcoming than my house. You shall like it there, Samuel, and I think your mother will, too. But do not tell her that just yet. She may decide not to, just for the sake of it."

Such a thing seemed to baffle the boy, but he nevertheless vowed secrecy and kept up his barrage of questions.

◆

Andrew felt pounds lighter as he traveled back to the inn. He had just come from the general's house, and most of his worries were eased. Except for that detail about her traveling with Titus Asinius.

Drusus greeted him at the door. "Well?"

"She is well," Andrew replied with a smile. "She had a son. She has gone with one of Jason's friends to Rome, to claim the Visibullis estate–apparently the steward has been in touch, and needed verification of an heir."

Drusus nodded, not looking surprised. "One of my servants came shortly after you left with a similar message for me. I am glad she went; it spares me from needing to do so too quickly. But still, I too should make the trip soon, to remove any doubts they may have of her." He sighed, glancing inside as if seeing through the walls to where Ester lay. "Go tell your mistress her grandson has been born. Perhaps it will bring life back to her soul."

Andrew moved to her room and knelt beside the bed. She had grown so thin, so pale. "Mistress?" He picked up her hand, the fingers lax. "Mistress, I just got the news. Abigail had her babe, a little boy. You have a grandson, Lady. Your husband and son live on."

Ester opened her eyes and smiled.

◆

For the first few days of the voyage, Abigail was so sick she could barely stand. But she soon got her sea legs, much to the relief of her companions, and was able to move about with relative ease. They were traveling on one of the ships that Caius Asinius owned, and it was a trading vessel. They occupied the only two cabins available for passengers, and both were rather cramped. Abigail had insisted on taking the smaller of the two, and Titus had insisted back that if she did that, Samuel would stay with him.

So she and Benjamin had their own little room, which had seemed quite cozy at the start, of which she was completely oblivious for the next hours, and which then began to suffocate her. For her own sanity's sake, on the fourth day of the voyage she fled to the decks, baby bundled up against the brisk sea air and nestled against her.

"Abigail."

At the sound of Titus's voice, she turned from her place at the rail, smiling when she saw her friend and Samuel drawing near. Titus did not return the smile.

"You should not be up here." He sent a scathing look at one of the sailors until he skulked away.

"I was about to lose my mind in that cabin. I needed fresh air."

Surely Titus could understand such reasoning—he spent most of his free time out of the close space. He sighed. "Well in the future, please only come on deck when I am with you. You are a bit of a novelty on board." He glared at another man who had lingered a bit too long with his gazes. "I am afraid these men will eventually decide staring at you is not enough."

Abigail blushed and cleared her throat, holding Benjamin a little closer to her. "One would think this little bundle would deter them."

Titus's look was dry. "Only if one thinks as a woman instead of a man. Be wise and cautious, my friend. Your beauty has not dimmed, and Jason is not the only man who could appreciate it."

Abigail searched his gaze carefully but saw only concern there, none of the things that had once made her blood chill whenever he looked at her. She nodded, docile again, and took a step closer to his side. "I will be careful. And I will only come out here with you." With a smile she added, "As long as you bring me at least twice a day, anyway."

Titus grinned his agreement and held out an arm to urge her into movement. He fell into step beside her, even put one hand protectively on the small of her back as they walked. Samuel attached himself to Titus's other hand, swinging it happily as he skipped along beside them. The boy's eyes were focused on the water.

Abigail looked up at her companion. "This evening I will resume our lessons, if you wish."

"I was hoping you would offer," he admitted with a smile. "I have spent the last days trying to sort through all you have already told me, but I have many questions. These Laws are all-encompassing; I fear I will never learn them all, and that at each moment of my life I will have to stop and wonder what it is I should be doing."

Abigail laughed. "That is not a bad thing, my friend. If you pause to wonder, then you will have paused to hear your conscience, the voice of God. But you remember the basics, do you not?"

Titus nodded, his face at peace. "Love the Lord first of all, and then my heart will bend in the right direction. Love my neighbors, and do unto them as I would have them do unto me." His gaze went hard, focused straight ahead. "It will not be easy. My life up until now has been dominated by those things God forbids. Women, drunkenness, violence. In moments like these, I feel as though I am capable of leaving it all behind. But when I am alone, facing Rome?" He shook his head in dismay. "I know not how I will resist falling into those habits once more."

"You will not be alone," Abigail swore. "Our God is everywhere, Titus. He is in us. And you heard what Tabitha said, that Jesus promised to send the Holy Spirit in his place, to comfort us and teach us."

Titus sighed. "I have not seen this Spirit. How will I know it?"

Abigail looked up into his face and smiled. "How did you know the messiah?"

Titus returned the smile. "He touched me."

She nodded, looking forward again. "His touch was fire, as was his blood on me. His Spirit will be fire, too. We will know, Titus. We will know."

THIRTY

The vessel rocked violently in the storm, the boards creaking under the strain and groaning with the effort of staying afloat. According to the captain, they were in no great danger; the storm was a mild one, he claimed, and they would weather it with no troubles. Titus believed him because he knew the man, and he knew that he spoke the truth.

Abigail did not look convinced.

Samuel was asleep as though it were nothing but a lullaby, and Benjamin had finally settled, too. He knew Abigail needed some rest, but she groaned every time she closed her eyes. Hence why she was sitting on the floor in his cabin, Samuel's head in her lap, the baby's basket beside her. Titus sat on his pallet and watched the lantern sway back and forth on its hook in the ceiling.

"I have been sick enough this past year to last me a lifetime." Her voice sounded tight, strained. "Must I *sail* back to Israel when this is done? Can I not simply will myself to be there, or strap myself to the back of a giant bird?"

Titus chuckled. "Before the storm began, you were claiming to have gained a love for sea life."

"I spoke prematurely." She put a hand on her stomach.

Titus patted the space beside him. "Come here."

She eased from under Samuel and crawled the few feet to his side. He slid a hand under her braid and gently massaged at the pressure in her neck. She sighed.

"It is your nerves that are making you ill," he said. "You must relax."

"That is what I am always told right before something unpleasant befalls me."

Titus bit down a chuckle. "Jason once said that you never complained. That you were perfect humility, modesty, and grace."

"He then proceeded to spoil me."

He smiled, though she could not see it. "You have no idea how tired I got of hearing your name. It seemed that every time I saw him, you were the only thing on his mind. I had to follow him around as he searched for presents, listen as he vented his frustrations with the walls you kept around you." He shook his head, breathing a laugh. "And once the others had seen you, it only grew worse. We could not meet without mention of Jason's Venus."

Abigail laughed outright. "Venus? I think you were a bit strong in your teasing."

"No. I think you simply do not realize how beautiful you are." His hand stilled on her neck, then fell away. Abigail turned to meet his gaze, her own questioning. He drew in a long breath, wondering at the trust he saw in her eyes. "I certainly never made it a secret that I found you attractive. I think I made you blush every time we met."

She surprised him by smiling. "You were certainly shameless."

"If you had been anyone's but Jason's," he began, but then shook himself to halt that thought. "But for all that, I could not understand how he had let himself fall in love with you."

"Neither did I." Sighing, she leaned against the wall at her back. "I thought he would tire of me quickly. I wanted him to. But it seemed that no matter what I did, he found something in it to pursue. If I held aloof, he would take it as a challenge. If I treated him normally, he would take it as encouragement. If I argued with him, he would find it entertaining. And then the baby." Her eyes fell on Benjamin, and she smiled.

Titus watched the little one's chest rise and fall. "I thought you a fool for not welcoming what would secure his affections. And I thought him a fool for caring."

She rolled her head along the wall to face him again. "And I despised you for once convincing him to go to another woman. For making him feel guilty for staying at home with me instead of going into the town with you."

Regret filled his veins. "And for all that, he loved you anyway, and remained my friend."

She nodded. "He was a good man."

Titus mirrored her in agreement, but then just studied her for a long moment. "On your wedding day, I accused you of not loving him."

A sheen of tears glistened in her eyes. "You were right. I did not love him. I had come to be fond of him by that time, but I could not let him past the pain he had caused me. Even at the last, I had not given him my heart as he wished it. I suppose I loved him in a way." She dashed at the tears before they could fall. Drew in a quivering breath. "Not as I should have."

He could manage no accusation. "You made him happy, whatever your emotions. I am glad of that."

"Now," Abigail tacked on with a hint of a grin.

"Yes, now." He smiled too, but it soon faded. "I see, now, what I could not before. That you are a person, not just a slave. A human, not just a woman. You have intelligence and conviction and wisdom. And that the Hebrew way is not so incomprehensible."

Abigail reached out and patted his hand where it lay on the floor between them. "You have proven yourself to be much more than I ever gave you credit for. I thought you the worst of all Jason's friends. But of all Jason's friends, you are the only one who let himself be changed by all that happened."

He took his hand from hers so that he could put the arm around her and draw her close in companionship. "It surprises me, too." He gave her shoulder a squeeze. "But it has at least gotten your mind off the storm."

She elbowed him in the ribs, undoubtedly instantly aware of it again.

Titus grunted, then laughed. "Sweet as honey, that Abigail. All humility and gentle modesty." She grinned in response as Samuel was wont to do, and Titus sighed at the sight. "How old are you, Abigail?"

Abigail paused for a moment, as if she had to calculate. "My birthday passed this year without any attention. Fifteen. And you?"

He let his lips tip up in a crooked grin. "I remember when I was fifteen. It was a good year. Bithia came to us that year." He glanced down and found her eyes lit dryly. "I think you do not care about that, though, do you? And I should try not to think of those things anyway, I know. I am in my twenty-eighth year. A few years older than Jason."

"But still younger than most centurions. I suppose the five of you all were. Put ahead by politics, and brought together by that circumstance."

"Indeed." Titus sighed, resting his head against the wall. "The seas are calming."

Abigail hummed her agreement, then let silence hold the room. Minutes later she asked, "Did you not like the military, Titus?"

He did not have to think through his answer. "No."

"Why not?" Exhaustion weighted her voice, and her head came to rest against his shoulder.

"I did not like having to answer to somebody else for my every move."

"But we all have to answer to someone." She yawned. "At least in the military, there are others that must also answer to you."

Titus smiled at her logic and reached with his free hand to smooth a stray tendril of hair from her cheek. "And in Rome, I have servants that do the same."

She blinked rapidly, much as her son had done earlier when fighting off sleep. "Surely not so many."

"Not so many fewer."

Abigail hummed for a moment. "The wealthy Asiniuses. Your father was consul until recently. 'A family destined for greatness.'" She chuckled to herself. "'But the son is a bit intolerable sometimes. He thinks himself too good to serve as a soldier.'"

Titus did not know whether to be amused or amazed. "Where did you hear such gossip?"

Her eyes slid shut. "I read Jason's letters to his mother sometimes."

Her breathing was growing deeper, and Titus knew she would soon be asleep. "Abigail, did Jason not write his letters in Latin?"

"Mm. I always thought it rather rude. He knew his mother could not read it."

Titus just watched her for a moment, smiling softly as she drifted off. "Abigail," he whispered, knowing she would not hear, "I have never met anyone quite like you."

He watched her a moment longer, then lifted her gently and carried her to her own room, putting Benjamin beside her after a second short trip. Bidding the two sleeping beings a good night, he went back to his pallet. Slumber did not come so easily to him.

Thinking back on it now, he was sure Jason had mentioned his parents' rather strange decision to educate their slaves, even the girl. Until this moment, though, he had given it no thought. It had been none of his concern that they could read or write. And when he had first seen Abigail, anything beyond the charms of her body simply did not interest him. Even that time when she had spoken with them of her one God, of what his Son would be like, it had been easy to put aside her wit and knowledge the moment she closed her mouth.

Weeks ago, when she had written that note to her fellow slaves, it had struck him as odd for only a moment; after all, it had been in Greek. But apparently she was also literate in Latin, and undoubtedly in Hebrew as well, if she had the other two.

It was no wonder Jason had ceased to see her as a slave after spending so much time with her. Most of the noble women he knew were not as learned as Abigail seemed to be. But whether or not her skills would endear her to Rome he could not tell. Because the point remained that she was a Jewess, had been a servant in a Roman's house. The families he knew would not be so eager to welcome her into their circles.

But they would not have to, after all. They would have to welcome only her son;

and he would make sure they did so. He would stay in communication with Abigail even after she went back to Israel, and he would see that the boy received the education he deserved; Samuel too. He had a sharp mind, and it should be hewn. Abigail would surely see the wisdom of sending them to Rome for their schooling, and when they came, he would gladly welcome them, take them under his wing.

It occurred to him as sleep finally came that he was looking quite far into the future all of a sudden. It was an unsettling realization, for he still was not so clear on what he would be doing with his life in the next year. But, he supposed, that was one curiosity easily satisfied. All he had to do was wait and see.

◊

By the time the ship arrived in port at Ostia Antica, Abigail had once again decided she liked life on the sea. Looking out in all directions and seeing the vast world of water underneath her, the edge of land just within sight, the gulls flapping overhead and crying out their complaints. She liked the salty air and the shimmer of sun upon the swells.

They arrived early in the day, but they still had a bit of a journey before they reached Titus's home. There was a veritable entourage awaiting them, which he pointed out from the rails before they were permitted to leave the ship.

She surveyed the collection of slaves, horses, and carts that stood inland a few hundred yards, amid the bustling of the small city. "Why are there so many?"

"I am the son of the house. And a rather demanding one in the past. They would wish to anticipate my needs; and moreover, the larger the procession entering Rome, the more attention it gets. My father will wish my homecoming to be something that gains notice."

"Oh." Abigail held Benjamin a little closer to her and pulled Samuel back against her legs.

Titus smiled and put a hand on her shoulder. "You have nothing to fear, Abigail. You are my guest, and Jason's widow. They may look at you with curiosity, but you will be treated with respect." He laughed outright at the look she sent him. "You are a mistress now. You must grow accustomed to being held in respect."

"I was a slave for most of my memory, Titus. If not for Jason, I would be one still. I would have married a slave, I would have remained a slave."

Titus snorted and looked out at Ostia again. "As Jason pointed out to me in one of our many conversation on the matter, you were born free. And you are far too good to be the wife of a slave."

"That slave was my first and dearest friend."

Titus looked at her again. "Andrew? Are you in love with him, Abigail?"

Abigail sighed, not missing the censure in his voice. "No, Titus, I am not in love with Andrew. But he is my friend, and I love him. I will not endanger my son's future standing by marrying a slave. Do not worry."

A smile slipped onto Titus's mouth. "Well, you cannot blame me. Your husband did it."

Abigail rolled her eyes. "To ensure his son's future standing. It was a very different situation."

He granted that with a tilt of his head, then turned when the captain called out their permission to debark. He nodded his acknowledgment to the man, then smiled into Samuel's grin when the boy took his hand excitedly. "Here we go. We shall be in Rome within the hour."

Abigail had to stifle the urge to run back into her cabin and hide.

They left the ship, their luggage having already been taken to Titus's slaves. As soon as they were on dry land again, one of the elder servants rushed forward, falling onto a knee with head bowed in front of Titus. "My lord and master. It is with deepest pleasure that I welcome you home."

"I have only been gone a year, Vinius," Titus said with humor. "Do not injure your bad knee on my account."

The man seemed taken aback by the show of concern.

Titus chuckled, motioning with a hand. "Rise, good servant."

Abigail watched as the man obeyed, his face proving the discomfort caused by his knee. His gaze wandered to Abigail before he cast his eyes to the ground.

"This is Abigail Visibullis," Titus said by means of introduction. "You may remember my friend, Jason."

"Of course!" Vinius beamed a smile.

"This is his widow, and their child."

The servant's smile vanished. "Widow? My lord, I had not heard of his death. My condolences. Mistress," he then said, bowing to Abigail, "your husband had my deepest regard. I serve your pleasure with willingness."

"Thank you, Vinius." She hoped he heard her genuine appreciation in her voice.

Titus's brows were drawn. "The head servant in my father's house has not heard of my best friend's death? I have forgotten much about my father's habits, it seems. I wonder if even my mother knows."

"Your father shares with us what we need to know." Vinius studied the ground.

Titus grunted and nodded in the direction of their horses. "Let us be off, Vinius."

The servant was quick to obey, leading them to their transportation and pointing them to where they could sit in most comfort and watch the scenery pass with the most luxury. Titus nodded his approval and held Benjamin while Abigail was helped into her place, then gave the child back and hoisted Samuel up, following him soon after.

They were all menservants who had come to greet their master, and Abigail felt their gazes on her more than once. If she happened to turn in their directions, though, they were always quick to look away. She found her spine straightening of its own accord and glanced down at her son for fortification.

"Did Jason not tell you that nowhere in Rome was there to be found a beauty to compare to yours?" Titus asked with a smile, his words soft so that his slaves would not overhear.

"Jason said many things to try to flatter my vanity."

Titus chuckled. "Flattery it may have seemed, but it was probably all true." He glanced briefly but sternly at one of his men who was looking their way. "It would take more control than most men have for them not to look at you, Abigail. You will have to be understanding."

She lifted her chin. "From what I have heard, women are not lacking in your household, Titus. Perhaps you should remind your men that I am not a novelty, as I was aboard your ship."

Before Titus could respond, Samuel began his customary catalogue of questions, asking about everything from the name of buildings they passed in Ostia to the kinds of plants growing alongside the road to Rome to who was who among his slaves. It kept the two adults occupied until they entered through the massive gates of the city Titus dared to call home.

THIRTY-ONE

"Mistress! The runner has arrived! Your son will be here in moments!"

Aquilia Asinius smiled. "Go see that cook has the meal prepared." The servant hurried away, and Aquilia reached to smooth down a curl of her silver hair. She took a single glance in the mirror, long enough to verify that she looked her best. Each tress arranged. Paint carefully applied to her face. Stola draped just so. Jewels telling the world who she was. Satisfied, she headed for the door of her chamber.

She moved slowly through the house, knowing it would be a few minutes before Titus arrived. As she went, she looked at every piece of furniture she passed, making sure all was clean and perfect. She was not disappointed. She arrived in the front room just in time to hear the commotion that preceded the opening of the massive door.

Her calm fled when her son's form filled the entrance. She flew to embrace him. "My son!"

"Mother. I have missed you." He held her close, then drew back enough to look at her, his smile genuine. "You are a vision of loveliness."

Aquilia smiled at the compliment, but then another figure caught her eye. A woman. Her smile fell from her lips. "Who is that?"

Titus turned to include the woman, giving Aquilia a clearer view of her. She lifted her chin. Had she expected her son's habits to change while he was away? Obviously they had not. He cleared his throat. "Mother, this is Jason's widow, Abigail, and their son Benjamin."

Not what she assumed, but no better. Aquilia did not return Abigail's smile, and she did not reach out to make any greeting. She just shifted her words to Latin. "This is the Hebrew slave that ruined your friend? Why did you bring her here?"

Titus glanced at the girl, though her face revealed no emotion. "She needed to come to claim the estates for her son. I told her she could stay here until the matter is settled."

Her mouth fell open. "Have you lost your senses, Titus? Are there not enough women in my house for you and your father to entertain yourselves with? Must you bring in another to tempt him into shame?"

Titus's face turned instantly into the granite creation Aquilia saw more often than not. "She is Jason's widow, Mother."

Aquilia sliced a hand through the air. "She is a slave. And while your father respected your friend, you know well he will not consider a claim on such a creature now that he is dead!"

Her son rolled back his shoulders into the fighting stance she knew all too well. "Mother—"

"If my presence here is going to cause problems, I will simply stay elsewhere." The words startled Aquilia not just because the girl dared to interject herself into the conversation, but because she did so in Latin. She even smiled. "I am certain there is either an inn nearby, or the steward of the Visibullis estates would consent to me staying there."

"No." Titus folded his arms across his chest. "You will not stay in a public house with no guard, nor will you throw yourself on your servant's mercy. We will claim Benjamin's inheritance through the legal channels, and when you go to his estates, it will be as mistress, not beggar."

Abigail looked at him with amusement. Amusement! In the face of her son's determination? Had she not seen the stone of his countenance, she would have though he had softened while in Israel. Perhaps this slave was just too stupid to know when not to argue.

"Titus, I will not allow you to be generous at the cost of your home's peace."

His eyes gained an ironic glint. "There is no peace in this home, and there never was. You will cause no more trouble than would find us anyway. My father may be lecherous, but he is not the worst of the men I know. You would not be safe in the city unescorted."

"She will not be safe here, either." Aquilia threw her shoulders back. Her son respected the woman, it was clear. Which meant that unless she wanted to antagonize him his first hour home, she had better aid his efforts to protect her. "Not as an independent woman. You must let your father think she is yours, Titus, it is the only option."

Titus did not look shocked by the suggestion, but he did not look convinced by it either. "She is Jason's widow."

Aquilia sighed. "And since when does that affect your desires? Was not Aria Flavius's betrothed? Was not Cornelia Lusius's sister?"

Titus said nothing, just clenched his jaw.

Aquilia lifted a brow. "If she stays here it will be as your protectorate. She can stay in the procoeton attached to your chamber."

"The only way out of that room is through mine," Titus objected.

Aquilia rolled her eyes. "Precisely. It is the only way in, as well."

He considered for a moment. Sighed. Nodded. "Let it be as you suggest, Mother."

Aquilia inclined her head, then looked at Abigail once more. "Whatever is she wearing?"

Titus and Abigail both looked at her garment with surpise on their faces. It must have been traditional Hebrew apparel, but it would not do here.

Her son cleared his throat. "Jason bought you some things after the Roman fashion, did he not?"

The girl nodded. "Shall I change?"

"Please." Aquilia made no attempt to hide her distaste.

The girl once again proved she had no sense by smiling. She put a hand behind her back. "Come, Samuel. Titus will show us to our chamber."

Aquilia drew in a sharp breath when a boy emerged from behind her. He was a lovely child, all golden curls and large eyes filled with trepidation. As for what he was doing here . . .

"Titus, tell me you have not gained a taste for boys."

Titus laughed. She had not honestly thought he had, but such beauty raised questions. Her son shook his head. "Jason bought the boy to save him from such a fate. Although Samuel has become more a son than a slave."

Aquilia made her thoughts on that clear with another pointed look at the girl, but she only shrugged. "I speak Greek more than anything. Child. Slave. They are the same word. The lines become blurred."

Titus choked back a laugh.

Aquilia let out a repulsed breath and turned away. She had not seen her son so jovial in fifteen years . . . and knew not what to think about seeing him so now. With *her.* "Settle in, my son. Come see me once you have had a chance to refresh yourself."

Abigail had never seen a home the likes of this one. She trailed Titus through the vestibulum and fauces, through the middle of the atrium, and toward the peristylium. The fact that his chamber was off the garden told her it would be larger, more ornate.

It certainly was. She had heard Jason once complain about how close the bedchambers could be in a Roman house, but she felt none of that in this cubiculum. The ceiling was vaulted, the air flowed in from the garden, and bed and windows were dressed in fabric she knew well had cost a fortune.

Titus grimaced when he opened another door, presumably to the servant's quarters attached to his. "This will far too cramped for all three of you."

She came up beside him, Samuel still holding one hand while Benjamin nestled against her chest. She smiled. "It is larger than the room I grew up in. We will be fine here."

"I will have a more comfortable mattress brought in. And arrange for a pallet for Samuel. Are you certain?"

"Quite." She stepped out again and looked around her in appreciation. "Titus, your home is beautiful." Her eyes landed on a small statue on a table in the corner of the room, then moved as if drawn magnetically to the gardens outside.

"It is. That is about all it is, as I think you will soon discover." He surveyed the room as if for a flaw. "It will do, I suppose. Are you sure you will not mind the lack of an exit?"

Abigail shook her head, but still she had to sigh.

Titus's face softened. "What is bothering you, my friend, if not that?"

Abigail hesitated only a moment. "Titus, are you going to tell your parents? You have changed, and they will notice."

Titus sighed, sitting down absently on one of the chairs. "I should, I know. But it will be difficult to explain to them."

"Especially if your father thinks I am your lover." She held his gaze firmly, though she felt heat stain her cheeks. "I appreciate the delicacy of the situation, that you feel I must be protected. But promise me that after I leave, you will clear up this fallacy."

Titus nodded, looking relieved. Probably at the permission to put off the task until then.

She was not finished, though. "Besides, I am not convinced he will believe this. My seventy days of mourning will not be complete for another fortnight, not to mention the forty days of purification following the birth." When he smirked she narrowed her eyes. "What?"

"My father is hardly educated in the laws of your people, Abigail. Such things will not occur to him, I assure you." But it did, at least, cause him to study her. "It has only occurred to _me_ that you have not been wearing mourning."

"One of the physicians said we should not," Abigail said softly. "He said it was only furthering Ester's depression. And I did not think about it once Benjamin was born."

Titus nodded, then stood. "Well, take a few moments to get settled, and I will do the same."

Abigail nodded. But she had no idea how to settle into this place.

⸙

Caelia gasped when she heard that Titus was returned. She hurried from the room she shared with two other women and dashed in the direction of her master's chamber. To say she had missed him in the past year would be an understatement; she had counted the days until his return once Caius had announced he would be back soon. To be sure, she hoped he had thought of her with less frequency. She was still less than anxious to be the cause of a deeper rift between Titus and his father. But now that he was back, perhaps it would signal the end of her nights with Caius. Perhaps she would be his alone again.

Something within her told her it would not happen that way. Before, Titus had been the only man she had known, and that was why he kept her to himself. But now she had been defiled by another, by many others if truth be told, and he would probably not be so eager to claim her as solely his. But at the very least, she would get to enjoy his arms once more, feel his lips warm against her flesh. . . she closed her eyes in delectation, opening them again quickly so she could speed to her destination.

Perhaps now his friend would return soon, as well. She smiled. The single kiss she had bestowed on him had told her that Jason Visibullis would appreciate a chance to spend some of his time in her company, and she would not mind spending some of hers in his, either.

She came to the doorway and smiled anew when she saw Titus within. He was even more handsome than she had remembered, with that darkest brown hair, muscles tanned from working outside, the proud bearing that struck fear into every heart that came across him. He was the epitome of what a man should be, a model of the gods. She stepped into his chamber.

"Master."

Titus looked up, something indiscernible flashing in his eyes. She was suddenly aware of the way she was dressed, more provocatively than he had ever permitted. No desire flashed in his eyes, but surely that was just his usual Stoic control. "Caelia."

She took the acknowledgment as invitation, closed the distance between them and wrapped her arms around him. She kissed him soundly, but he did not respond. Instead of crushing her against him, he held her a few inches apart.

"Titus." She had expected his distance . . . but still it pierced. "I have missed you."

He seemed amused by the statement. "Were you lonely, Caelia? I find it hard to believe, knowing my father."

Heat flooded her cheeks even as she lifted her chin in pride. "You knew what you were forfeiting by leaving. But you are back now, Lord, and I welcome you eagerly. I will come to you tonight–"

"No." He disentangled her arms from around his neck and forced her a step away. "You will not come to me tonight, nor tomorrow, nor the day after."

"But my lord, you never refused the others, though they were shared. Why should you refuse me?"

Titus sighed, his jaw clenched. "It is not that."

"Then what is it?" She planted her hands on her hips.

A melody of laughter rang out, decidedly feminine. Caelia walked a few steps until she could look through the doors and into his servant's room. A woman swayed into view, bouncing a baby on her hip. "Who is *that*?"

The woman looked up, revealing a face that made Caelia's blood boil. Of course Titus would have found the most beautiful woman in Israel. But why did he bring her home with him? The child? Was it his?

Titus looked that way even as the woman wandered back out of sight. "Abigail Visibullis."

Caelia spun to him, eyes wide. "Visibullis?"

"Jason's widow."

Her amazement only grew. "Widow?"

"And their son, Benjamin."

"Son?"

Titus bit back a grin. "Have you forgotten your command of Greek in my absence, Caelia?"

She opened her mouth, but it took a moment to find words. "It is only that I did not know, master, either of his marriage or his death."

He nodded. "I brought her here to claim the estates for her son."

Her eyes narrowed. "She is lovely."

"She is indeed. Jason was quickly the envy of us all."

Anger made her shake. "Well, you never waited long to take what you wanted." She spun to the door. "When you tire of her, Titus, you know where I will be."

✦

Titus watched with mirth as Caelia stormed from the room. "Indeed, Caelia, I know where you will be," he said to where she had been. Feeling eyes on him, he looked over to find Abigail leaning against the door to the procoeton. "Do you see, now? Our involvement is quite believable, however false."

Abigail rolled her eyes. "I think you enjoyed that, Titus Asinius."

Titus only grinned. "I am only a man, my friend."

Abigail grinned, shook her head, and turned.

A slave filled the doorway of his chamber. "Master, your father has arrived home."

Titus nodded with a sigh. After Abigail he called, "I must go down and meet him, Abigail. Get yourself settled in up here."

Hearing her agreement, he left the sanctuary of his room in favor of what he was not so sure would be a warm reunion. His father was one thing he had not missed when in Jerusalem. It seemed that they could not be in the same room without bursting into the flames of argument. It made it so that in past years, Titus simply avoided his sire whenever possible. They did not understand one another, could never agree, and were hence always disappointed in what the other did, thought, or said.

But Titus had prayed for forgiveness for his own insolence and had tried to forgive his father's, too. It seemed that now he would be tested, to see whether or not he had been sincere enough.

Titus met his father in the atrium and made himself smile. Caius stood at the same height that he did, had the same build and gait. His hair had turned to an iron gray, his face was creased with lines that only added severity to his appearance, rather than age. He was by all accounts a dignified personage; most held him in fear. What terrified Titus was that he knew he would look the same in thirty years, though being similar to the man was the last thing he desired. He could only pray he would not be hewn by the same tides.

"Father."

Caius's face lit with a smile that matched Titus's; partially forced, partially genuine, partially wary. "Titus, my son." They approached one another and embraced. "You look well. Jerusalem seems to have agreed with you."

"It is good to be back in Rome. You look well too, Father."

Caius simply nodded at the observation. A hand clapped to his shoulder, he led him toward the impluvium. Its fresh waters glistened in the sunlight streaming in from the opening above. "Vinius met me at the Forum to tell me you had arrived." A glint Titus well remembered entered Caius's eye. "He tells me you brought a woman with you. One with a child?"

Titus took one last breath of peace. He knew very well his father's smile would soon fade. "Yes, Abigail Visibullis. Jason's widow. It is his son."

Caius froze midstep, turned to look him in the eye. His smile had become a straight, unyielding line. "You brought the Hebrew slave into my house? The one who was the ruin of your closest friend? Fool."

Titus bore the epithet without so much as a wince. "Would you have Jason's legacy be lost to his only son, Father?"

"Of course not."

"Then it was necessary that Abigail come to Rome to lay her claim for her son."

"*Jason's* son is then naturally welcome under my roof. The whore is not. Toss her into the streets where she belongs."

Motion caught Titus's attention a second before Abigail's voice rang out. "As I already told your wife, I will gladly stay elsewhere. But my son will go wherever I do."

Titus and his father both looked at Abigail, and both drew in a sharp breath at the sight of her. She had changed into one of her Roman costumes, and had changed just as quickly from lovely Hebrew mother to seductive goddess. The cloth draped in becoming folds over her curves, the jewelry complementing the tone of her skin. Titus forced himself to swallow and to remember that she was his friend now. That behind that perfect body was an intelligent, caring soul.

Abigail entered the atrium and stopped directly in front of his father. "I am not a whore," she stated calmly, authoritatively. "I am no longer a slave. I cannot control what you think of me, but you will speak of me with more respect."

Titus mentally lauded her, at least until a glance at his father showed only heightened interest. The last thing they needed was for Caius to decide she would be a challenge worthy of conquering.

"I spoke amiss." Caius somehow made the apology sound as though he had not changed his mind a whit. His eyes did not leave Abigail. "Forgive me, fair one."

She made no response, measuring him and obviously finding him lacking. When Titus held out a hand, she put hers in it and stepped close to his side. It was a move gauged to lay down the boundaries, and it apparently worked, for Caius's eyes sparked with something new. Not exactly respect, but it resembled it.

They had been speaking in Greek, but Caius turned to Titus and said in Latin, "In your letters, you wrote only of your disapproval of Jason's woman. You neglected to mention her beauty."

Titus glanced down at Abigail only briefly. "I saw no reason to discuss beauty I did not possess. She was Jason's."

"No longer." He ran his eyes over Abigail just as Titus had the first time they met, and Abigail stepped closer to Titus now as she had to Jason then. Protectiveness surged again. "You have taken her to your bed?"

Titus arched a brow artfully. "Would I take the widow of my closest friend to my bed?" He laced his words with enough sarcasm to elicit a knowing smile from his father.

"If you have not," Caius said, "you are a fool. You know I would."

"You would. But you will not."

Caius nodded his deference to Titus's claim. Turning away enough to break the tension, he said in Greek, "I imagine your mother has made sure a meal is ready, and you must both be hungry. Come, let us dine."

"We will join you in a moment." He watched as Caius nodded and walked away. Titus breathed a sigh of relief and looked down into Abigail's face. She was still looking in the direction his father had gone, and if her expression were any indication, her thoughts were not very pleasant. He gently cupped her chin. "He will not touch you, Abigail."

She nodded, but her features did not ease.

"Where are Samuel and the babe?"

As hoped, Abigail's face softened and brightened with a smile. "Benjamin is asleep, and Samuel is being introduced to the other boys in the house, and Antonia, with whom he went, promised to see to his meal."

Titus smiled. "She was my nurse. Mother must have sent her up; your children will be well cared for in her hands."

"She seemed very gentle, kind." She sighed. "Hers was the only polite reception I have encountered within these walls."

Titus squeezed the hand he held in encouragement. "The worst is over, my friend. Now all you have to do is work on smiling instead of scowling when I look at you."

She smiled now, but with teasing in her eyes. "As long as you keep looking at me as you have been instead of as you once did, that will not be a problem."

Titus propelling them both toward the triclinium and food. "Then perhaps we should find you some less becoming clothes."

THIRTY-TWO

"Inside?" Abigail looked dubiously at the tiny room Titus indicated. Her nose wrinkled. "Is that sanitary?"

Titus sternly held down his laugh. The corners of his mouth nevertheless tugged up. "Yes, Abigail. It is far cleaner than an outdoor facility. And far more convenient as well."

Abigail nevertheless shook her head. "Rome is such a strange place." She peered into the room but did not step in. "Relieving yourself *indoors*. And you call the *rest* of the world barbaric?"

He lost the battle to the laugh and put a hand on Abigail's shoulder to urge her forward.

She absorbed the sound with a smile. If the stares the servants sent their way whenever he laughed were any indication, it was not something he had habitually done in this house. Hopefully they would grow accustomed to and fond of this new Titus. "It sounds as though your father has much planned for you these next few days."

He sighed, rubbing a hand over his face. "My father has much planned for me for the next few *years*. Running the shipping companies, the slave trades." At the wince she could not hold back, he sighed again. "Sorry. But these wars we have fought have secured many lands for Rome that still burst with miscreants. The numbers that are caught and sold are vast. But beside all that, he also expects me to be active in politics. Go to the Senate hearings, run for offices. . . he will not be happy until I, like he, have a consulate on my list of accomplishments."

"And is that what you want?"

Titus led them into the back garden behind the house. The sun was bright and warm, the plants a riot of color and scent, all blending together in a scene that made Abigail smile. She said nothing, however, just waited for Titus to respond. At length, he did. "I know not what I want. I did not like the military life, but I have been rebelling so long against my father that I have already decided I will not like this, either. I suppose I should give it a chance to win me."

Abigail chuckled, then closed her eyes to breathe in the sweet scent of myriad blooms. "You have lovely gardens. I think I could very easily get lost out here and be content never to be found."

"This was Jason's favorite spot as well." He led her down a stone path, pointing toward a granite sculpture. "Our garden nymph. She bears a striking resemblance to you, Abigail."

Abigail stopped before the artwork and tilted her head to the side critically. The figure was nude, but for sculpted flower petals arranged over her that did little to hide her shape. The eyes were closed, head falling back as if to better receive the touch of wind, perfume of blossoms. Her lips were curved up only slightly, her body young and firm, her face at peace. Abigail shook her head. "I do not see it."

Titus chuckled. "These next few days will be hectic, indeed. But tomorrow I will dispatch a missive to Arminius to let him know you and your babe have arrived; I expect he will be in touch as to what you need to do. We will have to make time to go out there soon, I know."

Abigail nodded soberly. "I must thank you, my friend, for all you have done to help us. If it were not for you, Benjamin and I could both have died, or been left abandoned at the least. And coming to Rome would have been all but impossible on our own."

"I am only glad I was there to help."

Abigail pressed her hand lightly against the arm it was resting on in acknowledgment of her gratitude, but then looked toward the house. "Benjamin will be waking soon, and he will be hungry. I should go in."

With a nod from her friend, she moved back inside.

♦

Titus sighed and sank down on the chaise positioned near him. He would be able to protect her from his father with their current arrangement, it was true. But he had a feeling it may take more than a little bit of prayer to give him the strength to protect her from himself. It was true he was far more temperate now than he had been a few months ago, but he was no less a man. Seeing her in that lovely garment today had only made more obvious what he had never attempted to deny: Abigail was the most beautiful creature he had ever seen. Getting to know her, liking her, feeling responsible for her did not change that. If anything, it would only complicate the situation more.

But he certainly had enough respect for his late friend to honor her period of mourning, and that would guarantee the chastity of even his thoughts for the next fortnight. Luckily, she would be leaving soon after that.

His brow furrowed. Traveling back to Israel would be no easier than traveling to Rome would have been, and this time he could not go with her. He would have to find someone to accompany her; someone huge, intimidating, strong. . . and a eunuch.

♦

The day was bright and warm, the sky an unbroken azure spreading out above them in a peaceful canopy, the land a brilliant green rivaling an emerald in its clarity. Outside the city, nature's smells predominated, the scents of civilization receding and being replaced by that of fresh growth, damp earth, clean air, and promise. It was a day for breathing in with joy and exhaling in contemplation. It was a day to relax, to marvel at the beauty in this world God had fashioned.

But Abigail could not calm the nerves in her stomach long enough to appreciate it. It was her fourth day in Rome, and they were heading out to the Visibullis estates to meet with Arminius and discuss the necessary legal moves. She was terrified. She knew not what she would do if they questioned the truth of her claim.

Titus's presence beside her was her one anchor. Even now he gave her a soft smile of encouragement and reached over to rest his hand on hers, cradling Benjamin's head. His thumb brushed through the downy locks of the baby, who gave a toothless grin that made Titus's lips turn up even more.

"I hope Samuel is having fun," Abigail said on a sigh, wishing the sensitive child were with her now to offer his innocent smile and his simplistic wisdom.

Titus shifted his smile from Benjamin to her. "I am certain of it. Antonia will keep a close eye on him, but he will enjoy the markets. You would too. I shall have to take you out into the city soon, Abigail, you have been closeted up in the house since your arrival."

Abigail smiled in contentment. "I have yet to get the fill of your library. I began Epictetus's *Discourses* yesterday before you arrived home."

"Ah, one of the founding texts of Roman thought. And what do you think of our State's philosophies?"

Abigail shrugged as she considered. "I agree with some of the tenets, I admit. The idea of a sphere of choice strikes me as true in many ways; that there are simply things I cannot influence, and it is needless to worry about them. But what Stoicism does not seem to take into account is that emotions simply *exist*. And that they have profound effects. Perhaps I cannot control you, but does that mean that a heartfelt appeal would evoke no response that would allow you, with your larger sphere of choice, to make decisions to affect what I would will? I think not. I think the human heart, and the human condition, is much more than a collection of individual's spheres. I think we are all bound together by something far deeper than circumstance."

"Christ did teach, according to Tabitha, that we should go out of our way to help those who need it, acting on faith that others would do the same for us. He preached love above all, and that does indeed seem to reach far outside the walls Stoicism forces us to erect." He sighed. "But I have been a Stoic forever, it seems. I was brought up with those precepts, raised to be a statuesque pillar unable to be bent by the winds of trial."

She tamped down her smile "And you did it very well. You not only kept your distance, you forced everyone else to keep theirs. But were you stronger then, Titus, or are you stronger now that you bent your knee to a higher authority and admitted that God's sphere of influence is all-encompassing? That he can affect what we cannot, but that through prayer and our Savior's sacrifice, we have achieved the ear of that omnipotent God?"

"Your rhetoric is flawless, my friend. I readily admit that you are right." He glanced at the countryside, then lifted a brow her way. "But one thing you would do well to glean from Epictetus's philosophies: there is no point in getting nervous about a situation such as the one we are approaching. The truth is well outside your control, and it will speak for itself. Be calm."

Abigail drew in a deep breath in an attempt to obey. She cast her eyes around her as she exhaled, able to appreciate even through her nervousness that the land they were driving over was beautiful. The foliage was lush, the air sweet with spring, the sun bright and warm upon her. "Are we close?"

Titus nodded, pointing toward a grove of trees. "Beyond that copse is the villa. It is a lovely place, Abigail; the Visibullises have long been a respected family in Rome. Cleopas's father, I believe, had a falling out with Augustus, but up until then they were among the leading families." He grinned. "There was a day not so long ago when they were above the Asiniuses, I know. This estate reflects that. My father would kill for such property."

Abigail arched her brows in consternation. "I hope you exaggerate, my friend."

Titus chuckled, giving her hand an encouraging pat. "Have no fear, small one. He is not in line for this one at any rate."

Abigail gazed down into Benjamin's face. He watched the world roll by with large eyes, and his curiosity made her smile. "For my son's sake, I am glad the Visibullises have such a place. Benjamin deserves to have every opportunity open to him. I know not if he will choose to live here or if he will remain in Israel, but the choice will be his, just as it was his father's, and his father's before him."

"What do you think of Rome thus far, Abigail? Jason said you would not take to it."

She sent her eyes around her once more, then smiled. "I did not think I would. And I still do not know that I would want to live here, so far away from all I call home. But I concede that I was premature in my judgements. Rome is a lovely place. At the very least, I am glad I came, that I have seen it." She met Titus's gaze. "And you? Do you still detest Israel as you once did?"

A single corner of Titus's mouth tugged up. "I find it impossible to loathe the place that saw me make such changes in myself. But I am afraid it is less the land itself I appreciate as the culture it was imbued with. Which is, I grant, what I disliked most in the beginning. I have come full circle."

"Indeed. Well, you will always be welcome in our home, wherever it may be. Know that, my friend. Be it this estate we approach now or our home in Jerusalem, you will always be greeted as a friend. I promise you that."

"The same to you, Abigail. If ever you need anything, for yourself or Benjamin or Samuel, I will gladly help you. If either of them wishes to come to Rome, I will happily take them into my counsel and do all I can for them."

"That is good to know." She meant it, though she could not yet contemplate a day when the tiny bundle in her arms would be striking out on his own, without her.

"There it is." Titus motioned toward an impressive structure as they drove within view. It stood magnificently etched against the horizon, proud and strong and promising to last twice as long as it had already been.

The final minute of the journey was made in silence as she took it all in; there were vast fields in the background, where Abigail could see grapevines and grains, animals grazing far away to the right. There were many smaller buildings all around, which Abigail could only assume to be the dwellings of those who worked the estate, perhaps stables or storage areas as well. As the wheels turned over the unevenly paved ground leading up to the villa itself, several people appeared to greet them, smiles on all three of their faces.

"My lord Asinius." The central man bent with deference at the waist. "It is good to see you once more."

"Arminius," Titus greeted as the vehicle rocked to a halt, "I am glad to be here again as well. I would only that the circumstances were different."

"Indeed." The steward's face fell. "I was deeply struck by the terrible news of my masters' deaths." His eyes moved to Abigail and the bundle in her arms. "It followed so soon after the joyous news of Jason's marriage and approaching child. Mistress, allow me to help you down."

Abigail smiled her gratitude and handed Benjamin momentarily to Titus so that she could descend more easily, then took the baby back.

"You are as lovely as my young master claimed," the elder man said with a soft smile. His gaze fell fondly onto the babe, who offered a happy grin at the new face. Arminius chuckled. "What a charming babe your son is. I can see Jason in him."

"As can I. My husband spoke well of you, Arminius. I am glad to meet you."

The old man actually blushed at the compliment. "And I you, Mistress. Come, let me show you the villa."

Titus had climbed down by then as well, and he fell in beside her and Arminius. The steward studied her as she studied the structure.

"It is lovely. It is no wonder Jason longed to return here." She smiled, knowing he would revel in the words of his late masters. "Many an evening he would regale me with stories of his time in Rome, of this place. But my imaginings fell far short of the mark."

Arminius looked around as if he had never seen the place before. "It is a most gracious estate, to be sure. It has been my pleasure to serve here so long. But it has been too long without a master present. I had hoped Jason would return before long."

Abigail cast her eyes down. She had not the heart to tell him that Jason would not have returned, and that it was because of her. "Titus tells me I will have to offer proof that Benjamin is Jason's son."

Arminius nodded. "Legally, yes. But the word of an Asinius will go far, and Titus wrote that he was at your wedding and can vouch for you."

"She also has the jewelry that was Jason's inheritance," Titus added. "But you said that others had already come forward claiming to be heirs? I suppose they have backers whose word is worth as much as mine."

"Not quite." Arminius smiled. "There have been several, yes. But most could not possibly be true simply because of incorrect timing, not to mention that neither Jason nor Cleopas mentioned them once, whereas Abigail here was an oft-spoken of figure in their correspondences."

Abigail looked surprised by this. "Cleopas never even mentioned this estate to me, though. I did not know of it until Jason brought it up."

Arminius shrugged. "It is of no consequence. They mentioned you, which is all the authorities will care about. It should not take long for the rabble to be cleared out."

Titus nodded, obviously satisfied. "We will both be at your disposal throughout the process, of course. We will do whatever is necessary to ensure that Jason's son receives the benefit he is due."

"Thank you." Arminius inclined his head and darted a gaze from Abigail to Titus. "If I may say, my lord Asinius, I am grateful to you on my masters' behalf for seeing my new mistress to Rome. A beauty as great as hers would find danger without a guardian."

Abigail felt herself blush. Titus only grinned at her. "My friend, a beauty as great as hers manages to find danger even *with* a guardian. But I swore to Jason she would be taken care of, and I will keep my vow."

Arminius nodded, halting them before the exit to a stately portico. "I could tell from his correspondence that he cared for you very much, Mistress."

Hearing the man several times her age continually referring to her by that title made the uncertainty creep up Abigail's spine, but she just straightened it in response. "I miss him greatly. And his father. Our lives altered too quickly that night; I fear I will not know how much it sent me reeling until I finally come to a halt."

Arminius nodded again, then lifted a hand to indicate the scene before him. "The vineyards will have a good year. There will be more than enough to store for the household and to sell. A fine vintage, surely, that will fetch a dear price. Our wines are known throughout Rome for their sweetness and strength."

Abigail looked out, noticing that there were many men bent over the vines, pruning, she supposed, though she knew nothing about the process. "How many do you have working in the fields?"

"There are twenty in the vineyards themselves. Three that specialize in running the winery. Fifteen more working with the vegetables, plus the shepherds and cowherds, the stablehands, and those serving as lesser stewards under me. Our total number is seventy; only a few are designated for the villa, though, so if ever you wish to stay here, Mistress, we will need to swell that number. You would not be safe here, I fear, without a larger staff. There are no women other than the workers' families to see to you, and hence too many men to trust." Arminius looked abashed at having to admit that.

Abigail smiled at his honesty. "I thank you for that wisdom, Arminius. If ever I intend to stay here, I will be certain to heed your advice. It is not a present worry, though. I must return to Israel soon to attend my mother, Ester. When I left, she was not well. The deaths of Cleopas and Jason were too much for her."

"I am sorry to hear that. Please, give her my wishes of health."

From there they continued the tour, but it was not until they had traveled all through the villa and were back where they started that Arminius cleared his throat. Abigail could tell by his posture that he was about to put forward something important— whether it be a test of her or a simple desire for information she knew not. "Mistress, my masters had both begun writing to me of a teacher whose lessons they rallied to, a man who was called Jesus, and whom they claimed was a Christ come to save the world, Jew and Gentile alike. Do you know of him?"

Abigail smiled, her eyes wandering to Titus, whose gaze encouraged her to share honestly all she knew. "Yes. I heard the stories my husband and father told, though I never heard the rabbi teach myself. But I have since learned many of his teachings. You see, the day they were to crucify Jason and Cleopas's murderer, they executed in his place this teacher. I had gone to see vengeance done, and instead I was witness to the death of a blameless man." Her eyes slid shut, and she tilted her face upward. "I will never be the same. I saw the agony on his face as he died, and it was the agony of the world, that he took on his shoulders to lighten our burden. A stray drop of his blood landed on my flesh, and I felt my soul washed clean of its sins."

"He is dead, then," Arminius said in a mournful tone, which inspired her to open her eyes again.

It was Titus who answered. "No. No, he is no longer dead. On the third day, his tomb was empty, and many have professed to seeing him alive. The Jews, of course, say his body was stolen, but I posted the guard myself. The Christ lives, Arminius. He has triumphed over the grave, and Abigail and I both believe it means we, too, will triumph over death. We will not be cast down to Hades with every other soul, we will be taken to the bosom of the Lord himself, there to live for eternity."

A tear traced a crooked path over the creased cheek of the loyal servant. "And my masters?"

"They believed." Abigail held Benjamin to her with one arm so she could reach out with the other and rest her hand on Arminius's shoulder. "Even now, they are with our Lord in Paradise, preparing a place for us. If you accept that truth, my friend, that Jesus the Christ died for your unrighteousness and rose again to deliver you from it, then you, too, will see the glory of heaven someday."

"This gift would be offered to a Gentile servant?" The steward shook his head. "It is too precious to be wasted on jackals. I just rejoice that those I served will be blessed in eternity."

Abigail smiled. "Titus is a Gentile. I was a servant. If the gift can be extended to us, why not to you? Our Lord did not preach health to the healthy, but to the sick. He did not feed the filled, but the hungry. It is those who need him most for whom he came, so if you desire him with a full heart, Arminius, he will not refuse you. The true God knows each of his children by name and will welcome you into his embrace."

"If this is true," Arminius said in a shaky voice, looking from her to Titus, "then how steep must be the cost. What must I do, how much must I give, to take this gift for myself?"

Titus shook that suggestion away. "A gift has no price. As we were taught, his yoke is easy, his burden light. All the Lord requires is a contrite and humble heart that will seek his will in all things. For some of us," he admitted, "that was the hardest thing he could ask. But I am learning what he wills, my friend, and I see that when I submit myself to him, he raises me up."

"All you must do is believe." Abigail squeezed the old shoulder under her hand. "Believe with your heart and confess with your lips that Jesus is the Lord, the only Son of the only God. If you do that, he will guide you in all the paths you will take."

"I do. I do believe. Since the first word my master wrote of this man, there has been a stirring in this weak heart." He covered his chest with a wizened hand, the tears coming faster now. "I asked him to tell me all he knew, and he faithfully did, but I feared with his death would come the end of my learning. I know not what to do, or how to pray to your God, Mistress, I know only that my heart shouts at me to embrace these words you speak. Teach me, I beg you, how to beseech this God."

Abigail glanced at Titus, then said, "Our friend, who taught us, said that Christ instructed his disciples to pray a certain prayer. Shall we pray it?"

The steward's nod was decisive. "Yes. Please, Mistress, teach me."

She let her hand fall down to grasp his, her eyes closing even as Titus's hand settled on her shoulder. "My Lord and Father in heaven," she whispered, not knowing if the very words were right, but knowing she remembered the meaning, "let your name be set aside as holy. Let us dwell in your words and your laws, let us seek and do your will here, as your servants do it in heaven. Give us all we need this day to serve you, and help us have the strength to forgive those who have wronged us, even as you have forgiven the wrongs we have done. Help us to follow your path rather than that of temptation and evil, since you are our deliverer and shepherd. For you hold the heavens and the earth in your hand, and we give you the glory for all."

"My Lord and Father in heaven, we come before you humbly today, as your servants." Titus's voice echoed in the room, sounding full, bright. "You know our hearts, you see that though different in the eyes of the world, we three have come together to seek your name. In this land of sin, Lord, we need your touch on us all the day. Grant us your eyes, that we may see the right path. Grant us your ears, that we may hear you whisper your truths. Grant us your heart, that we might reach out with love and understanding to those around us. Grant us your Spirit . . ." His voice wavered, the emotion in it pulsating. The hand on her shoulder vibrated with something that matched a harmonic within her. "Grant us your Spirit!"

A sudden heat entered the room, as if the wind had been chased out by a gust of fire, yet a cool touch brushed her face. Gravity pulled on her as if she were at a great height, and she fell to her knees along with the others, close together, body bearing down as spirit lifted up. Abigail opened her eyes, her breathing fast and short, and saw tongues of fire above the heads of each of her companions and saw from the movement of their eyes that there was one above her as well.

"Jehovah!" She sobbed, bending over until her forehead touched the cool marble of the floor, the baby cradled in the space between her and the ground, not so much as squirming against her. "Blessed be the name of the Lord!"

She heard the men crying out praises to God, praises hushed by emotion but moving along the stone that their heads, too, were pressed against until it reached her ears. Arminius's gnarled fingers still gripped hers tightly, she still felt the weight of Titus's hand upon her shoulder blade. But most of all, she felt a presence within her, one so strong she could barely breathe, one so gentle she felt laughter bubble up. She never wanted to move, never wanted to lose the intensity of this moment, even as she thought that it would surely consume her totally if it remained over her much longer.

At length, the Spirit eased away, breathing became more regular, and Benjamin gurgled out a half-hearted protest at his position that brought them all up with smiles. Abigail sat back up onto her knees as Titus helped Arminius to his feet.

As she stood, she followed Arminius's gaze to the entrance of the chamber, where a fourth person stood up, confusion on his face. Arminius cleared his throat. "My son, Helius."

Helius stumbled forward, eyes large. "Father . . . I came in to fetch you, and there were flames dancing in the air! I tried to cry out a warning, but I was struck down to the floor. What was happening?"

"The baptism of fire and the Spirit." Titus put an arm around Abigail and pulled her to his side. "Tabitha said that the Lord promised it would come. It has."

She looked up into his gaze and smiled, then turned her face back to Helius. "You have witnessed a miraculous thing here today. I am sure your father will explain it to you."

"Yes. Yes, I understand now, and I will tell my whole household so that they all might believe with me. Run to your mother, Helius, and tell her to gather your brother and sisters together this evening." He inclined his head once more to Abigail and Titus as Helius sprinted out the door. "As your servant, I am already indebted to you. But for sharing this glorious promise with me, I find myself even further in your graces. Mistress, you are my master's daughter, and your son is his son. There is no one on this earth I would rather serve than you. I will handle this matter of inheritance with as little bother to you as possible and send word when all is done."

She gave him a soft smile "I thank you for that. As your mistress, I am blessed to have such a faithful steward. As your sister in Christ, I rejoice in the salvation of your soul. As my father and husband did, I will keep in touch with you regularly, Arminius, not only about the estate, but about our lives. I am honored to call you my friend."

Tears clouded the old man's eyes once more, and he dropped to a knee to take and kiss her hand, then rose up to place a tender kiss on the baby's head. "Safe travel back to Rome this afternoon, and to Israel when you have cause to go. Your mother's health will be in my prayers to our God."

"And you and your family will be in mine."

Arminius clasped Titus's wrist when he reached out his hand. "You will be blessed for taking care of her. You do honor to the memory of your friend."

Titus's head inclined to an angle too humble to be habitual to him. "As do you. How the Visibullises found a man so honest I will never know, but they were blessed indeed. We will be in touch."

"Peace go with you."

As they walked outside, Abigail wondered how it could not. The peace filled her so completely that there was surely no room left for anything else.

THIRTY-THREE

Aquilia looked up in surprise when her door burst open, the surprise turning to consternation when she saw it was her husband that stormed in. He had not so much as stepped foot in her chamber in a year, and when he did, it was certainly never with a pleasant intent. Usually to insist she change something that displeased him. Never, *never* for a good reason.

He strode over and wrenched the embroidery from her fingers.

"Caius! What are you doing?"

He tossed the fabric to the floor for one of the maids to pick up in a scurry before he could step on it. "What has happened to our son?" He looked ready to call fire from Jove down on her for whatever it was she must have done.

Aquilia's silver brows drew together. "Stop towering over me like the Colossus and firing accusations. What are you talking about?"

Caius kicked the handmaiden out of the way so he could pace, ignoring the whimper of pain she made when she collided with a sturdy table. Aquilia curled her fingers into a fist.

"He has *always* been impossible," he raged, arms gesticulating in anger. "I expect it of him. And he is no less stubborn now, but there is something more. As if he thinks himself better than us."

He spun back to face her. "Tell me you did not notice it at dinner this evening. Tell me you did not see how he looked at that *slave* as though she were a goddess dangling blessing before his nose."

Aquilia forced her fingers to relax and lounged back against her chaise. "As usual, Caius, you are overreacting. Certainly, I see affection between them, but that is no surprise. She is his lover, and he her protector."

Caius practically hissed as he devoured the space between them again. He grabbed her by the shoulders and pulled her several inches off the chair, his fingertips biting so painfully into her arms that she cried out before she could think that she did not want to grant him that satisfaction. "You never should have let that whore into our house. She has proven herself already to be a poisonous serpent just waiting to strike. Jason already fell to her venom, I will not see my son do the same!"

He released her, and Aquilia struggled to maintain a measure of grace as she collapsed back into the pillows. She did not rub the bruises on her arms. In fact, she regarded him cooly, without flinching. "Do you want her that badly, Caius?"

His hand fisted, he even pulled his arm back a bit. But he did not hit her. He knew well that if he ever did, she would walk out of his house so quickly that he would have no time to stop her and so loudly that all of Rome would know it within an hour. "How dare you, woman! I come here with concern for our son, and you drag up your pain at not being able to satisfy me?"

Aquilia rolled her eyes. That particular barb had lost its sting a decade ago. "You come here concerned only because you see that Titus cares for her. And since he has taken the loveliest women in Rome to his bed and never been inspired to care, you think that this one must have some rare talent to inspire a fondness in our son where none was possible before. You are jealous, Caius, because you know if you touch her Titus will not forgive it. But you see that young, supple body, and you think you must possess it."

Caius narrowed his eyes. "To hear you talk, I almost think *you* want her."

She just gave him an icy smile. "It is not inconceivable that you would have forced me to find my pleasure elsewhere, even in another woman. But in reality, you have ruined pleasure for me altogether, Caius. I want her only to be out of my house, and soon enough she will be. In the meantime, I only want *you* to stay away from her before you force yet another rift between you and your son."

Caius measured her for a moment then spoke from between clenched teeth. "You know nothing, woman,"

He stormed from her room. Aquilia just watched him go, then motioned for the maid to hand her embroidery back to her. Life as usual in the Asinius house.

♦

Caius raged through the peristylium. His next destination was Titus's room, but he took a detour on the way to the quarters of the female slaves. His blood was boiling, and he would need to expel his wrath if he wanted any sleep tonight.

"Qira!"

A door opened, and a slave stepped out. She was nude, her long red locks hanging wet about her, sticking to her breasts in a way that had him ready to take her then and there, if he had not had another task looming over him.

"Master." Her eyes were on the ground.

"You will join me tonight. Go now and wait for me."

"Yes, Master."

He turned and walked away again before he could see her go back into the chamber she shared with two others. He headed now for Titus's room, fully prepared to tell his son that he had better get his fill of the Hebrew now, for once she left, she would never be welcomed under his roof again.

He didn't bother knocking on his son's door either, just opened it and walked in. Not with quite the energy he had entered Aquilia's chamber, but still forcefully enough to gain the attention of the two occupants. Caius sneered. There they were, not in bed as he had half expected to find them, but sitting on the chaise, facing each other, their hands intertwined. The way their heads snapped up upon his entrance, he supposed they must have been bowed. Doing what? What were they looking at that was so interesting?

"Father." Titus's tone reflected no surprise. His fingers did not release Abigail's. "I thought we had agreed years ago that you would announce yourself before entering my chamber."

Caius let his eyes sweep over their joined hands to make it known he did not like seeing such warmth, then leveled a hard gaze on Abigail that had just enough raw desire in it to terrify her, he figured. "I would like to talk to my son alone."

"In the face of such a gentle request, I know not what you can do, Abigail, but graciously acquiesce." He turned his gaze on her, and it softened. "I will let you know when he has said his fill and it is safe for you to return."

Abigail dared to smile, even squeezed his fingers before getting up and moving quietly into the procoeton.

"What is it?" Titus asked with a sigh, not bothering to stand.

Caius pointed at where Abigail had gone. "That whore is going to destroy you as she did Jason if you are not careful. I have seen the way you looked at her this evening, and I will not have it, Titus. If you wish to take her to your bed, fine, but you will *not* take her into your heart, and she will not step foot in the house again once she leaves for Israel. Have I made myself clear?"

Titus did not reply for a long moment, his gaze riveted on Caius's face. "Abigail is my friend's widow, and you will treat her with respect. And for the record, Jason was not destroyed by her; he was happier as her husband than I have ever seen him. Though I hardly expect to be graced by the same favor, I would count myself blessed if I ended up with a morsel of his happiness in my own life, be it from the hand of Abigail or anyone else. But as for returning, I can promise you I will not argue on that count. Because I *do* care for her, and I will not subject her to this disrespect any more than necessary. She is my friend, Father; we have shared a common grief and found from it a common joy. And if that distresses you, then it is your problem to deal with and not mine."

Caius opened his mouth to rebut, but got nothing out before his son continued.

"And Father?" The smile Caius was more familiar with returned to his countenance, the one that combined menace with power. "I saw the way *you* looked at her this evening, too, and I will not stand for *that*. It drives you to madness to see someone so beautiful, conversing intelligently, looking at you with disdain. You want her, but you will not have her. If a whore, she is *my* whore. Have I made myself clear?"

Most of the rage abated, but the concession tasted no more pleasing. "I have no need to steal a woman from my son's bed." He made a point of looking at the bed, neat and still made up from that morning. "It is all women are good for, we both know that, and there are plenty to choose from. What I find curious, Titus, is that you have been so deferential to her emotions in the days that she has been here. I am not so convinced you are satisfying her body." He gave a wicked little smile and turned to the door. "And I cannot have unsatisfied women in my house."

♠

Titus's hand had clenched into a fist that he carefully uncoiled as his father left the room. He must get a rein on his anger, dismiss that part which came from the dent in his pride. Focus on the offense he took on Abigail's behalf, even at the opinion on women in general. Just not on the insinuation that he could not please a woman. It would do no good to get upset about something when it would lead his mind down dangerous paths.

He did not hear Abigail reenter, only noticed her when she took her seat again and covered his tensed fingers with a small hand. "I did not intend to eavesdrop, Titus, but hearing myself called a whore made me freeze where I was." There was a smile in her voice, and it lured his gaze from the door to her face. "My friend, I appreciate your defense, and I even thank you for claiming me as your own. I will do my part and seem as satisfied as is humanly possible."

That won a grin from Titus, though he tried to hold it down. "I do not wish to shame you like this, Abigail. You are a woman of virtue, and I hate to besmirch your name, even in my own house. Especially in my own house."

Abigail tilted her head. "When in Egypt, Abram told Pharaoh that Sarai was his sister instead of his wife, in order to save his life and her virtue. I do not see why you claiming your friend as your lover to do the same is any different. I am not shamed, Titus. I am protected, and I thank you. I think the important thing here is *you*. I do not wish to make your father your enemy."

Titus sighed, running his thumb over her knuckles. "I fear that was done long before you entered my life, dear one. We have never gotten along, and I know not how it could change."

"We will add it to our prayers." She reached for his other hand too, putting them in the same position they had been in before the interruption. "You were praising the Father for giving us peace, and for sending us his Spirit to comfort us."

Smiling, Titus nodded and bowed his head again, letting the words seep through his consciousness before coming out his lips. By the time he spoke, a soft voice into the quiet room, he had aligned himself once more with the Spirit that hovered still in the back of his being.

◈

Samuel tugged on Abigail's hand, his eyes wide with excitement. "Mother! Mother, *look!*" He pointed at a huge beast that was standing a good distance off.

Abigail looked, and her eyes widened too. She turned to Antonia. "What is it?"

Antonia followed their gazes and smiled. "An elephant. No doubt brought over after one of the African campaigns. There are a few who think the novelty will make them money, but I assure you, they are more pleasant from here than they are close up. Their stench is as big as they are."

Abigail chuckled, and Samuel bounced up and down a bit in excitement. He did not ask for a closer look, but he strained to see over the people who kept passing in their way. Abigail picked him up, since Antonia held the baby, to give him an extra few inches.

"Look at his ears!" He giggled in delight as the beast twitched the giant flaps of flesh. "See, Mother, I *told* you the markets were more exciting than at home."

"I think for everyday, I prefer the relative quiet of Jerusalem." She slid Samuel back to the ground but held his hand once more as they began to move. "Although this is certainly a pleasant diversion. Are we shopping for anything in particular, Antonia?"

"Only your pleasure, Mistress. The young master instructed me to get you out of that library for a day and to see some of the sights. Bithia suggested maybe you would want to see some of the games that will be on next week, but I said I doubted it. Bloodbaths, that is all they are, and not fitting for a lady's sight."

Abigail had certainly heard enough about the gladiator fights in the Coliseum to know that the nurse was right. Violence could hardly be a game to one whose life had been turned upside down by it. "I will likely only be here for another week, anyway." Her eyes moved from stall to stall and vendor to vendor. "Arminius informs us that all is going smoothly, and the false testimonies have been dismissed. Titus is beginning to keep an ear open for news of ships sailing to Israel."

"And slaves to take you there," Antonia added with a knowing nod. "You will need at least one strong eunuch to see to your protection."

Abigail would have loved to deny that particular necessity, but having been in the streets of Rome for half an hour, she could not. It was unnerving, how many men stared openly at her. Her only reassurance was the huge African that followed them a few steps behind, his head above everyone else's and his arms, bigger than most men's legs, crossed forbiddingly over his chest. Any troublemakers would surely steer clear of the man they called Panther.

"Oh, look at these." Antonia urged Abigail to a table that had necklaces strewn over its top, the colors and stones so many that she couldn't begin to name them all, yet most were apparently not too precious, if all laid out so carelessly.

"Pretty." She touched a purple rock with a finger.

"Amethyst," the vendor replied with a grin missing a few teeth. "One of the rarest gems, and a favorite of ladies. It is said to protect against intoxication from wine and keep a man faithful."

Antonia snorted. "With Titus, you may need that, Mistress. Especially if you expect him to pine for you when you leave, although certainly I have never seen him look at a woman with so much caring."

Abigail's smile felt tight and forced, and she drew her hand away from the table altogether. "I do not need an amulet, thank you."

Antonia arched a white brow. "Come child, I have heard stories, and even Hebrews have jewels of significance."

"Hebrews." The vendor recoiled as if the word warned of leprosy rather than a nation. "I was cheated by Hebrew merchants more often than I can count."

"If it happened more than once, it is your own fault, and I feel no pity." She looked back to Antonia. "And I did not mean to say I judged the jewel itself, only that I do not think any object capable of achieving what a man does not wish to be so. Our traditions do not give jewels powers, only worth."

The man narrowed a single eye to give him a rather strange appearance. "You are Hebrew? You speak Greek like a Roman."

She gave him a smile. "Because I was raised in a Roman house that happened to people itself from Israel."

The vendor's features returned to normal, the toothless grin back in place. "A prettier Hebrewess I have never seen. I will cut the price of the amethyst in half for such a face as yours."

Abigail rolled her eyes. "Keep your charm of wine and women, friend, the jewels my husband gave me are better cut, and I wear them little enough as it is."

Not that any vendor would let it go at that. "But the lady's husband will not pine, says the servant, and so she will get no more jewels if she does not ensure his faithfulness. Or perhaps more, if she is one to accept them as apology?"

"I tire of this." Abigail sighed and motioned for Antonia and Panther to move on with her.

"Is Titus your husband now, Mother?" Samuel asked with curiosity.

Abigail smiled down at the boy. "No, Samuel, Titus is only my friend."

"Oh." He sounded mildly disappointed, and Abigail squeezed his hand.

"You will miss him, I know," she said softly to him, "and so will I. But Titus belongs here in Rome, and we in Israel."

He nodded, though it seemed her words had only made him sadder. Abigail let it go, figuring the markets were not the place to have a serious talk with a six-year-old boy.

They spent the next couple hours browsing, and by the time they returned to the Asinius house, Samuel had cheered, and Abigail had forgotten about the episode. Until, of course, Titus returned home from his day at the Forum and Samuel practically pounced on him.

"Titus." He sounded serious as the man scooped him up in his arms in greeting.

Titus smiled into the frown that knit together the fair brows. "Yes, Samuel?"

"Why will you not pine for Mother when we leave?"

Abigail had been changing Benjamin and now stepped into the room afraid she was either going to laugh or choke. "Samuel! That is not a question to be asking him."

Titus just chuckled and didn't take his eyes off Samuel's serious face. "And who said I would not pine for your mother when she left?"

"Antonia." The boy paid no attention to the flame she felt in her cheeks. "She said Mother should get an amethyst, even though you love her."

She nearly coughed with the humor and humiliation that lodged in her chest. "That is not quite what Antonia said."

Titus grinned at her. "I imagine it is close enough, given how well Antonia has known me in the past."

"But Antonia is under false impressions that Samuel does not understand, so Antonia says things that little ears should probably not overhear."

"What does the size of my ears have to do with it?" Samuel asked in confusion.

Titus looked to be struggling to contain his laughter as much as she.

"What your mother means, Samuel, is that Antonia may have said some things that are not a reflection of the truth. Because I will miss you and your mother terribly when you leave, and she will not need an amethyst to make it so. But Antonia cannot know how much I love you both, because she has not been through all that we have together. Understand?"

Samuel looked relieved as he nodded, sending curls bouncing. He wrapped his little arms around the man's neck. "But Titus, if you *do* decide to be Mother's husband, you will be my father, too, right?"

Titus laughed, probably at the shade of red Abigail's face must be. "Yes, Samuel, I imagine that is the way it would work."

"And Benjamin?"

"I would also love him as a son," Titus said with a hint more seriousness, "though he would retain the name of his father. I would never try to end Jason's legacy."

Samuel, looking fully satisfied, wriggled to be put back on his feet. He scurried out the door in search of the boys of the house.

While Abigail closed her eyes and took a moment to draw in a deep, calming breath, Titus approached and lifted Benjamin from her arms. "He is a child, Abigail," he said softly. "Do not be embarrassed by what spills forth from his young lips. He only wanted to be reassured that he was loved, that the mother he loved was loved, and that the brother he loved was loved, but I figured I had better also remind him that the father he loved was loved, too."

The complexity brought a smile to Abigail's lips as she opened her eyes to look on his face. "You are a good man, Titus Asinius. I never would have guessed at how patient you have proven to be with the children."

"I would not have either." He smiled down into Benjamin's cherub face.

"You will be a better father, someday, than the one you have had to learn by. You will surely love your own children more than you love mine, and even with mine you are wonderful."

He chuckled. "But yours are perhaps easier to love because they have none of me in them. My own will undoubtedly share my stubbornness and drive me to madness with it, which is perhaps why I have so long ignored my mother's prodding to look for a wife."

Abigail returned the smile, her hand settling comfortably on his arm as he held her son. "But the time is coming, Titus, when look for a wife you must. And you must promise me that when you find her, you will invite me to the wedding and provide a long enough engagement to give me time to arrive. I would share in such a joy with you."

His face sobered, his eyes searching hers. "But how will I find a suitable wife in Rome, Abigail? I am not fool enough or vain enough to think I could maintain a faith when surrounded totally by unbelievers. I will need a wife who believes. But I daresay that at this moment, the only such woman in Rome is you."

"Truth travels quickly. Already Arminius and his family believe, and they will tell their friends, and soon there will be a church forming in Rome as we heard was forming is Israel. You will not be alone here. But even if you were, as long as you seek God earnestly, he will sustain you."

Titus reached out to cup her face tenderly. Gratitude shown in his eyes. Gratitude and something else she could not quite define. "How is it that such a beautiful, delicate flower is never bent by the winds of doubt?"

Abigail leaned just a bit into his hand. "I have been bent double, Titus, until I thought I would break. Perhaps it has made me stronger, or perhaps I am now only in a calm between the storms. But this I know: our only hope to escape it is through our Lord."

For a moment, she thought he would kiss her. She could almost convince herself that the glint in his eye was akin to the one Jason had gotten so often, right before claiming her lips. But he pulled away, dropped his hand. "In this last week or so we have, Abigail, we should resume our lessons. There is surely much I have not learned."

"Yes." She looked to her son, afraid he would see the disappointment in her eyes. Benjamin was asleep. "Tonight after dinner. I will make sure Samuel joins us, too; I have not been attending to his lessons as I should."

"You have been busy learning yourself. You have practically devoured our library."

"And I will miss it when I leave." She made sure her tone was just as light as his as she took Benjamin back. Titus trailed her into her room, where she would put him down for his nap. "I will pine over those books, Titus. And my longing for their knowledge may even remind me to miss you a little, too."

Titus smiled but said nothing until they had returned to his room. "I think I may have found a eunuch to purchase, but I did not want to make a decision without you. You should see him for yourself."

"Meet him, you mean." The corners of her mouth tugged up. "*Seeing* a man will not tell me much about his loyalty, will it?"

Titus smiled in return. "I suppose not. Meet him, then. He has been serving these past years in the house of an acquaintance of mine, as the guardian of the daughter. But she has just married into a house that has no need of her slaves, and her father has no need of this one, either. He has always served her with devotion, I know, and I find it hard to imagine anyone serving *you* with anything else, since you treat them as your equals."

She grinned. "They are my equals. Not only because I was a slave, but because we are all the children of God, and we should not be judged according to our fortune or misfortune."

"You are of course right, as always," he granted. "But there are few enough others to share your view that you stand out as an extraordinarily kind and deserving mistress. Which was my sole point."

"Then your point is granted. What is this man's name, and when shall I meet him?"

"His name is Phillip." She was almost surprised he knew that detail. "And you will meet him tomorrow, if that is to your lady's liking?"

"I like it very well," she said with a muted grin. "And now, my lord Asinius, I would like you to take me on a stroll through your magnificent gardens, as soon as I call Antonia up to watch over the babe."

"I submit most gladly to your wish." To prove it, he called for Antonia himself while she prepared herself to go outside once more.

THIRTY-FOUR

Phillip did not remember much of childhood. Some vague impressions of running free through the forests of Germania, but that was all. He had lived through only thirteen winters when the Romans came to his land and captured his tribe. He remembered the fear that snaked through the trees, the courage that the warriors called upon to face it, and a bloody fight that stripped him of his father, his brothers, his uncles, his cousins. The last time he saw his mother and sisters, they were being raped by the Roman soldiers, three of his sisters dying of it, the youngest only nine years old. He remembered looking into his mother's eyes and seeing her command: Live!

He had a different name before he was in his thirteenth winter, but he would never speak it now. They had called him Phillip because he had attempted an escape by stealing their horses, creatures supposedly so loyal to their masters that theft was not a worry. He had been caught, of course, having never so much as ridden a horse before that day, but for the rest of the journey back to Rome, he had learned of the magnificent creatures, how to care for them, ride them properly, speak to them. He had hoped he would end up somehow with these beasts.

Instead, he had been treated as though he were one. The castration he had completely blocked from his mind, but he recalled the humiliation of being sold. His first master had been a merchant that needed laborers to load and unload all of the wares from ship to land and back again. It had been grueling work, but it had paid off. He had grown strong and large, and when his master died and he was sold again, he was intimidating enough to be made a guard.

He had come to this house when he was in his nineteenth year, and the girl he was assigned to protect at all costs was nine. She reminded him of his smallest sister, and he honored her as though she were. Even as she grew up and grew insolent and cruel, he served her faithfully. To do otherwise would be to die, and that was the one thing he would not do. As long as he lived, he was obeying his mother's last command.

When his mistress became engaged, he was not unhappy, even knowing it would mean his service here was complete. She had made a good match, and the man may even have a chance at making her happy. And secretly, deep inside, he was glad to be rid of her.

He knew his sale must be impending, but obviously his master saw no need to keep him informed of how it was going. But he was not surprised when he was called early that morning and told to go to the atrium to be examined by a prospective buyer. He simply dressed in his usual garments, designed to display his muscle more than any other purpose, and went where he was bidden.

When he entered the room, he recognized the man. Titus Asinius, once a friend of his mistress's older brother. His mistress had entertained a crush on him for a while. Heartless was the best word he knew of to describe him, but Phillip could not see the same ice in his face now that he had always seen before. Curious.

But not his place to wonder.

The woman he had never seen before. He would have remembered such beauty. This would be the one he was meant for in these proceedings, he knew. A face so fair was in danger, and the child she cradled in her arms gave many reasons why her life was important. Asinius's wife? Phillip doubted it. He imagined even he would have heard the gossip if the mighty Titus Asinius had been wed.

"Here he is," his master said when Phillip entered the atrium. "Germanic. He has always served loyally."

The woman nodded, and he stood tall and straight so that she could examine him. But her eyes did not roam over his body; they sought out his face. She handed her babe to Asinius and stepped closer to him.

"Hello, Phillip." She spoke in a warm alto voice that he imagined would soothe the child and send shivers up many a man's spine. "My name is Abigail Visibullis."

The lesson of speaking only when necessary had been beaten into him, so he just bowed his head in deference.

The woman smiled. "Do you speak, Phillip?"

"Yes, Mistress."

She tilted her head up to look into his eyes. "What languages?"

"My native Germanic and Greek." He knew his accent was not perfect, even after so many years in Rome. "A very little Latin."

Abigail nodded again and turned back to his master. "Can you give me a few minutes to speak with him, my friend?"

Phillip was surprised when the man agreed without hesitation. He was usually not one to take orders, nor was he one to not have his hand in every part of a transaction. But he left soon after.

Abigail turned to him again with a smile. "Please, have a seat."

He did not sit often, and it was uncomfortable. His post was usually in the corner of a room, standing as if a piece of the furniture, ready at any moment to spring forward and defend or kill. The only time he did not stand was when he slept. But she had asked him to sit. He sat.

Abigail smiled again. "Phillip, I will present myself honestly, and I will then ask you if you think you can serve me with your whole heart. First of all, I am a Hebrew. My parents died when I was a small child, and I was sold into slavery. A Roman prefect purchased me, and I became his wife's companion."

Not what he expected, certainly. He blinked.

"This Roman's wife was also a Hebrew, and she wanted a girl to teach, to share her days. My mistress taught me the Laws of our people, and my master taught me the laws and the language of Rome. Though a slave, I was raised to think all men are equal, no matter their lot in life or where they were born. And when I married their son, a Roman centurion, they raised me from my slavery altogether and called me a mistress along with those I once served.

"Months ago, my husband and his father were both killed in an uprising in Jerusalem. I came to Rome with my husband's friend," she said, nodding toward Titus, "to claim his estates for our son. On my way here, I had Titus to protect me. On my way home again, I will have no such friend. But I do not plan to return to Rome for more than a visit, so if you agreed to serve me, you would make your home in Israel. I would ask you to learn the laws of my God and to listen with an open heart to the faith that I hold dearer than life. I served my masters with love, not from duty, and that is how I wish to be served if served I must be. I would not ask you to do anything I can do myself; only to step in when my strength or abilities fail. The choice is as much yours as mine, Phillip, and while I would see the money I give your master to be buying your freedom, not your life, if you cannot see it that way, and if you would not freely help me in return for all your physical needs, then I will not make this transaction."

She halted and regarded him evenly, obviously waiting for a response. But what response could he possibly make? Here sat this beautiful woman, saying she had once been as much a slave as he, claiming to want to free him if only he would protect her from her enemies. Here sat this beautiful woman, looking at him as though he were her friend, never so much as questioning his ability to do the labor he had been trained for, only asking if he could soften his heart.

That was harder for a man like him than killing. But she seemed to think he could accomplish it, and strangely, that inspired him to think that perhaps he could, as well. His gaze flitted to Titus, and he wondered if maybe this girl had something to do with the softening in *him*. He was holding her son tenderly, and the hard mask he had always associated with the man was absent.

Phillip nodded. "I would serve you eagerly, Mistress, no matter where you go. I will listen to whatever words you wish to teach me, and take them into my heart in hopes that it becomes like yours."

She gave him a brilliant smile. "Then we will get along well. Right now, my entourage consists of you and a six-year old boy whom my husband bought but who has since become my son. When we return to Israel, we will join my mother's house, where there are three others. Andrew, who is probably about your age, Simon, the head of slaves who has always been like a father to me, and his wife, Dinah, the cook, beside whom I served happily for many years."

Phillip nodded again but had to ask, "But does Mistress not have a handmaiden? I am able to protect you, but not to see to your personal needs."

Abigail's smile turned wry. "Mistress has been a handmaiden too long to know what to do with one for herself, my friend."

"But Phillip has a point, Abigail," Titus said from behind the couch on which she had sat. "If you truly want to make the journey in safety, you must project the image of an affluent woman to whom an affront would mean trouble. The more servants you travel with, the safer you will be."

Abigail sighed and looked at him over her shoulder. "Titus, I had *no* attendants on the way over, and in spite of your multitude of warnings, I met with no problems. I grant that I cannot travel alone, but Phillip certainly strikes me as perfectly capable of protecting me without the help of a girl who can only braid hair and bathe my feet."

"On the way over you were with me, on a ship that I owned, with men who were all either under my employ or owned by my family. If they had touched you, their lives would have been forfeit, and they all knew it. But you will not be sailing back on one of my ships, and I will not be there to strike fear into the sailors. Phillip may certainly intimidate, but they would fear only immediate pain, not the far-reaching kind. Make them think you are important, and you will command respect, as well."

Abigail rolled her eyes. "But I am *not* important, and there would *be* no far-reaching effects!"

"Oh yes there would." The severity of Titus's assertion raised him a notch in Phillip's esteem. "If a hair on your head is harmed, I will personally see that the perpetrator is aptly punished. And as a wise woman said to me recently, a lie meant to save is not a crime, anyway. Letting a ship full of people think you of a higher status than you think yourself is certainly no worse than letting my father think you significantly worse than you are."

Abigail sighed again and answered Phillip's curious gaze. "We had to tell Titus's father I was his lover in order to protect me from Caius himself," she told him almost wearily. "It is not true, but it serves the purpose, and you will have to be aware of it, at any rate."

Phillip nodded his assent, wondering as he did so how Titus, whose reputation he well knew, managed to have her under his roof *without* making it true. His respect for both of them grew, and he found himself grateful that these two had been the first to speak with his master about his purchase. If he was going to be sold, he could not imagine a more perfect woman to be in service to.

"Well." Abigail stood up so she could take the baby back into her arms when he began to fuss. "Phillip, I will not ask you to stay in here while we negotiate the price. I do not want you to feel insulted when I negotiate your master ridiculously low." She delivered this last part with a grin that had one tempting his lips as well. "If you could kindly go outside and try to look defensive when your master sees you?"

The grin tugged a little more, and Phillip had no problem in giving her allegiance even now, before the sale. He would just as soon let her pay less for him than he was worth so that she would have more money in the future. "I will make him think I have shamed him, so that he is eager to be rid of me, no matter the price."

Abigail laughed, softly enough that his master would not hear, but warmly enough for it to reach into his heart. "Go, my friend. And Titus, look displeased."

Titus already did. "I can negotiate this for you, Abigail."

She waved that away. "I have been haggling for years. I may never have bought a person before, but no one ever paid less for oranges than I, and I practically stole the purple Mistress sent me after."

Phillip buried his mirth and left the room.

♦

Titus watched Abigail's face change as Phillip left the room. By the time Otho returned, looking wary and apologetic, his friend had pulled a mask of contempt over her serene features.

"He is arrogant and stupid," Abigail proclaimed. "How can you even have the audacity to proclaim him a worthy slave?"

Otho pressed his lips together. "He has served my daughter well all these years."

"Yes, and now he will not serve another with loyalty. I tried to be kind, and he made it clear I was inferior to your daughter." She made a face, as if trying to control her temper, and sighed. "I will be honest. I am leaving in but a few days, and I need the protection. I imagine your man will at least fend off the thieves and rapists for me, but

I do not look at this as a long-term investment. I will sell him again the moment we land in Israel and I have my own loyal slaves surrounding me once more. But I can promise you now that the insolence that *creature* showed me will gain you no higher price than what I am willing to offer in my desperation."

She named a figure so low Otho had no choice but to be insulted. "He is worth four times that!"

Abigail did not so much as waver. "He is worth a fourth that."

Titus stifled the urge to laugh and instead reverted to his well-known scowl. "Do not even spend that much of your son's inheritance on such a man."

"What choice do I have?" She managed to put frustration into her gaze "I heard just this morning that Marius Tansitus is selling a eunuch. Let us go and see him, he can surely not be any worse."

Abigail sighed, looking weary now. "You would drag me all around Rome on this mission, with no concern for the babe or me. If you want to look elsewhere on my behalf, Titus, go ahead, but I would rather return home and sleep."

"Very well then." Titus held out a hand as if to help her rise. "Let us return home, and *I* will see that you do not waste Jason's son's money."

Otho held up a hand. "Wait. I will cut my price in half."

"That is still twice as much as I am willing to pay." As if in on the scheme, Benjamin began to fuss. Abigail sighed. "I will raise my offer by a fourth."

"Abigail!" Titus let his hand fall to his side. "You will not!"

"I accept." Their host all but tripped over his words.

"Give him the money, Titus. And have that wretch get his things and follow us home. I will be waiting in the chaise."

Titus made a point of sending her an irritated look as she strode for the door, but he obediently doled out the sum–so low he almost ruined their act and chuckled in delight. "You have gotten lucky today, Otho. In the future, you should advise your slaves that if they speak to buyers as he did, they will meet your lash before they can leave your house."

"He has never been anything but respectful." Otho appeared almost pained.

Titus almost felt pity for the man. Though it was his own fault for being so easily swayed. He shrugged.

Otho shook his head in defeat and began to move toward the door. "I will go supervise his packing, make sure he takes only what is his."

Knowing Panther was watching over Abigail outside, Titus said, "I will join you, to make sure he takes nothing Abigail will not need him to have." And to make sure Otho did not belatedly take his advice and give Phillip a parting whipping.

✦

Titus tried to ignore the strange sensation that settled over him when he finally got an affirmative answer. He'd been asking the question every day for the past week, ever since Arminius had given the word that the estate would be settled without need of Abigail's remaining in Rome.

"Just arrived an hour ago," the man said, his accent crude to match his face. "Sails for Joppa again in four days, Lord."

"Thank you." Titus nodded and turned away, wondering why the news made his spirits plummet. Of course, he would miss Abigail. She had become his friend, his teacher. They had spent the last evenings together, praying and discussing the Law, and Titus had never felt such a peace in his soul as he had in those moments. And he would miss the babe, and Samuel. But that was surely not enough to cause this tightness in his chest.

"It is about time," Caius said from beside him as they walked back to the house. "I swear to Jove, that girl is a curse, and if she stays in our house much longer, we will feel it."

Titus rolled his eyes. His father was not one to prattle on about the gods, so he was not fooled for a moment. "Which is to say, she distracts you terribly, and since you cannot have her in your bed, you want her out from under your roof."

Caius sent him a withering gaze. "I am a man, Titus, and if you are really as close to her as you say, surely you would understand her charms."

An alarum sounded in Titus's mind, echoing in his ears. "Why do you say 'if,' Father?" He tried to keep his tone casually belligerent, as it would usually be if someone insinuated he had not been able to conquer his latest prey.

Caius's shrug was entirely too calculated to be meaningless. "It is a strange sort of intimacy I see between you. Not what you usually share with your lovers."

"Abigail is not my typical lover." He kept his tone cool. "Her emotions are more fragile after her loss, and as you yourself taught me, one must indulge the heart if one wants to keep the body."

"I just wonder who is controlling whom. I see you tending her emotions, but I never see her tending your needs. Or do the Jews have a problem with displaying their loyalty in the form of kisses to be seen?"

It seemed a safe excuse. "They do, at that. I never once beheld Jason's lips on Abigail, though there was proof enough they had been there. I know better than to expect her to share in public what she deems appropriate only in private."

"Is it that, Titus? Or is it that she has been hiding behind her mourning and has not let you touch her at all?"

Titus forced himself to remain calm, knowing it was the only way to protect his friend. "I promise you, she has refused me nothing I have asked for."

"But have you been too much of a coward to ask for what you want?"

Titus stopped to glare at his father. They were near home now, only a minute away, and Titus did not want to arrive during this conversation. "You sound like an adolescent boy telling his friend he will not believe he has a lover without proof. I thought you well past such immaturity."

Caius smiled, but there was nothing pleasant in it. "The slave needs to learn her place, Titus, and if you have not shown her that she is nothing but a whore in spite of her son, I will. The babe is my guest. She is not." That said, he moved forward again with long, quick strides. Titus had no choice but to follow. He walked up to the door, which opened before him. "Timothy, where is Abigail?"

"Resting in the courtyard." The slave answered so quickly that Titus wondered if his father had someone watching her at every moment. The thought did little to calm his anxieties.

"Ah." Caius nodded, smiled, and turned to his son. "I believe I will go the library for a while, my son. I will see you later."

Titus narrowed his eyes as his father walked away. The library looked out into the courtyard, which meant in effect that Caius was going to keep an eye on Abigail himself. Which was to say, it was Titus's opportunity to offer the proof Caius demanded. With a determined gait, Titus headed for the peristylium.

He breathed a little easier when he immediately spotted Phillip standing in the shade with his eyes on Abigail. She had chosen a chaise that was set up for the sole purpose of enjoying the sun's rays.

Titus walked outside, seeing the platter of food beside Abigail, little enough eaten to tell him it had been recently delivered. He turned to Phillip. "Have you had your meal yet, Phillip?"

The large man greeted him with a brightening of the eye if not a smile and shook his head.

"Go ahead."

As the eunuch obediently headed inside, Titus slid over to Abigail, whose sleepy eyes had come open at his voice. She smiled up at him. "I did not expect you back so soon."

Titus sat beside her on the chaise. "A ship from Israel has arrived. It sails for Joppa in four days."

"Oh." A flicker crossed her face that made a pleased whisper travel up his spine, something glad that she seemed no happier about the impending separation than he. Her smile looked forced. "Good. I am eager to get home."

Titus reached out and brushed a stray tendril of hair from her brow. "We have not found you a handmaiden yet. We will have to look with more diligence tomorrow."

She nodded her acquiescence, and Titus drew in a deep breath, saying in a whisper, "My father is determined you will not leave without learning that the Asiniuses think you nothing but a slave. He demanded proof that I have already taught you that, Abigail. He is watching now from the library."

She did not look that direction, but he felt a shiver run through her. She searched his face, settled her gaze on his eyes. Smiled. "What is your plan to convince him?"

He smiled too, trying to make it look as though they were merely exchanging a teasing conversation. "I must kiss you, dear one." He followed his words with the action before she had a chance to respond.

He knew that he could not move with caution, otherwise it would not look as though it was a regularly occurring practice. So he took her lips quickly, lightly, teasingly, then again as his hand settled on her waist, then a third time with a smile, lingering. His lips parted hers even as her arms came around him.

It felt as though his blood flamed. He melted under those small hands that were on his neck, his back. His hand slid around her, up her back, pulling her closer until she was pressed against him, his body noticing with approval that she pulled him closer too, even as his mind screamed at him to remember this was only an act. Which meant if he wanted it to stay that way, he had better end it soon.

Figuring his father had seen enough, Titus scooped her up and carried her into his room, knowing the dimness of the interior would hide them from view. He put her on her feet, though it took more than a moment of self-lecture to convince his lips to pull away from hers.

Their arms were still around each other when he looked down into her eyes, as hazy as his. "Perhaps," he said breathlessly, "that was not such a wise idea after all."

"Probably not." Abigail pulled his head down to hers again. Her kiss was intoxicating, hungry, and he returned it as greedily as she gave it. When finally she pulled away, it was with a long breath. "I am sorry. I should not have done that."

Titus smiled and buried a hand in her long, silken tresses. "I am not sorry. I have wanted to kiss you since the first time I saw you. You are lucky that I now have the strength to stop at that."

"You have grown much." She gave him a luminous smile. "I am proud of you, Titus."

He returned the smile, but he knew it was not so bright. "I cherish that, my friend. But even though I respect you more than anyone I know, it is probably a blessing that you are leaving soon. I am only a man, and you challenge my strength constantly."

A hint of a blush stole into her cheeks, but she neither pulled nor looked away. "I suspect you are right. For I am only a woman and not above temptation either."

A rather dangerous thing for her to say to him when she was still in his arms. But luckily the sound of hurried steps approaching his door was enough to convince him to step away rather than devour her lips again. As soon as the knock sounded, he called out, "Enter!" and hoped that he looked more composed than he felt.

It was Phillip, and he carried a letter in his hand. "From Israel."

Titus took it quickly and broke the seal. "It is from Drusus Visibullis," he announced, which drew Abigail to his side so that she could read the missive with him.

The first news the letter contained made her cry out in joy. "She improves!" She smiled first at Titus, then at Phillip. "Praise God."

"There is more. They are coming to Rome." He let the hand holding the letter fall to his side and looked over at the happy woman beside him. "He instructs you to remain here with me until they arrive."

Abigail stilled, her eyes landing on his. What had passed between them a minute before passed again now. "For how long?"

Titus shook his head, handing the parchment to her to see for herself. "He writes that he will not leave until Ester is well. It could be weeks or months, Abigail."

She drew in a careful breath as she read it. "Arminius promised that the legalities would soon draw to a close and the estate be proclaimed Benjamin's. Perhaps we should stay there."

Titus sighed. "You have not the staff, and it would probably take months to find slaves suitable. They must be selected with care, Abigail, for your life would be in their hands."

"Then what do I do?" Her tone crossed frustration with a plea. "I am not welcome in your house, Titus, certainly not for an indefinite period of time."

"Do not be ridiculous."

Titus turned in surprise to see Caius standing there, a heartless smile on his face. "You are of course welcome in my home. You are Jason's widow, the mother of his son." His hard gaze flickered to Titus. "And mine has obviously found pleasure in you, so you may remain just where you are. I will not hear of you taking an unnecessary risk. I will inform the slaves that you are until further notice a part of my household."

He left again, and Titus followed him out, stopping him with a hand on the elbow a few paces down the corridor. "Father, what is this about? Your motives are never so pure, and I would be a fool not to question them."

Caius plied his arm away from Titus's grasp. "I saw how easily she went into your arms, Titus. I will see for myself that she does not go so easily into your heart."

Titus let him stride away, but he could not move. He could not help but think that his father's warning was a bit too late; she had taken up residence in his heart long ago.

THIRTY-FIVE

Abigail finally took pity on Samuel when he tried to hold his eyes open with his fingers and keep looking down at the letters she had written. Laughing, she put an arm around his shoulders. "Enough, my son. You have done well this evening. You should go to bed."

Samuel dropped his fingers from his eyes and slumped against Abigail. "Sleepy."

"You played hard today. But you still tried hard on your lessons, and I am proud." She kissed his brow. "Go get ready. I will be in in a moment."

Samuel nodded and slid off of the chaise, then shuffled in the direction of the exit, apparently headed to relieve himself. Abigail smiled and let her eyes move over to where Titus was immersed in a book, Benjamin asleep against his chest. Her smile only grew as she walked over to claim her slumbering son.

"You should have put him to bed when he fell asleep." She lifted the baby, loving the way he snuggled against her.

Titus looked away from the manuscript with a smile. "He seemed happy enough, and he did not bother me."

She nodded. "Send Samuel in when he returns, please." She moved to their small room, putting the baby gently into his basket. He nestled in easily, and Abigail stood there a moment just looking at him. Each day he seemed to grow a little more beautiful, and she was beginning to see his personality emerge. The way he would fight sleep if she put him down when still awake, wanting so desperately to stay with her, but the way he clung to it and did not want to wake up when she came to rouse him from a nap.

He was beginning to look more and more like Jason. It made her heart skip now and then when he looked up at her with those innocent eyes and she saw her husband reflected there. She would be lying if she said she did not miss Jason. He had been her life's axis for the last year. And now his death took that central place, and everything she did revolved around the glaring fact that she was his widow.

Tears surged without warning, and she squeezed her eyes shut against them. She was not a very good widow. It had only been months since he died, and here she was dreaming of another man. She knew it was wrong–more than that, it was pointless. It was certainly good and right that she and Titus had become friends, that they had not only gotten past the mutual disdain they had once had, but had actually come to like one another, to help one another grow in their new faiths. What was not acceptable was the way her heart had begun to flutter whenever he was near, the way it raced when he smiled at her, the way her blood had boiled when he had kissed her earlier that day.

She had no business falling in love with Titus Asinius. It was not only stupid, it was unfair. She had not had these feelings for Andrew, who had loved her so purely and genuinely, she had not had them for Jason, who had ended up sacrificing a career and a home to make her his. Why should she feel them now, for a man as out of her realm as the very sphere of the stars? Nothing could come of an interest in Titus. Even if he felt an affection for her, even if it was as strong as this thing blossoming in her heart, it would not matter. Titus was not like Jason. He was not half Hebrew, he did not have parents that would encourage him to make her his wife. They could never marry; it would destroy his family, and he would be ostracized.

So marriage being out of the question, all they could share was a friendship. It could not be let to deepen into anything more. It would only hurt them both in the end, or tempt them to sin, neither of which was acceptable. If he must kiss her again before his father to keep her safe, then of course it was a risk worth taking, but she would not be so foolish as to again initiate an embrace. She had learned this morning that it was too dangerous, the feelings he ignited in her too powerful to be trifled with.

Her thoughts were interrupted when she heard Samuel's entrance into Titus's room and the man's laugh as he picked up the boy and hoisted him onto his shoulder. Abigail had to smile as she saw Samuel's tired grin as he "flew" into the room as though a bird, arms stretched wide in his glide. Titus lowered him to his pallet gently, pulling the blanket up over him.

Her breath caught in her throat. It was no wonder she was falling in love with him. He acted like a father to her children, even the one who had been but a slave. When she had first met him, he had not even known how to speak to a child. Now he was a hero in Samuel's eyes, simply because he was always there, willing to listen, willing to love him.

"Good night, my dear little man." Abigail knelt beside Samuel and kissed him softly.

Samuel yawned. "I love you, Mother,"

"And I love you," she replied as she stood.

"Good night." Titus put a hand on Abigail's back to lead her back into his chamber, where they would have their own study session. He closed the door softly behind him, so that their voices would not keep the children awake.

"What time tomorrow would you like to begin the search for a handmaid?" Titus asked as they both took their usual seats.

Abigail lifted her brows. "Why bother, now? I will not be traveling back on my own; I will not need such a large retinue for myself."

He gave her a muted grin. "Abigail, the point remains that you are now a lady of means, and as such, you should have an attendant."

"Titus," she rejoined with a sigh, "if have a maid I must, I would rather choose one from among my own people, since it is in Israel that I will be spending my days."

"In other words, you will not go in search tomorrow, you would rather just calmly wait for Ester to arrive so that you can fall back into the habit of waiting on *her*."

She sighed again, her gaze weary. "How is it that the man who was once the firmest advocate of me keeping my place is now the first to balk at the prospect of me returning to it?"

Titus just smiled and picked up her hand. "Because, sweet one, I was once blind to everything but politics, but now I have been blessed with a vision that allows me to see you in all your worth. You are not a slave, Abigail, you have not the soul for it. And it would pain me to see you slip back into old habits."

"You need not worry." She squeezed his fingers. "Ester was the first to raise me above my status, and she will not let me slip back into it now that I have given her a grandson."

Titus was quiet for a moment as he nodded his concession. "You have really missed her a great deal, have you not?"

"She is my mother. She is the woman who raised me and taught me and loved me for half of my life, the half that saw me make the biggest changes. This is the first time I have been away from her for more than a day since Cleopas brought me home. How can I help but feel as though part of me is missing? And not knowing how she fared until today—it has kept part of my mind in constant prayer."

"You have hidden your concern well." His tone hinted at disappointment. "I knew you must miss her, but you have never let yourself show anything but what the moment calls for."

"Titus," she said softly, meeting his gaze with warmth, "that is not so. It is just that I cannot let myself think about her much, or I would worry needlessly. I know she is in the Lord's hands, and I have had faith that she is taken care of. And that faith has allowed me to focus on what is happening here, things that I certainly need to give attention to. I have not been hiding my feelings from you. I have simply been keeping them at bay, even from myself."

He nodded, his face relaxing. "I suppose I shall have to practice that, so that I do not walk around somber and depressed when you finally leave me."

There was a seriousness in his voice that she decided to dismiss. "Come, my friend, we both know you are the master of that already and were long before we met."

"No. I simply did not feel anything I thought it necessary to hide before we met. But now?" He shook his head, then reached out to touch her face, slide his hand through her hair to the back of her head. "Now, my father would disown me for feeling the things I do for you."

Her heart accelerated, even as she willed it to be reasonable. "Is it so unacceptable that I am your friend?"

His smile was sad, it seemed. "My friend? Yes, that would be bad enough. Far worse is that a woman he sees only as a slave has become the mistress of my heart."

"Titus," she breathed, half in reprimand, half in longing.

"I am in love with you, Abigail." He gazed long and deep into her eyes. "I, the first to condemn Jason for letting his involvement get emotional, have fallen completely in love with you."

Tears flooded her eyes, blurring his earnest image. "Why do you say these things to me? Why do you shift the balance of our friendship for something that cannot be?"

"Perhaps because I cannot bear the thought of never acknowledging the purest emotion I have ever felt. And perhaps because I need to hear you say it in response."

She shook her head, hoping to clear it of all that was happening. "I cannot. It shames me to feel things for you I never felt for my husband."

"But this is not shameful." He moved a thumb to catch one of the tears that spilled over. "We have come to this love by doing things that are right. We have grown together, we have learned together. We have become equals that you and Jason could never be because of how your relationship began. There is no blame in that."

Abigail sighed and averted her gaze, wondering at the trembling that began somewhere inside and worked its way toward her limbs. She realized with some surprise that it was terror. "No blame, perhaps, but much fear. How can I let myself feel this, when I know it will end only in loneliness and pain? We have no future, Titus. I know that. But losing you will hurt too badly if I let us explore these emotions."

"Must it?" His gaze was intense enough to make her question her own beliefs on the issue. "Must a relationship end in consummation in order for it to be worthy of pursuance? Can we not find something beautiful and fulfilling in each other that will remain with us for life, even though we cannot marry, or spend those lives together? Surely, Abigail, it is better to know fully what God has blessed us with here, so that we can thank him for it, than it would be to ignore it and never give voice to his amazing gift."

A smile tugged at her lips, drying her eyes. "My friend, I know not whether you have just struck upon a profound truth or perhaps simply made the weaker argument the stronger with your rhetoric. Have you been reading Aristophanes?"

Titus laughed. "I have not." Then he leaned over before she could anticipate his move and brushed his lips over hers lightly, tenderly. "Let us pray about this, Abigail. The Lord will guide us in the path we are meant to take. If you are right, and these feelings are best left forgotten, then he will help us forget them. But if I am right, and they are better explored, he will teach us how to strike the balance to make us both stronger and better for having felt them."

She nodded, her lips burning from his gentle touch. "But until we hear his wisdom, it may be best if you do not kiss me again. It indicates that you already assume the answer and are hence not so open to the Lord's will."

His grin was teasing. "I am not assuming, Abigail. I am merely exercising faith."

She shook her head at his logic, but still she had to smile. Cautiously, she reached out and let her fingertips rest against his cheek. "I do love you, Titus," she said softly, knowing from the gleam in his eyes that he was glad to hear her say the words. "I am not sure what this love will do to me, but I will not deny it."

Titus used the hand still buried in her hair to draw her closer, then rested his forehead on hers. "I will not hurt you. I give you my pledge to that, my love." He closed his eyes. "Pray with me."

She, too, closed her eyes. In the moment before he began to speak, she let the sensations register, the warmth from his close proximity, the scent of him, the feel of his skin under her fingers. In that heartbeat, she only wanted to draw closer, to put herself as close to him as was humanly possible. In that heartbeat, she was not so sure that keeping an emotional distance would be possible. She found her heart yearning with his that it be the Lord's will that they feel this love.

"Our hallowed Father," Titus began in a low, warm voice whose quiet strains had no problem reaching her ear on their way to heaven, "guide us now as you have been doing for so long. You led us through darkness and pain, and now you have brought us to this new juncture. We praise you, Father, for your unfailing strength and wisdom. And now we ask you to hear this new plea and give us answer. You brought us together as your servants, my God, and you know these feelings that have arisen in our hearts. Help us to make the right decisions, to go through each day according to your will. Neither of us wants to hurt or be hurt, neither of us wants to do anything you would not have us do. Please give us your wisdom now, Father, and help us to handle ourselves righteously and blamelessly. We ask these things in the name of your Son."

He fell silent without actually ending the prayer, as had become their habit. For the next minutes they sat still as they were, their hearts open to the movement of the Spirit, their minds sending unspoken thoughts to God. By the time Abigail opened her eyes, the familiar feeling of peace reigned inside, though she knew not what answer it was supposed to give. They shared a soft smile.

Titus eased away. "We shall keep praying. I imagine with something this important, our Lord may see fit to make us contemplate it a while without simply providing an answer."

"Perhaps." She knew that she would be thinking about it, and that every thought would turn into prayer. But she also knew that the chill that crept in the moment he moved away was a rather strong answer in itself. A minute later she decided to retire instead of attempting another lesson, and Titus did not argue.

She made her way to her room with a heavy heart. And the question burdening it most was not just a query on the appropriateness of her feelings anymore. Now she was also wondering if God would let such strong emotions grow, only to forbid them expression.

Phillip stood in his usual position against the house, eyes flitting from where his mistress sat on a bench to where Samuel ran with a few servant boys in a game of chase. He surveyed every possible entrance to the gardens behind the house, listened to what may be coming from within.

Abigail turned her head to him with a smile. "What do you think of while you're standing guard, Phillip?"

Never had he had a master who solicited his thoughts like she did daily. Learning how to answer had taken him a few days. "I keep my thoughts open, Mistress, so that I will notice all that is going on around us."

Her smile turned almost sardonic. "I envy you the ability to do that. For as long as I can remember, my thoughts have run rampant whenever they may. I cannot seem to have a moment of rest without coming up with some new, often nagging contemplation."

"I have not the mind that you have. When you are teaching Samuel, I can see within you a deep wisdom, Mistress. But I was born to fight, not to think."

Abigail reached to pick up the beads that Benjamin had just dropped, handing them back to the baby with a kiss on his downy head. "And I watch you as I am teaching Samuel, and I see a mind that grasps all I say. One can be an intelligent warrior, my friend, it is quite possible. My father, my husband were such men. Do not deny the capacity the Lord gave you just because you were taught to ignore it."

Phillip felt a smile tugging on his mouth. She tended to have that effect on him, though he had practiced it rarely enough before meeting her. "Perhaps my lady simply finds gifts in those she meets that they themselves have never suspected."

"If so, then perhaps it is because those I meet have been trained not to give themselves credit where it is due." She offered him a friendly grin. "Admit it, Phillip. You have followed my lessons well, even those I share with Titus."

He had only had occasion to sit in on the latter once, but he could not deny her assertion. Everything she said, whether it be to the boy or the man, made perfect sense. He was still not certain if it was the material itself that was so reasonable or simply her way of putting it. He inclined his head in acquiescence.

"And what do you think of the Law and the Prophets?" She turned slightly on her bench so that she could better look at him.

Phillip glanced at her again, then looked away to make sure that Samuel was not falling out of the tree he had begun to climb. Seeing that the child was doing well, he allowed himself to form a reply. "I think that this God of yours is thorough and just. I do not remember much of the gods of my people, but I know that those the Romans serve cannot boast the same authority. What I cannot reconcile is the mercy you speak of. How can the same being be both perfect justice and perfect mercy?"

She barely hesistated. "By providing the atonement. He will not deny the need for justice, but he will also recognize that those who are truly repentant should be granted another chance. By accepting sacrifice, be it in the traditional form of animals and grains or the ultimate one of his own son, the Lord fulfills his thirst for justice while still being merciful. In a way, by man recognizing his own sin, he can be free of it. It is the growth God is encouraging, the striving for excellence that comes of making a mistake, confessing and repenting of it, and going out to live more righteously. He wants his children to be with him, to commune with him. We cannot do that as sinners, though, so it is only through purifying our own hearts that we can achieve that union that both we and he yearn for."

Phillip nodded but was saved from having to form an immediate opinion by the sound of footsteps inside. He recognized them immediately. "Titus is home."

◆

Titus strode outside, his eyes finding Abigail's form. His burden felt solid and monumental in his hands.

"Welcome home, my friend. How was your day?"

Titus grinned. "Fruitful. You will never believe it, Abigail, it is amazing. I was walking through the markets, and I came across a scribe I had bought manuscripts from before. He had somehow come across this." He put the package into her arms. "He said he berated himself for buying it, for keeping it, because no one in Rome would ever buy it. It is as though our Lord led him to it just for our sakes."

Expression intrigued, Abigail unwrapped the object, then stared at it a moment in absolute shock. "Is this—?"

"The Holy Scriptures." Titus had never had to battle the urge to dance as he did now. "It is in Hebrew, I cannot read it, but you can read it to us, Abigail. No more excuses for forgetting the details."

Abigail laughed even as tears flooded her eyes. Setting the tome aside reverently, she leaped up and threw her arms around him, pressing her lips to his. "It is the best gift anyone has ever put in my hands, my love. We will learn it together. I know there is much I never committed to memory as I should have, much I have forgotten. I do not know how a copy of the texts ever made it into his hands, but we will cherish this unexpected blessing."

"Yes." His heart galloped as she leaned up to kiss him again. Her lips lingered this time, and Titus felt all tension leaving his shoulders. His arms were loose around her, but she seemed perfectly content to stay within them. When she pulled her lips away, smiling, he smiled too. "I feel the need to point out that it was just *you* who kissed *me*, and that it was not therefore I that assumed any answers."

Abigail laughed. "I feel at peace with it, too."

"As do I." Titus released a contented sigh. "I know not how to explain it, but when I found the Scriptures. I felt it was my answer. I sought his word, and I found it. I pray I have not just read from this what I wished to."

Abigail shook her head, eyes agleam. "I feel it too. I prayed for an answer I could not mistake. The Scriptures are the one thing in the world that I cannot deny."

Titus was quite sure she had never been more beautiful than she was in that moment, as she gave him permission to love her. His heart, once a frozen block in his chest, was now so full and warm that he felt as though he might burst. "In that case." He leaned down and captured her mouth again, kissing her deeply.

Phillip snagged his attention with a low warning. "Caius is coming."

With reluctance, Titus pulled away. "I love you." Abigail smiled a moment before his father appeared.

"Titus. I need to speak with you." With that he turned and strode away again.

Titus shook his head. The fact that he was amused instead of irritated was surely a testament to the humors of love. "The tyrant calls. I will see you in a few moments, dear one."

THIRTY-SIX

Abigail got up to put the Scriptures back in a drawer for safe keeping. They had just put in two hours' worth of study, as they had every evening for the past week. It was late, and they were both tired. But she knew they would not retire quite yet. First, they would spend a few minutes in each other's arms, then say a prayer and go their own ways. When she turned back around, he held out an arm. She settled into his side on the chaise, and he kissed her temple tenderly.

"You are so beautiful," he whispered.

She smiled and turned her face up to his. "As are you." His lips closed over hers. One of his hands moved to cup her face, the other rested lightly on her back. Her heart still pounded every time he kissed her, but at least she was in better control than the first time. Still, she soon pulled away and rested her head on his shoulder, relishing the feel of his arms around her. "It has been a good week."

"It has. Although sometimes it is hard to believe that until seven days ago I had never kissed you. I just feel so. . . at home with you, Abigail."

The words brought her eyes up to his, though she had to shift her head to make that possible. She said nothing in response. As much as she may feel the same, it did not change the fact that their homes were in very different worlds. Who knew how much longer they would be together? To keep from thinking about it now, she asked, "Did Samuel show you his tooth?"

Titus chuckled, pulling her a little closer to his side. "Only about four times. And of course, I saw the gap every time he grinned, which was practically all evening."

Abigail chuckled too. "He is such a good child. Do you know, I think he is even beginning to win over your mother."

At that news, Titus lifted a brow. "I find that curious indeed."

Abigail smiled. "It is true. We were outside yesterday, as was she, only I did not realize it. Apparently Samuel came across her while he was playing, and of course it did not occur to him that he would be intruding, so he sat down and started entertaining her. I apologized when I found him, and she said nothing. But today, we were all out again, and she called him to her to finish telling her the story he had begun yesterday."

The tale brought a smile to Titus's lips. "My mother is a kind enough woman at heart. She just has so few chances to show it, in this house. Life has not been gentle with her, nor has my father." Titus untied the end of Abigail's braid and ran his fingers through her hair. "I noticed she actually spoke to you at dinner tonight, too. I was quite surprised. I think that is the first time she has done such a thing, and you have been with us for almost a month."

Abigail grinned. "I suspect she did it mainly to irritate your father. I heard them arguing earlier today."

"If they speak at all, it is to argue. One thing I learned from them is that a marriage for politics is quite simply not worth it if the parties do not at least like one another."

Abigail nodded her agreement but decided not to contemplate who Titus would end up marrying one of these days, when she had gone back to Israel. Instead, she considered his parents. "It is a pity they cannot get along. Ester and Cleopas loved each other so very deeply, and it made their years together wonderful and their house a peaceful place in which to reside."

"From what I understand, my parents never got along. According to Antonia, the hostility in this house has been there since the day they entered it."

"Your mother is beautiful, though. I am surprised your father . . ." she tapered off, heat rushing her cheeks.

Titus smiled. "My father likes beautiful women, it is true, but he likes only the ones he can rule. My mother has always been an independent woman. She had her own wealth, you see, and has never needed to rely on my father. Moreover, she brought him connections he needed, and he cannot tolerate being indebted to anyone. But they remain married because it provides them both with a necessary level of respect in the eyes of the city. Even if everyone in it does know that they would prefer to have nothing to do with each other."

Abigail shook her head. "Promise me you will never subject yourself to such a marriage, Titus."

"Oh, you have my word on that. Need I request the same promise from you?"

Abigail dropped her gaze and pulled away a bit. "I will never remarry. I am a widow with another man's child."

He rubbed a hand over her arm. "It is not the hindrance you think it. In fact, you may need to be careful. Your son has his inheritance, and you are beautiful. You may be just what many men are dreaming of."

Abigail straightened her spine and silently met his gaze.

Titus grinned. "I dream about you, my love, but not for those reasons."

"I know that. But then, we will never be married."

Titus's brows drew together. "It is not that I do not wish it, Abigail. It is simply not poss–"

She halted him with a finger on his lips. "I know. You need not explain what I myself have already considered. But the point remains: I will not remarry. My body was Jason's. My heart is yours. My soul belongs to my God. I have nothing else to give another."

Their gazes held for a long moment, and Titus buried his fingers deep in her hair. "Is it wrong of me to feel relief at that?"

Abigail felt herself smile. "No more so than it is for me to be jealous of your future wife, when you have not even found her yet."

He smiled, too, and leaned down to kiss her again. "We should pray. Then sleep. The day is catching up to me."

Abigail nodded and bowed her head to obey. They each took a turn speaking, sharing their thoughts and worship, and were soon kissing good night and standing up. Abigail glanced at the boys as she entered their chamber, smiling softly at both of them. She was truly blessed, in spite of all the dark times she had come through. She would have to keep focusing on that in the upcoming weeks, reminding herself of all of her blessings instead of worrying over what could not be helped. But at the same time, she needed to prepare herself for that inevitable moment's approach.

As she slipped into bed, she let her mind move over those who had been her life up until a few months ago; Ester and Andrew, Simon and Dinah. Right now, they seemed very far away, and terribly long ago. They had never even seen Benjamin, who was now the biggest part of her life. They did not know that she had put her faith in Jesus the Christ, they would probably not even believe her if she told them Jason had visited her while she was in labor. They were probably nervous about her being with Titus, because they could not realize how much he had changed. So they would certainly not understand if she confessed her love for him.

Sighing, she buried her face in the cool cover on her pillow and drew in a deep breath. She missed her family. It was a ball in her chest every time she thought about them. She missed the city she knew so well, the gold and alabaster beauty of her homeland. But something new bloomed alongside her love for Titus. Something that made her wonder if she was still the girl they knew, and if they would welcome the changes she had made. Something that made her question her ability to go back to the way things were.

She was not even certain anymore exactly how things had been. Those weeks after the uprising had been a blur, a collection of unpleasant impressions with that sheen of pain over everything. She remembered her resentment when Ester would not respond, she remembered the awkwardness with Andrew. Would he still hold that love for her in his heart? Did he still hope that somehow they would be together?

It was impossible now, for her son's sake if for no other reason. But it was something she would have to deal with when they were reunited, along with all the other issues that had been left dangling because of the unanticipated separation. It would be strange to face them all again now, when they had been living with different concerns for the past two months.

"Father, I give these cares to you," she whispered into her pillow. "Please protect them on their passage over, heal my mother, touch their hearts. Guide us all, and help me to handle the situation as you would see fit when we are together again." She felt a peace as soon as she spoke the words and breathed it in gratefully. Closing her eyes, she let go of all thoughts, all worries, and let herself fall into sleep. It was in the last moments of consciousness that she realized her period of mourning had ended that day, and that tomorrow would be her time of purification from giving birth. It was one more thing to remind her that even the Lord pronounced it time to move on.

◆

"You, eunuch."

Phillip turned at the unfamiliar voice. His shoulders tensed, even though it was a feminine voice that called him, probably not a direct threat to his mistress. But one never knew. After being in this house for several weeks, he knew that Abigail was despised by almost everyone, and that danger could lie anywhere.

The woman who materialized from the shadows was one he had seen only a few times, usually on his way to his quarters. Abigail refused to let him stay with her through the nights; he understood her need for privacy, but he also knew the darkness was the best time for dark motives. It was in the night that he had seen this woman emerging from her room, usually headed toward Caius's chambers. She was one of many women to make that trek, and most of them he pitied, knowing they had no say over their lives. This one, though, did not arouse any compassion. She held her head high, arrogantly, and walked around as though she were a mistress instead of a whore. There was pride in her eyes now, too, as she looked up at him. She held her spine straight, and still she reached only to his chest.

He said nothing, just waited for her to state her purpose.

She smiled. "I am Caelia."

He flicked his gaze through the open door he had been about to go through, where he could see Abigail just inside, sitting in the sun that came through the window, Benjamin nursing at her breast. He felt himself relax, since his ward was in sight. He disliked leaving her even on the errands she sent him on, at least when Titus or Panther was not there to watch her in his stead. She did not seem to realize that a threat could pounce at any moment.

Caelia followed his gaze, her eyes turning dry, then kindling. "Your mistress is a beautiful woman. Did you know I met her husband before he went back to Israel last year? A handsome man. Charming. I had no chance to get to know him, though; Titus was protective of me. Possessive."

Phillip regarded her evenly, wondering what her point was.

Caelia raised her chin another degree. "Now my master will not even look at me. And why? For *her*?" She let out a mocking laugh. "I know the laundress, and she assures me that if they are lovers, they hide it well, even from their sheets."

Phillip stiffened, and the woman smirked. "I have bribed her to keep the information to herself. But know this: I will tell Caius if I want to, and he will be so angry at the deception that he will take her and teach her her place. He will throw her into the streets and disown Titus for succumbing to her spells. He is not the man he was when he left, and it is all *her* doing!"

"What do you want?" Phillip demanded.

Her eyes smoldered, and it reminded him of his childhood, his aunt. . . she was a priestess, and this was the look on her face as she prophesied destruction. Almost unconsciously, he whispered a silent prayer to his mistress's God. For her protection. Not for his.

Her hands balled into fists. "I want Titus, and I will have him again. Tell your mistress that if she stands in my way, I will give her over to Caius, and Titus will be the one blamed for her death when I kill her in her sleep after he's through with her."

Moving with lightning speed, Phillip closed a hand around her throat, picked her up, and slammed her into the wall. He kept his voice a bare murmur. "You will die by my hand before you will raise yours against Abigail. You will not blame my mistress for your master's decisions." He noticed with satisfaction that her eyes were not so powerful when they were bulging, nor her lips so poisonous when they were gasping for breath. He released her as suddenly as he had grabbed her, and she slumped against the wall.

"Harm me, and you will die," she said through her gasps.

Phillip smiled. "I will tell Caius it was on Abigail's orders when she found you in Titus's arms, and he will slap my wrist and proceed to rejoice that his son is not so devoted to Abigail after all. He will buy three women to replace you, and you will never be missed."

She faltered for a moment, obviously wondering if he may be right, but soon regained her confidence. "We shall see. If I were you, I would not bargain my mistress's life on that possibility."

She walked away, and Phillip was left knowing she had scored a victory. He would not risk Abigail's life. Which meant he would have to make sure he was not alone in his plan.

❧

Titus slammed his fist against the wall. "I am such an idiot! I should have bribed the laundress myself."

Phillip folded his arms across his chest. "Regrets are not to the point, Lord. More pressing is what to do now that Caelia knows."

Titus sighed, raking a hand through his hair as he paced his chamber. "She will do it. I know her well, and she is a viper. If she approaches me and I turn her away, she will go to my father and tell him everything."

"Perhaps Mistress should leave this house," Phillip suggested soberly. "We can go to that estate of her son's."

"And you think my father will not find her there? It is the first place he will look, and he will be angry enough to follow her immediately. Will you fend off all the army he brings with him?"

"Then what?" More irritation entered his voice than Titus had ever imagined him displaying; proof, to his mind, of the slave's devotion to Abigail.

"I know not." Titus raked his hand through his hair and cursed. "Perhaps. . . perhaps I will just have to *not* turn her away."

"What?"

Titus spun around when Abigail's voice invaded the room. Guilt vied with frustration in his chest. "Abigail, this does not concern you. Go back to your room."

She looked at him as though he had taken leave of his senses. "Am I now your slave to be commanded? And is it none of my concern when you talk about taking another woman to your bed?"

"It is not what you think, Mistress." Phillip stepped forward, hand up in a calming gesture. "Caelia knows you and Titus are not lovers, and she has threatened to tell Caius of your deception unless Titus takes her back."

Her gaze stayed on Titus all through Phillip's short speech. "And you think the answer to this problem is doing as she demands? You would give up all you have worked for, you would open yourself to sin again just because she bids it?"

"Yes!" Titus practically roared. "To save you, Abigail, I would do anything. I will *not* let my father have his way with you."

Abigail regarded him cooly. "If your father forced himself upon me, it would be his sin, not mine. It would be painful, but the world would not come to an end. If you took Caelia, the sin would be upon *your* head, my friend."

He threw up his hands and spun away. "She would kill you. And you would speak to me of *sin*?"

"I love you!" Abigail cried in return. "Would you have me stand aside while you sacrifice yourself for me? While you give yourself to another? Am I to believe that when you are in her arms you would find no pleasure there? I have been there, Titus.

Even knowing it is wrong, even trying to keep yourself pure of sin in such a situation, it is impossible. And you would put yourself into it willingly, so how could you even *hope* to stay free of sin? And once in its clutches, how will your motives remain untainted?"

Titus's jaw clenched in anger. "What would you have me do? Let the old lecher ravish you?"

"I would have you find a better answer."

"How?" He paced again, but the bitterness still caught him, swamped him. "Shall I pray, Abigail? What good will it do? I have been praying, seeking God earnestly for months, and I am rewarded with *this*."

"Titus." Her rebuke was so soft that he had no choice but to halt if he wanted to hear her. "Will you lose faith at the first obstacle? Our Lord has not abandoned us. This is surely not as big a problem as it seems to us in this moment."

Titus sighed, his shoulders slumping in defeat. "If this is a test, I know not how to pass it, my love. You are in my care, and you hold my heart. I cannot see you hurt. I would sooner condemn myself than see you in pain."

"Do not say that." She moved to him, wrapped her arms around his waist, and pressed her cheek against his chest. "Please, beloved. More than your protection, I need your faith. It is God who brought us together, and through serving him that we have grown so close. If you give up on him, why should he not give up on us?"

He sighed and held her close. "I will not give up. Forgive my doubt. I spoke in passion, but it is not truly my heart. I *will* pray and await an answer. I will not take this upon myself."

He kissed her, kissed her again. "Just please do not dismiss this, Abigail. It is a serious threat."

She nodded, snuggled against him. But it did nothing to quiet the worry inside him.

♦

Aquilia picked up the cup of warm drink from the table before her and leaned back, surveying the two silent men with whom she dined. They would be off to the Forum soon, she knew, doing whatever it was men did all day. She took a sip of the brew, wondering if she should try to be tactful or not. Deciding it would be far more entertaining to see her husband's irritation at her question, she turned to her son. "Is Abigail not joining us this morning, Titus?"

Titus's head jerked up, his eyes narrowed a moment before he regained himself. "No. She did not sleep well last night. She had only just fallen into a sound slumber when I left. I already asked Antonia to make sure a tray was sent up for her a little later."

Aquilia was tempted to smile at the annoyance that flickered over Caius's face at Titus's casual intimacy with the Hebrewess. "I hope she is not unwell. I was considering visiting with her a bit this morning."

Titus put down his knife and stared at her. "I . . . know she would appreciate that."

"Excellent." Aquilia motioned one of her maids over to her. "Go help Antonia with the children. And when Abigail is awake and up for company, come fetch me."

The girl hurried away, and Aquilia smiled into her husband's scowl before looking to Titus again. "Have you heard anything more from the Visibullises?"

"No. I am not certain we should expect to hear from them again before they arrive, either. But I begin to expect their arrival any day now."

"Good," Caius pronounced. "The sooner that harlot leaves my house, the better."

"You may speak of your own women that way, Father," Titus said calmly, "but I will thank you not to attach such names to mine."

"I have watched her with the children." Aquilia studied her son, hoping his father would not see in his eyes what she could see so clearly. "She is a wonderful mother. Caring and patient, but firm. She will raise Benjamin to do honor to Jason's memory."

Caius made his usual grimace. "If she wishes to honor her husband's memory, she should leave the boy in Rome with a guardian. You would do well, Titus, I see how you fawn over the babe."

Titus rolled his eyes. "Abigail would not leave her son. Nor would she consent to staying in Rome. Therefore Benjamin will return to Israel with her until he comes of age to decide for himself if he wishes to return to his father's country. And at that time, if he does wish to come back here, I will certainly step in and offer him my benefaction." He stood up. "If you will excuse me, Mother, I would like to say goodbye to my guests before I leave."

Aquilia nodded her assent, smiling into her cup as her son stalked away. Caius was practically steaming.

Her husband focused his foul humors on her. "What was that all about? I thought you only wanted her out of here."

Aquilia was not about to tell him her real reasoning. "And soon enough she will be. I would rather not have it said that I had a guest in my house for so long without showing her any kindness."

"She is not our guest."

Aquilia smirked and stood. "She is not yours, perhaps, but she is our son's. It will not injure you if I have an hour's conversation with the Jewess." She waved a hand at him as she headed for the door. "Go play in your politics and your intrigues and your business, Caius. Do not concern yourself with me."

She left the room before she could hear his response, and though she did not rush to her quarters, she also did not linger near him. She had a few household tasks to see to this morning, and she figured that by the time she was done them, Abigail would be up and ready to see her.

Her prediction proved to be the case; she had no sooner sat down to her embroidery after seeing to her duties than her maid came in to inform her that the young mother had sent her to say she was welcome to join her at her convenience. Aquilia nodded and put down her needle, rose from her chaise, and headed for her son's rooms.

The door to Titus's room was open. Abigail sat at the small table finishing off a glass of juice. Samuel was entertaining the baby, Antonia keeping a watchful eye over them both. In the corner stood the eunuch they had bought, looking formidable and impenetrable.

Abigail smiled when she noticed Aquilia and stood. "Good morning. I am so glad you stopped in."

Aquilia smiled. "I should have done so long ago. Forgive my negligence." She turned her smile on Samuel, who had scurried over to her. "Hello, Samuel. How are you today?"

"Well. Look, my tooth is beginning to grow back in, and now another is loose!"

Aquilia laughed even as she bent down for a closer look. "Why, so it is. Pretty soon you will be as toothless as an old man."

Samuel laughed in delight as Aquilia turned to Antonia. "Maita is going to the markets; she suggested you might like to join her and bring the boy."

Samuel bounced up and down and looked over at Abigail. "May I go, Mother? May I, please?"

Abigail smiled. "If Antonia wants to go."

"I would love to." She reached out for Samuel's hand. "Come, my boy, we shall go get ready and leave the ladies to talk in peace. Kiss your mother goodbye."

Samuel did as he was bidden, hurriedly, and ran from the room with Antonia on his heels. Abigail watched him with a smile and shake of her head. When they were gone, she looked back up at Aquilia. "Please, sit down."

They both did so, and once they were seated Aquilia wasted no more time. "My son is in love with you."

Abigail just looked at her for a moment, then drew in a long breath. "Yes. And I am in love with him. But you need not worry about what that will mean. We both know it can go nowhere, and we have no plans for changing that. I will return to Israel with my mother, and he will stay here and look for a suitable wife."

Aquilia leaned forward. "I was not afraid that he would follow Jason's lead and marry you. I am more concerned about what will happen if Caius realizes Titus is so attached to you. My husband hates you as much as he desires you, Abigail. He was very fond of Jason. When we received the news of his decision to marry you, Caius was enraged. He had entertained high hopes for him and saw you as his downfall. Up until then he had been fully prepared to pull the same strings for Jason as he had for Titus, getting him out of the military and back to Rome."

Abigail's shoulders rolled back. "Yes, Jason spoke highly of him. Although I am sorry to say I have yet to see the generosity my husband mentioned."

Aquilia breathed a laugh. "Surely you did not expect it, Abigail. You were a slave. Jason married you only because of the babe. We cannot forget that as quickly as the Visibullises."

She inclined her head. "I did not expect it. Having met Titus a year ago, having seen the cold man he was, I knew his family could not be much different. If your son warmed up to me, it was only because of the situation we found ourselves in. Mourning Jason, watching his murderer be released. He had promised my husband he would see I was taken care of, and he did that. He is still doing that. If Jason had not made him swear to it, I have no doubt Titus would have been content to forget that I existed."

Aquilia lifted a brow. "Perhaps he would have. But he does not care for you now simply because of a promise to Jason. Indeed, I would say Jason has very little to do with the things he feels for you. The question now, Abigail, is what really happened to my son as he mourned for Jason, watched his murderer be released? He is not the same man who left here, who wrote us, who you yourself just mentioned. This new Titus is far from the cold man you said you met a year ago. What happened to him?"

Abigail drew in a long breath, obviously considering. "Much happened that day when Barabbas was released, Aquilia. We both watched an innocent man hang in that murderer's place, a man who was nothing but a teacher who had offended the officials.

We heard that same man, unjustly put to death, forgive those who did it to him. Can you imagine how small that makes you feel? Lusting for revenge, and hearing a dying man forgive his tormenters?" She shook her head at the memory. "The very earth shook at the crime. Most of the crowd fled, but I could not. My labor pains began. Titus saw me, came and helped me up. He took me home, but no one was there. They had moved Ester away, and I knew not where they had taken her. He stayed with me because he was afraid of failing Jason, afraid I would die if he did not get help. He stayed by my side the whole time, the following days, and we talked of all that had happened. The midwife had been a follower of this teacher who had been crucified, and she taught us his lessons. They made sense to us, so we decided together to live by them."

She shrugged, as if anything could be so simple. "The changes your son has made he made because he chose to be different. He chose to put aside his bitterness. It really has very little to do with me."

Aquilia measured her silently for only a moment. "Perhaps. Perhaps he will remain as he is now once you leave. Perhaps he will revert back to the man he used to be. Either way, I was not certain you realized how different he truly is now. He is smiling, laughing, seemingly taking joy from life. Before he lived only for pleasure, but it never brought him contentment. He has never treated anyone with the respect he shows you. Which brings me back to my initial concern. It is only a matter of time before Caius picks up on this. Be careful, Abigail, and advise Titus to do the same. If he keeps looking at you so warmly in his father's presence, he will bring an explosion down on his own head."

Abigail shook her head. "If Caelia does not beat him to it."

"What?" Aquilia's spine snapped into alignment. "What does that wench have to do with anything?"

Abigail briefly explained what had passed between Caelia and Phillip the day before. Aquilia's brows drew together. "I had not realized he had refused her, or any of the others for that matter. Will you try to tell me you have nothing to do with *this*, either?"

Abigail sighed. "It is part of the teachings of that man I spoke to you about that one should refrain from sexual relations until one is wed. Titus has been honoring that of his own accord. Although I will admit that last night, when he entertained the notion of accepting Caelia in order to silence her, I did not take well to the idea."

At that, Aquilia smiled. "I imagine not. It is hard to believe a man's motives to be altruistic when the 'sacrifice' involves giving himself pleasure. Just as it becomes hard to believe his words of love to you when he is making love to someone else."

Abigail flushed. "There is that. But also, I cannot tolerate the thought of letting her have her victory just because I fear your husband."

"You fear him with just cause." Aquilia drummed her fingers on the table. "But Caelia you have no reason to fear. I will take care of her myself, and with pleasure."

"How?"

A cold smile twisted her lips. "Quite simple. I will tell her that if she ever mentions this again, either to you or Titus or Caius, she will find herself the play thing of the gladiators. I have sent troublesome maids to the arenas before, and I would not hesitate to do so again. I imagine all of Caius's whores know that, which is why they all try not to displease me." She stood. "I will go see to her. In the meantime, pass my advice along to Titus. And so you know . . . I have come to respect you, Abigail. You must be an amazing woman, if you have made my son's heart thaw. I will understand his mourning when you leave."

✦

Caelia clutched the door until her knuckles were white, resentment burning in her chest as her mistress strode away. She wanted to slam the door closed, but she could not. She wanted to claw Aquilia's eyes out, but she could not. She wanted to scream, to lash out, to destroy that Hebrew witch, but she could not. Not yet, anyway. She would not disobey her mistress's command, because she knew for a fact her threat was a meaningful one.

But there would be another opportunity, sooner or later, to get her revenge. And until it presented itself, she would simply be patient.

Ever so quietly, she closed the door.

THIRTY-SEVEN

Titus knew relief. It had never occurred to him that his mother would prove the answer to his prayers about his father, but he whispered his gratitude to God. He only wished he had found the time to discuss it with Abigail the day before, so she could have allayed his fears earlier. Some guests had come over the previous evening, ones who he could not in good conscience ignore. He invited her down, but she had declined. He had not minded, though he had missed spending time with her. By the time he had retired, she had been asleep, so it was not until the following morning that she managed to tell him about her conversation with his mother.

"You were once again right, beloved." He hugged her tightly. "We had only to pray, and we received an answer. I never should have doubted."

She smiled up at him. "We all doubt. It is getting past it that is important."

He returned her smile then, unable to resist, leaned down and brushed his lips over hers.

"How was your evening?" She posed the question guilelessly, but Titus still had to narrow his eyes. The family that had joined them for dinner had been an upstanding one, one whose daughter was just of age to be wed. It had not been a whim on his parents' part to invite them over with their children, and Titus had been fully aware that both sets of parents were considering whether or not he and the girl would be a good match. He suspected that her brothers would not like the idea; he had been friends with both of the eldest, which meant that they knew his reputation.

"What?" Abigail prodded when he did not answer.

Titus blinked away his thoughts. "It was a matchmaking venture. One would think they could at least wait until you left before they started this nonsense."

Abigail sighed. "That reminds me. Your mother advises that you be more careful about how you look at me in front of your father. She says it is all too obvious that we are in love."

Titus gaped. "My mother said that?"

Abigail nodded placidly, absently smoothing down his toga. "I will never get used to seeing you in all this cloth, Titus. I still expect you to be in your uniform every time I see you."

Titus chuckled and tugged gently on her corresponding stola. "And every time I see you, I expect you to be in. . . that delectable blue thing."

Abigail laughed and dug her fingers into his side, though she only got one good tickle in before he pinned her hands behind her back and pulled her against him. He proceeded to kiss her soundly.

"There. That will teach you."

Abigail laughed again. "Oh yes. I have learned my lesson well. If I want you to give me an exceptionally good kiss, I should tickle you."

He kissed her again just to make sure the instruction stuck, then stepped away, holding onto one of her hands as he did so. "Are we ready?" He propelled them toward the door as he asked. They had been planning this outing for a week and half, and he was looking forward to showing her around his city.

"We are ready. Antonia has the children, Phillip is outside the door, ready to take up residence in my shadow, I watched you grab some money, and I can think of nothing else."

"Marvelous." He pulled her through his door, where Phillip was waiting to fall in behind them, and out the front. He tossed a smile her way. "How is it that we have yet to go out together, except that one time to the villa?"

She smiled back. "You are out with your father every day, and when I have gone out, it has been with Antonia. I suppose when you have a day with nothing pressing to do, you take the opportunity to stay home."

"True." Though he had never done so before, he had to admit. He had run into a few of his old friends, and they had seemed a bit offended by his preoccupation. It reminded him rather forcefully of his own response to Jason when he had acted in this very way.

Abigail must have read his thoughts. "I seem to have that effect on people."

Her tone said what her words did not: that she had that effect because they desired to be with her but were still ashamed to admit it openly. Titus squeezed her hand in denial. "We are going out. And we can do so anytime you wish to, beloved."

She renewed her smile. "Perhaps you should wait to see me in action before you promise that. You may be quite embarrassed to be seen with me, Titus, I am shameless when I am haggling. Is that not right, Phillip?"

Phillip chuckled. "The merchants run for cover when they see her approaching; they all know she will practically steal their wares, but always in such a way that they are happy to part with them."

Titus laughed as they approached the door that a servant opened wordlessly before them. "I saw you in action with Otho, and yet still I am willing to go with you to the marketplace. Shall I play the part of domineering lord again?"

Abigail smiled up at him sweetly. "It is what you are best at."

He laughed again and pulled her closer to his side, knowing that if the rest of the day could continue in the same vein, they would have a marvelous time.

They had been browsing the stalls for an hour before Titus actually stopped her at one, his eye on the necklaces. Abigail looked at him curiously. "What has caught your eye, Titus?"

Titus picked up a length of gold with delicate craftsmanship.

"Titus, no."

He hushed her with a smile. "Indulge me, Abigail. I would like to give you something to remember me by." He fingered the pendant with a grin. "Amethyst, right?"

She flushed. "As if I need any token to help me remember you."

He glanced at the merchant, who had come to attention. "I am going to ask you how much this is, and you are not going to waste my time with your outlandish prices. Take whatever number that is in your mind right now and cut it in half."

The merchant smiled slyly and named a number entirely too high. Titus sighed and replaced the necklace. "You have wasted my time. I will find my lady a token elsewhere."

He turned, pulling Abigail with him.

Naturally, the shopkeeper called him back with a shout of a number half as large as the original one he had mentioned, and Titus turned back to finish the negotiation. He got what he deemed a good price for it, even if Abigail did tease that she could have gotten it for half *that*.

"Be silent and wear your gift," Titus ordered with a grin, slipping the gold chain over her head. She obliged.

They had wandered half an hour more before an entirely too-familiar voice intruded upon their attention.

"Titus! I was hoping to run into you."

Titus froze and sighed, then turned to face his father. "Father. I thought you were spending the day at the baths."

Caius waved that away. "Come, son, I need your opinion on something."

Titus arched a brow in question, but Caius was already sidling through the crowds. With a glance at Abigail, who shrugged, he led them after him. By the time he realized where they were headed, his father had fallen in beside them again and had the audacity to take Abigail by the arm, proclaiming, "Actually, Abigail, this will interest you as well. You are still looking for a handmaiden, are you not? I believe I spotted a few Hebrewesses in the lines."

Abigail looked at Titus over her shoulder as Caius led her onward. He clenched his teeth together. "She does not need to go there, Father."

"Nonsense, Titus," Caius returned with an innocence that spoke of deviousness. "If I have learned anything about women, it is that they are never satisfied until they have control. If you were to pick out a slave for her, she would hate the girl. If you let her come and choose for herself, she will be satisfied. Is that not true, Abigail? Would you not prefer to decide for yourself who will serve you?"

"Not there," Titus maintained.

But it was too late. They were already on the edges of the slave sales, and Abigail recoiled. Still, Caius pulled her onward, and Titus could not stop him, short of tugging on Abigail's other arm and turning her into a human rope. Opting to spare her joints, he squeezed her hand in encouragement.

◆

Abigail was not certain quite what she expected Caius to do. Proclaim her a slave too and offer her to one of the traders? No, not with Titus there. Was he simply trying to humiliate her? Perhaps, but that seemed too simple. Seeing no other option, she held her tongue and her patience and followed him.

Caius stopped the group before a line of assorted peoples, their nations and races apparently as various as their sizes. He headed straight for one small woman. Under the grime, her hair may have been blonde. Under the pain, her eyes may have been blue. He grabbed her by the jaw and turned her face to Titus. "What do you think? Germanic, they tell me. Fine bones. Once she's had proper meals for a week or two, I think she would be quite lovely."

Abigail looked at Phillip, whose fingers were curled in fists. In all probability, this girl was from a far different place than the village he had come from, but she knew he would see her as a sister in that moment. Catching his eyes, all she could do was shake her head slightly, hoping he saw in her gaze that she shared his compassion. She watched him deliberately relax.

Turning her head back around, she caught sight of the girl. She was in another line of slaves, and she stood out. Most of them had had their heads shaven, but she still had long hair, falling in dark tresses to her waist; most of the others were filthy and looked malnourished, but she was clean and healthy, albeit pale and terrified. Abigail could tell at first glance that she was an Israelite. She stepped free of Caius, who released her without thought, and walked the few paces to the girl.

She spoke in Hebrew. "What is your name?"

The girl looked up as though shocked to hear the words, her eyes reflecting a fear that had Abigail's heart racing in sympathy. "Miriam."

Abigail smiled gently. "A lovely name. The sister of Moses, one who stood with faith beside him. It is a strong name, one to live up to. My name is Abigail."

"David's wife." Miriam looked sideways at the man guarding this group, as if afraid to be caught speaking.

"Where are you from, Miriam?" Abigail knew no guard would dare to punish a slave for answering the questions of a prospective buyer. She tried to put her confidence in her words so that Miriam would feel it, but she was not certain that she succeeded.

"Hebron." Again, her voice was barely a murmur.

"I am from Jerusalem." She, too, looked at the guard. Keeping her words in Hebrew, she asked, "How much are you asking for this girl?"

The man looked at her as though she were a sea creature. Abigail smiled and turned back to Miriam. "He does not speak Hebrew. So I want you to tell me why you look at him with fear. Perhaps it has something to do with the reason you have not been shaven, or let to starve?"

Miriam's hands shook, and she kept her eyes downcast. "He has not touched me, Mistress, I swear. He just–is a businessman. My hair, my skin. He said I would fetch a higher price if I showed up in Rome pretty, and that it would be higher still since I was a virgin."

Abigail felt her blood boiling up. "I am certain of that. Miriam." She waited until the girl's eyes came up to hers. "How old are you?"

"This summer will be my sixteenth."

Abigail smiled again. "You are older than I, though I would not have thought so. I already have a son, I am already a widow. I was sold for the first time when I was eight."

This brought Miriam's gaze up with a snap of surprise. "You were a slave?"

Abigail nodded. "Until my master's son married me. I need a handmaid, Miriam, but what is more, I need a friend, a sister from my homeland. Will you come with me, serve with me? I need a maid mainly for appearances, I will not ask you to do what I can do for myself. If you consent, I will buy you; I will look upon it as buying your freedom. If you decide you do not want to remain with me, you may leave, but it is my hope you stay beside me, helping me in return for your material needs. Would you agree?"

Miriam stared at her blankly for a moment. At length, she articulated carefully, as though in pain, "Mistress, if you are sincere in your proposal I would be a fool to deny you. Do you think I do not realize that if you walk away from me, some man will buy me in a minute and make me his whore? I am actually surprised that I stood here for five minutes without drawing attention, thanks to the way that guard has kept me. If you wish me to serve you, I will do so happily, and I will praise Jehovah for watching over his daughter when she thought he had forsaken her."

Abigail smiled. "Then it will be done. What languages do you speak?"

Hope began to kindle in her eyes. "Hebrew and Greek."

Abigail nodded her approval, then turned back around. She found Titus watching her. He would not have understood the words, but he still seemed to grasp what had happened. With a smile, he turned to the guard.

His words were in Greek. "My lady has taken a fancy to the one with hair. How much?"

The guard looked at Abigail and Miriam as if noticing for the first time that they were standing there together. His look was as hostile as possible without actually spitting on Titus. "Forget it, friend. No matter what you offer for her, I guarantee some lord will come along willing to pay more. That one is for a bed, not for braiding hair."

Titus pasted his old smirk onto his face. "Let me ask you again, friend, how much for the girl?"

His sharp tone drew the man's attention as his softer one had not. He sent his eyes over Titus, then drew himself up as if preparing for an introduction. Obviously, he saw in Titus one of those lords willing to pay for a girl to warm his bed. He named a price. The usual bickering ensued, but the slave merchant would not budge much.

"Give it to him," Abigail pronounced after a few fruitless moments went by.

Titus looked at her as though she had taken leave of her senses. "It is too much, Abigail. You can get another girl for a third that price."

But her hands already shook with fury. "I am sure I can. But I promised Miriam I would buy her, and I will not renege on that. Give him the money. I underpaid for Phillip, I can afford to overpay for Miriam."

With only one sigh of protest, he drew out the money and handed it over, then supervised as the man untied her from the line and handed her over. Caius rejoined them, looking rather pleased, though the scraggly Germanic woman he had in tow did not seem to be the cause of his smile. Titus arched a brow.

Caius's smile only grew. "A pretty wench," he said in Latin, nodding toward Miriam. "I am glad to see you have decided to diversify, Titus. And I am beginning to understand your taste for the Jewesses."

Abigail wanted to retort but could think of nothing biting enough. So she took Miriam by the hand and led her to where Phillip stood. She introduced them, instructed them to remain together on the walk back to the Asiniuses' house, and moved back to Titus's side.

He gave her fingers a squeeze. She concentrated on using the walk to calm down.

As soon as they arrived home, Caius announced, "We need to attend a small business matter quickly, Titus. Leave the women to get settled in and come with me."

Abigail gave Titus a reassuring smile when he looked down at her. "I will get Miriam settled in and see you later."

The two men soon left, and Abigail's smile faded. She turned to Timothy, who was leading the Germanic woman away, and stopped him with an authoritative voice. "I will need a room for Miriam which is not with all of your master's women. With your mistress's maids, perhaps?"

Timothy's expression was pained. "There is more room with the others–"

"I am sure there is always more room with Caius's wenches, but my maid will not be one of them. If there is no room with Aquilia's girls, I will insist Miriam be put in the guest chamber beside Titus's room. Do you think your master would approve of *that*?"

Timothy apparently decided Abigail was angry enough to do it, for he pasted humility onto his face. "Mistress's head maid has just been married. She had her own small chamber, which is now free. The other maids were hoping to get it, but I am sure they will be understanding, since it is only for a brief while."

Abigail nodded, satisfied. "Phillip, will you please go with Miriam to see that she gets settled in, and then show her to my room? I want to check on the children."

As the servants moved to obey, Abigail went toward Titus's cubiculum. She found Antonia and her wards in the peristylium. Samuel and one of the other boys were playing with marbles, and Benjamin was watching with apparent delight. The sight was enough to restore the smile to her face and most of her previous good mood. She took the baby from the nurse's arms and went inside to feed him. As he suckled, the rest of her spirits were restored, so that by the time Miriam and Phillip appeared, she was once again calm and peaceful.

Miriam's face lit up when she saw the baby, and she sat at Abigail's feet with a smile. Abigail introduced her to Benjamin, and then called in Samuel to meet her as well.

"When my mother arrives in Rome," Abigail said once Samuel had run back outside, "you will meet the rest of the servants beside whom you will serve." She told her about all of them, then about herself, how she came to be where she was now and even the current situation. Then she asked, "What about you, Miriam? What is your story?"

The maid got a distant look on her lovely face. "I was born a slave. My mother was my mistress's handmaid, and when I became big enough, I began helping her in the chambers of my mistress and her daughters. Her husband, my master, was away a lot, out with his flocks. They were wealthy, with great herds. As it seems you have experienced, Mistress, wealthy men tend to think the world is theirs. The last time my master returned home, he suddenly noticed that I was no longer a child. My mistress had been planning my marriage to another of the slaves, but she was a jealous woman. When she saw her husband looking at me with desire, she decided being the wife of a slave would not hinder my master, so she opted to sell me. The very next day, I was gone. My mother treated me as though it was my fault, as though I had tried to allure the master." She shook her head, tears burning in her eyes. "I did not. But it did not matter. I was sold to that trader you bought me from. I was lucky, I suppose, that he thought me worth so much, otherwise I would have starved like the others, or perhaps been taken by the men in his employ."

Abigail reached down and grasped Miriam's hand. "The Lord keeps watch over his children, Miriam. And if he is willing, we will soon return to our homeland together. You will love my family. They are kind and generous." She smiled and tickled Benjamin. "And the only master is not much of a threat."

Miriam smiled at the baby's deep belly laugh.

Samuel burst into the room. "Mother! Come see!"

Abigail tucked Benjamin onto her hip and stood. "Excuse me, my friends."

Phillip followed Abigail with his gaze but felt the maid's attention shift to him. "Is she as worthy of my devotion as she seems?"

He smiled without taking his eyes off his mistress. "More so. I have been with her for a month now. She is not only fair and honest and compassionate, she is genuine and selfless. She is not quite convinced that she is any better than a slave herself. But she is." He glanced at Miriam, smiled a little. "Speaking for myself, at any rate, she is far superior. She could not offer me freedom as she did you, given that she needs my protection, but I would have taken great pleasure in refusing her. I will gladly serve out my days with her. Life with her will be better than any you could design for yourself."

Miriam smiled too, and folded her hands in her lap. "I know how to be nothing but a slave; I would never choose to throw myself on the mercy of society. And seeing the love she inspires in you, I am sure I have much to thank my God for. I will honor her all of my days."

Phillip nodded his approval and focused on Abigail fully again. He need not have worried about this girl's devotion, he knew. One could not feel the merciful touch of Abigail's hand without loving her.

Titus drummed his fingers on his arm in impatience. He knew he was practically glowering, but his father did not seem to mind. He just kept speaking with the group of men, laughing and exchanging harmless barbs.

"You must all join me this evening," Caius proclaimed to the joy of his companions, who immediately agreed. Titus mentally moaned. "I will break out that wine I have been wanting to try. Bring your wives, I am certain Aquilia would like the company."

That, at least, was probably true, and it almost surprised Titus that his father thought of it. Often, he was just as happy to have the men come over by themselves, so that they could engage in whatever debauchery they pleased without fearing the ladies' interruptions.

The group of men agreed and disbanded, and Titus sighed, thinking they would finally get to leave. Or, at the very least, he could tell his father that *he* was heading home.

Before he could do more than open his mouth, another gentleman approached. "Ah, the Asiniuses!"

"Cornelius Cossus." Caius greeted him with a smile. "How fortunate we should happen across you; I was just extending my invitation for entertainment tonight to many of our mutual friends, and I was hoping to invite you and your wife as well."

Cornelius laughed in delight. "I would like nothing better. I had resigned myself to a dull evening at home, but this is a large improvement." He turned to one of the slaves dogging his steps. "Run home and tell your mistress we will be joining the Asiniuses this evening. In fact, just have her meet us at their home, I will simply go along with them now. If you do not mind, Caius."

Caius waved away the concern. "Of course not. We were just heading back. You remember my son, Titus, of course."

They clasped wrists amid pleasantries that Titus did not feel. He knew well why his father was making this particular reacquaintance: Cornelius Cossus was one of the current consuls, and if Caius wanted Titus in politics right now, this was the man whose favors he should win.

"Yes, of course I remember Titus. Tell me, my young friend, how was Israel? I know the emperor grows continually impatient with the troublesome Jews. Are they as rebellious as the communications make them out to be?"

Much as he hated to admit it . . . "Quite nearly."

Caius shook his head. "His friend, Jason Visibullis, was killed in an uprising, along with his father. Both were upstanding soldiers; it is a true tragedy."

Cornelius looked as though the news struck him near to his heart. "Yes, I had heard. It pained me greatly. Did you know, Cleopas Visibullis and I used to be great friends. We were in the academy together."

His father was never one to let such an opportunity pass by. "Cleopas's grandson, the heir to the Visibullis estate, is with us even now; he is only a babe, Jason never even met him, but the mother brought the child here to claim his inheritance."

Cornelius nodded, a familiar glint in his eye. "I hear he married a Hebrewess. A shock, really; most of us were willing to forgive it of Cleopas, but for Jason to repeat the mistake?" He shook his head. "I have heard that the girl was a startling beauty, otherwise why would he have done such a fool thing?"

"You will see for yourself." Caius's laugh grated on Titus's nerves. "She is certainly a temptress, is she not, Titus?"

Discomfort stirred, but he could not bring himself to dismiss the consul. He smile felt strained, but he forced it out. "A lovelier woman I have never met. Jason was the envy of all of us."

Cornelius laughed. "And knowing your reputation well, Titus, I am sure you were swift to comfort her in her loss."

The tension within him multiplied. "She has become very precious to me."

"Yes." Somehow, Caius sounded more amused than displeased. "It seems my son has a heart within his chest after all. I am not sure where he got it."

Cornelius chuckled and clapped a hand to Titus's shoulder. "A heart is a good thing for a statesman to have, at least within measure. Although with Asinius blood in your veins, moderating your compassion is probably not a lesson you need to learn."

Titus had no response to that; he knew it was intended as a compliment, but his heart did not warm with the words. His father, of course, jumped on the chance to talk of his impending career, but Titus found it far easier to tune them out than to listen. They were soon home, anyway, and the moment they stepped inside, he excused himself to find Abigail and warn her of the consul's presence and the party that had been formed for the evening. Not surprisingly, he heard her voice coming from the back gardens. He followed its melody outside.

"Titus!" Abigail stood when he appeared. She was currently alone with Phillip, though he got a blur of motion in his periphery that he knew to be Samuel. He smiled at the sight of her, and it grew when she rushed up to him and threw her arms around him.

"She is wonderful." She pressed a soft kiss to his lips. "Miriam will fit in perfectly, and I am actually glad your father dragged me down to that wretched place." She kissed him again. "Thank you for not refusing to meet that outlandish price."

Titus chuckled at her exuberance and did not release her lips so easily when she moved them to his for a third time. It did not occur to him until he heard Cornelius's voice just behind him that his father and guest might follow him outside.

"I see the rumors were not exaggerated." Cornelius smiled as Abigail pulled back, obviously startled. The man sent his eyes over her, and his smile only grew when she blushed. "At least, I assume this is the mother of the Visibullis heir."

"This is Abigail Visibullis." Titus tried to convey support to her through a hand on her shoulder. "Abigail, this is Cornelius Cossus, one of the consuls."

Cornelius inclined his head to her. "I hope the lady will be joining us this evening."

"Father has arranged for a dinner party," Titus informed her when she looked at him in question.

"And he would be most pleased if you joined us," Caius added.

Abigail drew herself up in pride. "I thank you for the invitation—"

"Splendid!" Cornelius interrupted. "It is settled, then!"

Caius's eyes glinted with challenge. "And you can have your new maiden serve you. It would be a good test of her abilities, I think."

Caius and Cornelius turned and headed back inside, obviously expecting their word to be carried out. Abigail leveled an accusing gaze on Titus.

He let out his pent up breath. "It will be well, Abigail. All of the men are bringing their wives, which ensures the propriety of the event." He squeezed her shoulder gently, then leaned down and pressed his lips to her forehead. "Simply tell Miriam she will assist the maid that usually serves you; it will give her a chance to learn, but she need not be left to founder on her own. Is that acceptable?"

"Well, I suppose." She sounded begrudging at best.

"Thank you." He kissed her softly, then drew away. "I should go join them before Father plans out the next ten years of my life without me. I will be sure and greet Samuel and Benjamin before Antonia takes them for their dinner."

Abigail sighed in frustration. "What has gotten into him? He has never been so eager to join his father and his guests before."

"The consul is an important man," Phillip provided from the shadows. "If Titus has any intention of beginning a career in Rome, he needs to make friends like Cornelius."

Samuel and Miriam chose that moment to race up to them, Antonia following at a safer, slower pace, obviously glad to have younger legs to keep up with the child. Samuel threw himself at Abigail, and she swung him up into her arms with a laugh.

"Did I hear Titus?" He gave her neck a giant squeeze.

"Yes, but he is in with a guest now. We will go in now and get washed up for the meal; he has promised to come say good night before we go. But Antonia will have to put you to bed tonight, my son. Titus needs me at dinner with him."

Samuel's face fell. "Must you?"

"So it seems." Though internally she asked the same question. Determined to talk with Titus about it when he came to the boys, she pasted a smile on her face and put Samuel on his feet. "Come, you are filthy."

Samuel rallied enough to chatter all the way inside and made no fuss when Antonia subjected him to a good scrubbing at the wash basin. It gave Abigail a chance to turn to Miriam.

"It has been suggested that you assist with serving me tonight." She said it softly, making it clear Miriam could refuse. "You would not be alone, just working beside the girl who is usually there. Her name is Valenia."

Miriam bowed her head. "I will be honored to serve you tonight, Mistress."

Abigail's frowned at the easy acceptance. "Are you certain you will not be too nervous with the crowd? I know I was terrified at my first meal with my mistress, and then again at the first Roman gathering I was asked to serve at."

Miriam smiled warmly. "I have been serving all of my life, Mistress, I will be fine."

Abigail sighed and nodded, then changed the subject. "I have no idea what I should wear." She smiled when she realized she sounded much like Ester always had when about to meet new people. "Come, we will go through what Roman garments I have."

She opted for full Roman styles, a simple dress but with extravagnt hair and generous jewelry. The result, as she looked in the glass, would have been well worth the time had she actually cared about impressing the guests who would no doubt be staring at her in curiosity, trying to figure out why Jason had forfeited his career for her. By the time she heard Titus's voice, she was convinced that going downstairs would be an enormous mistake.

He stepped into the room, eyes widening upoing spotting her. "Abigail. How is it that every time I think you have reached the pinnacle of beauty, you manage to surpass it?"

She did not so much as smile at the compliment. "I need to speak with you."

Titus's eyes glittered with what looked suspiciously like mirth. When Samuel attached himself to his leg, he mussed the boy's curls and gave him his attention. "Be a good boy for Antonia tonight and do whatever she tells you. And help her with your brother."

"I will," Samuel said solemnly. "But must Mother go?"

"She will be in once you are in bed to kiss you. And she will only be in the tablinum, not far."

That seemed to satisfy the boy. He nodded, gave Titus a fierce hug, and turned to help Antonia calm the baby before he could fuss. Titus turned back to Abigail.

She folded her arms over her chest and pitched her voice law. "I cannot do this, it is absurd to expect it of me. The only Roman parties I have ever been a part of, I have been serving at. To expect me to suddenly be a guest–"

"Is understandable, given how perfectly I have seen you conduct yourself in many different situations." He put his hands on her shoulders. "Fair one, Cornelius was a friend of Cleopas's, and he wishes to speak with you, to share his memories and hear about his later years."

She relaxed a bit. "But will he be the only one there? I am afraid of being a spectacle, Titus, that everyone only wants to see me to marvel that Jason would have dared marry such a wretch."

He moved his hands to either side of her face. "You are not a wretch. You are a beautiful, loving, amazing, intelligent woman, and I love you."

Abigail deflated. "And I love you."

"Then do this for me," Titus pleaded. "If I am truly to make a place for myself here, begin a career, then I need to establish a good relationship with the men that will be out there tonight. If the consul wants to speak with Cleopas's daughter, then I must try to convince her."

Abigail sighed. "If it is Cleopas's daughter he wishes to speak with, I have no problems. If it is the slave that Jason shamed himself with, then I cannot go out. Because the slave is still too much of me, Titus, to try to hide it. And I will not injure my husband's memory by proving to his critics that he was foolish to marry me."

"You will honor Jason." He pulled her closer and kissed her deeply. When he eased away from her, it was with a smile. "You will be lovelier than any other woman here tonight. You cannot know how proud I am to have you with me. I remember coming to that luncheon of Jason's, I remember seeing you beside him and feeling the jealousy burn within me." He grinned. "I remember being the recipient of your biting rhetoric as you debated with us about God and his Son. And now here we are, Abigail, having come full circle. We have both seen that Son, we have both changed so much, and now it is my side you will be at. It will be all the others burning with jealousy."

Because they would all think her his lover. The thought did not make it past Abigail's lips, but it still sent a chill down her spine. Much had happened since that day he spoke of; they had indeed changed a lot. But she felt the same nervous anticipation now that she had before Jason's friends arrived, and for a moment she saw the same cold statue in Titus that she had as he walked into her master's house. It vanished quickly in the face of the warm man she loved, but even the memory served to make her unsure of her proper place here. Was she really going to the dinner as Jason's widow, or as Titus's mistress? Was she going to be received as a free woman, or as just another man's possession?

"Go kiss the children," Titus bade softly, pulling her from her reflections. "And then we shall go out."

THIRTY-EIGHT

Abigail entered the tablinum on Titus's arm, tension wracking her. Already a multitude of people were here, spilling from the large room into both the atrium and the peristylium. She had no idea how the kitchen slaves had managed to pull such a feast off, but trays of food and drink circulated as if the party had been planned a week ago.

Aquilia, who stood beside her husband as if they did not despise one another, was the first to notice them. She smiled, but it did little to cover the gleam in her eyes. "My son. Come, get reacquainted with Marcus Priscus."

"Yet another father of an eligible girl," Titus muttered for Abigail's ears alone, even as he smiled and led them over to his parents. He reached out to clasp the man's wrist. "Marcus, it has been several years since I have had the pleasure of talking to you."

The man's toga told her he was a senator. "Indeed, although your father has made certain you were never far from our thoughts. How did you like the military?"

"Let us just say that it has given me a renewed appreciation for civilian life."

"Abigail." Aquilia drew her aside and then propelled her even farther away. "Cornelius has been most eager to speak with you. He grew up with Cleopas, you know."

"Yes, Titus mentioned it." Se tried to keep her nerves in check, but it had not occurred to her that she would be separated from Titus.

"He could be a huge help to Titus."

"Yes, he mentioned that as well."

Her cynicism was apparently not lost on Aquilia; she sent her a sharp look. "I am merely trying to encourage you to be cordial."

"Of course." Abigail said no more, since they had only a few more paces before they were at Cornelius's side.

He looked up at them in greeting. "Ah, here is the guest from afar. My wife, Claudia."

Abigail greeted the new woman, noticing that she had the same cool, aging beauty that Aquilia possessed. She also noticed that with only a few adept maneuvers, those two women had managed to separate themselves and head to another part of the room.

Cornelius was still smiling, and Abigail did not know if there was anything less than honorable lurking under his placid face or not. Deciding she should not assume the worst of anyone, she forced herself to relax as he invited her to sit with him.

Cornelius waited for her to settle onto the couch beside him before saying, "It is so lovely to have this opportunity to meet you. I was terribly upset when I heard of Cleopas's death, and Jason's too. It has been many years since I saw my old friend, but one does not forget the brightest days of one's youth." He laughed lightly. "Not that you are old enough to know that as well as I. But in a few years, my friend, you will understand that truth."

Abigail smiled and made some agreeing noises.

It was all the encouragement Cornelius needed to continue. "Tell me, how was my old friend these past years? I had heard, of course, that he married a local woman, and naturally I met Jason when he was in Rome, but the details have been few."

Figuring her family was something she could speak of easily enough, Abigail settled in and relaxed in reminiscence.

Titus laughed at whatever it was the man beside him had just said, but his eyes moved around the room in search of Abigail. She had sat with Cornelius for almost an hour in conversation, eating little and drinking less. When Cornelius had finally left, Marcus's wife had moved to the seat beside Abigail and struck up another conversation. He had watched Abigail's body language to try to divine the nature of the talk, but it was apparently friendly enough, for she had laughed sincerely without tensing. He was glad she was getting on so well, but still, he wanted to maneuver himself to her side as soon as possible.

"Titus!"

Titus turned with a smile at the familiar voice, unable to help laughing when one of his oldest friends barreled toward him. "Lucius." He steeled himself for the enthusiastic embrace that Lucius did not withhold. "You are back from Ephesus."

Lucius looked down at himself as though amazed to see that truth. "So I am. And you from Israel. When we got the news that the Asiniuses were hosting a party tonight, I told father we simply had to come. We are late, I know, but it seems it does not matter." He looked around at all the people milling about, smiled again. "My sister asks after you."

Titus rolled his eyes. "How is she enjoying married life?"

Lucius's amusement was wry. "She is not. She finds her husband a bore, which is not unexpected when one marries a man as old as one's grandfather. But when one is convinced that only a man in his dotage will forgive one's lack of innocence . . ."

Titus fended off the old accusation with a raised hand. "It was years ago, my friend, and your sister did not seem so concerned about her 'innocence' at the time."

"I shall take your word for it." Lucius did not seem overly concerned as he scanned the room. When his gaze halted on Abigail, his brows flew up. "Delicious. Who is she?"

"Abigail Visibullis." He expected jealousy to surge, but instead it was pride that filled him. "You remember Jason? Abigail is his widow. I brought her here from Israel so that she could claim Jason's inheritance for their son."

Lucius grinned. "Yes, I am sure that was your only reason. I had, of course, heard that Jason married a Jewess. Was she not a slave?"

"It depends on your definition of the term. Jason's parents raised her as their daughter, educated her, clothed her as a gentlewoman. Jason, obviously, did not feel inclined to regard her as a sister, though."

Lucius sniggered. "I should think not."

Their continued gazes in her direction brought Abigail's eyes up, and when she saw Titus, she flashed him a smile.

Lucius shook his head. "I did not realize they were hiding such beauty out there in barbary."

Titus breathed a laugh. "Call her a barbarian when she can hear you, and you shall find yourself the recipient of a nicely delivered lecture on civilization through the ages of the Greeks versus the unbroken chain of law of her own people. If you are lucky, she will throw in a few musically rendered lines of Homer, and then compare them to Virgil's attempt at modeling it."

Lucius laughed. "Come, friend, you must introduce me to this paradigm of charm." He started in her direction, leaving Titus little choice but to follow. As if foreseeing their lack of need of her, Marcus's wife stood and moved away, exchanging a few words of greeting with the two younger men as she passed them.

The couch was not designed to hold three of them, but Lucius did not seem too concerned about that. He merely sat on one side of Abigail as Titus claimed the other, exclaiming merrily, "Titus tells me you can sing the Greek poets."

Abigail glanced at Lucius, then looked with curiosity at Titus. He had pulled her closer to his side to keep as much space between her and Lucius as possible and then left his arm around her waist protectively. "Strange, I do not think Titus has ever heard me sing the Greek poets."

Titus smiled at her and accepted a glass of wine from one of the slaves. "Perhaps it is just that I have heard you speak _of_ the poets, and your voice is always a song." When his friend laughed, Titus took a sip of his wine. "You would have loved to hear her the first time Jason invited us to his home, Lucius. She chastised us as lawless pagans, subtly rebuked us for staring at her, and proceeded to teach us about our own religious figures so that we were truly ashamed at having not realized ourselves the things she pointed out."

"You _were_ lawless pagans." Her expression combined amusement with a hint of irritation. "You spent every moment you could carousing in the city, and you made my husband feel guilty for opting to stay at home with his family."

"She knows you well, I see." Lucius grinned and motioned for a slave to refill his wine. "You should have seen him here before he left, my friend. There was not a party he did not attend, a woman he did not seduce, a wine he had not tasted–and still he was one of the most stubbornly reasonable men I ever had the hardship of knowing! I could not once instigate a fight with him, and trust me, I tried. I even had good reason once or twice, but he would never rise to the bait. Now if his _father_ dared to insult him, that was a different story."

"Enough of your reminiscing, Lucius. Abigail does not wish to hear about my ill-spent youth."

He knew Abigail truly did not wish to hear about it, but Lucius apparently thought the comment indicated its opposite. With another laugh, he leaned closer to her. "He was the envy of every man in Rome. Not only was he known to have the most beautiful slaves awaiting his every whim at home, he seemed to be able to merely quirk his finger and have any noblewoman willing to throw aside her virtue and invite him into her chamber."

Feeling Abigail's shoulders tense, Titus interjected calmly. "That is enough, Lucius, take pity on the lady. You will offend her sensibilities with such talk."

"I only thought to make sure that she truly does know whom she has aligned herself with." Lucius took a long draught of his drink.

Abigail put a hand on Titus's knee, aligning herself with him even more. "I know Titus. I know the kind of man he was. And I also know him as a man far different from the one you describe."

Lucius arched a brow and looked over her head at Titus. "Really? How interesting. I have never known him to hide his nature."

"Nor have I." Abigail smiled. "But even the most lawless of boys can grow into decent men."

Titus heard her defense of him with an amused smile. He had a hard time focusing on her words, though, with her hand on his knee. He could feel the warmth of it through the layers of cloth, it seemed, and the awareness only grew until he could feel her nearness at every nerve ending. As Lucius rejoined and directed the conversation along a different path, he felt her relax again and took the chance to draw her a little closer, until her back was resting against his side. She darted a curious look at him over her shoulder once, as if wondering what he was up to, but she was soon turned back to Lucius, laughing at something he said. Her hand stayed where she had put it. It alone told him she was not as relaxed as she seemed, since the longer Lucius prattled, the more tense her fingers became.

"Are you all right?" he whispered into her ear when Lucius's attention was diverted by a tray of food.

"Fine. Why do you ask?"

He chuckled. "Because you seem to be trying to reshape my knee."

Abigail loosened her grip abruptly, and would have removed her hand had he not covered it with his own. "Sorry."

"I do not mind." He measured her for a moment. "You have not eaten much."

She pressed a hand to her stomach. "I cannot. Miriam has tried to tempt me with everything here, but I would rather just wait until later, or tomorrow."

He nodded, since Lucius had made his selections and turned back to them again. At that point the party was in full swing, and Titus marveled at how large it had become. He had somehow managed to forget how easily a small gathering could turn into something so massive in his father's house. Many of the guests had settled onto couches or chairs by that time, more furniture having been brought in quietly as more people arrived. His father was not far from him, seeming deep in conversation with Cornelius Cossus.

After another hour, Abigail shifted beside him. "Excuse me, I must go tend Benjamin. I will be back in a few minutes."

Titus nodded, moving so she could rise. He exchanged a glance with Phillip to direct the eunuch to accompany her, and the two slid from the room.

Lucius sipped again from his wine. "Once again, Titus, you have outdone us all. She is devoted to you." He gave an exaggerated sigh. "A pity. I would like to see what she hides under that stola."

"I am glad you waited until she left before you announced that." Titus motioned for a slave to refill his cup. He was not sure how many he had already had, but it was a fine vintage.

Lucius laughed. "I am not a complete scoundrel, Titus. At the very least, I realize that saying such a thing to a woman will ruin any chances I may have to begin with." He grew suddenly pensive. It was not an uncommon thing for him, shifting moods so suddenly. "It is not fair that you have her, Titus, your mother is even now trying to find you a wife."

"Abigail will return to Israel soon. I have a feeling my mother is wise enough to wait until her departure before insisting I wed."

"You have no respect for the property of your friends." At least his proclamation was quiet enough not to draw the attention of any of the other groups nearby. "You take whatever you want, never considering to whom it actually belongs."

Titus felt his brows draw together. "You are mistaken in that, Lucius. When she was Jason's, I honored that bond. If I take her now, it is because that claim no longer exists. Jason is gone. I miss him, but he is gone. Abigail's mourning has passed."

"And how convenient that you are the one nearest her when it has. Titus Asinius, the tempter of the temptresses."

"I have not missed your moods, Lucius," Titus returned dryly. "Jealousy always makes you foul. Just accept that you will never so much as touch her and move on to another conquest."

Lucius brightened again, an impish smile on his lips. "Probably, that is not such a great loss. I suspect she is not nearly as talented behind closed doors as imagination would suppose."

Titus raised his cup to his lips and looked straight ahead. "Never in my life have I lowered myself to answering your prying questions. Do not expect me to start now."

Lucius laughed again, his humor restored, and was content to change the subject.

❧

Abigail took her seat beside Titus again after returning. She felt more at ease simply because the pain of needing to nurse had been relieved, but now she was beginning to feel tired. Her eyes sought Miriam and found her making the rounds with the other maids, a pitcher of wine in hand. The girl met her eye and lifted a brow in question, but Abigail gave a small shake of her head.

Titus and Lucius were deep into talk of politics, with the occasional reference to someone she had never met, so Abigail's mind wandered around the room. She kept looking over at her maid simply to make sure all was well with her. Twenty minutes after her reentry into the room, Miriam ended up by Caius.

Abigail's breath caught as the man raised his cup and slid a hand up Miriam's leg. He was not the first to touch the girl, but the others had made it look casual–a hand to the back, on the arm. Miriam had not seemed disturbed by those, but now her face froze in an expression Abigail knew well: panic.

She stepped away at the first possible moment, glanced toward Abigail. Their gazes clashed, and Abigail saw the panic mount. Miriam headed her way, eyes spewing apology.

Titus looked up at her approach too. "Ah, good. More wine, please."

Miriam lifted a trembling arm. Abigail stood, put herself between Miriam and Titus, and halted her with a hand on her arm. "It is not your fault," she said in Hebrew, softly. "You are not to blame for Caius's actions. If you do not calm yourself, you will spill the wine."

Miriam flushed, but some of the panic eased from her eyes. "I am sorry, Mistress."

Abigail smiled. "I am not rebuking you, my friend." In Greek she added, "Would you go check on my son for me? See if he has settled?"

"Of course."

Abigail pried the wine gently from her fingers. "Go." She watched for a moment as her shaken maid turned and left unobtrusively, then she turned back around to Titus.

He smiled when he saw her with the pitcher. "It has been a long time since you have poured for me, sweet one."

Abigail narrowed her eyes at him. "I think you have had more than enough to drink, Titus Asinius." To prove it, she handed the pitcher to a passing maid and then waved her away.

Titus scowled, but it was not long lasting. He put his empty cup aside, then put his hands on Abigail's hips to urge her back down beside him, pulling her as close as he had before. "It does not matter." He nipped at her ear, making her jump. "You are sweeter than any wine, anyway."

Abigail sighed, even if a smile tugged at her mouth. "You have most assuredly had enough to drink, my love." She elbowed him in the ribs to drive the point home.

Titus chuckled. "You may be right. Ah. My mother is taking the women away. I suppose that means you must leave me."

Abigail lifted a hand to rub at her neck. "I suppose so. I will only stay a moment with them, I think. I am tired."

"Do not retire before I get to say good night."

Abigail smiled at him and stood, said her farewells to Lucius, and left the room with Miriam, Phillip falling in behind.

Caius's voice grabbed Titus's attention. "What do you think of our Hebrewesses, Cornelius?" he was asking his friend, who was every bit as inebriated as he. "Pretty, are they not? The new maid is a fine creature, Titus picked her out."

Titus considered correcting his father on that one, but Cornelius replied before he could.

"The maid?" He laughed. "Why waste your time on the maid when you can have the mistress?" He raised his cup to Titus. "My compliments, my friend. An enviable trophy."

"Say thank you, Titus," Caius instructed with a sloppy grin.

Titus smiled; only his father could treat him like a child while congratulating him on a seduction. And in that particular moment, it was more entertaining than annoying. "Thank you, Cornelius." His obedient echo inspired laughter from both Cornelius and Lucius.

"The ladies are gone!" Caius raised his cup high. "Girls, make some old men happy!"

His friends cheered and laughed, and the servants that had been dedicated solely to pouring wine or offering food entered the room in a far different character.

"Who do you want, Titus? Take your pick, it is your first symposium since your return."

Titus shook his head. "I have heard no philosophy to make this a symposium, Father. And I will defer the first pick to our friend Cornelius."

"A deserving fellow! A wise son! I am a blessed man!"

"Amazing." Titus turned to Lucius as Cornelius beckoned a girl over to him. "My father loves me as much when he is drunk as he despises me when he is sober. Why has this never struck me before?"

Lucius laughed. "Probably because you are usually just as drunk, and not nearly so congenial. Your Jewess kept waving away the wine, Titus, you have not had enough!"

"No, I am quite satisfied." He looked around at the situation that could very easily get out of hand. "As a matter of fact, I think I may just slip away. I have enjoyed catching up with you Lucius; stop by again soon."

"I will. And give Abigail a kiss for me. Here." He pointed to his thigh with a wicked grin.

Titus breathed a laugh and shoved his friend lightly in the shoulder. Trying to avoid notice, he slipped out of the room and hoped that his father would be too diverted to notice his absence. That accomplished, he headed to his room.

He was not really very drunk at all.

⚜

Abigail kissed the sleeping faces lightly, smiling. "Thank you for watching them for me, Antonia."

The older woman smiled. "It is always my pleasure, Mistress. Both of the boys are well behaved."

"Go ahead to bed." Abigail put a hand on Antonia's shoulder in farewell. She then turned to Miriam and Phillip. "The two of you can go ahead as well. I would like some solitude, I think. Phillip, I want you to be near Miriam tonight. There are a few too many drunken men around for me to send her to her room alone. I will have Titus to ensure my safety up here, but I would rest easier knowing you were within call for Miriam."

Phillip folded his muscled arms over his chest. "We will wait for Titus's return before we leave you, Mistress. Let Miriam take down your hair, and I will watch for him."

Abigail sighed, knowing he would not budge on the matter. "Very well." She moved into her chamber, Miriam behind her. Getting her hair down was quick work, and Abigail found herself soothed as the brush was run through it. The evening had been a long one, and her nerves felt frazzled. She felt she had conducted herself well, and she had not been as self-conscious as she had feared she would be, but still it had been trying. The entire environment was foreign to her; she had never been a part of such a large gathering before, even at the general's house, and one so blatantly Bacchical was entirely unfamiliar. She had hoped she would have some relief when she went with the women, but a few minutes with them had told her it was not to be, that the ladies of Rome were just as capable of being coarse and vulgar as their male counterparts. She had left almost as soon as they all settled in. She had a feeling she would not be especially missed.

Phillip came to attention moments after Miriam put down the brush. "Titus is here. Are you ready, Miriam?"

"Do you need anything else, Mistress?" Miriam asked.

Abigail shook her head and gave her maid a smile. "Thank you for your help,

Miriam. And I am sorry if Caius upset you tonight."

Miriam returned the smile. "You cannot be held accountable for his actions, Lady. My only distress was anticipation of yours."

"Sleep well," Abigail bade, then turned her smile on Phillip. "And thank you for watching over her tonight."

Phillip nodded, then led Miriam from the chambers just as Titus entered. He headed straight for his bed and sank onto it, looking exhausted and tense. With a smile, Abigail went over and sat beside him, reaching up to try to massage away some of the tension in his neck. Titus sighed at her touch.

"You seemed to enjoy yourself tonight." Abigail's gaze followed her hands over his neck. How had she never noticed that it was so corded with muscle?

"Mostly. It has been a long time since I have seen Lucius."

Abigail smiled. "I can only imagine the trouble the two of you got into in prior days."

Titus breathed a laugh. "You should probably not even attempt that much, beloved."

"I did not expect you to leave the party so soon."

Titus shrugged. "It was about to get significantly worse than it had been, since the ladies left. I daresay I shall not be missed."

"Ah." Abigail continued to work on his neck, but he did not seem to be relaxing any. When he suddenly let himself fall backward onto the mattress with a huge sigh, she had to laugh. "You should see yourself, Titus. You did not look so exhausted when you had stayed up with me all night through my labor."

Titus smiled, eyes closed, and reached up blindly. Abigail took his hand in hers, though she was not sure if he was asking for help up again or simply wanting contact. She tugged lightly on his arm to see if he would assist her in the former goal, but he only chuckled at her attempt and, with one good tug, pulled her down with him instead. Though she laughed, her heart accelerated dangerously.

"You are a defeatist." She put a hand on his shoulder and tried to lever herself up. It was an impossible task, given the arm he had around her. "You need to sleep this off. I should go call your manservant to help you undress."

Titus's eyes had drifted open again, a half-smile played on his lips. He held her right where she was. "Perhaps you should help me yourself, beloved."

Abigail narrowed her eyes. "You have definitely had too much to drink."

"Or not enough." His smile turned roguish.

"Either way, I shall simply ignore that indiscreet comment so that you can look me in the eye in the morning."

"I can look you in the eye, now." He propped himself up on his elbow and attempted to prove it. But she could not meet his gaze, not knowing what she would see within it. Abigail cast her eyes downward, even when he put a finger under chin to tilt her face up to his. "Abigail." Still she refused.

A moment later he rolled her onto her back. Her eyes flew open now, which was undoubtedly his intent. But far too much desire filled his gaze, as she had known it would, desire she was not sure she could combat. Heart pounding, she closed her eyes again.

Titus caught his breath. Had she learned nothing with Jason? Did she not realize that she looked the height of desirable like this, eyes closed in innocence, lips parted ever so slightly, cheeks flushed? He felt the rise and fall of her breasts under him and let his breath out again. Curse her, if she was going to act this way, what was he to do? He lowered himself until he could taste her lips.

A whimper escaped, one that mixed fear with longing. Just as her hands curled into his tunic as if unable to decide whether to push him away or pull him closer. "Titus . . ."

"I must have you." He trailed his lips over her jaw. "I must, beloved, I can take it no more."

She gave one halfhearted push at his shoulder, shook her head. "Titus, no. You yourself said it would not come to this, that our love did not need consummation."

Titus met her watery gaze for a moment. "Since when am I the one to always be right?" He kissed her again, refusing to release her mouth until her hands clung to him. "We love each other so much, Abigail. What could be more natural than this?"

He had slid his hands up her sides, taking her arms with them and anchoring them above her head with one hand, then toying with her hair with the other. Her breath caught in obvious pleasure even as a tear spilled onto her cheek. "Do not try to tell me this is right, Titus. You know it is a sin. It is wrong."

"Perhaps," he whispered into her ear as he took the lobe into his mouth. "But feel it, Abigail. Is it not good?"

"Good and wrong cannot coincide." She trembled. From fear, desire, or the battle between them? "Pleasure is fleeting."

"That depends entirely upon how much of it you have scheduled." He smiled against her mouth, though it soon faded into another kiss. "I have never wanted a woman as I want you, my love, and I will have you. Tonight."

Her entire body went rigid. "Will you force me, Titus?"

He met her gaze head on. "Will you make me, Abigail?"

She sagged back into the mattress under him. "If you do this, I will hate you in the morning."

He smiled and kissed her gently. Hovering over her mouth he whispered, "You will not hate me, my love. You cannot. Your heart is mine, and nothing can change that. No matter what I do, you will love me, and you will forgive me."

More tears spilled over. "You are not being the man I love."

"I am the man I have always been." He kissed away the droplets. "And yet you love me."

"Titus–"

"Hush." He kissed her into obedience, kissed her until she kissed him back, kissed her until she was pliable. He kissed her as he undressed her, as he awoke her, as he took her. And then he held her close as she sobbed against him, held her until she had cried herself to sleep. Then he leaned over, blew out the lamp, and held her all through the night.

THIRTY-NINE

Abigail awoke groggy, confused, and sore. Dawn was a breath on the horizon and no more, and she stretched in the darkness to try to wake herself up more fully. That was when she became aware of the body beside hers. She suddenly remembered why her eyes felt swollen and stinging and let out a depressed sigh. How was it that she had been through all she had been through and still ended up in the same place she had been a year ago? Should she not have been stronger by now? Wiser? At least knowledgeable enough to know that no man was really as interested in a platonic relationship as he may claim?

"Where are you going?" Titus muttered, half asleep, when she started to ease away.

"Benjamin will need to be fed."

He nodded, and she could barely make out his smile through the predawn darkness. He reached out and smoothed her hair out of her face, kissing her shoulder. Tenderness welled up in her, quickly followed by anger at the soft emotions. She jerked out of bed and fumbled around for her tunic, slipped it over her head. She darted into the small room and picked up the stirring Benjamin. Samuel still slept soundly; she was grateful that he had not been awoken by her crying the night before and decided to investigate. Things were bad enough without having to explain to a six-year-old why she loathed herself.

She settled onto the bed and put the baby to her breast. Knowing her son was always affected by her moods, she attempted to distance herself from everything but him. Humming a psalm, she rocked gently until he had eaten his fill and dozed back into slumber. It was enough to make Abigail smile. Leave it to Benjamin to not disappoint her; he always stuck to his patterns. Hungry at dawn, but quickly satiated, then back to sleep for another two hours, when he would awake as starved as though she had not just risen with or before the sun to anticipate him.

After the baby was content, she cuddled him close and let her eyes slide shut. For a few moments, silence bathed her as her son settled back into sleep. Then the door opened almost silently, and Titus entered. He was either oblivious to the her immediate tensing or decided to ignore it. He simply smiled and lifted Benjamin from her arms. Once again, as she watched him cradle her son so affectionately, she felt overwhelming love for the man. Once again, anger followed quickly on its heels.

He held out a hand to her as he cradled the baby with one strong arm.

She had very little choice but to put her hand in his. Admitting she had intended to sit there and hold him half the morning would sound like a feeble excuse to avoid what had happened. No, she corrected herself, it *was* a feeble excuse to avoid what had happened. So she let him pull her to her feet.

Titus settled Benjamin down gently into his little bed, then opened the door and pulled her into his chamber before shutting it again.

"Titus, we need to talk," Abigail said softly as he pulled her deeper into the chamber, away from the sleeping children.

"I know." He stopped them beside the bed, then released her hand and began tugging at the tunic he had slipped on.

Abigail looked at him in disbelief. "What are you doing?"

Titus dropped the garment on the floor carelessly. "Getting back into bed. The morning air is cool, and I am still quite tired."

Abigail sighed and rubbed a hand over her weary eyes. Even without looking, she knew he had not moved to do as he had proclaimed. "You seem to be in no hurry."

"I am waiting for you to join me."

At that, she dropped her hand so that he could see the distress in her eyes. "Titus, what are you thinking?"

"It is rather simple." He sounded so calm, so cool. "I undoubtedly should not have done what I did last night. It upset you, and I am sorry that I lacked control. On the other hand, nothing has ever pleased me more than knowing you, and I find that my heart is not truly repentant. That means that even if I never touch you again, I remain guilty of it. And if I am going to be guilty of it, I might as well be enjoying it."

She blinked with fatigue. "That logic is shockingly perverse."

"But accurate." He reached out and rested his hands on her shoulders, pulling her closer. "Abigail, I love you. It is done now, you are my lover, there is no more reason to fight me."

He moved one hand to smooth down her hair, then left it at the back of her head, anchoring her as he stepped nearer still. "Do you still love me, Abigail?"

Something in her broke. She felt it, felt it crack, felt it crumble, felt herself sink into the hole it left behind. She did not know what she was doing to herself. But she knew the answer to his question. "Yes. I still love you, Titus."

"Good." He kissed her then, passionately, intimately, but not long. He soon stepped away, moved to sit on the mattress. But he held out a hand. "Come to bed with me, Abigail."

Feeling as though she were far removed from herself, she obeyed.

❧

Titus's satisfied smile turned to a sigh when the door opened. Not so much because they were being interrupted, but because Abigail jumped away from him in guilt at the first noise. He scowled as she tugged nervously on her tunic, though he had smoothed it over her curves just moments ago.

It was Phillip who pushed open the door, pulling a weeping Miriam behind him. Abigail rushed forward. "What is wrong?"

Miriam collapsed against her, unable to speak. Phillip shook his head. "He locked my door. It locks only from the outside. I heard her scream, but by the time I broke through the door, it was too late. The damage had already been done. I pulled him off her and knocked him unconscious." He sneered. "Seeing the condition he was in, I doubt he will even remember the episode."

"Who?" Titus demanded.

"Your father."

Abigail smoothed down Miriam's hair. "What a night."

Titus sent her a sharp glare, but Phillip apparently read nothing into the statement. "The last guests are just leaving. Caius only came moments ago. I brought her up here immediately."

"And she will stay up here." Abigail looked up at Titus; her eyes snapped with the same anger that pounded through him. "Your father can do what he wishes with his own women and I cannot stop him, but he will *never* touch any member of my household! Miriam and Phillip will move in with me."

Titus sighed. "Abigail, there are already three of you in a room the size of a closet. It is not possible to add more. They will move into the room next door, and we will not let my father know. We will let him think they are in here, and I will bribe or threaten whatever servants I must in order to convince him of it."

"How altruistic of you."

Her sarcasm bit him, but he could hardly blame her for it. "I am sorry. I admit this is my fault; I saw the way my father looked at her, and I did nothing."

Abigail sighed. Though he saw the war raging in her eyes, her expression ended up softening. "It is not your fault. I saw your father's reaction to her as well. It is why I insisted Phillip stay downstairs last night."

"And it is I that failed." Phillip rolled back his shoulders as if preparing them for punishment.

Abigail shook her head. "You cannot be expected to read his mind, Phillip. You did all you could, and I thank you for that." She stroked Miriam's hair. Thankfully the girl seemed to be calming down. "The only one to blame for this is Caius. No one else should be held responsible for the lecherous acts of a drunkard. Miriam, I am sorry. I promised you a life better than this, and then this happens in the first day."

Miriam wiped at her eyes, looking embarrassed at her own reactions. "As you yourself just said, you are not to blame, Mistress." She attempted a small smile. It was watery, but it got her point across. "It was not as bad as it could have been. If I had not been asleep when he entered, I could have stopped him myself, he was so drunk."

Abigail wiped away one of the tears Miriam had missed. "It will not happen again. Phillip, go see that Caius is delivered to his own rooms; wake his servants to carry him if you must. Get Titus's man to help you bring your and Miriam's belongings upstairs and put them in the next room." She moved to the eunuch and put a small hand on his large arm. "You have not failed me, Phillip. And worrying that you have in the past will only distract you in the future."

It was obviously the right thing to say to convince Phillip to dismiss his thoughts. With a nod, he exited the room again.

"Go wash up," Abigail bade Miriam gently.

Titus waited until they were alone again before speaking. "I truly am sorry, Abigail. This should not have happened to her."

"No, it should not have." She pressed her fingers to her eyes. "You should not have objected to moving them into my chamber."

Titus watched her for half a moment in silence. "Must we argue about this right now?"

"Why not? Why not discuss the actions of the son while we are on the topic of the father?"

Titus's felt the old storms gather behind his eyes. He approached her so quickly that she stepped back in fear, but he stopped her retreat with iron hands on her shoulders. "You will not compare me to him. I did not sneak into your chamber while you slept and rape you, Abigail. Every woman who has ever come to my bed has come willingly, and whether or not you regret your decision, it was still your decision."

"Barely! You pressured me." Her cry was quiet.

"Yes. And you gave in because you wanted it as much as I did." When tears gathered in her eyes, he cursed, dragging her against his chest and holding her with surprising gentleness, given his temper. "Do not cry, beloved. Please. I am sorry you fell in love with such a weak man, but you destroy me when you cry." He kissed the top of her head. "I swear, I will not pressure you again. If you come to me, it will be of your own choosing, and otherwise I will not touch you."

Abigail wept against him, her hands balled into fists around his tunic. "This is not how things are supposed to be."

Titus cradled her head. "Very little in life is, dear one." He tipped her head back so that he could look into her tear-stained face. She had no right to look so beautiful even as she cried. "I love you."

"And I love you." The admission sounded miserable.

He moved to kiss her, but before he could, he spotted Samuel entering the room. Titus straightened, smiled. "Good morning, Samuel."

The boy rubbed sleep from his eyes. "What is wrong? Everyone is upset."

Titus scooped the child up when he approached. "It is nothing for you to worry about, small one. My father has not been behaving himself."

Samuel settled into Titus's arms, resting his head on his shoulder. "Perhaps someone should scold him."

Titus chuckled. "If only it were so easy. I am afraid he is not as good as you, Samuel. He does not listen to our reproaches."

Samuel reached out to Abigail and touched a clinging tear with the tip of his finger. "Do not cry, Mother. Everyone is sad when you cry."

Abigail smiled at him and tried unsuccessfully to tame his curls with her fingers. "I am finished crying. Is Benjamin stirring yet?"

"He will be now."

Titus nodded to her. "Go tend him. I will help Samuel get ready."

⬥

Abigail shut herself into the small room and lifted Benjamin from his basket. Part of her had wanted to refuse Titus's command simply because it was a command. But she had obeyed. Just as she had earlier.

"Father, forgive me, for I am weak," she murmured in Hebrew, her eyes squeezed shut as she settled onto the bed. But somehow, her brief prayer echoed in her heart as more of an excuse than a plea for help. For though her mind may be repentant, her heart was still guilty. She knew it and wished it otherwise . . . even as she accepted that she would sin again.

Titus went out alone that day to answer a summons from the steward in charge of their shipping business, knowing his father would not so much as open his eyes until late afternoon after entertaining all night. He had gotten to know the business fairly well since his return to Rome, and he knew he could handle the problem. In fact, he had a better head for it than Caius did, and his father had surprised him by realizing it. Perhaps he could convince him that it would be wiser to put aside political goals for a while and simply let him tend to this. He would rationalize it by pointing out that in another ten years he could double, if not triple the revenues brought in on their ships. With the added prestige of such wealth, it would be far easier to enter the political arena, especially since his father's peers would no longer think of him as a child. What he would *not* mention to his father was that with ten years and added wealth, he would be independent enough to dismiss Caius and his ambitions if he so chose. Assuming the old man had not drunk himself to death by then anyway.

This plan struck him as ideal, even plausible. Having a course of action eased some of the burden of the future from his shoulders and made his step a little lighter. He knew that when he returned to the house he would have entirely different problems to deal with, but for now he would develop his idea, reasoning through it until there were no holes for Caius to point out.

The first step would be winning the allegiance of the steward and other men in his employ in the shipping end, and he figured he was already well on his way to achieving that. The better the decisions he made, the more they benefitted, and the more they looked on him with respect and loyalty. He took it as a good sign that already the missives they sent were no longer addressed only to Caius, but now to the Asiniuses. In another month, he would see if it was his name alone on the top. And best of all, his father would not wonder if he were trying to usurp him; Caius would like nothing more than to spend his days in the Forum and let the money-making end of things be taken care of by someone else. Logically, this should suit them both. It made so much sense that Titus began to wonder why neither of them had considered it before.

He settled the matter he had been called to deal with in very little time but spent several hours there acquainting himself with the details of the operation, talking to the men who worked for him, anticipating other problems likely to come up. By the time he left, he felt confident that he could indeed increase their income tremendously by working out a few kinks and making a few minor changes. It made his mood light, and he held onto that even as he returned home.

"Where is my father?" he asked Timothy as soon as he entered the house; servants were still dashing around trying to return order to the place after last night's feast, though he suspected they were in more need of sleep than the masters.

"In his chambers, Master. He has just awakened and called for food."

"Good." Titus headed in the appropriate direction with long strides and soon arrived at his father's rooms. He knocked on the door. It opened before him. "Good afternoon, Father."

Caius glared at him. "What is good about it?"

His obvious pain brought a smile to Titus's lips. "Seeing you paying for your revelries, for one thing. For another, I was just down talking with Quintilius, and we took care of the difficulties the Corinthian authorities were giving us. You know, I enjoy such work as much as you loathe it. I would be happy to handle the businesses from now on, so that you are free to concentrate on politics."

"Fine. Is that all?"

"No." Titus let his face turn hard. "If you touch Miriam again you will find yourself in far more pain than you are in right now. She is not yours. You have no right to her."

Caius scowled. "Will you keep them both to yourself, Titus?"

"I will keep Abigail to myself. Miriam is no more mine than she is yours. It was Abigail who bought her, Abigail who owns her, and it is Abigail alone who has the authority to give her to a man. She is a handmaid, not a concubine. To make certain you respect this, we have moved her in with the boys, and Phillip will be guarding them. See that you do not give the slave another reason to crack your skull."

Before Caius could muster up a reply, Titus strode from the room again.

He found Abigail and the children and the servants outside and spent the rest of the afternoon with them. Well, he spent the afternoon with Samuel. Abigail rarely looked up from the book she had brought out, and even when she did, her eyes were distant. It was only a small relief to see that it was not just him she kept herself aloof from, but everyone. Her answers to Samuel were monosyllabic, she showed no interest in Antonia's story from the markets that morning, and she did not so much as mutter a complaint when Phillip and Miriam hovered over her. When they ate with his mother, his father still not feeling up to leaving his room, she was silent. He followed when she put the children to bed, hoping she would talk to him once they were alone.

He waited on his chaise while she got the boys settled, straightening when she came out into his room, dismissing Miriam and Phillip. He stood. She turned to him, and her hollow eyes suddenly sparked. He was fully expecting another argument to begin. Instead, she walked over to him calmly and pulled his mouth down to hers. Her lips were hungry, and her hands impatient.

He decided not to try for conversation after all.

❧

It was the second night in a row Titus has accepted an invitation from Lucius to join him at some gathering in the city. The night before, Abigail had stayed up with a copy of a dialogue until his return, when she could convince her servants to leave her. This night, she found herself considerably irritated. They had been in Rome for many weeks and he had never left her alone of an evening. Yet when she accepted him as her lover, he went out? It was insulting. So rather than finding some excuse to stay up, she granted Miriam permission to sleep in her room, sent Phillip into Titus's, and went to sleep.

His return awoke her. She heard his voice, Phillip's muffled answer, and she sat up in irritation. If it woke her up, there was a good chance it would wake the children as well. Furious, she exited into his chamber, more irritated still when the moon's angle told her it was only an hour or two before dawn. She felt Miriam come up behind her.

Titus was glowering at Phillip, who was saying, "I will not leave her alone with you when you are in this state. You are worse than drunk if you think I will."

"And you are worse than a slave if you think I would hurt her. Can a man not have privacy in his own room?" His words were slurred, and he only just noticed her. Looking her way, he did not so much as smile. "Hello, sweet one. Why do you not tell your lackey to leave us?"

Abigail stepped out from behind Phillip and put a hand on his arm. "It is all right, my friend. You and Miriam may go."

Phillip bristled. "He is drunk and not in control of himself. I will not leave you with him like this."

"A slave and a eunuch dares to judge me!" Titus let out a mocking laugh. "Come here, my love, so I can show him that I will not hurt you."

Abigail stared at him for a long moment as he stood there, his hand extended to her. His face was a cold mask, familiar but not a part of her better memories. It occurred to her only then that she had not so much as seen him smile at anyone but the children since the night of his father's party, four days ago.

She stepped calmly toward him. "Keep your voice down. You will wake the children."

"Mistress!" Phillip objected.

Abigail put her hand in Titus's when she was near enough, letting him pull her close and cover her mouth with his own. He tasted so strongly of wine that she was afraid she would get besotted just from kissing him. She pulled away when it became clear he did not care to.

"You are drunk." She put as much distance between them as she could, though his arms were firmly around her. She ended up leaning her head back so that she could look up at him.

"I am not."

"You are."

He seemed to consider. "Maybe a little."

"Quite a bit, from where I am standing."

Titus shook his head. "I am not very drunk. You would know if I were; when I am very drunk, I am very mean."

Abigail arched her brows. "And insulting Phillip is not mean?"

He all but growled. "He will not leave."

Abigail sighed, seeing no peaceable solution to this dilemma. Finally, she turned her head toward her servants. "Phillip, take Miriam and go to bed."

"Mistress," Phillip tried one last time, obviously distressed, "I realize you love him, but can you not see that he is not himself? Would you have him make a whore of you?"

Abigail let her gaze fall straight ahead. "I already have." That rendered him speechless, so she said again, "Please, Phillip. Take Miriam and go."

He obeyed, glaring threateningly at Titus all the while. Titus did not seem to notice, however, as he was too busy glaring in turn at Abigail. "Do not speak of yourself like that," he said as the door closed behind the servants. "You are not so low, dear one. I love you."

"Do you?" She moved her eyes back to his, searching them as she had done on two occasions before. Once, she had found him lacking. The second time, she had seen potential, something in him to make her hope. This time she was far too confused to make sense of what she saw. "I believe you do, Titus, somewhere inside you. But you are letting yourself fall into your old habits. And the old Titus thought of me as nothing but a slave."

His face hardened even more. He clenched his jaw, and she wondered if he was fighting her words or his own reactions to them. "I know you are not a slave. I love you."

Her lips curved up, but it was hardly a smile. "You say that as though the mere statement can bend reality. Yet you treat me as though I am but another of your wenches to be taken at your convenience and ignored whenever you have something better to do. I have barely even seen you in the last two days, Titus."

"Two days is not such a long time."

"It is when I have nothing to do but sit around and wait for my lover to come home."

Quite suddenly, his eyes lit with pleasure. "You have missed me. Why did you not simply say so, rather than try to make me feel guilty?"

She wanted to shout, "Because *I* feel guilty! Because I need to know that you are capable of feeling it too!" Instead, she quietly sighed, letting her eyes slide closed. "It is late. I am tired. I do not like to be awakened by the roars of a drunken man."

"I was not roaring, and I am not that drunk. Though it is late, and you are tired. My suggestion would be to go to bed."

She nodded, prepared to turn back to her room and do just that. When Titus picked her up and carried her the few steps to his bed instead, she let out a frustrated breath. "Titus!"

He placed her on her feet long enough to pull her tunic over her head, then scooped her up again and deposited her on the bed. "You will be asleep soon," he promised her with a crooked smile as he stripped himself and settled beside her. "Think of me as your lullaby. I will soothe you and tire you and keep you warm and content."

She may have had better success in mustering an objection if he had not already figured out what sensations overwhelmed her. She fell asleep once again in his arms.

But that night she dreamed of the earth shaking, of thunder rolling in, of the midday sky turning black as night. She dreamed of a colorless world, with naught to brighten it but a single glistening, perfectly formed drop of blood that hovered in the air like the sun. In her dream she stirred, reached, tried to touch the crimson sphere, but it evaded her. In her dream she wept, stretched, demanded of God an explanation for why he withheld his salvation. Just before she awoke, she looked down at her own dream-created feet and saw that it was she who was moving away. And the drop of blood fell onto the world, erasing the darkness and leaving it bright as morning again.

But still she stood in the shadows.

FORTY

Titus ran his fingers through the hair splayed over his chest, twisted it loosely around his forefinger, let the wave fall free again. Abigail slept as soundly as the children in the next room, and he was glad. Truly. She had seemed restless these last few days, even though he had refused any further invitations from Lucius for social activities. Staying home with her had not pacified the irritation he seemed to chafe within her. The last three nights she had been tossing terribly, caught in the throes of a bad dream. He had held her each time as she awoke shaken, trying to soothe her, but she had not even told him what haunted her in her sleep.

Tonight he was the one suspended in unrest. He had gotten a couple hours of slumber earlier, but now, perhaps an hour or two before dawn, he was wide awake. Loath to disturb Abigail, he tried not to stir.

A boring undertaking. His mind would not halt long enough for him to fall back asleep, but it did not come up with any particularly riveting thoughts, either. So he lay there and played with Abigail's hair and tried to tell himself that there was some external cause to her recent moods aside from him. Perhaps they were even normal; after all, he had only really known her for a few months, he certainly had not seen every facet of her being yet. And had Jason not complained often enough about her attitudes?

His brows furrowed. He did not want to compare his relationship with Abigail to Jason's. She was not his slave, he had not forced her to this, he did not hold her life in his hands. She had good reason to remain distant from Jason. And she had not loved him. Their current situation was quite different; she was just not acting like it right now. Perhaps it was because she was not yet accustomed to it, to him, to feeling these things. Perhaps she felt guilty for finding another so soon after her husband's death. Perhaps she was afraid of what would happen once Ester arrived in Rome.

All likely reasons; none of them the real one. But he did not want to think about the sin. He knew that every night they spent in each other's arms was wrong. Knew it, believed it. But the conviction, if present, was buried so deeply within him that it could not move him. One part of him said that he was making terrible mistakes, but another, louder part said it made no difference.

When blinded with pleasure, it was easy to push aside the guilt. Every time he looked at her and realized anew that she was his, that was all that mattered. He loved her as he had never loved another. Why should they not enjoy what they could while it lasted?

The knock on the door made him drop the lock of hair around his finger. It was still before dawn; what reason did anyone have for coming to his door? Hoping nothing was wrong, curious, he slid his arm out from under Abigail and eased out of bed.

Slipping his tunic quickly over his head, he strode to the door. Opening it revealed a servant standing with a lamp, his father illuminated by its glow. Titus drew his brows together. "What is it?"

Caius's gaze moved past Titus and into the room, undoubtedly to where the silhouette of Abigail's figure was visible in the moonlight. "I am sorry to interrupt you, my son."

"I was not asleep anyway." Titus pitched his voice low to try to avoid disturbing Abigail. "What is it?"

Caius turned his attention back on Titus. "You may remember that over a year ago one of our ships disappeared. We assumed it sank in a storm. I have just received word that it pulled into the harbor, and they assumed I would want to meet it right away; who knows where it has been or what it will have on board. Since you have been the one handling that business this past week, I thought you would like to accompany me."

Exploring what happened to a mysteriously vanished ship or spending the next few hours trying not to toss restlessly–it was not such a hard decision. "Give me a moment." He turned to the slave. "Help me with my toga."

The servant put the lamp down and hurried to assist Titus in dressing. He did not miss the way his father's gaze kept moving to the bed, though. It was only partly to prove a point that he moved and sat down beside Abigail once he was dressed. Brushing her hair back, he said at an almost-normal volume, "Beloved, wake up for a moment." The light and motion in the room had begun to stir her anyway, so it was not difficult to get her to blink her eyes open. Titus smiled. "I am needed at the shipping yards, a craft we thought was lost has returned. I know not how long it will take me down there."

Abigail nodded drowsily. Titus moved his smile down to her lips and kissed her gently. "I love you, Abigail," he murmured quietly enough that his father would not hear. "I will see you later today." He stood again and moved to join his father and the slave.

&

Abigail awoke with a gasp when something pounced on her.

"Mother!" Samuel's huge grin erased the instant worry. "Why did you not tell me?"

She pushed herself up, trying to clear the cobwebs of sleep from her mind. She had risen once to feed Benjamin, but the pull of a warm bed had been too great. She had fallen asleep again, and now it was far later than her usual time to rise. "Tell you what, small one?"

"That Titus is now your husband! That means he is my father. He said so!"

Abigail sighed, a pain clenching her heart. She closed her eyes against the picture of the boy soon to be disappointed. "He is not my husband, Samuel."

Confusion etched itself into his countenance. "But. . . you. . ."

His look at the bed told Abigail clearly how he had come to this erroneous conclusion. She barely stifled a groan. Why had she come back in here after Titus left, knowing how tired she was? She should have anticipated that Samuel may awaken before her this morning.

A lie sprang to her lips, escaping before she could think to stop it. "I came in here after feeding Benjamin to talk to Titus. He was gone, so I sat down to wait for him. I must have fallen asleep." At least she was still clothed.

Samuel apparently saw no reason to question the explanation, but his grief was obvious. He slumped down and curled up in her lap. His face was buried in the blankets still covering her legs, so it was only the slight tremor that moved up his back that told her he was crying. Abigail felt the new, carefully constructed shell around her heart shatter. It felt as though it took her heart with it.

"Do not cry, my son." She ran her hand over his head, fighting back tears of her own. "I know you want a father. And Titus loves you as though you were his son. It is just that I cannot marry him, dear one."

"Why not?" Samuel cried. "You love him. He kisses you all the time."

Abigail let her head fall back against the wall behind her. "It is not that simple. Even if he wanted to marry me, he could not. His father would not approve."

Samuel snapped up, looking furious as he faced her. "Then why does he act with you as my father did? Why does he kiss you and say he loves you, why does he touch you if he cannot be your husband?"

She should have realized her sensitive child would have seen and understood far more than she had expected. And looking into the warm brown of his eyes, golden flecks magnified by the tears still clouding them, she felt the stab of responsibility that she had been ignoring. She was the one this boy looked up to, the one who guided him, who taught him right from wrong. And how was she to give him lessons on the Law in the morning and then sin knowingly as soon as she put him to bed? Something solidified within her, something that brought a peace with it even as it hurt. "He should not. And he will not any longer. You are right, Samuel, unless he is my husband, he should not act that way."

It was certainly not the solution Samuel had hoped for, but he subsided. For a moment, he let her soothe him, let her dry his tears. Then he leaned up and soothed her in return, made her tears begin to fall.

"He will always love you, Mother," he murmured as they held each other. He could not understand the words he spoke, but that made them all the more striking. "Even if you anger him, he will love you."

She wiped at her eyes, gave him a kiss on the forehead, and finally realized that Phillip was in the corner of the room in his usual position. She had no idea when he had come in but assumed it had been while she still slept. "Where is Miriam?"

"She went to get your breakfast and bring it up, Mistress." Phillip's voice did not betray any concern, but the flash in his eyes did. "When you still slept, we assumed you would want to take it up here. She should be back directly."

Abigail nodded. "Thank you." She heard a hearty cry come from the other room, so she swung her legs off the bed and stood.

She was just finishing feeding Benjamin when Miriam arrived with food for the rest of them, and they ate in relative silence. As soon as Samuel was done, Abigail asked Miriam to take him and Benjamin to Antonia for a while.

Samuel drew his brows together. "What of our lessons?"

"We shall do them a little later," Abigail said softly. "If the clouds on the horizon are any indication, it will be raining this afternoon. Go play now, and we will do our lessons when you cannot be outside."

Samuel apparently thought that was a fine arrangement. He gave Abigail a kiss and fell in beside Miriam with no argument. The girl carried the baby in her arms tenderly but darted a worried look at Abigail over her shoulder on her way out.

Abigail sat mutely, her eyes fixed on some point straight ahead, her fingers toying absently with the fruit on the plate before her. She was not hungry, but taking little pieces of the meal from plate to mouth at least provided her with something to do with her hands. Her few, distracted actions stood in marked contrast to the thoughts flying through her mind.

She knew what she had to do. She felt the persuasion within her, felt the Spirit hovering just beyond the edges of her reserve. All she had to do was open herself that small crack, and he would come flooding back in, calming the place that had been raging within her. She knew that. And she intended to do it. But first, she closed her eyes and looked back across the last few days. She had been unhappy, but that was not what she thought about now. No, what upset her the most was that Titus had been unhappy, too. She was not certain he realized it, but their actions had hurt him as much as they hurt her. He had reacted by doing the only thing he knew to do: reverted to his Stoic roots and refused to accept into his sphere everything he did not want to influence him.

Unfortunately, that happened to include everything that had brought them together to begin with. It had resulted in a man unwilling to feel but unwilling to admit to a lack of his feelings, one who let himself want but would not grant that he had needs beyond that. She saw again his smile that morning. It had been true, it had been warm, but it was the only one like that she had seen in all these days. He needed her to stand firm as much as she did.

Miriam slipped back into the room, and Abigail opened her eyes, looked at both of her servants. Her soft words drew their startled gazes to her. "I owe you both an apology. For the past week, I have faltered greatly. I have not been a deserving mistress or a worthy friend. I have been a hypocrite." She blinked back a few tears. "Forgive me, my friends, for teaching lessons I did not obey."

Miriam had tears in her eyes as well. "Mistress . . ."

Abigail shook her head and stood up. "Please, give me a few moments." She turned and quickly exited through the door to the courtyard, knowing neither Phillip nor Miriam would actually leave, but needing at least the appearance of solitude. Outside, she fell to her knees on the cool ground.

"Father, forgive me." Her words flowed into the ground in Hebrew. "I knew what I did, yet I did it anyway. I deliberately turned from you to chase after my own desires, I put Titus above you, and now I feel the emptiness that my actions have caused. Come back to me, Spirit! Forgive my sins and fill me with your peace."

The Spirit descended upon her as heavily as it had the first time, pressing her down further into the ground until she was lying prostrate, her arms over her head. She wept, but the tears were cleansing, washing away the bitterness and the resentment.

"Give me strength. Give me strength to face him, Lord. Give me the strength to stand and maintain my position. Soften his heart, please, so that he may hear me and choose the same path. Please," she beseeched on a broken sob, "please do not let this be the end of our love."

A breeze whispered over her, and the rain began to fall. It washed away her tears and soaked her with heaven's.

The returned ship did not hold so many secrets as Titus would have liked. Or if it did, they were all locked within the minds of the few sailors still alive, and those minds were not in very good shape. There were five men that they found on board, and all of them had to be carried ashore. It was a wonder that they managed to sail back into the harbor at all in their current condition.

The ship itself was not in much better condition. All of the stores were depleted, which was certainly not surprising, and the goods they should have had after their last voyage were gone. That was not surprising either, given the many months of time they were missing. No one knew what kind of situations they encountered or what they had to do to get out of them, and the men were not speaking. In fact, most were tossing around in delirium.

Titus and Caius stayed several hours, supervising the transfer of the men into clean quarters and fetching physicians to look at their conditions. They stayed while they unloaded everything on the craft and went over it from bow to stern, trying to find a clue as to where it had been. Again, not much information was forthcoming. At noon, they both turned the reins back to the steward and headed home to eat.

Titus was informed upon his return that Abigail and Samuel had just finished their meal, so he went ahead and dined with his father before going in search of her. They took the time to continue mulling over the mysterious reappearance of their ship. In spite of anything and everything they found or could not find, it was an unexpected turn of good fortune to have it back; even if it returned empty, it was still one more ship that they could repair and send back out.

"I am headed to the Forum in a about half an hour's time," Caius said as Titus stood once he was finished eating. "Will you be joining me?"

"Probably." He wanted to talk to a few other men of his acquaintance who owned similar companies and see if they could offer any insights into what most likely happened to his ship. "I will meet you down here then." At his father's nod, Titus headed for his room.

At the peristylium, he saw Caelia. She was simply standing there where courtyard met hallway, not moving. When she spotted him, a feline smile curved her lips. Titus sighed and braced himself for whatever she might have to say.

"Good afternoon, Titus." She ran her eyes over him with the same appreciation they had always held.

Titus waited a moment to see if she would say more, but she did not. When he drew even with her, he stopped. "What are you doing here, Caelia?"

Her smile became even more smug. "Just watching, my love."

He made an arrow of his gaze. "Watching?"

She hummed her agreement. "And now that you are back, I will simply wait."

Titus clenched his jaw. "And what is it you will be waiting for?"

She shook her head.

Not in the mood to deal with her, Titus turned away and walked to his door.

"She is not in there."

Titus turned back around to face her. He was not surprised to learn that Caelia knew where Abigail was. He would not have been surprised if she always kept tabs on her, as a matter of fact. "Very well. Where is she?"

Caelia lifted an elegant, tapered finger and pointed a door down, to the room Miriam and Phillip had moved into. She said nothing, and Titus did not try to get her to. He simply moved the extra steps, knocked, then opened the portal.

He stopped abruptly just a step inside, his eyes hard and all-seeing. He noticed, for instance, that there were far too many possessions taking up residence in there to be only the property of the slaves. He noticed that in addition to the bed, there were three pallets on the floor. He noticed that the basket that was Benjamin's bed was in the corner. And he noticed that the three people who turned to face him at his entrance looked like warriors ready to do battle until the death.

"What is going on in here?" His voice was calm, deadly calm, coldly calm, familiarly calm. He knew his face reflected the same stolidity, and he did not care. Could not care.

Abigail moved a hand, and Miriam and Phillip both moved quickly past him and out the door, closing it behind them. Titus did not so much as glance at them. His full attention was on Abigail.

"If I had spoken to you first, I knew you would have talked me out of it. But I cannot do it anymore, Titus, it is killing me inside."

He did not have to ask what "it" was. Though he had to wonder how she could destroy him so peacefully. "If I could have talked you out of it, it is because you do not really want to do it. You are letting your emotions get caught up in details, Abigail. Being with the man you love should not kill you inside."

Abigail clenched her eyes shut for a long moment, and Titus had the uncomfortable impression that she was holding back a storm of tears. He was relieved when she opened them again steadily. "The man I love is not my husband. He never will be, because there are more important things to him than me, and I understand that. But knowing a man that is not my husband is a sin I will never commit again."

Anger surged up, hot and comfortable. It was the only emotion he could trust right now. "Abigail, you are being absurd! It is not my fault that I cannot marry you, so why should we be punished for it by having to keep a distance between us? No woman has ever made me feel the way you do. Does that not count for anything?"

"Even if your family were not an issue, you would not marry me." Something akin to anger flashed in her eyes, too. "Yes, you love me, I know that. We have something amazing between us, Titus, but it is not enough. We are too different. Look at us. In the past week we have shown ourselves for who we truly are: you are a fine, popular Roman man of nobility, with business concerns and invitations to all the events in the city, and you thrive on that. But I am a Jewish woman raised with strict beliefs, and I have spent too many years as a slave to feel comfortable in a crowd that I am not serving. Surely you remember what Aristotle said about relationships between unequals."

"I do not care what Aristotle said!" Titus roared. "It is irrelevant anyway. In the important matters, Abigail, we *are* equals. You yourself have affirmed that. You are my teacher–"

"What lesson have you learned at my hand?" She tossed out an arm in a defiant show. "I teach you the Law and you disobey it, I teach you the Prophets, and you decide their wisdom interferes with your pleasure. I cannot live like that, Titus, not if I want to keep from falling into the same despair I knew with Jason. Why did Jesus bother making the sacrifice he did if I am going to refuse his salvation?"

He dared not step closer lest he do something he would later regret. "This is not about salvation. This is about you being angry that I will not do as *Jason* did and be badgered into making you my wife."

"I never asked to be made his wife." Her voice broke on a sob, but she did not stop. "But I will not be made your whore."

It infuriated him that she would say that again when he had already told her he did not want to hear her speak of herself that way. He forced himself back into his icy rage. "I did not make you a whore. If you are, you chose it for yourself."

Abigail's fists balled up and pressed against her legs. Her spine was rigid. Angry and hurt and determined, she looked more beautiful than ever. "This is not how I wanted to handle this." Her voice was so tight it sounded like a plucked string. "I am sorry I lost my patience, that I grew angry. I hoped to reason with you, to remind us both of the decisions we made on Golgotha. I had hoped that we could return to the path together, help each other."

Titus regarded her for a long moment. "If you think I can be your friend again without touching you, you are mistaken."

"That was my fear. That was why I moved in here. Phillip will be guarding me all night. Attempt to touch me again, and I will not be able to keep him from doing what he has wanted to do all week."

Titus balked, sneered, and started to turn away. "I do not need you so badly that I would force my way into your room. There are plenty of women willing to satisfy me if you are not, Abigail."

"Titus."

He paused at the door but did not turn around.

She was silent a moment, though he swore he could hear each painful pound of her heart. Surely it was not his own—surely his had stopped beating altogether. "Please, do not shun Samuel because of me. He adores you, and it will upset him if you ignore him because of your anger with me."

Titus made no reply, he simply wrenched open the door and surged outside, slamming it closed again behind him. That she thought she had to remind him not to be a monster with the child was as insulting as the threat had been. He stormed past Phillip and Miriam, who gave him a wide berth and hurried back to their mistress.

He spotted Caelia standing just where he had left her, looking expectant and eager. At least some women seemed to retain their loyalty; certainly, she had gone to his father when he was away, that was only to be expected. As a slave, she had no say over that. But had she not been waiting as soon as he returned? Had she not been hoping to return to him, to be his again? And even over the past months with Abigail present, she had not given up that hope.

He did not hesitate. He strode to her, pulled her to him, crushing her, and devoured her mouth. She responded as though he were the first taste of water she had received after a month in the wilderness. He ended the embrace as abruptly as he had begun it, stepping away. Part of him wanted to command her to wait for him in his room that night.

Perhaps he would have, had the kiss stirred anything but revulsion within him. "Go back to my father, Caelia. You have nothing I want."

FORTY-ONE

"She is worse today."

Phillip could not argue with Miriam's whispered observation. For the past two weeks, Abigail had been withdrawn. It was understandable. Her fall from Titus's favor had given the rest of the house a reason to snub her, so even appearing at meals was impossible. Miriam had to fetch all of her food from the kitchen and bring it to her so that she would not have to face Aquilia or Caius or Titus. The one time she had gone out, none of them had looked at her, and the servants had actually avoided her, too, as though she were not even there. It had been debasing, and Miriam had held Abigail as she wept afterward. She had not repeated that torture since. The next day she had attempted to send a missive to Arminius to try to make arrangements to move out to the villa for her remaining time in Rome, but that had proven an even greater trial for her; Titus had intercepted the message and proceeded to corner her and rail at her stupidity and lack of concern for Jason's child's life.

Phillip had seen her flinch when he called Benjamin simply "Jason's child." It was what Caius always referred to him as, as though her part in his creation was null. She had retorted with a claim that if he was so concerned, he should volunteer to send an appropriate entourage with her for their protection, but Titus had gotten that cold smile on his face. He had said that she had already gotten more than enough from him.

That night, Abigail had taken off the amethyst necklace she had been wearing under her tunic and had Miriam slip into Titus's room when no one was there and leave it. Titus had not so much as appeared in the same room as her since. That had been a week and a half ago. Abigail had tried to be strong after that, and probably would have done fairly well had it not been for Samuel. Titus had started out still seeing the boy daily, laughing and playing and hearing of his day. But in the past week, those visits had tapered off as Titus spent more and more time away from the house. Samuel had started to sulk, and nothing Abigail could do raised his spirits.

"Do you think it is because of Samuel?" Phillip asked just as quietly, wishing his mistress did not look so broken inside today. She sat with her shoulders hunched forward, as though too tired to straighten them, and her head was bowed. The silent movement of her lips told him she was praying. She had been doing a lot of that lately. He could not see that it did much good, but the one time he had made that observation, Abigail had gotten a strange smile on her face and told him he had no idea how bad it would be otherwise.

Miriam shrugged. "I do not think it is only that, but who is to tell? There is much burdening her spirits. Titus, the children, concern for her mother. Who is to tell if this is something new or just the rest weighing heavily?"

Phillip's jaw clenched. "You have no idea how much I would like to break the nose of that—"

"Hush." But Miriam smiled. "If she hears you, she will scold."

They watched her for another minute in silence before the maid sighed. "Perhaps it is Caius. He has been lurking about when he has no cause to, just looking at her. Perhaps she is concerned he will try something, now that Titus does not seem to care."

Phillip tilted his head in thought. "I daresay Titus would care quite a bit if his father touched her. He may be angry, but he is not indifferent. Though you may be right about the concern that could cause Abigail."

Miriam nodded, but then her face grew worried as she glanced through the open door into the house. "Titus is coming."

Phillip did not need to turn to follow her gaze to feel the approaching presence of an angry man. Moreover, he did not waste time with looks, he simply moved stealthily forward so that Titus could not barrel past him and lay hold of Abigail. He did not actually draw close to his mistress, since she liked to maintain the feel of independence, but he was near enough to be able to leap to her aid if necessary.

It was not necessary. Upon reaching the door, Titus came to a sudden halt, scanned the immediate vicinity, and headed for Phillip, not Abigail. When he was beside him, he pitched his voice down so that the mistress would not even hear him.

"Be wary tonight, Phillip," he warned with sparking eyes. "My father has already begun drinking, and it is Abigail's name that falls off his tongue. Do not trouble her with this in case it is nothing, but bar the door after she falls asleep, and keep careful watch."

Phillip nodded firmly, pressed his lips together.

Titus looked over at Abigail, shoulders still bent, head still down, lips still moving. "She looks terrible. Has she been eating?"

"As much as we can make her." Miriam stepped up beside Phillip. "If you wish to ease some of the shadow from her eyes, try spending some time with Samuel today."

Titus turned his piercing eyes on the maid. She actually flinched, and it brought a cold half smile to his mouth. "I will do that now. He is with Antonia?"

She nodded. Titus looked at Abigail again, and this time, the touch of his gaze brought her head up. Phillip watched as emotion flashed through her eyes before settling into something between resignation and pure emptiness.

Titus spun away. "See that she eats more."

Once he was gone, Abigail cleared her throat. "What did he want, Phillip?" She wrapped her arms around herself as if she were cold, though the day was warm and bright.

"To discover where Samuel is. He is going now to see him."

Abigail's face relaxed only a degree. She stood. "Good. Benjamin should be awaking soon. Let us go in."

Phillip and Miriam followed. The maid shook her head. "It does not appear to be worry over Samuel."

Well, if it was over Caius, he actually hoped the old man tried something tonight so that he would have an excuse to bash his head against a wall and erase that worry, too.

He kept that reflection to himself.

Abigail knelt down in front of her trunk and pulled out a length of cloth from the bottom of it. Squeezing her eyes shut, she fingered the tassels of Jason's prayer shawl and whispered the same prayer that had been on her lips for the last three weeks. "Jehovah, ease my worry."

So heavy it all weighed. The pain of losing Titus. The fear of his father, who had grown no bolder but also would not relent in his stares. The concern over Samuel's injured feelings, which had eased only slightly when Titus spent that single afternoon with him last week.

And the other. Dear Lord, the other.

"Mistress?" Miriam settled beside her and put a warm hand on her shoulder. Phillip had gone to check on Samuel in the back garden.

"Yes, my friend?"

Miriam's brows were creased, her hesitation obvious. "Mistress, I do not mean to pry, only to serve you as best I can. You are so dear to me, more like a sister than my owner, and . . . may I ask you something?"

Abigail only nodded. She knew that whatever Miriam requested to know, it would be out of her devotion.

Miriam cleared her throat. "I know every woman is different after the birth of a child. Some do not get the return of their courses until they wean, others right away. I have noticed that in the month I have been here, you have not experienced any bleeding. Is this normal since Benjamine was born?"

Tears surged Abigail's eyes, two escaping before she could blink them away. "No." She drew shuddering air back into her lungs. Her fingers linked through Miriam's. "They returned two months ago. And then . . . I am afraid, my friend. I am terribly afraid that I carry Titus's child, and I will be ruined if I do. My son will be ruined."

"This is what has been causing you so much distress." Miriam wrapped her arms around Abigail's shoulders and held her. For just a moment, Abigail let herself weep into her friend. "Perhaps it is simply your despair that makes you late. I have heard of such things. I myself was a bit late this last time, out of my fear from that night with Caius. Or perhaps the nursing is still having an effect after all."

"Perhaps. I have been praying it is that. But every day I awake and wait and nothing happens." She turned her eyes on Miriam. "What if I am pregnant, Miriam? How will I look my mother in the eye? How will I return to Israel? Who will respect Benjamin if his mother . . ." She stopped herself with a hand over her mouth, trying to hold back another sob.

"Hush." Miriam smoothed back Abigail's hair. "It will be all right. In spite of his anger, Titus loves you, Mistress. He will take care of you if you have his child. Perhaps he would even marry you."

Abigail wiped at her tears and breathed a dry laugh. "No. That is one thing he will not do. But he would think I expect it of him because Jason chose to marry me, and he would grow angry." She shook her head. "If I am with child, Titus will not be happy. He will be furious."

Miriam sat up straighter, thunder in her eyes. "And why should _he_ be furious? He is the one who manipulated you into his bed, _he_ is the one who chose the time to do it, _he_ is—"

"That is enough." Her loyalty made her smile a bit though. "I am just as guilty as

Titus. But let us wait a while longer before we resign ourselves to this. It could be as you say, I could simply be late in my cycle. And until I am certain, neither of us will say anything to anyone."

"Of course." Miriam fell back to her knees and kissed Abigail's hands. "I will do your will in all things, without question."

Abigail smiled truly for the first time in days. "The Lord was smiling on me when he led me to you. You are my friend, Miriam, and we both know you do my will only when you agree with its benefit for me, and I thank you for that as well. I have very little use for people who do only what they are told."

Miriam returned the smile and stood once more. "I disobey only because you expect it of me."

"You disobey because you realize how unwise your mistress can be. But in this I suspect we can agree. It is best for the suspicion to remain a secret until it is proven or disproven."

Miriam nodded, her face serious.

Good. She would undoubtedly add her prayers to Abigail's. Perhaps it would urge the Lord to answer sooner.

Abigail was just putting Benjamin back down after his first feeding of the day a week later when the nausea struck. She barely made it to the facility down the hall before she fell to her knees, retching violently. Even though her stomach was empty, still the heaves shook her until she was reduced to an exhausted ball on the ground.

Tears burned her eyes to match the acid in her throat, and she pounded the floor with her fist. "Why?" she cried in Hebrew, rolling onto her knees again but unable to sit up. She rested her head on the cool floor, then covered it with her arms. "Why do you do this to me, Jehovah? Must I pay the rest of my life for one week of sin? I repented. Lift your heavy hand from me, I beg you, I cannot handle these consequences. *Eli! Lama sabachthani?*"

She felt small, warm fingertips run over her arm, her hand, onto her face. "Why do you cry, Mother?" Samuel asked into her ear, curling up beside her. "Is it because Titus does not love us anymore?"

Abigail unwrapped one of her arms from her head so that she could put it around Samuel. "Not us, my son. You he still loves. It is me he hates."

Samuel buried his face in her shoulder. "If he hates you, then I will not love him."

"Never stop loving anyone, Samuel, or you will be as bad as the one who hurts you." She kissed his forehead weakly. Moving her eyes, she saw Miriam and Phillip both standing a few steps away. "Help me up, please."

They did so, and once Abigail was standing, albeit without much strength, she looked at Miriam. "I well remember this illness. I will tell Titus today."

Abigail paced the chamber slowly, singing to Benjamin as she rocked him in her arms. She had spent most of the day in thought and prayer, but still anxiety balled up just below her throat, threatening to overwhelm her. Much of what would happen to her in the next years of her life relied on what Titus would say when he walked in and she told him she was pregnant with his child. If he wanted to have anything to do with the babe, whether it include a relationship with her or not, then she had no choice: she must stay in Rome. She could not ask him to give up everything to follow his child back to Israel, especially when Abigail had access to an estate nearby.

On the other hand, if he wanted absolutely nothing to do with any of them, she would have to consider how she was going to protect her family from the harsh rule of the Sanhedran. She could always claim the pregnancy was the result of a rape; it would be a lie, but it would be a lie that would protect her children. Still, it was one whose very idea weighed heavily on her conscience. How could she claim that the babe was a result of violence?

The third possibility was moving somewhere else entirely, somewhere where no one knew that her husband had died before the second child was conceived. Somewhere where she could claim to be a widow, true enough, and simply never share that the two babes she had birthed had different fathers. But she could not ask Ester to leave the only place she had ever known, and she could even less contemplate spending the rest of her years absolutely alone, without anyone she loved. If she stayed in Rome, she would be without her family, she was sure, but at least Titus would be nearby. Even if he never wanted to speak to her, she would know he was there. He would answer her call if she ever truly needed him.

Like now.

She pushed that from her mind. She fully expected Titus to be angry, but she prayed he would calm quickly so that they could discuss the possibilities for her future. But she would not judge his immediate reaction as being an indicator of his true decision. She, after all, had had weeks to consider this possibility, to adjust to it. For Titus, it would be a slap in the face.

"He comes." Miriam rushed from the window facing the street. According to the plan they had already laid out, she took Benjamin, and she and Phillip left the room and went outside to the garden to make sure Samuel did not decide to dash inside to visit her or Titus.

Nerves dampened Abigail's palms and accelerated her heart. She forced herself to quit pacing, listening instead for the approaching footsteps of Titus. He would have to walk by this small cubiculum, no matter where he was going within the house. She would call him in when he did.

"How unprecedented. Abigail, alone."

Abigail spun around to see Caius standing only a few feet away. She had forgotten this room was connected to another; it had not concerned her, because she was only interested in Titus, who would arrive from outside. She had not considered that Caius was already home and could find her here. She was more irritated than afraid, however. Titus had to be approaching even now.

She squared her shoulders. "I am waiting for Titus. And I need to speak with him in private, so please leave."

Caius smirked and took a few steps closer. "Have you not caught on? Titus does not want you. He wants nothing to do with you. He keeps you here now only for the babe's sake, so what could you possibly have to say that would interest him?" He reached out and ran a hand down her arm.

She slapped his hand away. "Do not touch me!"

He grabbed both of her arms and dragged her against him. "I will do as I wish with you. You are nothing but a slave and a harlot." He gave her a hard shake. "Why should I not just kill you now? The boy would be better off without you. Why should I leave my son in your talons? Why?"

He shook her again, and the fear surged up when she saw the violence in his eyes. "Please!" She tried to break free of his hands, tried to push him away. All in vain.

"What new trick do you have in mind now, whore? Why must you speak with him, what do you have planned?"

"Nothing, I–"

One of his hands around her throat cut her off. She gagged, trying to gasp for breath, clawed at his hand.

"Tell me." He relaxed his grip enough for her to gulp in the air so quickly it made her cough.

Wheezing, she saw little choice but to reply. "I carry his child."

She knew a momentary breath of relief when he released her. It was followed by blinding pain as he backhanded her in the face, sending her reeling. "Conniving witch!" He caught her by the shoulder only to hit her again. Dizziness flooded her head, blood flowed from her nose, and the ground rushed toward her. She heard a cry of pain that must have been hers, but she was not aware of actually opening her throat to make the noise. The hard stone of the floor struck her and sent a bolt of agony all up her right side. She barely heard the shouts that filled the room over the rush of blood in her head, but she felt clearly the foot that kicked her in the stomach with all its force, once, then again.

She doubled up at the pain.

Titus had hit the room a few seconds before Phillip, so he was the one to drag his father away from Abigail, leaving Phillip to rush to his mistress to see if she was all right. He threw Caius into the wall. "How dare you lay a hand on her?"

"You would thank me if you had any sense." Caius knocked his arm away. "She will manipulate you with this child just as she did Jason, she will talk you into marrying her just because she carries your whelp. I will not have it! Better to kill her myself than to have the Asinius name lost to a Jewish slave."

"Touch her again, and it is you who will die." His jaw muscle clenching, he turned back to find Phillip lifting an almost-unconscious Abigail in his arms. "Take her to her room and clean her up." He turned to the door, where Miriam had just rushed up in. "Go tend her. I will make sure Antonia takes the children inside."

Mainly he needed to have a few moments to let that last explosive minute sink into his consciousness. While he waited for reality to catch up, he headed toward the garden. Samuel was standing just outside staring at the door, from which he had no doubt heard the cries of his mother.

"Titus!" The boy launched himself at Titus's legs. "What is happening to Mother?"

Titus picked him up and help him close. "My father hit her, but she will be fine." He wanted to believe that, though from what he had seen, the blows had looked hard enough to knock down a grown man, to say nothing about a slight woman.

"I must go to her."

"No, not right now." Titus held him still when he would have squirmed to his feet. "Let Miriam and Phillip tend her first. I will take you to her soon, but for now you must go with Antonia and help her with Benjamin. Will you do that for me?"

Samuel looked torn, but at length he nodded somberly.

"You are a good boy." Titus put him back on his feet. To the concerned nurse, he said, "Take them both and go to Panther. My father is in a rage, and I would put nothing past him."

Antonia moved to obey. Titus headed for the bedrooms. A few steps from her door, he stopped.

Abigail was pregnant. That was what the entire drama came down to. Not pausing to discern what it was he felt at that realization, he moved with renewed energy to her door, not even bothering to knock before entering.

She was sitting up, perched on the edge of the bed, her arms wrapped around her middle as Miriam dabbed at the blood on her face. Her left eye was already swollen almost closed, a mottled red that promised to turn dark with bruising in a few hours. Just looking at her made him ache. He held his ground until Miriam murmured, "There, the bleeding has stopped." Then he stepped forward.

"Leave us." Titus spoke softly enough that the loyal servants would not fear to obey him. He stood aside to let them pass but did not advance into the room until the door closed behind them. Even then, he took only a few steps before halting again. Abigail sat without moving, her good eye focused on him, and waited silently for him to speak. It was just as well that she did not immediately launch into excuses. He wanted simple answers. "How long have you known?" He tried to soften his tone, but he had a feeling some of his anger slipped out, if her slight recoil was any indication.

"I have suspected it for a few weeks. I was not sure until this morning, when the nausea began."

Titus's fingers curled into a fist, but he had the good sense to hide his hand in a fold of his toga to keep her from noticing. "And were you planning to tell me this, or simply go to a local harlot and try to poison yourself, as you did when you learned you were carrying Jason's child?"

Abigail flinched and turned her head away, struggling to keep her breathing even. "How can you even ask that, seeing how I love my children?"

"It is reasonable enough. I will not abandon all hopes of a career and marry you. But your honorable status of widow is tainted and ruined if you have a child that obviously did not belong to your husband. You will be outcast everywhere. Your son will suffer."

"He would if I were to die by poison, too. And I could not choose the life of one of my children over the life of another." She shook her head vehemently, though it must have hurt her. She raised a hand to her temple and winced. "I know what this child will cost me, but it is ours. I will have it, and I will love it." She paused a moment to let that sink in. "I was only out there today to tell you I was pregnant. And to ask you what your will is. If you want me to leave and never bother you again, I will. If you want your child close enough for you to visit, I am prepared to move to the villa permanently."

Titus regarded her with disbelief. "You do not want to live in Rome, you have said it yourself."

She returned his gaze with her good eye. "I will not take your child from you unless you command it. Things have changed, Titus. I will never be accepted back into Israel now. They were not very tolerant of me as it was; do you not remember how the Pharisee offered me to Barabbas? I do not wish to find myself stoned."

"But what of Ester?" He could not imagine that she was suddenly so willing to give up all that she had been holding dear.

"Ester will understand my decision. She will hold that it is fitting for a woman to leave her family for her husband. I know," she then added quickly, raising a hand slightly to fend off the words that had leaped to his lips, "you will not marry me. I would not ask it of you. But as I swore to Jason when I was given to him as his slave, I will swear to you now. You may treat me as you will, but I will honor you as my husband and lord for the rest of my life." Her lips trembled. "I love you, Titus. After you, there can be no other."

He shook his head. "How is it that honoring me as your husband involves forbidding me to touch you?"

Abigail raised her chin a notch. "I honor and love you enough to try to spare your soul the sin to which I tempt you."

Titus dug his fingertips into his palms. "Even now, when you are willing to stay here, when you are willing to give up all other parts of your life, when you are willing to have my child in spite of ostracization, you are not willing to budge on this?"

"You do not understand." Her whisper sounded fierce, colored by her bruises and her passion. "As a man, you are not judged for this, but I am. By having your child, I submit myself to scorn and hatred, while you receive slaps of congratulations on your back from all of your friends. You have the freedom to walk away from this situation, and I cannot stop you. The world will not forgive me, Titus. But God will. He will only if I repent earnestly, and it is only then that I can forgive myself. Tell me, my love, how would you have me live if I have not even that? How am I to stand against the scorn of society without the strength of my God?"

Titus had nothing to say in response. He nodded to acknowledge that he had heard her, then he gave in to the instinct he had been fighting for the last few minutes and went over to her. He sat beside her on the bed and put an arm around her, drawing her gently to his side. It was the first time he had touched her in a month and a half, and he did not want to hurt her.

"I love you," he whispered into her ear. The words relaxed her a degree, and she let herself be molded into his light embrace. "That will never change. Know that, no matter what happens." He put a finger under her chin to urge her face up, careful of her injuries. "I will have to think about this, Abigail, and consider my options."

She gave a small nod. "I know."

He brushed a feather-light kiss over her cracked lips, then drew away. "I will not keep you waiting long. Lie down, rest, and I will talk to you again tomorrow."

But it was panic that lit her eyes instead of agreement, and she pulled away. "No. I will not stay here another night, Titus. Did you not hear him? He wishes me dead!"

How many times must he say the same thing? "It is not safe for you at the villa."

"It is far less safe for me here. Look at me, Titus." She held a hand to her face. "This is what has become of my obedience to you on this matter. I will not endanger myself or the children or your babe by remaining any longer in this house."

She stood to prove her point, and he mirrored her, not sure whether he intended to argue the point or admit defeat. He had the chance to do neither. She no more than straightened before she cried out in pain and doubled over again. She would have fallen in a heap on the floor had he not reached out quickly and caught her.

"Abigail!" he called, even as Phillip burst through the door. She did not seem to hear him. Agony was etched onto her face as it had been not so many months ago, the first time he had held her in his arms. "Abigail, speak to me."

"Titus, there is blood." Phillip's voice was saturated with horror.

"The baby." Titus knew he sounded as terrified as he was, but he did not care a whit for Stoicism at the moment. He picked her up and put her back on the bed as he shouted, "Go for a doctor! Take Timothy with you, he knows where to find the best. Hurry!"

Phillip's quick footsteps pounded away. Miriam appeared to help him position Abigail on the mattress. When they tried to shift her, she groaned and curled up in a ball from which they could not urge her, arms and knees drawn up to protect her abdomen.

"I will kill him," Titus muttered, seeing the stain of red grow on her garment. "If she dies, so will he."

Miriam looked up at him out of narrowed eyes. "She needs your support right now, not your anger."

Titus uncurled one of Abigail's fists so that he could weave his fingers with hers. With his other, he soothed the hair from her face. "Help is coming, my love. You are strong, all will be well."

Miriam drew in a long breath. "We will need rags. I will stay with her, I know what to do. My first mistress miscarried, and I was with her the entire time."

"She will not lose the baby," Titus corrected her with burning eyes.

Miriam gazed at him silently for a moment. "We will need rags to staunch the blood regardless. Go get someone to fetch them, Titus, and have them bring fresh water."

"You go. I will not leave her."

Miriam stared him down in frustration. "Titus, this is a woman's problem, and I know far better how to handle it than you. Nothing will happen to her in the three minutes it will take you to accomplish those errands, and the servants will obey you far more quickly than they will me."

That last was enough to convince him. He eased away, freed his hand. "You are right. I will be back immediately, beloved." He kissed her fingers.

By the time he reached the door, he was at a run. And he felt a dark enemy chasing him, biting at his heels with every step. Speed would not help him escape it, running would only propel him into its talons.

He dropped to his knees in the middle of the corridor, then fell prostrate on the floor. "Lord, return to me!" he cried with anguish that tore his soul in two. "Forgive me and return! Do not punish her and the babe for my sins, I beg you!"

He felt the Spirit whisper over him, and the cleansing it brought took away his breath. A moment later, he found himself back on his feet, a single impression present in his mind:

Hurry.

FORTY-TWO

Titus rushed back from the servants' hall, orders given, his mind looping endlessly in fervent prayer. He did not even know anymore what he was praying, but he knew that the Lord understood the cries of his heart. He knew, too, that his heart wanted nothing more than to be beside Abigail, and not just in this moment. But he did not have time to think about anything right now.

He was just entering the main part of the house when Caelia called out from behind him, tears in her voice. "Titus!"

Reluctantly, he turned. He saw her running toward him, still gathering her clothes about her, tears coursing down her cheeks. "Your father–he forced himself upon me–"

She had reached him and latched onto his arm. He pulled away from her. "I do not have time for your antics, Caelia. Abigail is lying upstairs, the life of our child bleeding out of her, because of my father's violence. At this moment, I am not too concerned about whether or not he has found his pleasure with you."

Her tears dried rather quickly. "Child!" Her lips snarled, malice gleaming in her eye. "I hope she dies with it! She only wants to manipulate you–"

Titus grabbed the wrist she was reaching out toward him and pressed in a place that brought her to her knees in pain. "You will never say such things about her. And if you value your own life, you will make every attempt possible to keep your face out of my sight from now on."

He spun around and strode away, ignoring the curses she spewed at him in a language he did not understand. He had made it to the courtyard before he was hailed again, this time by his mother. He paused with a sigh as she approached.

Curiosity covered her face. "What is going on?"

He motioned her to join him as he continued toward Abigail's room and informed her briefly of what had happened. A glance at her face showed him that she had paled with the news. She stopped outside the door through which groans could be heard.

She seemed to struggle a moment with what she wanted to say. At last, she threw back her shoulders. "Go, see to her. I will make sure a wet nurse is found for Benjamin, and I will have the children and Antonia moved into my chambers. Caius would not look for them there. I doubt he would harm Benjamin, but Samuel is another story. Titus," she said when he reached for the door. Her eyes were serious. "Send me word when the physician arrives. I will light a candle to Juno for her."

Titus shook his head. "For all else I thank you, but do not utter a word of Abigail to Juno. If you wish to pray, pray to her God, not yours."

Aquilia seemed shocked by that suggestion. "I do not know her God!"

"He knows you." Her offered her a fleeting smile, then entered the room. He found Miriam and Abigail right where he had left them. He took his place and her hand again.

"The supplies will be here in a moment."

A servant arrived with rags and fresh water a minute later, and soon after that Phillip returned with the physician. A scholarly looking man, the doctor stopped beside the bed and looked down at the woman curled up in pain. He glanced at Titus. "Before I determine how best to help, perhaps you should inform me of what happened to this girl?"

Titus knew the man thought he had done the damage, though a mere physician would not dare to voice any disapproval. "My father happened. He would have beat her to death if I had not come in. She is with child."

The doctor looked at the blood-soaked rags and sighed. "Judging by the look of her, she was not very far along. Miscarriages are common in early pregnancy, keep that in mind, Lord."

Titus suddenly realized the man was fearful, and for good reason. He had friends who had ruined physicians who could not save their family. He made his voice soft and moved to give him access to Abigail. "I know there is only so much in your power, my friend. Please, just do what you can for her. I realize. . ." he choked on his own words. "I realize you may not be able to save my child. Please, just try to save Abigail."

The doctor took the place Titus had vacated and examined her for a few moments. Amid her groans and whimpers, he shook his head. "The pain is great for her, and will probably not abate for many hours. She will be weak for a while and should not be touched." His pointed look at Titus told them what kind of touch he was speaking of. Titus did not bother to inform him that such things would not be happening in any case. He moved his gaze to Miriam. "Keep her clean, bathe her regularly, and see that she remains comfortable. Unless infection sets in, she should be up and about in a week or two."

Titus nodded, wondering if her heart would heal as quickly as her body. He ushered the physician out soon after, paying him for his time though in Titus's opinion he did little to help. Stepping back into Abigail's chamber, he felt oppressed. Daylight faded from the sky and the air coming through the window was cool. The tension was thick and brutal. He fell to his knees beside the bed and rested his forehead on its edge.

"Forgive me," he whispered, to Abigail and to God. "The first obstacle I faced, and I stumbled. And not only did I stumble, I took with me on my fall the best gift I had ever received. My Father, I do not deserve your mercy. She does. Not for my sake, but for hers I ask you to put your hand upon her in healing." His hands, linked above his head on the mattress, clenched into fists of affliction. He heard Miriam and Phillip slip out of the room. "Lord God, you know my heart, in its weaknesses and its desires. You know that my love for her is pure, even if my wants are not. I have lied even to myself this day, this past month. My mind would have me cry out to you, 'Why do you punish her for my sins? Why did you not see my hidden desire and respond to it instead of my words?' But my soul knows that these thoughts are unjust. You have given us all freedom, and we abuse it. My father's actions are not your will, yet I trust they will work to your good. Please, Father Jehovah, forgive me. And please, too, give me the strength to forgive my tormentors, even as your Son did."

He halted, unable to find the words to put to the stirring of his soul. Rather than try and fail in that, he let silence fall around him, his heart inclined toward heaven. He felt a feather light touch upon his head and looked up to find Abigail trying to look at him through one swollen eye. He picked up her hand from where weakness had made her drop it right in front of him and kissed her fingers gently.

"The baby?" Abigail murmured.

Titus shook his head. When she closed her eyes again and turned her face away in pain, he felt his heart clench within him.

"I am sorry." She winced, gasped. "I prayed selfishly when I realized it this morning. The Lord heard and punished me."

"No." He got up and sat beside her so that he could put a hand on her face to urge her to look at him again. His smile felt small, soft on his mouth. "Abigail, the Lord hears your heart, not your words. And in your heart, you would never wish an innocent dead for your own convenience, I know that. Surely God, in his wisdom, knows that you did not mean any selfish thoughts. Just as he surely knows that this is not the best way to save you from ruin. The blame for this is divided among us, my love, between us and my father, but it does not touch Jehovah. He knows, just as I do, that I would have married you. There is no way I could let the children suffer for my actions. This would not be his answer."

Abigail shook her head degree by degree. There were tears stinging her eyes. "I would not marry you out of duty, Titus."

He smiled anew. "It would not have been duty, Abigail. I love you. I want to help you raise the children; Benjamin, Samuel, and all those we would have together. I want you to be the mother of my sons, dear one, and I want my daughters to walk with your grace." He saw her cracked lip quivering with emotion, and he leaned down and brushed a kiss over it. "Rest now, beloved. We will speak more of this when you are better. We cannot move you until then, but I will use the time to make the villa safe for you. And I will make sure that Phillip and Panther are both here at all times to watch over you."

"The children?"

He smiled. "With my mother. They will be taken care of. Now rest. You lost much blood."

Abigail closed her eyes to obey, but she soon opened them and looked at him. Something in her face relaxed. "I have missed seeing that peace in your eyes, Titus."

He wove their fingers together. "I have missed feeling it there. I was simply too stubborn to realize it." He drew in a long breath. "I am sure I will make many mistakes, my love, many not so bad as this, but perhaps some even greater. I cannot promise otherwise. I do not understand the faith as well as you, I do not know all the laws I should obey. But I can promise this; I will not make the same mistake again. And I will never close my heart off to God as I did this past month."

Abigail gave his fingers a weak squeeze and let her eyes slide closed. "I love you."

"I know." He sighed. "It is the greatest blessing of my life."

Titus had succeeded in avoiding his father almost entirely over the intervening two weeks, as he attempted to come to some conclusion as to the best resolution of the situation. He was simply not ready to deal with him, to face him, to speak his mind. Instead, Titus dedicated his efforts to strengthening his business connections and arranging for Abigail's move to the villa. Everything was coming together beautifully, which was an answer to his continual prayers. That also meant, however, that the impending altercation with his father could be put off no longer.

He drew a deep breath in as he went in search of him, knowing well where to find him at this hour of the day. The evening meal would take place in an hour, so Caius would be sipping his wine, relaxing to the strains of music one of the slaves would produce. Titus found him exactly as he expected, but still, the mere sight of him caused him pause.

What right did Caius Asinius have to lounge on his chaise without a care, when Abigail was still trying to heal from the injuries he had inflicted? How could he smile at a slave girl like that when the woman Titus loved still fought tears every day over their lost child? His hand balled into a fist, but he murmured a prayer for calm and strength and only stepped into the room when he felt it descend upon him.

"Titus." Surprise colored Caius's tone. He gave a cold smile. "You have been avoiding me, which is too bad. I have been wanting to apologize."

Titus straightened his spine, knowing there was no remorse inside his father's heart. "Indeed?"

Caius nodded, that terrible smile still in place. "Oh, yes, indeed. I heard the pregnancy was terminated, of course, but still, I am sorry. I would have wished the whore to die as well. Then you would have been thanking me for freeing you from her spell."

He felt his fingers curling into a fist again. "I will thank you anyway," he said carefully, gaining Caius's undivided attention with his words. "Your cruelty has opened my eyes, and I have finally decided on a course of action. I am going to marry Abigail." He already had the certificate drawn up, though he knew convincing her would be a task. She would think only of his sacrifices at first. But he would prevail.

Caius stilled, his smile fading. "You will not."

"I am offering no choice." Titus stared down the man who absently swirled his chalice of wine. "There is nothing you can do to change my mind. If you decide to disown me and keep me from the family business, I cannot stop you, but it will not stop *me*. And you know Rome will talk, if you do that. There is no other heir. If you disinherit me, everything you worked for will revert to the state when you die."

Caius made no overt move, but his fingers tightened around the cup, and his jaw clenched. "You would throw away your life for that wench?" Without warning, he dashed the cup to the ground. The slaves jumped, but Titus did not so much as budge. "You are an Asinius! You have responsibilities!"

"And I will not walk away from them unless you force me to. I will marry Abigail. You cannot stop me. I am a grown man, I do not need your permission, and I am certain I can make my own capital if you refuse me any of yours. There are several improvements that could be made to the Visibullis estate that would provide a steady income for us."

Caius's face mottled in rage, and he surged to his feet. "You would steal the wealth of your friend, as you steal his family?"

"Of course not." Titus crossed his arms over his chest. "I would use my earnings from the military to make a few purchases that I would join to his estate, and I would live only from the profit it produced. I would not touch Benjamin's inheritance for myself. And that only if you followed through on your threats. It is your decision, Father. I just want you to know your choices. You can deliver to me what is mine, or you can refuse. Either way, I will marry the woman I love. We will leave this house as soon as we can.

I have already found many suitable servants for the villa, and it will not be many days more before all is in place there for her arrival. A few more days, Father. What happens between us from there is up to you."

Caius sliced a hand through the air. "I did not raise you for such insolence!"

Titus smiled, amused. "Actually, you did."

Caius calmed suddenly, his eyes burning with repressed emotion. His voice was even, hard, and unforgiving. "Have it your way, Titus. Go with your whore. Manage my business, too, I will not have Rome saying I turned my back on my son over something as insignificant as a Jewish slave girl. But I will never acknowledge her as your wife, and neither will Rome. You will crucify yourself with this decision."

Titus's lips twisted upward. "We shall see about that. If Abigail has any talent, it is inspiring love in those around her. I am glad to hear you will not destroy our businesses by forcing me from them. But I am sorry you will not be a part of my family."

He turned and strode from the room.

⸙

Caius watched his retreating form with a bitter scowl. It had been two weeks since he had that wench whimpering at his mercy, and he had not so much as caught a glimpse of her or anyone in her circle since. He knew that his wife was with them almost incessantly, that most of the slaves were siding with them, too. "I should have killed her when I had the chance."

"There is another way."

He turned at the familiar voice, smiling when Caelia appeared. Her face was a mask of serenity, but her eyes roiled with hatred. It pleased him to see her like this, as she had been on a few other occasions. It lent her a fire that translated well into passion. "And what is that?"

She moved her lips into the semblance of a smile. "It is simple enough in principle, but it may require a bit of orchestration in practice. You must be ready to seize the moment whenever it arrives, Master."

Caius's heart lit with the same spark. "Tell me."

⸙

"The bruises are all but gone. Another day or two and the marks will have vanished. By that time, I will have the villa ready for you, my love."

Abigail smiled and turned into the hand with which Titus caressed her face. She cradled Benjamin, trying to urge him into sleep. "Thank you, Titus. I know you do not wish me to leave your side, but this is the best decision."

"I know." He smiled and leaned over to kiss her softly. "The morning after next, I will have to make a trip that will keep me away for two days. I have located a man wanting to sell two ships for a very reasonable fare, but he will only deal with the owner, not my steward. The new business this will procure will ensure my independence from my father, Abigail. These will answer only to me."

"That is good," She nodded, but her brows drew together. "I hate that I have come between you, Titus. I want to believe your relationship has a chance to improve once

I am out of his sight and his mind, but that will require a great effort on your part."

His expressiona implied it was one he would not make. "Our relationship was bad long before you entered the scene, beloved. I will never please him entirely, and there is no use in mourning that."

She drew in a deep breath, let it out again slowly. As she recovered over the past weeks, Titus had made a conscious effort not to discuss anything trying with her, she knew. But there were many things they needed to talk about soon. At the top of the list was what she was going to do when Ester arrived in Rome. She could not really imagine going back to Israel now, after all she had been through with Titus. But she had to face the fact that he would never be hers. It would surely be far less painful to think of him moving on if she were on the other side of the sea.

A knock on the door interrupted her thoughts, and Miriam went to open it. A moment later, Aquilia and Samuel entered together, the boy holding the woman's hand and chattering away happily. Aquilia was smiling.

"Good afternoon, Mother." Titus got up from the chaise he had perched on and went to kiss her cheek. "Did you enjoy your trip into the markets?"

Aquilia nodded with a smile at Samuel. "We had a lovely time. Samuel was telling me about a rather interesting thing that happened while you were in Israel, though. Something about a vision you all had of Jason?"

Abigail and Titus exchanged a somber look. "It was not a vision," Abigail said softly. Her brows drew together. "At least I do no think it was. We all saw him, even the midwife."

Aquilia regarded her evenly. They had spent many hours talking during her recovery, and Abigail had shared much of her beliefs. But often Titus's mother balked. Like now. "How is this possible?"

Abigail's eyes slid shut. "Because it was a day for the miraculous, my friend. A day when the world turned upside down. When the scriptures were rewritten. When the dead rose again. I did not realize it at the time, but as my son was being born, God's was resurrected. New life. A new world." She smiled, but it felt almost sorrowful. "And yet it is trapped within this old one. How long will it take for the truth to spread?"

"As long as it takes for believers to travel with it," Titus answered with a smile. "We have already brought the word here, to Rome. Who knows where else it has reached? All I know is that the truth does not need anything but itself to be recognized. God will speak into the hearts of his children."

Abigail nodded and looked back to Aquilia, who seemed perplexed. She smiled. "You are listening, my friend. That is good. You have spent many years serving your gods, and it is not to be expected that you revise your views in a day. But you are in my prayers."

Obviously unsure how to respond to that, Aquilia turned to Samuel with a smile. "Tell your mother what we saw in the markets, Samuel. She will enjoy the story."

Samuel settled beside Abigail on the chaise, and she prepared herself for a tale of fun.

FORTY-THREE

Andrew stood for a long moment, surveying the house before him. It was not in his tastes. Then again, neither were any of the others around him. He missed the familiarity of their house by the Praetorium, the stark beauty of Jerusalem's hillsides. And yet he was glad they were here. They had returned to their home for a few days before setting sail, and it had been so. . . empty. The general had made sure everything there remained safe and secured, but it was still not the same. There was no laughter there anymore, no smiles, no wisdom. Instead, there was only that aching hole that Cleopas had left. The concern for Abigail. The stale smell of dried tears and hopelessness.

Things had improved over the months. He would never argue with that. Ester's recovery was almost full; there was still a shadow of sorrow in her eyes, and he suspected that would never abate entirely. But there was a light there, too. He was glad they had stumbled across the gathering of the disciples, that they had heard the one called Peter teach the crowds; so many of their questions were answered, and with the answers came the peace Ester had been searching for. Three thousand others had believed with them that day. The very thought brought a smile to Andrew's lips. The temple leaders had tried to quiet them, had forbidden the name of Jesus to be spoken, but it was no use. The word spread like wildfire, and churches were springing up all over Judea.

They were not in Judea anymore. With a sigh, Andrew took the last few steps to the imposing door of the edifice and knocked. Seconds later the door opened, and a slave stood before him, impassivity written on his face.

Andrew decided at first glace that he did not like the man. But he smiled anyway. "Greetings, my friend. I am Andrew, in service to Ester Visibullis. Is this the Asinius house?"

The servant's chin rose a notch, and displeasure entered his eyes. "It is."

Andrew nodded, refusing to read anything into the man's demeanor. "Is Abigail Visibullis still here? My mistress has arrived in Rome to rejoin her daughter."

The man opened his mouth, but before he could make reply, a more familiar voice met Andrew's ears from inside. "Andrew!" It was Titus. At least, Andrew thought it was Titus; his name was followed by a laugh, and Andrew was not certain he had ever heard Asinius laugh. But indeed, the large figure of Jason's friend soon appeared, urging the slave aside and opening the door wide. He was smiling, too, looking far more. . . pleasant than Andrew could readily remember seeing him.

"Lord." Andrew tilted his head to a respectful angle. "It is good to see you again."

Titus held out an arm to invite Andrew inside. "Likewise, my friend. Please, come in." Andrew followed him inside, wondering at that title of "friend." The Titus he had met before never would have ascribed it to a mere slave.

"Abigail will be thrilled; she has been praying for all of you night and day. How is your mistress?"

That brought a smile to Andrew's face. "Well, Lord. Her health has improved, and if she still greatly mourns the loss of her husband and son, she has found comfort in her faith, in what we have heard of the same teacher my masters had come to serve."

"Jesus, yes." Titus gave a knowing nod and a beaming smile. "We have been praying that the truth of his teachings would reach your ears, as well. Abigail and I both watched him die." A shadow flitted across his countenance. "It changed us both. And the midwife was one of his followers, so she told us all she remembered of his lessons. We heard of his resurrection hours after Benjamin was born."

This news brought mixed feelings to Andrew's chest. That the faith was shared brought him joy; that Titus had been with Abigail the entire time brought something else. He was not sure what to call it, but it was akin to apprehension. He decided to put that aside for now. "How are she and the babe?"

"Benjamin grows every day, and Samuel as well. Abigail . . ." He sighed. "Abigail is improving, but she had the misfortune of becoming the brunt of my father's anger. It so happens that if you had come three days later, she would not have been here. She is moving out to the villa as soon as I make the purchase of a few more servants."

Andrew's brows pulled together. "He hurt her?"

Titus nodded shortly, his jaw clenched. "We had bought her a eunuch for protection, but she had sent him away for a few moments, before I arrived home one day. We stopped him quickly, but not before he could bruise her. It was two weeks ago. She has not been without at least two able-bodied men for protection since, I promise you."

Andrew smiled in spite of the serious situation. "Knowing her as I do, that has been absolute torment. Abigail is an independent creature."

Titus chuckled. "So I have learned. Please," he then said, indicating the furniture. "Sit, be comfortable. I will go inform Abigail of your arrival. I trust Ester is near?"

Andrew nodded. "She was tired from the journey, so Drusus and Simon and Dinah took her to an inn and sent me to ascertain whether or not Abigail was still here. I am glad we did not miss her yet again."

Titus smiled and nodded. "Thankfully, Drusus's prompt missive arrived a week or so before she was planning to sail home. I will be right back."

◈

Titus felt determination possess his face. He was truly glad Ester had arrived; it would please Abigail. But at the same time, it brought to the fore a few topics that must be settled immediately. Titus had planned on waiting until he got back from his short trip two days from now to broach the subject, but he would have to revise that plan. He headed toward Abigail's chamber with a purposeful stride.

He stopped in the hall, however, and made a quick detour to his own room before returning to knock, then enter hers. He smiled to see Abigail reading from the Scriptures to Samuel and the others, translating it into Greek as she went. She paused when he came in and smiled up at him.

"I thought you were going to the Forum."

Titus smiled. "I met with a detour. I must speak with you, Abigail."

Curious, Abigail set the holy writings aside and stood up. Could she see his nerves? Hopefully not. She smiled and stepped close enough to rest her hand on his forearm.

"What is it?"

Titus darted a glance at the others–Phillip, Panther, Miriam, Antonia, and the children were all here. He would have preferred having this conversation in private, but he did not want to take the time to debate with them on the wisdom of sending them away. It would seem that his servants had all become rather emboldened under Abigail's influence. He focused his gaze on her. It was not too hard to do. She seemed to him now more beautiful than she had ever been, and he no longer knew if it was an actual improvement in her physical traits or the reflection of his love for her.

He linked their fingers together. "The villa will be ready for you when I return."

Abigail nodded. "You have already told me as much."

"Yes, I know," he said with a grin. "That is not what I want to discuss, exactly. But my love, your mother will be with you again soon. I must know what you plan to do when she arrives."

Abigail sighed. "I know not, my friend. I certainly recognize that you have put forth much energy and money to people the villa, and I know much of it has come from your own funds, even though I asked you to use ours. I would hate to have made you do all that only to leave soon. Not to mention that I would miss you terribly. But at the same time, I must recognize that my presence in Rome will only make it harder for you to go on with your life."

Titus lifted her hand and pressed his lips to her knuckles. "You are my life." His soft, fervent words elicited a frown from Abigail's brows. "Abigail, I know you will argue about the wisdom of my desires, but it will not change them. I want to marry you."

"You cannot." She looked frustrated when he moved their fingers to still her lips.

"I can. I know I have done nothing but deny the very possibility since you came here, but I was wrong. I do not care about a political career, I never really have, and my reacquaintance with that arena has strengthened that. I want to run my businesses, and I can do that quite well with you as my wife."

"But your father–"

"Will disapprove, but he will deal with it. I already spoke to him. He will not disinherit me, though he says he will not recognize you as my wife." He leaned down to kiss her softly. "I do not care for his opinion, my love. All that matters is that I will still have the means to provide you a good life, and it is the only life that will make either of us happy. My mother has granted her consent. Marry me, dear one."

He raised his other hand, in which he held the amethyst necklace he had given her what seemed like so long ago. He had all but forgotten that it was in his room, but now he slipped it back over her head.

Abigail's lips trembled, her eyes wide in stupefaction. Samuel bounced up and down, Antonia hushed him. Her gaze stayed locked on his. "Titus. This is a monumental decision. We need to talk about it, to pray about it, to think it through fully."

He gave her a bright smile. "I have been praying about it without ceasing, and I have received my answer in many different ways."

"But . . ." She changed her words into Latin and made them quiet enough for only his ears to hear. "Titus, what if I was damaged by the miscarriage? What if I can have no more children? You need heirs."

In the same tongue, he replied, "And I will have them. I plan to adopt Samuel. Even if the Lord chooses not to bless us with more babes, my line will continue."

She drew in a sharp breath. "Still," she fumbled, once more in Greek, looking down at the jewel around her neck. "I need to think about this. I will answer you when you return."

Titus laughed, drawing her gaze back up to his. "I cannot wait that long, beloved. I must have your answer now, this very minute."

She narrowed her eyes at him. "And why is that?"

"Because Andrew is downstairs." He stated it calmly, his smile still in place.

Abigail's eyes went wide again, and after a brief moment of absolute stillness, she made a lunge for the door.

Titus caught her by the hand to stop her, laughing again. "Not so fast, small one. I will not have you reuniting with your family until I am sure you will let me become a member of it. So very quickly, I will finish all I wanted to say. I have already made arrangements for us to live at the Visibullis villa, but off of the money I bring in, so that Benjamin's estates will remain intact. I would like nothing better than for Ester to stay with us. My mother may wish to join us too, since Father would probably make her life miserable when it became clear she supported our union. But you would be the mistress of the estate, my love. Of that there will be no question."

Abigail stared at him as if he were bereft of his sanity. "Are you quite serious about this? Have you truly thought out all the consequences of such a decision?"

"Fully." His voice was soft, gentle, sure. He met her gaze. "I love you, Abigail. In my heart, you are my wife. How could I ever marry another? The Lord brought us together for a reason, and I want nothing more than to praise him with you every day for the rest of my life. I want to teach him to our children with you, to spread his word to the empire with you. Abigail, if you cannot live here, in Rome, then I will go back to Israel with you." He cupped her face in his palm, and in careful Hebrew he promised, "'Wherever you go, I will go; and wherever you lodge, I will lodge; your people shall be my people, and your God my God. Where you die, I will die, and there will I be buried. The Lord do so to me, and more also, if anything but death parts you and me.'"

Tears filled Abigail's eyes. "That is what _I_ am to say to _you_." With a watery laugh, she covered his hands with hers and stretched up to kiss him. "I can think of no greater honor, Titus, than being your wife. The Lord has blessed me in giving me you. As soon as the arrangements can be made, I will marry you."

Titus was quite certain his joy was radiating from him as he leaned down to kiss her deeply, even as a cheer went up from their audience. He pulled his lips away only when Samuel launched himself at them, jarring the embrace to a halt with his happy cries. Titus laughed and pulled him the rest of the way into his arms. To his betrothed he said, "Go, greet Andrew. He told me the others are at an inn nearby. Miriam and I will bring the children down in a few minutes."

He nodded to Phillip to tell him to follow her as she dashed out the door. Phillip grinned back at him.

❧

Abigail wasted no time. She flew through the house, suddenly feeling better than she had in months. Her family was here, and she was going to marry Titus. Heaven smiled on her today. Of course, it would probably take a long conversation to convince her family of the wisdom of marrying Titus, but she felt ready to face that challenge. She was even ready to face the uncertainty of Andrew's emotions on the matter.

She guessed correctly which room he would be waiting in; she could see him standing and looking around without approval as she sped along. She smiled. "Andrew!"

Andrew turned with a huge smile. When she barrelled his way, he caught her up in his arms and spun her around. "Abigail!" He laughed, setting her back on her feet. He held her at arm's length with hands on her shoulders. "Look at you. You are more beautiful than ever, which has no doubt been tormenting the poor men of Rome."

Abigail laughed. "Perhaps."

"And you have no doubt eclipsed all the Roman women when you put on their styles." He grin as he glanced at her stola and intricate hair.

"Oh, absolutely." She gave him another hug. "Oh, Andrew, I have missed you all so much. Tell me, how is she? Better? I trust you would not have made the journey otherwise."

"Mistress is quite well. She still misses them, and she has been worried senseless about you, but she has been improving every day, eager to meet her grandchild." His smile was bright, unreserved, which eased some of the concern in Abigail's heart. "And from the impression I received from Titus, you will be happy to hear that after hearing a sermon of Simon Peter, the entire household has embraced the salvation offered by Jesus."

Her heart brimmed, overflowed. "That is wonderful. We have been praying."

Andrew nodded, sobering. He held her gaze firmly. "Much has changed, has it not? We have been living different lives these months. I must confess I was worried when I heard you were coming here with Titus, and I disapproved of Drusus asking you to remain in his house until we arrived. But the man who greeted me moments ago was not the man I remembered. How did this happen, Abigail?"

She smiled. "We were both at the crucifixion of our Lord, Andrew. The mob pulled me along with it, and he was in charge. We were both so moved by what we saw, by the sheer righteousness the Christ portrayed–and then, as the earthquake began, so did my labor. Titus took me home, stayed with me after getting a midwife. She taught us the words of Jesus, and we believed together. When Benjamin was born, I went to stay with Tabitha, the midwife. When Titus received the word from Arminius, he volunteered to bring me here." She shrugged. "We have grown together, learned together. We received the Holy Spirit together."

"Then he has truly changed," Andrew said with relief.

"He is even quoting Hebrew scripture."

He arched a brow. "A quicker study than I at Latin, then. What has he been reciting?"

She held his gaze steadily, somberly, and spoke the same passage Titus had spoken to her only minutes before. Seeing the question that grew in Andrew's eyes, she sighed at her halt. "Andrew, I am going to marry him."

He regarded her a moment without any reaction. He searched her eyes. "You love him?"

She nodded, the emotion filling her heart at the thought of him. Andrew smiled. "Then I wish you my congratulations, my friend. You deserve that."

Her relief coupled with disbelief. "You are not upset?"

He laughed softly. "If I had learned of this a couple months ago, I would have been fit to kill him. But as I cleansed my heart before Jehovah, I saw what I had been denying for too long. I have always and will always love you, Abigail, but I am not the husband the Lord intended for you. I chose servitude, but you have the heart of a queen."

"You are my friend."

He smiled into her assurance. "Yes. And I will always be your friend. I will also always be your servant. Speaking of which," he said, nodding toward Phillip, who was standing unobtrusively inside the door, "are you not going to introduce me, Abigail?"

Abigail smiled and turned to beckon Phillip forward. "Of course. Phillip, this is Andrew, about whom I have told you. Andrew, this is Phillip. I was forced to buy someone to protect me when I thought I would be returning to Israel on my own, and Phillip has been beside me ever since. He is a true friend."

Andrew and Phillip both smiled and clasped wrists, assessing one another and nodding.

"And it sounds as though the others are coming, too." She heard Samuel's buoyant voice, followed a moment later by Titus in the doorway, boy perched on his shoulders. Miriam, holding Benjamin, followed, Panther bringing up the rear.

"You remember Titus and Samuel, of course," Abigail said as Titus put down the boy so he could run to go give the man a proper greeting. With his usual energy, Samuel threw himself into Andrew's waiting arms. "And this," Abigail continued, drawing Andrew's gaze back up, "is Miriam, my handmaiden. She is from Hebron. And the angel in her arms is Benjamin."

Andrew nodded and smiled, but his gaze had not yet made it to the baby. It was lingering with appreciation over Miriam, who was blushing, smiling, and turning her attention deliberately on the babe. Abigail almost started laughing. Restraining herself, she settled for sharing a knowing glance with Titus instead, who grinned and draped his arm over her shoulder.

"Let us hope Ester agrees to staying with us," he whispered into her ear, "so that a suitable arrangement can be made for those two."

Abigail bit back her grin and spoke loudly enough to draw Andrew's attention. "And the giant behind her is Panther, another dear friend. He is Titus's mother's bodyguard, but she has been so kind as to lend me his services frequently."

Panther nodded, as did Andrew, but his eyes wandered away again rather quickly. This time, he looked at Abigail and Titus. "Mistress will be eager to see you. Our inn is on the outskirts of the city, though, and the hour grows late. What do you wish to do?"

Abigail looked to Titus for advice, and he was quick to provide it. "I suggest you plan on going tomorrow. As a matter of fact, I would recommend you take tonight and however long necessary in the morning to get everything here together, and make this your last night in this house. If time permits, you could all simply move to the villa tomorrow, or stay one night in the inn and go the next morn."

She lifted her brows. "Is everything ready there?"

Titus nodded. "With the addition of Ester's household, all should be well until I can finish the arrangements upon my return. And knowing you would have familiar company, I would feel far better leaving you with them than here."

"That sounds good to me."

Andrew nodded and put Samuel back on his feet. "I will go now before darkness falls and tell her that her grandson is beautiful and her daughter well. We will call for you in the morning."

They all said their farewells, Andrew's gaze lingering a bit longer than necessary on Miriam, and he was soon on his way. The rest of them headed for their rooms.

Abigail drew close to Miriam and took Benjamin. She could not resist a tease. "What do you think? He is handsome, is he not?"

Miriam blushed again but made no attempt to hide her smile. "It is an apt description. And I know from all you have told me that he is a good man."

"Good enough not to blame you for the violence of Caius, Miriam."

Miriam met her gaze steadily. "Is this your will, Mistress?"

Abigail smiled and took Miriam's hand. "My will is for you to be happy. Perhaps Andrew would accomplish that, perhaps not. But if our houses join together, you will have plenty of time to discover for yourselves if your hearts are suited to one another. I will approve either way. And in the meantime, we have much to do before the morrow."

A predictable chaos ensued as they attempted to get everything packed and ready to move, and it was not until nearly an hour later that Titus managed to pull her aside. "Would you like me to postpone my trip, my love? I could see you settled at the villa first, and then leave in a few days."

Abigail smiled her dismissal of that, though she rewarded his thoughtfulness with a kiss. "I would rather be selfish and have you go quickly so that you can get back and we can sooner be wed. Besides, I will enjoy the time with Ester, and by the time you return, we will have gotten caught up, and I will hopefully have convinced her to stay here with us."

"Here? Are you certain?"

Abigail nodded, certain her smile reflected her peace. "Hearing Andrew speak of the work being done in Judea made me realize that we are needed more here than there, my love. Right now, who in Rome but us and those we have convinced believe in Christ? Israel has his disciples, and while I would like to hear them myself, I feel as though God's plan is for us to be a beacon for him here."

"I feel the same." His eyes smiled into hers. "Is it any wonder I love you so much? Not many people would be willing to sacrifice their home for their faith."

"Perhaps, perhaps not." She tapped a fingertip to his nose and grinned. "But who said anything about a sacrifice? I will be with you, and you *are* my home."

He gathered her into his arms and held her close until Benjamin convinced them with a wail that it was time to take a break from their work and find their respective nourishments.

FORTY-FOUR

Caius watched from the shadows as his son bade Abigail goodbye with a warm kiss, a bright smile. He felt his knuckles tighten around the door, whiten in rage. Did Titus honestly expect him to just sit around and do nothing, say nothing, while he threw away all their family had ever worked for over that slave girl? If so, then he was more of an idiot that he had ever supposed.

He watched his son leave, watched the Germanic eunuch follow behind her as Abigail headed back inside to finish packing. He knew very well that she was as happy to be getting out of his house as he was to be getting rid of her. The only difference was that she would not be so happy in a few hours, and he would be ecstatic. Smiling, he looked over to where Caelia stood a few feet away and nodded. She nodded in reply without saying a word, then ran to the house's side entrance. It was Timothy's cue to follow Abigail back the hall.

Ten men followed Caelia back into the room, and he surveyed them critically. The one with the authority stepped forward immediately and bent a knee to him, but Caius did not acknowledge him right away. Eight of the others were his primary interest. They varyied in heights, but all were densely packed with muscle, and Caius figured they would suffice. At last, he nodded to the kneeling man, who rose.

"She should be here momentarily. See that you make it quick and quiet. The fewer of my slaves to know about this, the better."

"There is no need to worry, Lord," the man replied with a mirthless smile. "We are quite accustomed to handling more troublesome slaves than any woman could ever be."

"Good." Caius settled comfortably on a chaise to wait.

⚜

Abigail had no sooner gained her room than a knock sounded on the door, and she opened it again. The sight of Timothy did not make her smile. The doorkeeper was probably her least favorite of the slaves in this house. "Yes?"

Timothy made no attempt to look happy about being up here. "That slave of the Visibullis house who came yesterday has returned. He is asking for you."

"Andrew? I did not expect him so early."

Timothy shrugged, obviously not concerned.

Abigail sighed and looked around her; most of the packing was done, with the exception of the last minute things, so she certainly would not mind getting an earlier start than planned. The sooner she got out of here, the better. "I shall go speak with him. Hopefully, he is here to say they are all ready, and he can help us get everything outside. Miriam, Samuel should be back from saying farewell to his friends soon, but if not, we will send Panther to fetch him once Phillip and I return. Just try to get everything else thrown together here."

"Yes, Mistress." Miriam picked up Benjamin and smiled.

Abigail pressed a kiss to her son's round cheek and headed back into the hall, Phillip behind her. "I thought this day would never come. It seems I have been here forever."

Phillip hummed. "It has been quite a while. And not an entirely pleasant while."

Abigail breathed a laugh in agreement. She suspected there was a bounce in her step as she moved down the hall. And why not? The shadow was finally lifting; she could never forget all those she had lost in that brief stretch of time, but life was moving on. She would get to embrace Ester today, to introduce her to her grandson. They would take that son to the villa as the new master, legally and blessedly. In a few days, she would marry the man who captured her heart. She did not even attempt to keep the smile from her lips.

They neared the cubiculum where Andrew had been waiting the day before. Abigail's pace increased with excitement, and Phillip made his match hers. No one was in sight as she neared, but he could easily be at a window or seated. She moved into the room with confidence, Phillip a step behind her.

She halted abruptly when she felt the many presences within, a second before she saw Caius lounging carelessly, a smug smile on his lips. Time seemed to freeze. She heard the shouts of the men as they seized Phillip. From the sound of it there were many of them, but she did not turn around to look. She could not have. At that same moment two men grabbed her by the arms, though she made no protest to warrant their tight grips.

Her gaze leveled on Caius. "What have you done?"

He did not so much as stand to dignify her. "What should have been done long ago. You are a slave, Abigail, and I am selling you as my son would do if he had any sense."

Phillip roared behind her, and she had a feeling he was barely being restrained by those many men. "Peace, Phillip," she said over her shoulder. "Fighting will only please him. It will give him an excuse to have you killed. Be calm, and you will best serve me."

She saw Phillip still abruptly, though the men holding him down still looked wary.

Abigail turned her full attention on Caius again, trying to ignore the pain that shot through her arms. "I am not a slave."

He sneered. "You are and always will be. No dresses, no jewels can change that." He waved disdainfully at her attire, then turned his eyes on the men holding her. His words were in Latin. "Take her away, and see that no time is wasted in giving her to the men. My son will not fight to win back what is the gladiators' fodder."

Abigail felt her heart freeze, her throat constrict. Not the arenas. Surely he would not send her there. But he would. She saw it in his eyes. So in the same tongue she said hotly, "Titus will never forgive you for this, Caius, and he *will* fight. To him, I am not a slave. I am a woman worthy of love, and I will be his wife. But you—never again will he see you as his father." In spite of the shock on his face, the men began to pull her away. She shifted her words back to Greek. "You have lost him! It is your fault, not mine, and sending me to arenas will not change that."

Her eyes met Phillip's as they dragged her by, and she prayed that he would understand the message she sent. He inclined his head as if he had read her thoughts entirely, otherwise not moving. She looked for the first time into the face of one of her captors. It was hard, battered, and had the distinct look of one who sharpened his edges to keep them as rough as possible. She would receive no mercy from him.

"Father Jehovah," she breathed in Hebrew, letting her eyes slide closed as the men pulled her where they willed, "give them wisdom and strength in their reactions. Do not let this be the ending to the progress we have made." Trembling overtook her, and from the depths of her being she cried out, "Protect your daughter, Jehovah!"

"Quiet!" One of the men punctuated his order with a hard shake. He pulled back his hand as if to strike her, but the other broke in quickly.

"No, leave her unmarked. Volusius will be pleased with this one's beauty."

The second man leered. "As well he should be. Perhaps he will keep this one for himself. She is too good for the likes of the gladiators."

The first shook his head, saying as though Abigail could not hear him, "Asinius ordered her to be given to the fighters, so she shall be. Volusius would not dare to anger him."

The second laughed roughly. "If it is defilement of her he seeks, perhaps we should get started now."

Abigail felt the Spirit descend upon her, and she came to a halt in her path, surprising them enough that they stopped, too, rather than simply yank her forcibly along. She looked one in the eye, then the other. Calmly, she said, "Touch me, and forsake your lives. Are we understood?"

They tried to laugh off her threat, but she saw the shiver of fear run through them, saw something within them balk, scream, and shrink further inside.

She mentally said a word of gratitude to her God.

Phillip had not managed to escape from Roman soldiers once without having learned quite a bit about the art. It took no thought to remember the skill. When Abigail looked at him with that darting glance, he had known exactly what she expected of him; keep himself from being killed so that he could see to the protection of her children first of all, and then figure out a way to free her from Caius's schemes. The very thought of his mistress in the arenas . . . it did not bear thinking about.

He had remained still for long enough that the grips on him had begun to relax. He waited until he heard the door from the atrium open, knowing that meant they would be taking Abigail outside. That was his cue to break free–if he waited for the sound of the door closing again, it would be too late, since that would be when they decided what to do with him. So at that perfect moment, he lunged, so quickly and powerfully that no one saw it coming. He heard shouts behind him, but he did not pause to look over his shoulder. Instead, he ran out into the corridor and headed for the masters' rooms, ducking into another room first so that they would assume he had gone out or at least toward the side door. He went out a second entrance of that room, then through the servants' hall until he reached Abigail's rooms. He entered quietly and addressed his words to Panther.

"Caius has sold Abigail to the arenas. There were eight men lying in wait for me, but I just broke free. Take Miriam and the children to your mistress, I am going to follow mine. Have a loyal slave waiting for Andrew outside with the news, and get everyone to him and the villa as soon as possible. Do not let Caius know what you do. Understood?"

Panther had time only to nod his dark head before Phillip climbed out of the window and wound his way to the street. He barely glimpsed Abigail's head as she was lifted into a cart, but it was enough. He would follow, see exactly where they took her, and do all in his power to get her out again.

His power had never felt so lacking.

"God of my mistress," he breathed in a tongue he had not used since he had been taken from the land that taught it to him, "if you are there, now is the time to act. She speaks of you as just and merciful; mercy would see this undeserving punishment pass from her head. Justice would see her tormentors punished instead." He felt his jaw clench, his heart contract in pain. "Protect her, if you are the loving God she claims. Protect her where I cannot."

Volusius did not look up from the scroll he was reading as soon as he heard them enter. It never hurt to make his underlings wait a little longer to achieve whatever business they were there for. After all, he was the one in charge, so he would do things at his leisure. He took his time in deciphering the writing before him, then rolled it back up neatly and put it aside. Only then did he look up to see who had entered. Spotting the two he had sent out an hour earlier to the Asinius house, his eyes fell with expectation on the small woman between them.

"This is she?" He rose from his seat so that he could stride toward them. At his approach, his men dropped their hands from her arms. He noted that they had been careful enough not to bruise her alabaster skin, and he gave them a nod for their trouble.

"Yes, sir," the senior replied.

Volusius studied the woman. She was young, as he had expected, and beautiful, as were all the women that made their way here from that particular house. This one surpassed the others, though. He had never seen such features, and her hair was absolutely breathtaking: long and thick and glossy, dark and smooth. He stepped closer and put a finger under her chin to tilt her face up. It was unmitigated perfection, minus the defiance in her eyes. That would fade soon enough, though.

"A lovely face." His eyes ran over each inch of her countenance for a second time. Then his gaze followed her neck down. "Strip her."

"No!" She tried to protect herself even as one of his men held her still and the other ripped her clothes off with a single strong swipe. She was shaking, and tears coursed down her cheeks as she tried unsuccessfully to move her hair over her body to cover her. It would have worked much better had she not been pinned against his man.

Volusius smiled, in part at the protestations, in part at the sight before him. Her beauty did not stop at her face. Her breasts were full, firm, her stomach soft and flat, her hips setting off a small waist and leading down to shapely legs. He reached out, noting with a smile that she first shrank away, then halted when she felt the man behind her. She stiffened, closed her eyes, and averted her face. He picked up the jewel cradled between her breasts. "From whom did you steal this, wench?"

"From Titus Asinius." Her eyes, open again, lashed him with anger. "Why do you not call him in to reclaim it and see how he gratefully rewards you?"

Volusius snorted a laugh and let the amethyst fall back to its place. "I think I will let you keep it, instead. It will be interesting to watch her try to fight off all the other slaves over it, will it not?" He glanced at his men at this, and they both grinned their answer. He turned his attention back on her body. "I trust you are not a virgin."

Her cheeks flushed. "The Visibullis heir I birthed would testify otherwise."

Volusius moved with lightning speed, grasping her by the chin and pulling her closer to him, away from the man behind her. "You say that as though it should mean something to me, but let me assure you that the name of your whelp is nothing here. _You_ are nothing. Your stay here will be much more pleasant if you understand that right now. You are nothing but a slave and a wench to reward my gladiators." He released her as suddenly as he had grabbed her, then took a step back to sweep his eyes over her again. "Get her a tunic and take her down to the other women. There are games today, my fair one, and you will be the prize for the winner."

One of the men quirked a brow. "But Ares is fighting."

"And if he wins, then offer her to him." Volusius walked back across the room. "If he refuses her, then give her to the next best man." He sat, dismissing them.

🔸

Abigail found herself being pulled back out the door, and she felt shame wash over her as they led her naked down a corridor. They passed no one, but it did not relieve her discomfort. She covered herself as best she could with her hair, but she was relieved when they led her into a small room and handed her a coarse tunic. Slipping it on, she realized that it had been a long time since she had put on such unrefined cloth.

She had never been more grateful for any garment in her life.

"Hurry," the second man ordered when she took a bit too long smoothing it over her. "The games will begin soon, and we do not want to miss them."

"What work can you do?" The first propelled her back into the hallway. "Laundry? Kitchen work? Cleaning?"

"Any of it. I am best in the kitchen."

"And it would be a shame to ruin those fine hands with lye." The second flashed a dangerous smile. "The kitchen it is."

The first snorted. "It is surprising she can do anything at all. The other women we have received from the Asinius house were good for nothing but pleasuring a man."

"I am not from the Asinius house. I was a guest there, not a slave." She knew they would not believe her, but still she insisted. Seeing the look the two men exchanged, she sighed. "I am not claiming to have never been a slave. I was. But not there. When I served, it was in the house of Cleopas Visibullis, the prefect for the Tenth Legion. I was his wife's handmaiden, until their son married me. Now I am the mother of the Visibullis heir."

This obviously did not phase the second man, but the first stopped and looked at her. "Cleopas Visibullis? I served with a man by that name decades ago, in Jerusalem. I was transferred shortly after he married a Jewess."

"That is my master and father." A shard of light fell on her heart. She said a silent prayer of thanksgiving; it may not end up helping her, but having something in common with this man would hopefully not hurt. "Or was, before he was killed in an uprising."

The man put a hand on his hip and glared at her. "He stole that woman from me, you know."

Abigail felt her lips turn up. "You are not by any chance Mannas, are you?"

He narrowed his eyes still more. "I am."

She nodded. "My mistress and mother remembers you with gratitude for being the one to make possible the introduction to the man she loved with all her heart." She smiled. "She and her husband always remembered you in their prayers."

This made Mannas shift uncomfortably, and the other man rolled his eyes. "Are we going to stand around all day reminiscing, Mannas, or shall we deliver her to the kitchens and get on with it?"

Mannas took her arm again and began walking. "I heard that Cleopas and his son were killed in Jerusalem, but how, if you are who you say you are, did you come to be here?"

Cynicism colored her smile this time. "Here in this building, or here in Rome? I came to the latter to claim the family estates for my son, who was born a month after my husband's death. I was in the company of one his dearest friends, Titus Asinius, with whom he had charged our safekeeping as he lay bleeding to death. I come to the former because Titus's father was not very pleased to learn that his son had fallen in love with me and plans to marry me."

Mannas looked over her head at his companion, pressed his lips together. A moment later he pushed her into the kitchen and stepped away. But still she heard him murmur, "Nothing good will come of this. That woman will bring trouble upon our heads."

She could only pray he was right.

❧

The head slave in the kitchens stared down at her as though she were nothing but a rotting vegetable stalk. His massive arms were folded over a chest that was easily two of her, and he stood towering over her as though she were a child. "Another worthless wench from the Asiniuses. What did you do to offend the lady?"

"It was not the lady I offended, it was the lord." She tried not to back away. He was so large that even standing a fair distance from him, she felt as though he were encroaching on her space. But she had a feeling letting him know that would only make things worse.

The giant grunted and pointed to a corner of the room, where a woman stirred something in a huge cauldron. "Sophia came from them, too. Go help her, do whatever she says, and stay out of my way."

Abigail bowed her head in obedience and made her way to the corner, feeling out of place and minuscule in a world that did not care about her. She silently prayed, reaching her heart heavenward without being able to find any words to express her thoughts. Help, guidance, strength, courage, patience, wisdom... she needed some help in all of her virtues at the moment, so she dug inside and prayed that her God would make up what she lacked.

Sophia was probably once quite beautiful. As Abigail approached her, she now looked mainly wrung out, like a once-crimson cloth left too long in the burning sun. Her hair was stringy and dry, her skin pulled taught over unfattened bones, her features sunken and withered.

When she looked up, only an echo of a light appeared in her eyes. "New?"

Abigail nodded. "Caius Asinius sent me here. Goliath over there thought I should come to you."

Sophia nodded, not seeming very interested and probably not understanding the reference to the scriptural giant. She stirred her pot. "There are games today, so there is much to be done. The bread should be ready to knead soon, if you know how."

"Yes, of course." Abigail hoped she sound meek rather than confident. She did not intend to make any enemies among the other slaves if she could help it.

"For now, chop these." Sophia indicated some miscellaneous vegetables beside her.

Abigail picked up the knife, fully prepared to do as she was told without any complaint. Without any words at all, if necessary.

Sophia, however, looked her way again. "How is everyone? Antonia, Vinius, Panther?"

"Antonia and Panther are well. Vinius's bad knees have been keeping him resting more and more, doing mainly managerial work from his bed. I have not seen much of him at all, I am afraid."

Sophia nodded, darting a glance at her with a mouth twisted up. "The other women?"

"I have not seen much of them, either. Titus brought me into the house as his guest, though his father would not receive me as such."

"Ah, you were Titus's," Sophia said with a sigh, as though that was the truly important part of what she had said. "He is always possessive of those he chooses himself. It has caused contention between him and his father more than once. Then Caius takes whom he wills, Titus finds another, and the cycle continues. It is only when Caius becomes too attached that one of us ends up here." The faded woman looked around her. She turned her eyes back on her companion. "I assume you will go to a gladiator tonight."

"The winner." She heard the fear in her voice. "They mentioned a man named Ares."

Sophia took the opening for a new conversation with a slight smile. "Ah, yes, our legendary war god. Ares has been here for years, he is the favorite among the people. He hopes to win his freedom one day, to go home to his wife and children, or so I hear." She shook her head. "No one has ever seen such devotion in a man before. He fights fiercely, for a cause. It is custom here that the better the fight, the better the woman the man gets as reward. Ares has had the best of us offered to him, a newer, prettier one after every win, but he turns us all away. They have tried boys, girls, other men, but everyone is refused. They say he wishes to remain faithful to his wife, but let us be reasonable. No man is so strong for so long. Most of us think that he is simply. . . incapable of taking his pleasure."

Abigail felt her face heating once more. "And when he refuses? Then what?"

RoseANNA M. WHITE

Sophia shrugged. "Then the guards respond to his knock and take you elsewhere. Once you are relegated to the lower fighters, several elsewheres a night."

Dread coiled low in Abigail's stomach. She did not know how much indignity she would have to suffer, but she decided there and then to do all she could to avoid it. Not only for her sake, but for Titus's, her children's. She would not be the only one hurt if what looked inevitable happened. It could very well eat at Titus, and it would be something the boys would remember until they understood. Even as she thought out what must be done, tears gathered in her eyes.

"Do not waste your energy on tears," Sophia said, gentleness in her tone. "They help nothing and only anger those in charge."

Abigail dashed quickly at the offending droplets. "I am sorry. I just miss my sons and Titus."

Sophia's hands paused in her task, eyes wide. "You have Titus's son?"

Abigail drew in a shaking breath. "No. No, I have my late husband's son. Jason Visibullis. I am his widow, and Titus brought me to Rome to claim the estates when Jason and his father were both killed."

Sophia stared at her blankly. "Jason is dead?" Her words were no more than a whisper.

A chill moved up Abigail's spine at the recognition she saw in Sophia's eyes. "In an uprising in Jerusalem six months ago." She waited a moment, trying to convince herself not to ask the question that spilled forth anyway. "You knew him?"

Sophia nodded, looking back to her cauldron, her chest rising and falling a bit too rapidly. "He came by often. Several of us . . ." She halted, as if debating whether or not saying what was on her mind would offend Abigail. She apparently decided it did not matter much. "Titus gave several of us to him over the course of the years. He was a kind man. A gentle lover."

Abigail concentrated on her vegetables.

She felt Sophia's gaze on her profile. "He must have loved you very much, if he married you. What I heard of the men's conversations led me to believe Jason would never wed a Hebrew."

A soft smile pulled at Abigail's lips. "His conversations led me to believe the same, Sophia. Moreover, I was only his mother's handmaid. But he did love me very much. And you are right. He was a kind man. A good man."

Sophia shook her head in remonstrance. "And yet you say it is Titus you miss, not your husband."

This time, Abigail did not flush. She just looked up at the older woman without even stilling her hands in their task. It may have been a while since she worked in the kitchen, but years of skill did not simply fade forgotten from one's fingers. "I do miss Jason. He changed my life more than I could have ever dreamed; but that made it difficult for me to open my heart to him at the time. Titus, though, has changed with me over this last half year. We became friends."

Sophia arched an unbelieving brow. "Titus is never the friend of a woman. Women are but to be conquered and taken in his eyes. And if his friend married you, a Jewish slave, he would harbor nothing but hatred for you. The Asiniuses had high ambitions for Jason."

"I know." Abigail moved the cut vegetables aside with a quick swipe and picked up a few more. She did not see the point of saying more. She knew very well she would not be believed.

A moment later, an unmistakably large shadow fell over them. Abigail stiffened, suddenly wondering if talking was forbidden and she would meet with the consequences for it, but she did not stop her work. Perhaps he was simply checking up on them.

That idea fell flat when his meaty hand came down and gripped the top of her head. He at once pulled her head back and leaned over her so that she was looking into his face upside down. It may have been comical had it not been terrifying.

"You are good with a knife," Goliath said, indicating the considerable pile of vegetables before her.

"Yes."

He moved her head back into the proper position, then turned her toward another corner of the room, where a stack of cheeses stood. "When you finish the vegetables, slice the cheeses. This thick." He held up fingers in front of her face to illustrate. "All of them."

"Yes, sir."

He removed his hand and turned to glare at Sophia. "You would do well to learn a few things from this one."

He sauntered away, and Abigail sighed, closing her eyes briefly. There went her hopes of not making enemies among the slaves. Without even glancing up again, she set to work with a fury.

FORTY-FIVE

Ester looked from one man to the other. "What do you mean, she is gone?"

"I am sorry." Caius Asinius offered a smile that fell short of sincere. "It shocked us all to find that she had left, but it was unmistakable. Her things were gone, clothes and jewels and everything, when we awoke this morning."

Ester did not narrow her eyes in suspicion. She did not have to. She just regarded him unflinchingly and recalled everything her son had told her about this man. She straightened her shoulders and held Caius's gaze. "Where is my grandson?"

"I do not know. She must have taken him with her."

"I see." Ester let her eyes move over the room. It was beautiful, far lovelier than the place she had called home for so many years, but she wanted nothing more than to escape its oppressive walls. She looked back to the owner, whose eyes refelcted his home's ice.

Her family had been tampered with enough. She did not need this arrogant Roman interfering with what happiness she still had available. "You are obviously not as smart as you would have me think, Caius Asinius, or you would know that Abigail would never run away on the morn of our reunion. You would know that I am her mother and that she would not react to me as *your* slaves do to you, because she is *not* my slave, she never was by your definition. So whatever you have done, you will not convince me you were not the one behind it. And though I may not be able to make you pay for it, I will certainly not let you get away with it."

She turned and strode from the room, Andrew, Simon and two of Drusus's men surrounding her. She headed for the door that would take her outside.

"Wait!"

It was not Caius's voice, but a woman's, so Ester obeyed. She turned to see who was obviously the lady of the house rushing up. There was a younger woman behind her, clutching a bundle to her chest as they hurried, slaves protecting them as well.

The woman came to a harried halt in front of Ester. "I am Aquilia, Titus's mother. Titus is out of town, Phillip, Abigail's bodyguard, has not yet returned with news of her, but I swear to you we shall get her back." She motioned the girl behind her forward. "This is Miriam, Abigail's handmaiden. And this is Benjamin."

Ester looked with awe at the small boy who gazed back at her with infant interest out of Jason's eyes. She reached out to take him, holding him close to her chest. "You are beautiful, my child." She closed her eyes against sudden tears.

"I recommend taking him and Samuel and Miriam to the villa at once," Aquilia went on. "My people know the way. In fact, I would ask to be allowed to come with you. I will not spend another day under the same roof as that monster."

Ester looked up at the woman. She saw a rich and bejeweled Roman noble, one who had probably never known a day of want in her life. She saw a sad and empty woman who had never had a day of happiness in her life. She smiled. "I can think of nothing better. How soon can you be ready?"

"I am ready now." Aquilia returned the smile.

"Ready for what?" Caius appeared in the doorway. He looked from Ester to the babe in her arms to his wife to the handmaiden.

Aquilia made no reply. She simply turned and began issuing orders for her things to be brought out, then moved to Ester's side and ushered her out the door.

He grabbed his wife's elbow. "You will go nowhere! Would you make a laughingstock of this family?"

Aquilia pulled her arm free and glowered at him. "You have already succeeded in that, Caius, by forcing your son to choose between his father and his heart. Because there was never any question, and all of Rome knows it. If this family suffers, it is no one's fault but yours."

Moments later, a woman brought out Samuel, and a processions of slaves followed with the rest of the belongings to be moved. Caius sputtered, though he calmed somewhat when a provocatively dressed slave slid up behind him and put a hand on his arm.

Aquilia raised her brows at them. "I considered sending you to the arenas as a parting gesture, Caelia, but I decided it was more fitting that the two of you poison each other. I have no doubt you shall feed on each other's misery until one of you kills the other. I wish you all the worst." She spun away, leading the procession outside.

Ester said nothing about that parting exchange until they were well on their way. "I hate to think that my family has come between yours, my friend."

Aquilia gave a humorless laugh. "My family was in ruins at its start. All yours has done is make us see that there is something better to be had." She met Ester's gaze. "Titus is completely in love with her. No thing, no one before Abigail has ever inspired him to be so strong and kind. Your daughter has saved my son. I feel as though I owe you for that, knowing as I do that it was the love of you and your husband that made her into the woman she is."

At that, Ester had to smile. "Thank you, my friend; but you are mistaken in that. The heart Abigail has was the heart she came to me with. She suffered much in the first years of her life, but it only made her soul great. I am not surprised to hear that your son loves her. Everyone does."

Aquilia nodded and drew in a breath. "They plan to marry."

Ester's eyes widened in surprise. "Marry? But she has been a widow only–"

"They know that." She reached over and rested her hand on Ester's wrist. Ester had a feeling that such a sign of compassion was unfamiliar to the Roman, but it meant all the more for that. "But when you see them together, you will understand. Their hearts are one. They need each other. That is the news that pushed Caius over the edge of his anger with Abigail."

Ester covered the elegant fingers with her own. She kept her gaze on their hands as thoughts whispered through her mind. At last, she said, "Then there is only one thing to do. We must pray."

⚜

Her breasts were so sore and heavy with milk that Abigail wanted to do nothing but wrap her arms around herself and moan. Every time she blinked, she saw Benjamin, and it only made the pain that much worse. It was evening by the time Goliath slanted a glance at the stains seeping through her tunic. As darkness was falling, Abigail found herself shoved into a small room without any explanation. A moment later, a baby was put in her arms who was fussing healthily. She knew not whose child it was or why she was in the arena compound, and she did not ask. She simply gave her a breast and let her own tears fall as this one innocent child took the milk that should have gone to another. But knowing Benjamin would be cared for, Abigail comforted herself in that she was helping *some* babe, at least.

She wanted her own.

As soon as the child had eaten her fill, the same slave that had put the girl in her arms reappeared to take her back. Abigail was not given much time to wonder about where she was to go. A man she had not seen before appeared and beckoned for her to follow him. "You go to Ares. Come."

Afraid to do otherwise, she obeyed. After minutes of walking, they entered what seemed to be a corridor of cells. Judging by the space between the doors, Abigail decided they could not be much larger than the closet she had called her room for most of her life. But behind these there was no familiarity, no trunk of small treasures, no peace and solitude.

"Let your hand rest upon me, Jehovah." Abigail prayed silently, her lips moving though she let no air take the words from her mouth. "Protect me and deliver me, I beg you."

The guard stopped in front of a door at the very end of the corridor. Without a word to Abigail, he knocked quickly, inserted a key into the lock, and turned it. Opened it, pushed her inside. She was still regaining her balance when the resounding thud of the closing portal shook the room. Abigail's eyes adjusted quickly, so that she could make out the man kneeling below the one window in the room, as if in prayer.

Abigail fell to her knees, too, and bowed until her forehead kissed the cold stone floor. "Do not cast me out, Lord." Her voice trembled

Through the hair that had fallen over her, she saw him turn his head partly, as if irritated at the interruption. The profile he presented showed a nose obviously broken at least once, a scar running from midcheek to ear, and a hardness born from a life of violence. "You will not flatter me, woman. Knock and leave, I will not be your lord."

Abigail's fingers clenched tightly, until her nails dug into her palms. "I have heard that you accept no one. And I do not ask to be an exception to that, no matter your reasons. I ask for your protection, Lord. If you send me away, they will give me to one who will not refuse. Please. I only wish to remain faithful to my betrothed until he comes for me."

Ares stood and turned to face her. "Rise, woman. I am not a god for you to bow to."

Abigail lifted her head. Sat up. Then rose to her feet. They stared at each other for a long moment.

"You are a Jewess," he pronounced dryly.

She did not know whether it was hope or fear that sprang up in her. "And you are a Samaritan."

Ares folded muscled arms over his chest. "What an interesting turn of fate, that one of the chosen shows up in the prison of a dog to beseech him for her virtue."

Abigail did not so much as look away. She raised her chin a degree and returned, "Indeed. How blessed I am, that the Lord has brought me to the door of one who recognizes his sovereignty, when so easily I could have been given to a heathen."

Ares' face did not relax. He looked her up and down, but Abigail did not feel the same dart of lust from him that she did from the other men that had examined her that day. "You are deluded, Jewess, if you think you will ever get out of here. For five years I have been training and fighting within these walls, and I have watched the women rot and die from the treatment. And one with your beauty will be used the more roughly for it."

"I know that." Tears threatened to clog her throat, but she swallowed them away. "But my betrothed is an important man in the city, and when he discovers the betrayal that brought me here, he will come with all force necessary to save me. I promise you, you will be rewarded if you help me."

"There is no reward that can entice me but freedom, and freedom is something only the emperor himself can grant. Tell me, Jewess, are you betrothed to the emperor?"

She saw no reason to answer such a question. "You have a wife and children. They are in Samaria, I presume?"

Ares only lifted his head, as if awaiting a blow.

"Tell me who they are, and I will see that they are well. I will do this no matter your decision concerning me, because I know what it is to lose a husband, to lose a father. To fear not seeing my child again." She searched his eyes, looking for something, anything that would tell her she was reaching him. She saw nothing but the same even brown that had been looking on her for the past minute.

A long silence passed. Abigail's gaze fell to the floor, her shoulders slumped. She felt despair crouching just behind her.

Ares' voice split the air as an awl. "How long since you were in Israel?"

Startled by the question, she looked back up. "Six months."

Ares tapped a finger against his arm. "Before I was captured, there was a man named John who traveled around the land, baptizing people in the name of one to come. My family and I heard his lessons with a yearning heart. Tell me, do you know what became of this man?"

Abigail grimaced. "John the Baptist was beheaded by Herod."

Ares sighed and turned away, his eyes seeking the moonlight that streamed down through the window. "And what of the one whom he proclaimed? Did he ever follow?"

"Yes." She could not hold back a small smile. "Yes, his name is Jesus, and he walked the land for three years teaching and healing the sick. As the Scriptures promised, he was taken and put to death. I saw them nail him to a cross, I watched his agony as he died. And I rejoiced with my whole soul when he rose resurrected on the third day. The messiah has come, my friend, as John promised he would, and he brought with him the baptism of fire and the Spirit. This was only days before I left for Rome."

The gladiator looked at her again, his gaze probing this time. He nodded. "I can see your belief." He hesitated a moment, then seemed to resign himself. "What is it you want me to do to help you?"

She tried to keep joy from leaping up prematurely. "Let me stay. I will stay out of your way as best as I am able."

Ares drew in a deep breath. "I have been very careful these years, Jewess, not only to remain faithful to my wife, but to make certain everyone knew that I was. This will destroy that reputation."

Abigail took a moment to contemplate that. It seemed she fell into this situation entirely too readily these days, having to appear to be one man's lover to keep from becoming another's. But Titus had volunteered, and this stranger was obviously hesitant at best. Was it too selfish of her to ask him to sacrifice five years of work for *her*, someone whose people had tormented his for centuries?

"On the other hand," Ares continued, "that damage will not actually hurt me at all, especially since I know well that they say it is not by choice I refuse everyone they send here. Whereas if I send you away, the hurt to you will be actual and severe." He pondered for a moment, then odded slowly. "What is your name, woman?"

"Abigail." Relief swamped her when she saw the capitulation in his eyes.

"And how old are you? You look young to be speaking of one husband lost, a child, and a betrothed."

"I am fifteen."

"Still a child," he pronounced with a surprising hint of a smile. "Or so I would like to think. I left my daughter ten years old, but she would be your age now. I cannot imagine her married, or with a babe of her own." He reached out a hand in greeting. Only once she had slowly placed her fingers in his did he say, "My name is Jacob. You may stay in here tonight and as many nights as they bring you here, and I will make no protest. In return, I ask that you tell me about this messiah John spoke of."

With a grateful heart, Abigail complied.

◆

Volusius looked at the guard in disbelief. "He what?"

"Kept the girl," the man stated again. "I waited an hour for the knock, but there was none. It seems our Ares was only waiting for his Aphrodite to come along to tempt him."

"Let us just hope there is no Hephaistos to rain fire down this time, shall we?" Volusius tapped a finger against his lips in consideration. "I am impressed. She is certainly lovely, but I did not expect that to influence him. It never has before. She must be quite the temptress." He straightened, his decision made. "Where is she now?"

"In the kitchens."

"Bring her to me. I will take her out to observe the morning's practice with me. Perhaps seeing the one who managed to make a lover out of Ares will inspire the others to actually become a challenge for him."

The guard nodded and turned away.

◆

Jacob tested the blade and handed it back. "Sharpen it more," he advised, picked up the next. "This one is good." Replacing it, he picked up a third. He tossed the sword from one hand to another. "The balance of this one is all wrong."

The smith smiled, revealing several missing teeth. "Then be sure someone else gets it, Ares."

Jacob smiled in reply and picked up one of the dulled, blunt practice swords. "And give them an excuse for their ineptitude? Never, my friend. I win because I am the best, not because my tools are."

The man shrugged and went back to work. Jacob turned to begin the training. He was still tired from yesterday's games, but that never earned him a day off. But it had, over the years, earned him the position of instructor rather than mere participant in these practices. Scores of men were in the walled compound, all of them potential enemies, all of them his students. He had to teach them what he knew just as others had taught him, not so that they could win or lose, live or die, but so that they could entertain the masses while they did so. They had to learn how to make death come slowly to their opponent, how to tease and play when they had the upper hand, how to prolong every fight when they were the underdog. Sometimes the crowds were merciful, and they would live in spite of a bad day.

Then there were the days when the victor found himself in the middle of the arena when the lions were released into it.

Jacob had not grown up a shepherd without learning how to fight off a few lions. He had not emerged unscathed from his fight with them in the arena, but he had emerged the favorite of all of Rome. That was when they had started calling him Ares, God of War, with the sword of death always poised ready to strike in his hand.

He just wanted to go home and tend to his flocks again. He wondered if they would even be intact if ever he did make it back. How could he expect his family to get along without him? His son was still a child, not even twelve years old, and his daughter was not a shepherdess. They had probably had to sell the flocks to have enough money to live on. He hoped it was enough.

Movement along the wall caught his eyes, and he looked up to see Volusius. It was not odd for the man to observe morning routines. But seeing the figure behind him gave Jacob pause. His sword fell to his side as he watched Abigail being prodded along behind Volusius. In moments, all of the gladiators were looking toward the wall.

Volusius smiled down at them. "A little enticement, men." He reached for Abigail and pulled her up beside him. "A morsel that even Ares found worthy of his attentions. Whoever among you does the best today in practice will have the chance to plant your seed in her belly tonight!"

A chorus of very male cheers went up, and Jacob watched as Abigail flushed and turned her face away. For the life of him, all he could see when he looked at her was the little girl he had not seen in half a decade. Was his little Mary growing up to be anything like the woman-child he had spent hours talking with last night? Had she fallen in love with some lucky man, as Abigail had with her Roman? Most unthinkable still, had his wife been forced to marry her off already? Could he even now be a grandfather? He did not feel old enough to have a child with a child. But he felt decidedly too old to see Abigail as anything *other* than one.

The man closest to him, known as Tiger, elbowed him with a smile. "Go easy on me today, Ares. I would like a taste of that."

Protective instincts flared up, and Ares gripped his sword tighter. "I think not." He practically snarled as he barked out, "Into formation! The first man I see gawking at that wall is going to get the broad side of my sword against his head!" In proof, he gave a light thwak to the nearest staring man. Amid laughter and joking, the warriors took up their positions.

Jacob glanced up at the wall only once. Abigail's eyes were on him, appreciative and smiling. She moved her lips, but he knew she did not speak aloud. It would not have mattered if she had; her words were Hebrew, and no one else there would have understood. But he did, and it lent him a little extra strength.

"I pray for you."

It proved enough to keep her safe for another night.

FORTY-SIX

Titus breathed in the cooling air of autumn with a sense of foreboding. Business had gone well; he had acquired the vessels, and they would be in his fleet soon, the revenue they brought in added directly to his. It would be enough to ensure financial security for him and Abigail. But still, there was a snake of dread coiled around his heart as he trotted his horse over the road leading to the Visibullis estate.

"Father God, please grant me peace," he prayed softly into the morning air. "I know that all is in your capable hands. Still, I have this terrible feeling. If it is your Spirit, then please guide me in the right actions. If it is not of you, please ease my heart."

The only answer was the whisper of the breeze through the trees. Not satisfied with that, Titus picked up his pace. A minute later, the villa came into view. His horse did not seem to mind being urged into a gallop for the last stretch. In front of the house, Titus swung down as his mount still pranced to a halt. A servant emerged to take the reins as Titus headed for the door.

"Titus!" It was Andrew who threw open the door with a relieved expression on his face. "We prayed you would come here first."

"What is wrong?"

"Your father sold Abigail to the arenas."

"What?" The word exploded from his lips and brought Titus to an abrupt stop.

"The women do not know," Andrew said softly, obviously urging Titus to mirror his volume. "They know he sent her somewhere, obviously, but not where. There were eight men holding back Phillip when they took her, but he escaped and followed her. He spent two days trying to find a way in, but there is nothing he could do. He said to send you directly into the city, that he would meet you at the gates."

"I am on my way." Titus spun back toward his mount.

"Titus!"

At his mother's voice, Titus halted. He was not surprised to see her here. "Mother. You have seen to the children?"

"Ester and I, yes," Aquilia assured him as she hurried up. She wrapped her arms around him fiercely. "You must hurry. We are so worried about Abigail, and the children are distraught. Do whatever it takes to get her back, Titus."

"I will." He looked over her head to see Ester standing not far away. The last time he had seen her was when he came to deliver the news of death. She had the same look about her now as she did the moment the door had opened then; panic just below the surface, hope fighting to keep its place even though pain lurked. "You will have your daughter with you tonight," he swore to her.

A wash of peace covered Ester's eyes, and she nodded. "Go with God, my son."

Touched more than he cared to examine at the moment, Titus nodded too and released his mother so that he could take his horse back from the waiting servant.

"Godspeed," the young man wished him as Titus vaulted into the saddle.

Titus said something that he hoped expressed his gratitude and pressed his heels into his horse's flanks. The ride into Rome was not very long at the quick pace he set, but every second felt like a year as he worried about the woman he loved. He should have known not to leave her for even a moment before she was safely at the villa, but he had been foolish enough to think that an hour would make no difference.

Once he reached the nearest gate, he reined his horse to a halt and scanned the crowds for Phillip. He did not spot him until he was literally at his side.

"My lord." Phillip grabbed the bridle of the horse and caressed the beast's nose. "I prayed you would come this morning. She has already been there two nights. You spoke with Andrew?"

"I did." Titus swung off his horse so that they could proceed on foot and talk as they went. "You know not where in the arena she is being kept?"

Phillip shook his head. His jaw clenched. "She should not be there at all. If I had been doing my duty–"

"Eight men, Phillip. It seems to me that you are amazing for escaping from their clutches at all."

"Every time it has mattered, I have failed."

"No." Titus smiled in spite of the anticipation sparking to life within him. "Who but God can know how many dangers were avoided because of your presence? You can be blamed for none of the sorrows that have befallen her, Phillip. The important thing is that we get her back. Once she is my wife, there will be nothing my father can do. All of Rome will know I have wed her, and they will not be able to turn a blind eye to his doings."

Phillip measured him evenly. "You know what they do with women at the arenas, do you not?"

Titus's felt his eyes harden into the way they had been most of his life. "I know better than most how harshly a whore is treated, yes, and I know my father would have sent her there to fill that description. But if you are implying that I may change my mind about marrying her because of what she is likely to have been through in these two nights, you are mistaken. If anyone is to be punished for this, it will be my father, not Abigail."

"What will you do?"

"The only thing I can with a clear conscience. Absolutely nothing. Never again will I step in his house, exchange a word with him, or acknowledge his existence. He has made his choice. I am no longer his son."

Phillip nodded. They walked quickly in silence for a moment before he asked, "And what of the officials at the arena? What will you do about them?"

Titus's grin felt edged with danger. "Well, my friend, that depends entirely upon how cooperative they prove to be."

Phillip's lips tugged up to match Titus's. It seemed he, too, was looking forward to the prospect of a confrontation. Sometimes only a hint of indulgence could tame the savage in a man's soul.

Mannas had a hard time believing it was chance that led him past the entrance gates at the very moment that Titus Asinius charged up the steps. If it was fortune, it was decidedly bad. He would rather be anywhere else. As it was, he stepped aside and hoped that the furious man would not even see him.

Such luck was not destined for him that day. As he strode by, Titus grabbed him by the shoulder and forced him forward with him, not even sparing him a glance. "Volusius," he demanded in a stony voice. "Take me to him."

Mannas nodded, but he had a feeling it did not occur to Asinius that he would do anything but agree. It was not an unsafe assumption. Mannas darted a look at the second man, recognizing him as the bodyguard that he heard had gotten away. He hoped fervently the man would not recognize him. He suspected Asinius would not object to the eunuch breaking a few bones in vengeance.

"This way." Mannas indicating a narrow, steep set of steps. He chanced another look at the young Asinius. At the moment, he had the same look of impenetrableness that his father was famous for, along with an extra touch of ferocity for good measure. Mannas decided to be glad it was Volusius, and not he, that would feel the brunt of this one's anger. Maybe he could even secure a little extra leniency for himself. "I heard that you just returned recently from Jerusalem, Lord. I served there myself, many years ago, alongside Cleopas Visibullis."

The hand on his shoulder tightened. "You are an idiot. You just admitted to me that you know who I am, and hence why I am here, which means you know for whom I come. And if you know of Abigail, it is because you have seen her. And tell me, my fellow legioner, how is it that you looked upon my betrothed without offering her your assistance?"

Mannas forced down a swallow. "I. . . did not know she was your betrothed, Lord, only that she–"

"Enough." Titus punctuating the command with a shake. "Where is Volusius?"

Having reached the top of the steps, Mannas indicated the appropriate chamber. He hoped to be released, but Titus apparently decided it would be a more impressive entrance if he barged in with the man's own guard in hand.

No, it was not a day of fortune for Mannas.

◆

When Titus flung the door open, Volusius looked up in surprise. The man stood, outrage on his face.

Titus released the guard and charged the man. "Where is she?"

Volusius scurried behind a large piece of furniture. "I know not of whom you speak or why you are here. Please, I am a busy man, and I have much to do. If you have business with me, we can make an appointment."

Titus's answer was to kick the table between them out of the way and walk through the void it created so that he could grab Volusius by his tunic and lift him a few inches off the ground. "Abigail Visibullis," he said with exaggerated patience. "My father had her delivered to you the day before yesterday. Where is she?"

"I–I do not know that name." Volusius clutched at Titus's arm.

"Then let me clarify. The most beautiful woman you have likely ever seen, young, with my amethyst around her neck and my babe in her womb." The falsehood was meant to get a reaction, and get it he did. He watched Volusius's blood drain from his face.

"Truly, Lord, I know not of whom you speak. But I will inquire. I will find her for you if she is here, and I will contact you. Please, go home and rest, and I will do all I can."

Titus dropped the man without warning. "See that you do." He turned and strode from the chamber with the same force he had entered it with, signaling Phillip to follow. As soon as they were outside, having slammed the door closed behind them, Titus ducked into the nearest empty chamber and pressed himself out of sight. Phillip followed suit as Titus eased the door closed after them. At the slave's arched brow, he just shook his head.

From the other chamber they could hear Volusius exclaim, "Well get her! Bring her up here and let her answer for herself. If that wench births an Asinius child here, that man will kill me!"

Titus smiled the answer to Phillip, who smiled in return. Minutes passed, silent minutes during which Titus leaned with perfect confidence against the wall as he waited. Phillip kept flexing his wrist as if hoping he would soon need to exercise it with a few blows.

At last, they heard two sets of approaching footsteps, one the heavy tread of a man, the other the softer one of a woman. Phillip immediately tensed, but Titus held up his hand to signal him to wait. It would be best not to show themselves until there was no hope of the guard escaping with Abigail. As the sounds drew nearer, Titus reached for the door's latch, and Phillip slid into place beside him. When the footfalls were almost directly in front of them, they threw open the door and stepped into the hall.

He watched as Abigail glanced up, the resignation on her face transforming instantly to joy. "Titus!" She launched herself into his arms before the guard could so much as respond and let out a trill of laughter. "I knew you would come!"

"Of course I came." Titus cradled her head against his shoulder. He drew it back enough to kiss her soundly. "Are you well? Have they hurt you? I swear, if anyone laid a hand on you, I shall–"

"Hush, my love." Abigail silenced him with a gentle finger over his lips. She was smiling, and he decided she would not be smiling if she had been treated poorly. "Jacob, known as Ares, the one they gave me to, is faithful to the wife he left behind; he would not touch me, but he let me stay with him so that they would not give me to another. The Lord was with me, Titus." Her eyes sparked with joy. "In fact, this Jacob had been a follower of John the Baptist, he of whom the scriptures spoke as 'a voice crying in the wilderness.' I told him of Christ, and he believes."

Titus laughed, barely noticing as Volusius came out of his chamber with a thundercloud on his face and spoke to the guard, who turned and left. He gave Abigail a squeeze. "The Lord was with you indeed."

She chuckled and rested her head against his chest. "How are the children?"

Titus smiled. "I did not see them in my rush to find you upon my return, but from what I understand, they are well, though missing you. It seems our mothers have struck up a friendship; they are all awaiting you at the villa, beloved."

Abigail drew in a long breath. "You saw Ester? She is well?"

He nodded. "She looked worried, but strong. A bit older than I remembered, but still lovely and graceful."

"What did she think of Benjamin?"

Titus laughed. "Fair one, I was there no longer than a minute. Andrew told me what had happened the moment I dismounted, and I was on my way again a heartbeat later. I rushed to the gates, where Phillip met me."

Abigail then pulled away from him to go embrace her loyal servant. "Thank you, Phillip. I knew you could get away from them and follow so that you could tell Titus exactly where I was."

"I should have done more," Phillip returned.

"No." Abigail pulled away and looking up into his stern countenance. "The Lord was with me, my friend. I have no doubts that he led me here so that I could meet and speak with Jacob, and he was watching over me every moment to ensure my safety." She looked over at Titus. "I promised him that I would see that his family in Samaria is safe."

At that moment, Titus would have promised absolutely anything to the man who had protected his betrothed. "We will do that and more, my love, for this man."

Two sets of heavy footsteps sounded on the stairs, and a moment later the guard came into view. Titus vaguely recognized the man beside him as a gladiator he had once cheered on. The warrior smiled when he saw them.

"I am Jacob. You must be Titus." The fighter approached with an outstretched hand.

They clasped wrists, and Titus smiled in return. "I am. I want to thank you for protecting Abigail for me."

Jacob smiled at her. "It was my pleasure. I only hope another has done for my daughter as I did for her. And she has taught me much in these two days."

"She is a good teacher, indeed." Titus tucked her under his arm again.

Phillip was looking with a good deal less warmth at the guard. "You! You were the one to take her from the Asinius house."

The guard took a step back.

Abigail reached out to put a steadying hand on Phillip's arm. "He only did his duty, Phillip. He had no way of knowing that I was not the slave Caius claimed me to be. But once he knew, he was as kind as he dared to be."

The guard looked as surprised to hear this as Phillip did. Titus buried a smile. He knew well that Abigail had a tendency to see more in a man than he could see in himself. "She is right, Phillip. The lackey is not to be blamed. It is the master who must answer for his wrongdoing." He turned and focused a burning gaze on Volusius, who also stepped back. "I realize you were answering to my father, but that allegiance will do you no good. I promise you that in a matter of weeks, my father's power will fade. And then you will answer to me, Volusius. You had better be ready to pacify me when I come for reckoning."

Volusius made no reply, so Titus turned to Jacob again. "I will see that your family is well, as you have seen to mine. Join your prayers to ours, my friend, and hopefully soon they will all be answered."

When Jacob nodded his acceptance, Titus let his hand rest protectively on Abigail's shoulder in preparation for leaving. He looked at Volusius but nodded at Jacob. "If I hear you have harmed him in any way because of this then you will pay with your life, and my friend here," he said with another nod toward Mannas, "will find himself with a large promotion and your former seat. Understood?"

Volusius only nodded. Titus turned away and let his smile escape. He led Abigail toward and down the stairs, Phillip close behind. In minutes, they emerged into the daylight and headed for home.

Abigail held Ester close, tears streaming down her face. There was so much to say, but she could find no words to say it.

Ester sniffed and pulled her tighter still. "I am so sorry, my daughter. I nearly gave up after Cleopas and Jason were killed, but it was not for lack of love of you. The darkness was just so heavy . . . but it was the hope of seeing you again, of meeting your son, that brought the light back into my life. I am so proud of all you have done."

"I have missed you, Mother." Abigail pulled away enough to dash at her tears. "You cannot know how much."

"I can. I missed you as much, my daughter. Look at you; motherhood has made you all the more beautiful. Or perhaps it is love that has done it?"

Abigail laughed and blushed and hugged Ester close again. "Both, I suspect." She kissed Ester's cheek. "It feels like much longer than it has been since I last saw you."

"That is because we did not even know how the other was faring. And because so much has changed." She sighed and studied Abigail's face hungrily. "Ever since the day Cleopas brought you to me, the day Jason left, I have seen something in you. Something unsatisfied, bitter, unyielding. Something that you buried, but which fueled you, kept you meek when you would have been bold, a servant when you would have been a mistress. That is gone from your eyes now."

She had not realized Ester had seen so deeply into her heart all this time. "Yes, it is gone. The Lord washed it away with his sacrifice."

Ester reached down to clasp Abigail's hands. "I am glad. I always saw in you a spirit that would rise up, as the women in the Scriptures who were called on by Jehovah to perform a great task. I rejoiced when Andrew told me we serve the same Savior."

"As did I. I prayed for you every day."

Ester nodded serenely, looking around her at the estate that had been her husband's for all those years, though he had chosen to remain always by her side in her land instead of enjoying it. "The Lord has blessed us, that I know. Most mornings, I still wake up and sorrow for all I have lost. But I have come to thank the Lord, too, for all he has given me." She met Abigail's gaze again. "Aquilia has told me of your plans to marry Titus. I could see in a glance that he is much changed, but I simply never would have thought, knowing the kind of man he had been–"

"I know." Abigail laughed. "I would not have thought, either, Mother. But the man he has become! It is amazing to behold. He loves the boys so, and he serves God and his Son with a full heart. I hope you will come to understand my choice, and I pray you do not mind our living here."

"Of course not. In fact, I was hoping that *you* would not mind *my* living here, as well."

Abigail's eyes widened. "Truly? You would want to leave Jerusalem?"

A hint of pain entered Ester's eyes, and Abigail saw the added age of which Titus had spoken. "There is nothing left for me there. I cannot go back to that house, and I have no family, few friends. No, child, my place is with you and Benjamin and your family. If you will have me."

"Nothing would please me more." She heard a familiar shout coming near and smiled anew. "And I am certain Samuel will agree."

The boy burst onto the scene, flinging himself at her. She caught him up and hugged him close.

"You are back!" He wrapped small arms around her neck. "I missed you, Mother! Where were you?"

She kissed his forehead. "Making a new friend. But I missed you as well."

Samuel grinned up at her. "Titus says that tomorrow he will become my father."

Abigail grinned in return. "Did he? That is good news. He tells me that tomorrow he will become my husband, too. We are blessed, Samuel."

"It is I who am blessed." Titus entered the room at a slower pace than the boy, but with the same contentment on his face. He carried Benjamin in his arms, who let out a happy gurgle when he spotted her. Baby arms stretched out to her, and Abigail put Samuel on his feet so that she could cuddle the babe to her.

Titus watched with a smile and turned to Ester. "I just spoke with Drusus, and he said he will not tarry long before returning to Judea. He also said you did not plan to join him. I pray that means you will remain here with us?"

"Unless you would mind. You may begin to think there are too many mothers around, you know."

Titus chuckled and reached over to pick up her hand. "Never. Especially since one more follower of Christ can only be a blessing under this roof."

"In that, my friend, we are certainly in agreement." Ester look at the man Abigail loved and sighed. "I trust you realize what a gift her love is. She does not give it lightly, though she inspires it with every smile."

"I know." Titus released her hand and picked up Samuel, who rested his golden head upon the large shoulder. He smiled at Abigail, and she grinned back. "We shall forge ourselves into a family, one bound by cords stronger than blood. But through the blood that brought us together. We shall serve together, love together, teach and learn together . . . we shall change the world together."

Abigail stepped closer to his side. "The psalmist said that 'weeping may endure for a night, but joy comes in the morning.'" She looked to the bright sun outside, and the others' gazes followed. "It is morning in Rome. Let us dedicate ourselves to sharing our joy."

There were no words that needed to be said. The Spirit said it all for them as it covered the room.

EPILOGUE

He had been traveling for a long while, and his horse was weary. He was weary, too. Wishing for the youth that these memories reminded him of, Menelaus rolled his shoulders back to loosen the tight muscles, trying to tell himself that he had no reason to feel so old. He was not, really. It was only the hours of travel and the news that met him at every stop that made him feel that way. But it just seemed wrong to be so aware of the age creeping in; this should have been a day of rejoicing, of gladness. It was the first time he had stepped foot in Italy in over a decade.

His memory of the road was blurred at best, but he was certain he was on the right one. It was well worn from hooves and feet, and the man he had asked two miles back had assured him he was headed in the right direction if the Visibullis estate was his goal.

It still tasted like mockery on his tongue. The Visibullis estate it may be in name, but everyone who spoke of it knew that it was the Asiniuses who made its name known at all. Menelaus spat the dust from his mouth. The anger was not as strong now as it had been ten years ago when he heard of the marriage, but it was still present. What right did they have to forget Jason, who was a better man than Titus could ever hope to be? What right did he have to take his wife, what right did she have to give herself to another? And the boy–the boy deserved to hear of his true father every day, not to forget him in the face of that pretender.

He rounded a bend, and the villa came into view. He reined his horse to a halt for a moment and simply looked at it. Even from this distance, he saw that it was bustling with activity. He knew from word along the way that it was more a town than a simple estate these days. It had become a haven for all the Jews when Caesar declared it illegal for them to live in Rome itself, and for the followers of that Nazarene, too. Menelaus was still amazed that the new religion had spread so quickly, in spite of all that the authorities tried to do to halt it. What was so impressive about a crucified carpenter? Or did they all believe those ridiculous stories about his supposed resurrection?

He spurred the horse on again and even urged it into a canter to get him there a bit faster, promising the beast a rest and food and water once he delivered him to the villa. Apparently the dust he kicked up was spotted a good ways off, for as soon as he came to a halt in front of the house, there were servants there to take the reins from him and offer him water. He drank.

"May I assist you, friend?" A man strode up. He was tall, muscled, older than Menelaus but looking far more energetic.

Menelaus drew in a long, cautious breath. "I am looking for Titus and Abigail Asinius. I am. . . an old friend. Menelaus Casicus."

The man smiled as if he recognized the name. It was possible, Menelaus granted, but not likely. They had no reason to speak of him to their servants.

"Of course. I will take you to my master. Mistress is tending the children, but I will inform her you are here. I am their steward, Jacob, and I am at your disposal."

Menelaus nodded as his eyes took in everything around him on the walk into the house. It looked to be prosperous, that was beyond doubt, but it did little to ease his mind.

Titus should not be enjoying Jason's prosperity.

The master came through the atrium as they entered it, and his face lit with immediate recognition. He smiled, and Menelaus frowned. He could not ever recall seeing Titus smile like that, but the lines it formed around his mouth proved he did it often.

"Menelaus!" Titus laughed, hurrying the last few steps to clasp his wrist and clap a hand to his other shoulder. "My friend, it is so good to see you! We have prayed for you regularly." He turned with bright eyes to the steward. "Did I not tell you I felt that the Lord would bring him here soon, Jacob?"

The steward smiled. "You did, Titus, and I never doubted. Shall I go tell Abigail?"

"Please. But on your way, you had better stop to see your daughter and her little one. He is standing."

With a proud grin, Jacob departed. Titus turned back to Menelaus with a more sober expression. "I have kept myself informed of your whereabouts. Lentulus and Apidius have come to visit whenever they could, but you I have not seen since Jerusalem. You have been on my mind much recently, my friend, and I felt deep within me that you have some contentions to settle with me."

Menelaus scowled. "You have felt that, have you?"

Unperturbed, Titus nodded, his dark eyes studying him. "We can talk now, or you can rest first. You are welcome to stay as long as you wish."

Menelaus's brows drew together. "You are very generous with what is not yours."

Titus actually smiled. "You would like to talk now, then. Very well. Allow me to assure you that I have touched nothing of Jason's estate except to improve it, and it is all Benjamin's. I live off my own revenue, as do Abigail and the children. When Benjamin comes of age, he will come into his wealth and find it more than what it was when he was born."

Menelaus breathed a humorless laugh. "You always had to be superior, did you not, Titus? But when Jason had something better, you simply took it."

A light of sadness entered Titus's eyes at the accusation. "I took nothing, Menelaus."

"You married his wife and raised his son and moved to his villa. You support his mother and harbor his people."

Titus spread his hands, palms flat. "And I am wrong for this? For taking care of his family as he asked me to do? For increasing what he left for his son, for protecting those he had come to identify with before his death?" He shook his head. "You are angry for many reasons, my friend, but that one is not valid."

Menelaus was too irritated to think of a proper retort. And he was distracted by the boisterous shouts of young boys that drew ever closer. In curiosity he watched as a pack of them burst into the room, the tallest screeching to a halt in a way that was vaguely familiar.

Titus, too, had turned to see the boys come in, and he smiled. "Perfect timing, my sons. We have a guest. This is Menelaus."

"I remember you," the tallest and obviously oldest spoke up. Menelaus saw the burnished hair falling in curls, the almost too-perfect features, and felt a whisper of recognition that he could not place. The young man grinned and elbowed the younger boy beside him. "He served with our fathers in Jerusalem. He was your father's best friend, and he came to see Mother and Grandmother after the uprising."

The younger boy's eyes widened as Menelaus's narrowed. "You knew my father?"

Menelaus knew a moment of begrudging respect. Apparently he had been wrong to assume that Titus had erased all knowledge of Jason from his son's mind. "Benjamin?"

The boy nodded vigorously. He must be, what, ten now? Menelaus suddenly saw Jason in his smile, carefree and confident. He stepped forward and reached out to clasp hands as a man would have, and Menelaus found himself smiling in return. "You look like your father."

Benjamin smiled again. "I know. Mother and Grandmother tell me that all the time. I look like Grandfather, too."

"Yes, you do. You would make them proud."

Benjamin did not seem surprised to hear that opinion. "They say that, too." He motioned to the group behind him, indicating the oldest first. "That is Samuel, and my little brother, Jason. He is named after my father."

Menelaus looked to the youngest boy with a serious gaze. He was probably around six and kept shifting from foot to foot as if impatient with the holdup in his race. Little Jason, Titus in miniature, nodded without much interest, and Menelaus found his smile returning. He looked to the fourth boy, around the same age as Jason.

"That is Mark. He is Andrew and Miriam's son." Benjamin looked to Titus. "Did someone tell Mother he is here?"

Titus nodded. "And since I am certain he will stay at least one night, since the hour grows late, you can all run along now and visit with him more later."

The group of boys all smiled and took off again, leaving Menelaus to watch after them. "Samuel–the boy Jason bought just before his death?"

"Yes," Titus said with obvious affection. "I have adopted him. He is growing into a fine man, and he helps with the younger ones without complaint."

Menelaus decided to release his resentment in favor of curiosity. "How many children do you have?"

Titus's chest puffed, but with a far different pride than Menelaus was used to seeing in him. "Three of my blood. Jason, of course, and his older sister Ester, who is almost nine, and the babe, Cleopas, who is two."

Menelaus studied Titus without expression. "You have named your children after the Visibullises instead of your own family?"

A hint of the old Titus entered the man's face. "I stopped calling my father family when I married Abigail, and nothing changed before he died five years ago, so I see no reason to favor his memory in such a way. We named a daughter after my mother, but she did not survive a month."

Menelaus marveled at the sadness in Titus's eyes. Uncomfortable with such talk, he searched his mind for something else. "I was surprised to hear of your enterprises here. It was my impression that Jews and this new sect called Christians are not favored in Rome."

Titus smiled almost too cheerfully. "Indeed. I suspect a large part of that is our fault actually; the emperor became rather intrigued by Abigail, and when she refused him, he grew angry." Titus shrugged. "He will never send his soldiers here, though, he respects her too much. As long as our brethren gather with us, they will maintain at least a modicum of safety. It is more than they find elsewhere, and not only because of the frustrations of Caesar."

Menelaus swallowed any reaction to the first part of that story. "Yes, I know. They meet with persecutions everywhere, though I have heard tales of even their persecutors being converted."

"Paul of Tarsus, yes. He writes us that he wishes to visit our church here, but the Lord has not ordained it yet. Still, many mutual acquaintances have made their way to us, and we keep each other updated on the growth of the church in the various countries."

"So you are a Christian, too, then?" Menelaus asked in disbelief.

Titus's smile was not proud now, but something just as strong. "I was one of the first, my friend. Christ gained my faith when I watched him die that day I should have been watching Barabbas. It was that that drew Abigail and me together."

He was not certain if that news made the present any easier to understand or not. Menelaus could not grasp this new man he saw in his old friend. Before he could think up any adequate response, movement caught his eye, and he turned to see Abigail enter the chamber.

If possible, she had only grown more beautiful since the first time he had seen her. He realized only by seeing her now, mature but still young, how close to being a child she had been ten years before. He realized too, seeing her dressed in Roman styles with gold glistening against her simple garment, that she looked more appropriate as mistress here than she had as slave in Jerusalem. She approached him with a resplendent smile and held out a hand. He took it.

"Welcome, my friend," she said in the same alto voice he remembered. "We have prayed you would come. Jason would have wanted us to keep in better communication."

Hearing her say it, he knew it was true and felt a stab of guilt. "I know. How is his mother?"

She chuckled. "She is having a marvelous time chasing around her grandchildren with Titus's mother. She will be eager to greet you, but she and Aquilia are out visiting another friend at the moment. I expect them back soon."

"I look forward to seeing them both again." Menelaus smiled, even when Abigail stepped comfortably into the space Titus made for her at his side, his arm around her.

"How long can you stay? Are you only on leave?"

Menelaus shook his head. "No, I have been released from service. I know not where I will go from here."

"Then perhaps you will find no need to leave at all." She said it with such satisfaction that Menelaus found himself wondering if maybe she was right. "Any who come to us are welcome to stay."

"Come." Titus held out an arm, indicating the rest of the house. "Let us give you a tour while a room is prepared for you. I think you will be intrigued by all we do here."

Menelaus fell into step beside them, some of his exhaustion falling away and mirth taking its place. "And why is that? Are you running a small republic here to make Plato proud?"

Abigail laughed. "Our king has no need of philosophy, having the truth instead. But it runs as smoothly, and we like to think we have emerged from the cave into that light."

"Just be prepared," Titus added with a measure of sobriety. "As Socrates warned, seeing it upon leaving the darkness can be painful for a while. But it is worth it, when you can finally see it shine for all the world to see."

Menelaus looked around him, from the vineyards to the fields to the houses to the people, and felt a strange stirring within him that told him they spoke the truth. Which was odd. He had never expected to recognize such a thing if ever he found it.

DISCUSSION QUESTIONS

1.) Even as a child, Abigail exhibits a bitterness toward God, though she cannot deny his existence. Why is this her response to tragedy? How would you feel toward the Lord if you lost all you held dear?

2.) Abigail demonstrates pride by clinging to humility. What are some other surprising ways we show ourselves to be proud?

3.) Many of the characters respond to the tales of Jesus' miracles by assuming them gross exaggerations. How do we, centuries after the fact, put our faith in what some call only stories?

4.) Ester has a problem separating her desires from what is best for those she loves. Do you encounter this? How do you make the decisions?

5.) Abigail makes a decision to keep her shame private so that her friends cannot get in trouble too. Have you ever been a situation like this? How would you respond if in Abigail's position?

6.) Have you ever had split loyalties like Abigail did when faced with her feelings for Andrew and her sworn dedication to Jason?

7.) Can virtue be taught? (This is for all you Plato readers out there!)

8.) How would you defend the idea of one God and his Son to people who had been raised in a polytheist society?

9.) Do you feel Elizabeth had just cause to poison herself?

10.) If you discovered you were pregnant in Abigail's situation, how would you react?

11.) The longer Jason is back in Jerusalem, the more he finds the covenant his parents made with God pulling on him. Do you believe that the prayers and dedication of parents can affect the faith of a child? How do you think this works in Jason's life?

12.) Cleopas and Jason are the first to open their hearts to the truth preached by Jesus. Why do you think that is?

13.) What does Jason's prayer during the uprising say about his character?

14.) Why does Ester retreat into herself?

15.) Abigail ventures to the trial seeking vengeance and instead runs into forgiveness. Has God ever surprised you by meeting you where you least expected it?

16.) Abigail and Titus both see the truth of Christ's nature by feeling the power in his blood. How do you feel his power?

17.) Many amazing, miraculous things are recorded in the Gospels as happening during the hours of Jesus' crucifixion. Which do you find the most awe-inspiring? The most shocking? The hardest to grasp?

18.) Have you ever witnessed a miracle? What is your immediate reaction? Disbelief? Awe? Praise? Questions?

19.) Abigail and Titus become friends because of shared experiences; they say several times that it gives them an equality that allows a relationship to grow. Do you feel the deepest relationships are founded on equality (as Aristotle says) or something else?

20.) Is a lie acceptable when it's to keep someone safe?

21.) Abigail prays a version of the Lord's Prayer that is reworded to come from her heart. How would you reword the prayer to be personal?

22.) They see the coming of the Holy Spirit as it is recorded in Acts, with tongues of flame over their heads. How have you seen the Spirit come into your life?

23.) Have you ever faltered and fallen into the same sins as before you came to faith? Why do you think this happened to Abigail and Titus?

24.) How do Christians live with sin? What do they tell themselves?

25.) It takes tragedy to bring Titus to his knees. Has God ever used a terrible event to get your attention?

26.) They choose not to blame the Lord for their loss, but to renew their faith in him. What would your response be in this situation?

27.) What do you think fuels Caius's hatred of Abigail? How does God use his schemes for good?

28.) In the epilogue, they reference Plato's *Republic* and point out how it is painful to step into the light of truth after living in the darkness for so long. Have you seen this?

For more information on the history and texts referenced in this book, check out the Companion Guide at www.RoseannaMWhite.com. Just go to the Books link and click on "Companion Guide."